PRAISE FOR
JUST FRIENDS WITH BENEFITS

"My absolute favorite part of this book though had to be the group of friends. Made up of different characters, guys and girls, couples and singles with a variety of different jobs, they reminded me exactly of my friends. They were witty and loud and loving and they gave a perfect oomph to a romance story. I will definitely look forward to reading more from Meredith Schorr."

—SAMANTHA, CHICK LIT PLUS

"*Just Friends With Benefits* is a birdseye view into the life and times of the modern single girl. Stephanie is a character every girl can relate to as she navigates the rocky road to romance. Reading this book feels like a night out with your best girlfriend listening to her spill about her relationship. Author Meredith Schorr strikes just the right tone between hope and anxiety, desire and disappointment. I'm looking forward to reading more of Ms. Schorr's work in the future."

—JILL AMY ROSENBLATT, AUTHOR OF
FOR BETTER OR WORSE AND *PROJECT JENNIFER*

"Schorr created a cast of characters who could be plucked out of any of our lives. Again, what makes this story so relatable is the honest and raw look at a group of friends and all those personalities that contribute to the dynamics of the friendship — the guy who's obnoxious but lovable, the girl who's prissy but loyal, the inside jokes, the teasing, the pop-culture references…they all combine to make this a spectacular book. Meredith Schorr's debut novel *Just Friends With Benefits* was fantastic. Seriously, I loved it."

—KELLY, CRIB NOTES KELLY

"Meredith writes with wit, candor, humor and vulnerability that illuminates the struggles of dating and relationships. You can feel her pain. Anyone who is single or once was single can relate to this book!"

—NANCY SLOTNICK, DATING COACH AND AUTHOR OF *TURN YOUR CABLIGHT ON: GET YOUR DREAM MAN IN 6 MONTHS OR LESS*

"There were a couple major plot twists. Upon reading the second, I swore out loud. It was that unexpectedly awesome"

—JENN, BOOKSESSED

"*Just Friends With Benefits* was a very entertaining read – it was light and witty, and the relationships in the book felt very true and realistic."

—SARAH, THE BRAZEN BOOKWORM

"*Just Friends With Benefits* by Meredith Schorr is a fabulous chick lit novel that you won't want to miss this summer! I was really surprised that this was Meredith's first novel and can't wait to read more from this budding author."

—CATHY, LIP GLOSS AND LITERATURE

"There are plenty of laugh-out-loud moments in *Just Friends With Benefits*. It is a fast-paced novel with witty banter between the characters reminiscent at times of the dialogue on the popular television show *Gilmore Girls*."

—NANCY, THE CHICK LIT BEE

"*Just Friends With Benefits* is a fun take on the dating world and how Stephanie, whom a lot of women can relate to, deals with life and love."

—PIA, SO MANY BOOKS, SO HERE'S MINE

"Reading *Just Friends With Benefits* was a lot like revisiting some of my own life. I appreciated the realism Schorr brought to the story. And, as Stephanie figured out what really was right for her, I found myself wanting to know what story Schorr will share with us next."

—ASHLEY, THE BOOK FETISH

"If you're looking for a good chick lit book to read, *Just Friends With Benefits* is a perfect pick!"

—BECKY, OH MY GOSH BECK!

"This is one of those books you don't want to put down. I know I read most of it in one day! Really, a fun, fun read. I highly recommend this book to any and all lovers of chick lit!"

—LAURA, A NOVEL REVIEW

"If you're looking for a light, fun, humorous read, this one is definitely for you!"

—STEPH THE BOOKWORM

"It's about more than recapturing a missed love with someone from your past; it is about the friends who are with you through thick and thin and learning to value yourself and your needs/wants."

—MICHELLE, MICHELLE'S BOOK NOOK

OTHER NOVELS BY
MEREDITH SCHORR

BLOGGER GIRL

A STATE OF JANE

JUST FRIENDS WITH BENEFITS

MEREDITH SCHORR

Booktrope Editions
Seattle WA 2013

Cover Design by Loretta Matson

*This is a work of fiction. Names, characters, places, brands, media, and
incidents are either the product of the author's imagination or are used
fictitiously. Any resemblance to similarly named places or to persons living
or deceased is unintentional.*

PRINT ISBN 978-1-62015-158-7
EPUB ISBN 978-1-62015-254-6

For further information regarding permissions, please contact
info@booktrope.com.

Library of Congress Control Number: 2013948898

ACKNOWLEDGMENTS

For the original release of *Just Friends with Benefits*, I'd like to thank my family, specifically my mother, Susan Goodman, who provided much of the inspiration for Stephanie's mom; my older sister Marjorie Rigotty, who read several drafts of the book and blessedly lead me to the appropriate ending; and my oldest sister Melissa Stock, who practically taught me to read. I'd also like to thank my boss and friend Alan Blum for his constant encouragement despite countless rejections, and Ronni Solon Candlen, Abbe Kalnick, Shanna Eisenberg, Jenny Kabalen, Megan Coombes and Deirdre Noonan for being true blue pals. I'd like to extend warmest appreciation to the folks in my novel writing class at Gotham Writer's Workshop for their thorough and honest critiques and author, Diana Spechler, whose manuscript critique was so incredibly helpful. Finally, I would like to thank Pat Evans and Marilyn Kapp from Wings ePress for offering me my first publishing contract.

For the second coming of *Just Friends with Benefits*, I'd like to thank everyone at Booktrope, including but not limited to, Kenneth Shear, Katherine Sears, Heather Ludviksson, Jesse James Freeman, Beth Bacon, Loretta Matson, Katrina Mendolera, Adam Bodendieck and Victoria Wolffe. I'd also like to thank all of my writing buddies, especially Samantha Stroh Bailey and Francine LaSala, the various book bloggers who read the book and gave it such rave reviews and most importantly, the group of strangers who made me feel like family during a week at the beach in the Outer Banks the summer of 2007 and likely have no idea that they inspired a novel.

This novel is dedicated to my sister, Marjorie for her unconditional love and support, for never telling me only what I want to hear, for sharing my love and encyclopedic knowledge of *The Brady Bunch*, *Little House on the Prairie*, *When Harry Met Sally*, *Parenthood*, *Felicity*, *Bill & Ted's Excellent Adventure* and *13 Going on 30* and for her hatred of certain New York Yankees players who shall remain nameless.

PROLOGUE

CRAIG HAD PERFECTLY COIFFED LOCKS. Slickly combed and impeccably trimmed. I knew because every Monday, Wednesday and Friday morning, between 10:30 and 11:25, I sat behind him in "Introduction to Law and Criminal Justice" and stared at the back of his head. While Professor Blum gave his lecture, I fought the urge to kiss the nape of Craig's neck, where his brown hair came to a flawless straight line.

At the end of every class, Craig would turn to me, his white teeth sparkling, and say, "Have a good one." In that split second, I would imagine asking if he wanted to grab a cup of coffee or get to third base back in his room, but by the time I summoned the balls to choke out my standard, "Thanks, you too," he was usually out of his chair and no longer in earshot.

I knew Craig was a brother in Phi Alpha Omega since the back of his t-shirts always bore the letters "ΦΑΩ", and when my eyes weren't focused on Craig's immaculate hairdo, they were focused on his muscular torso. (I especially liked watching his shoulder blades ripple when he raised his arms over his head in a stretch.) When someone slipped a flyer under the door of my dorm room advertising a Phi Alpha Omega-sponsored happy hour at The Longpost Tavern, I dragged my roommate with me, figuring a few pitchers of Bud Light and a Mind Eraser shot might be just what I needed to garner the liquid courage to kick our relationship up a notch.

On the big day, I wore faded blue wide-leg jeans with daisies on the rear pockets, a white v-neck t-shirt and black platform shoes. It was a rainy night and so to avoid the frizz, my hair was smoothed back in a long ponytail. I was wearing Clinique lipstick a shade darker than the color of bubble gum and purple eye shadow to bring out the hazel in my eyes. I applied my best poker face, showed my chalked i.d. to the burly male bouncer and, with my roommate Jana in tow, walked through the crowded bar where Alanis Morissette's *Ironic* was blaring. Even through the smoky haze, I immediately spotted Craig standing by one of the tables built into the worn wall. He was laughing at his shorter friend, who was gesticulating like a mad man screaming about the end of the world.

My heart pounding, I turned to my roommate Jana and gestured toward the bar. "I need a beer."

"Me too." Pointing her finger in the direction of the bartender, the glare from her enormous mood ring practically blinding me, Jana said, "After you."

I led the way, looking behind me every couple of seconds to make sure I hadn't lost Jana in the crowd.

I heard her whisper to my back, "Is your man here?"

I whispered back, "Yes. But I can't talk to him yet. Too sober."

"Which one is he?"

On a mission to down my first beer, I pushed my way to the front of the congested bar and flashed my $20 bill. I hoped the bartender would equate Andrew Jackson's face with either a large drink order or a big tip, since pitchers were only $2.50 that night.

The bartender was an older guy who was mostly bald on top but wore his otherwise long silver hair in a ponytail. I secretly named him Rufus after George Carlin's character in *Bill & Ted's Excellent Adventure*. I absently tugged on my own ponytail, noting our similar hairstyles.

Rufus motioned towards me, "What can I get you?"

"A pitcher of Bud Light and two glasses, please. Thanks," I said.

As I watched him soak a dirty pitcher in soapsuds, rinse it with water and fill it with beer, I said, "Actually, can I also get two shots of tequila? Salt and lime, too?"

Rufus nodded knowingly. "Gonna be that kind of night, huh?"

Fearing it might take more than beer to afford me the altered sense of self-confidence required to utter a single word to Craig, I confided, "I hope so."

Jana, in the meantime, was poking me in the side. "Which one is he?" I whispered, "The tall guy in the flannel shirt."

After doing a 360 of the room, Jana blinked at me. "Not helpful."

I turned away from Rufus and pretended to scope out the entire bar. Among at least ten other tall guys wearing a flannel shirt, I spotted Craig. "Green flannel. Puppy dog eyes." I quickly turned back towards Rufus, grabbed our shots and said, "Ready?"

"Ready," Jana said. "To Stephanie finally making the moves on her lust man!"

When the lukewarm tequila hit the back of my throat, I shivered involuntarily and quickly sucked the juice from the lime. I chased the shot with a few hearty gulps of beer before asking Jana, "So, what do you think of him?"

Shrugging, Jana said, "Not my type. Too clean cut for me, but cute in a geeky sort of way, I guess."

Jana was a Goth wannabe. She dressed in all black and her makeup application consisted of thick black liquid eyeliner. Despite her attempt to look dark and brooding, her baby thin platinum blonde hair and big blue eyes made her look more like a tourist from one of the Scandinavian countries dressed up for Halloween. Jana preferred the local artsy lounges downtown to the fraternity college bars, but was sick of hearing me analyze Craig's intentions. When I'd insist it must mean something that Craig said goodbye to me and only me at the end of every class, she'd just roll her eyes. I wasn't sure if she really cared whether or not I hooked up with Craig or if she just wanted me to shut up about it, but she agreed to come with me that night for moral support.

While we drank our first pitcher, I half listened to Jana tell me about the fine, twenty-something teaching assistant in her Anthropology class and tried unsuccessfully not to check on Craig's status every couple of minutes to make sure he was still in the same place and not making out with some chick.

"Don't keep staring at him like a deer in headlights, Stephanie! It's so obvious," Jana said, shaking her head. "Either make eye contact and smile or don't look at him until you're ready. Hurry up, by the way. I heard Joe's going to Valentines tonight."

Willing myself not to look over at Craig again, I asked, "Who's Joe?"

"My hot TA! Have you been listening to me at all?"

I kicked off the stray cocktail napkin, which had attached itself to the back of my foot and muttered, "I can't concentrate. Sorry. One more pitcher?"

"You owe me one," Jana said, before heading back to the bar.

While Jana got Rufus's attention, I observed Craig standing quietly to the side as his friend monopolized a conversation with two girls. I wondered who he was thinking about and wished it was me.

I raised my hands to the sides of my head to make sure no stray hairs had escaped my ponytail. When Jana returned with our pitcher, I asked, "Do I look okay?"

Jana, who was more experienced with men and couldn't seem to relate to a college freshman who was still a virgin, snorted. "You're far prettier than you give yourself credit for. And I'd kill for those raven locks," she said. "Yes, you look great. Go for it."

My stomach dropped. "Aren't you coming with me?"

As Jana refilled her beer glass and topped off mine, she said, "No. You'll look cooler if you go over to him on your own." Then she motioned towards Craig and gently pushed me in his direction.

I momentarily missed high school when it was more than acceptable for my friends to accompany me everywhere, whether to the bathroom or to make a move on a new guy. I felt safety in numbers. I knew Jana would not be persuaded to tag along with me and since I was afraid Craig might actually favor Jana's Kelly over my Brenda, I took a deep inhale and approached where he was standing. I took one last glance behind me and made eye contact with Jana. She mouthed "go for it" and flipped over a napkin on which she had drawn the Nike swoosh logo and the words "Just Do It."

As the space between me and the back of Craig's green flannel shirt got smaller, I wasn't positive I'd survive the encounter, but then I remembered the time my voice cracked during my solo at the Spring Concert in fifth grade. It was years before my classmates stopped calling me Peter Brady, yet I was able to live through the experience and even maintain relative popularity throughout junior high and high school. Worst case scenario, Craig would humiliate me in front of his friends, but I knew I'd live through that too.

I tapped him on the back and when he turned around, said, "Hey. You're in my Criminal Justice class, aren't you?"

His initial reaction was a blank stare and feeling foolish, I pinched my arm hoping I was dreaming. But then he grinned. "Yeah, I am. I'm Craig."

I gave him a toothy smile, wishing I was cooler and said, "I'm Stephanie."

Craig extended his hand toward mine and I absently shook it while trying to think of what to say next.

"Who do we have here, Hille?"

I removed my hand from Craig's and looked at his shorter friend and then back at Craig. I repeated, "Hille?"

"No one calls me Craig," he said. "Hille's my last name."

"Who's Craig?" joked the shorter friend.

Hille looked from me to his friend and said, "Stephanie, this is Paul. Paul, this is Stephanie."

Torn between wishing he'd leave me alone to talk with Craig and relief for the facilitation of conversation, I said, "Hi, Paul."

His teeth were as pearly white as Hille's, only the bottom row was slightly crooked, Paul smiled. "Hi, Stephanie. Haven't seen you around these parts before."

I had been there for lunch once when my older brother Sam came to visit with his girlfriend Amy. Nonchalantly, I said, "I've been here a few times."

"You should come to our house parties. The more cute girls we have hanging around, the more guys who want to pledge us." Chuckling, he said, "Not that we'd let the pledges actually speak to you. They'd be too busy manning the keg or cleaning the toilets."

"So, who are you here with?" Hille asked.

"My roommate. She's over there." I pointed in the direction of where I had left Jana but her seat was now empty except for several rain-soaked umbrellas in varying colors and sizes. I looked back at Hille and Paul and said, "Well, she *was* over there."

"Maybe she went to the bathroom," Hille suggested.

"Or maybe she's with one of the bartenders on the dirty mattress they keep downstairs with the kegs," Paul said.

A smile playing at the corners of his mouth, Hille said, "Ignore him. He's a pig."

Hille's scarlet lips were wet like he just bit into a juicy apple and I wanted nothing more than to ignore his friend Paul. But Paul kept talking and the more he talked, the quieter Hille became. I played along mostly because Paul was entirely responsible for keeping up the momentum of the dialogue and without him, I was afraid the conversation would implode, along with any hope of a relationship with Hille.

"So, tell me Stephanie. Do you like live music?" Paul asked.

"Of course," I said. "Well, it depends on the band, I guess."

"Does it have to be a band? What about a solo artist?"

I had no idea where this line of questioning was leading and wished Paul would get to his point. "Again, it depends on the artist."

"Well, how about this artist?" Paul put his beer down. Then he removed his Yankee baseball cap, ran his hands through his dirty blonde hair and started singing, *"If it weren't for Cotton-Eye Joe, I'd been married a long time ago. Where did you come from where did you go? Where did you come from, Cotton-Eye Joe?"*

As he sang, he did a little jig and I looked over at Hille with my hands covering my mouth, unable to contain my laughter. Hille released a quick chuckle before shaking his head at Paul and taking another sip of his drink.

After his performance, Paul put his baseball cap back on and resumed drinking his beer. "So, what did you think?"

I clapped and Paul took a bow. "Amazing," I said. "When are you going on tour?"

Paul removed his cap again and bowed his head at me. "Any day now, pretty lady. Any day now. Wanna be a groupie?"

"Perhaps," I said giggling.

I briefly forgot Hille was standing there until he said, "I think it's time for me to head out."

I wanted to say, "Don't go" but figured that would be a bit much since I'd just met him. So I said, "Really? It's still early."

Paul slapped Hille on the back. "The guy's a nerd. Probably going home to study. Gotta maintain that 4.0 GPA."

"4.0, huh? I'm impressed," I said.

Turning red, Hille said, "Paul here exaggerates. Not going home to study. Just kind of beat, that's all. Nice meeting you, Stephanie. See you in class."

"Bye, Craig. I mean Hille!"

I watched him walk toward the exit, stopping momentarily to put his empty beer glass on the bar. Realizing my mission was unsuccessful and I had just about enough money to grab a slice of pizza on the way back to the dorm, I turned to Paul. "Well, I think I'm gonna head out, too. As soon as I find my roommate."

"Nah! Let me buy you another beer," Paul said. "Maybe I'll even sing for you again."

I pulled on my ponytail as if I thought it might have gone somewhere and locked eyes with Paul. Not waiting for an answer, he re-filled my beer glass and winked at me.

As *Sweet Caroline* played in the background and hordes of my peers chanted, *"Good times never seemed so good. So good! So good!"* I decided Paul's grayish-green eyes were kind of pretty, shrugged my shoulders and said, "What the hell."

ONE

AFTER THE WAITRESS UNCORKED the two bottles of wine we had ordered to celebrate Hope's twenty-fifth birthday, one red and one white, we chanted in chorus "Speech! Speech! Speech!"

The pale skin beneath her freckled face, already flush from the bottle of wine we shared at Eric and Jess's house, turned a deeper shade of red as Hope stood up to make her toast.

"Okay, okay. Simmer down, people!" Hope waited for us to stop chanting. We were all buzzed so it took a moment but eventually we stopped pounding our fists against the table, put down our utensils and let Hope speak.

"I want to thank you all for joining me at my birthday celebration." Turning to her sister, she said, "Although Jess, as my closest blood relative, you're kind of obligated. And Eric, as Jess's husband, you didn't really have a choice, either. And Paul, well if you want to get laid later, you had to be here, too. So, I'd just like to thank Stephanie for taking the train from D.C. to Philly to celebrate with me. Mwah! And Hille, it was very cool of you to drive here from New Jersey. You guys rock. Happy birthday to me!" Hope took a sip of her wine and sat down.

Standing up with his glass raised, Paul said, "Well, that speech totally sucked, but since you're practically ten years younger than the rest of us, we'll let it slide."

"Ahem! I'm only seven years older than her, not ten!" I protested.

Dismissing me, Paul said, "Same thing, Cohen."

I looked at Hille, who was sitting across from me and rolled my eyes. He smiled and gave me a knowing glance.

I smiled back thinking Hille was even cuter now than he was back in college. He was practically the only brother from his fraternity who didn't have a receding hairline and, unlike Paul, the years of drinking beer hadn't reached his gut.

"Are you listening to me, Cohen? I'm trying to make a toast here and you're all glassy-eyed like you just smoked up."

"Maybe I have. Jealous much?" I asked.

His eyes wide with interest, Paul said, "Really?"

"No. Not really. Resume your toast. I promise to listen."

Paul sat down. "Fuck it, I forgot what I was gonna say. Happy birthday to Hope."

Hope reached over and gave Paul a peck on the lips, which quickly morphed into a bona fide smooch-fest. I turned my attention towards Jess, but she had moved from her own seat onto Eric's lap and was whispering in his ear.

I took another sip of wine, hoping to drown out the reminder that not only was I the oldest female in the group, I was also the only single one.

About forty-five minutes later, I looked down at my plate, empty except for some blood that had leaked out of my skirt steak and a mouthful of roasted potatoes. I had room left in my stomach to either finish the potatoes or drink another glass of wine and I chose the wine. Noticing that the seat next to mine was empty, I asked, "Where'd Eric go?"

Hille said, "To the bathroom." Then he quickly glanced from Hope, who was deep in conversation with Jess, to me and winked.

"Oh, thanks," I said, feeling my face flush in response to his wink. "If you gotta go, you gotta go, right?"

When Hille responded with a flat, "Yeah, I guess," I wished I had said something else. I was usually much better with the witty banter.

Eric returned to the table and in a soft voice said, "We're all good."

I whispered, "That was too generous of you. Let me give you some money."

Looking at me with a confused expression, Eric whispered back, "What are you talking about? I told the waitress it was Hope's birthday and she's bringing out a piece of cake."

"Oh, I thought you settled the bill," I said, feeling stupid and a little disappointed.

Eric laughed. "I love you Cohen, but not that much."

Jabbing him playfully in the arm, I said, "What are you good for, Eric? You don't sleep with me and you don't pay my bills."

Pointing at Jess across the table, Eric said, "I can only handle one wife at a time."

Overhearing, Jess said, "I'm okay with sharing. But only if you share 'The Librarian.'"

"If you met 'The Librarian,' I bet you'd change your mind about that. And besides, we're not dating anymore," I said.

Frowning, Hope asked, "What happened?"

"I couldn't take him anymore. He was beyond dorky."

"I thought that's why you liked him," Jess said. "Didn't you say his quirkiness was what you found most appealing?"

Before I could defend my decision by telling Jess how The Librarian's recent habit of addressing me by such endearing nicknames as "dear" and "honey" after only four dates felt insincere and gave me the hebeegeebees, Eric asked, "Why do all of your boyfriends have nicknames, Cohen? The Librarian? Didn't you date 'The Mayor' last? What was Paul's nickname back in college?"

Interjecting, Paul said, "'The Horse,' for obvious reasons. And, not for nothing, but you can't exactly refer to these guys as Cohen's 'boyfriends' since her longest relationship since me was what, three months?"

Reddening, I said, "Three and a half. And thanks for rubbing it in." As if I wasn't already excruciatingly aware that I was seemingly incapable of maintaining interest in a guy or maintaining *his* interest in *me* for longer than fourteen weeks.

Saving me from further playful, yet painful, ridicule at the hands of my best friends, our waitress and three other waiters approached our table. Our waitress was holding a plate with a piece of chocolate cake with a lit candle on top and she looked uncertainly from me, to Jess to Hope.

Pointing at Hope, Paul said, "She's the one."

The waitress let out a nervous laugh and said, "Thanks," and placed the plate in front of Hope's seat. Then she looked at the other waiters, whispered, "One, two, three" and started singing an off-key version of "Happy Birthday to You" while we all joined in.

I scanned the crowded restaurant. Most of the other patrons had paused their own conversations to watch our spectacle. The waiters didn't wear red and white striped uniforms with suspenders and I had a feeling performances of this nature were not typical at this upscale venue. While Hope buried her face in her hands and slunk further down in her seat, I watched Paul hand our waitress a bill. I couldn't see how much, but guessed it was a Benjamin Franklin.

After Hope recovered, she blew out her candle and made a wish. Then the waitress took the rest of our dessert orders. I didn't order anything, but took a bite of Hope's chocolate cake, justifying that failure to do so would bring Hope bad luck.

"So, Stephanie," Hille said from across the table. "When are you coming to New York for work again?"

"Not sure, actually. But if do, I'll totally look you up again." I hadn't been asked to assist with a closing in my law firm's New York office in over a year but remembered the last time and how I'd met Hille for breakfast before I went back to D.C. "We'll do dinner, though... breakfast is boring." Silently cursing my tendency to lose all sense of coolness in Hille's presence, I looked down at my black suede boots under the table and added, "Not that *our* breakfast was boring, of course!"

Flashing me that sexy wink again, Hille laughed and said, "Dinner it is. And, yes, you'd better look me up, kid!"

TWO

BACK AT ERIC AND JESS'S HOUSE later that night, I helped Jess finish off another bottle of wine.

Her yellow pant pajamas matching the kitchen chairs she had insisted on buying to add a more country-flair to the kitchen, Jess said, "Paul lost some weight since the last time I saw him, although he's still got that beer gut."

"Somehow, I don't think that gut is leaving anytime soon. But maybe Hope will get him into shape. What is she, a size two"?

Jess shook her head of shoulder length red curls in annoyance. "Don't remind me. I'm on a permanent diet, yet my little sister gives up soda for a month and turns into a twig."

"She's one lucky chick," I agreed.

"Don't even start with me, Miss Size Four."

Eric, who had been outside smoking a cigarette, returned to the kitchen, straddled a chair backwards, reminding me of Raj from *What's Happening*, and said, "Not interested in this topic of conversation. What I want to know is when Andy's gonna dump Rachel's ass. I just got off the phone with him. His testicles will be the size of Raisinettes if they last another year."

I poured myself another glass of Fat Bastard Shiraz, a gift from Paul, and asked, "And how is that exactly, Raj?"

"She confiscated his porn collection again, Re-run."

"And we all know how Andy loves his porn," Jess said.

Eric nodded. "Frankly, if he wants to jerk off to porn, why should she care as long as he still screws her"?

I slammed my hands on the faded wood table dramatically. "See? That's why I'm so happy to be single. A boyfriend would only get in the way of my porn addiction."

Eric clinked his wine glass against mine. "Amen to that."

"So, where is Hille staying tonight?" I asked.

"At Hope's apartment with Paul. They're both going home tomorrow. Why?" Eric asked.

"No reason. Just curious, since I figured he wouldn't want to drive back to Jersey so late."

Now standing behind Eric, massaging his back, Jess kissed the top of his blonde head and asked, "Are we having breakfast with them tomorrow?"

"Yes and no," Eric said. "Paul and Hope, yes. Hille no."

"Why isn't Hille coming?" I'd never formally said goodbye to him the night before under the assumption that I'd see him again.

"He's gotta get back early," Eric said.

"Why? Is he dating someone?"

"I don't think so, but what does that have to do with anything, Steph? I think he has some work meeting on Monday morning and wants to be home early to prepare."

"Oh. So only Paul and Hope will be here for breakfast?"

Eric narrowed his brown eyes at me. "That's what I said, Steph. I think you're cut off."

I took my last sip of wine and got up from the table. Yawning, I said, "I was finished anyway." I kissed them both on the cheek. "Going to bed. Night guys."

In unison, Jess and Eric replied, "Good night."

Under the covers in Jess and Eric's guest bedroom, I wondered if people at the restaurant had assumed that Eric, Jess, Hope, Paul, Hille and I were on a triple-date. Although Hille and I didn't kiss or even sit next to each other at the table, he was sort of my date for the evening by process of elimination.

I wondered if Hille was a good kisser. I pictured him with his shirt off. Then I pictured me taking his shirt off. I bet he had hair on his chest but not too much, and I knew he worked out so he probably didn't have man boobs. Bigger boobs than mine was a definite deal breaker. He was so sexy when he winked at me. There had to be some reason neither of us had found "the one" yet.

As I drifted off to sleep, I replayed the events of that long ago night at the Longpost Tavern and imagined what the last thirteen years would have been like if Paul was the one to go home early and not Hille.

THREE

ON THE TRAIN FROM PHILADELPHIA back to D.C. the next day, I tuned out the little boy sitting behind me who kept kicking the back of my seat, and felt guilty for fantasizing about a past that didn't include my two year relationship with Paul. But I still wondered if Hille and I would've made a better couple. If we'd hooked up in college, would we still be together now or would we just be best friends, like Paul and me? Or would I hate him for cheating on me with some slut with bigger tits? Or would he hate me for getting between him and his 4.0 GPA?

Then I thought about the time Paul gave me a Charles Chips tin full of green M&Ms for my birthday. And I recalled how he waited over two months to have sex with me and barely pressured me at all. And I remembered all the hours we spent playing dirty Mad Libs. We had so much fun together and I had no regrets.

And if I had dated Hille, who was vehemently opposed to any vice that could lead to a black mark on his spotless record, I probably would never have smoked pot back in college. And since I did my best bonding with Eric playing "Risk" and smoking out of Paul's three-foot glass bong, dating Hille instead of Paul back in college might have meant I wouldn't be best friends with Eric now.

No, dating Paul back in college, and not Hille, was definitely the way it was meant to happen.

But that was then and even though I hadn't given it much thought in over a decade, I could definitely see myself with Hille now.

With my bag in tow, I exited the train and down the escalators. As I waited on the long but fast-moving line for a cab back to my studio apartment in Capitol Hill, my mind continued to wander to thoughts of Hille.

* * *

I was still thinking about Hille when I went to bed that night. Cold, I jumped out of bed and threw a hoodie over my t-shirt. Within minutes, my arms screamed for fresh air and I sat up, removed the hoodie and placed it on the foot of my queen-sized bed for easy access. I always had trouble falling asleep on Sunday nights and my vacillating body temperature was not helping. When I couldn't sleep, fleeting thoughts like whether I'd make it to the gym the next morning, how many emails I'd find when I got to work and what I'd eat for lunch morphed into dire concerns which, that night, included whether Hille liked me and when I would see him again.

It hadn't occurred to me since freshman year that Hille might like me. We'd hung out many times since college and he'd never once made a move. But then again, I never saw him wink at anyone except me. Maybe he was flirting. And he *did* ask when I was coming to New York again. He didn't ask all of us when we were going to visit his new apartment, he only asked when *I'd* be there for another closing. Maybe he wanted to hang out with me alone.

I wanted to hang out with him alone, too, but as far as I knew, my boss, Gerard, had no plans to send me to New York anytime soon. Maybe if I asked him, he'd let me go. I couldn't tell him I wanted to go because I liked a guy there, but I had an idea.

Suddenly, I couldn't wait to get to work. I looked at the clock radio on my night table. I wished it was time to wake up already but the bright green numbers on the display reflected that it was only 12:17. I turned over on my side and tried to relax. I couldn't, so I put on the free sleep mask I got when I flew to Prague with my friend Suzanne and hoped it would release the pressure under my eyes. I probably looked like the lone ranger but since I was alone, I didn't care. I still couldn't fall asleep, so I removed the mask and looked at the clock again. It was 12:26. I thought about what I would wear if I met Hille in New York for dinner. Would he believe I was coincidentally sent to New York so quickly after he mentioned it? He was a guy and probably wouldn't give it a second thought. Sometimes I wished I was a guy so I wouldn't think so much. Guys cared about three things: food, sports and sex. I wished I had a penis, a big penis, of course. And balls I could adjust while sitting on my couch with a beer watching baseball.

I didn't really want to be a boy. I'd probably be a girly man since I cried at commercials all the time and couldn't program my remote control or change the bag on my vacuum cleaner, but I did like the idea of not thinking so much. And if I was a guy, I'd probably have fallen sleep already.

FOUR

WHEN I ARRIVED AT WORK at 8:30 the next morning, I took the long way from the elevator bank to my office. Although the entrance to the right of the elevators was closer to *my* office, the entrance to the left was closer to Gerard's and I wanted to make sure he was in. He was already sitting at his desk reading a paper, his John Lennon glasses resting on the bridge of his nose, while drinking what looked from the outside of the cup like coffee from one of the sidewalk vendors. After devising my plan of attack into the wee hours of the night, I couldn't wait to talk to him, but I did. I hated being bothered first thing in the morning before I finished my coffee or sometimes even took off my coat, so I refused to do that to Gerard. Instead, I drank my coffee and looked at my emails, stopping every few minutes to check the time on my phone. I decided to call him at 10:33 because it seemed more random than 10:30.

It wasn't even 9:00 when I finished reading and printing my emails. As a senior corporate paralegal, I had my own office, so I took advantage of the time by practicing my speech out loud with my office door closed. I didn't want it to sound too rehearsed, though, so I stopped at 9:45 and prepared a closing binder. At 10:32, I stared at my phone until 10:33 when I picked it up and dialed 7190, Gerard's extension.

Gerard answered in seemingly good spirits, "Good morning, Stephanie."

"Good morning to you, too. How was your weekend?" I instantly wished I could take back the second part since as nice as he was, Gerard and I didn't really talk about non-business stuff. And besides, if he asked about my weekend, I couldn't exactly tell him I got shitfaced.

"And how was yours?" Gerard was saying.

"Very good, thanks."

"So, what can I help you with this morning?"

I pulled a stray hair from the side of my ponytail and twisted it into a knot. "Actually, I wondered if I could speak to you when you had a moment. No rush." *But please let's do it now.*

"Sure. Why don't you come by now?"

"Great. I'll be right there." After hanging up, I removed my hair from the ponytail and brushed it straight. Then I checked my reflection in my metal letter opener. It was kind of blurry but clear enough to confirm that I didn't have lip gloss on my teeth. I grabbed my legal pad and a pen and headed to Gerard's office.

He was on the phone, but motioned for me to sit in his guest chair. "I love you, too" he whispered before hanging up and turning his attention to me. He smiled and said, "So, Steph, what did you want to see me about?"

I felt my heart pulsating beneath my black sweater. I had chosen black in case I started sweating. "Well, in preparation for my annual review, I've been thinking about some goals I'd like to set for myself." I paused and waited for Gerard's reaction.

"That's great, Stephanie! Anything you'd like to share now?"

"Actually, I'd really like your feedback."

Gerard locked his hands behind his head. "Shoot."

"Well, I've been working here for over six years now and I've definitely learned a lot. I enjoy working for Bartlett, Pinker and Wood and would like to continue my tenure here."

Gerard laughed. "Well, I'm pleased to hear that. You're an asset to the department and I wouldn't want you to leave us."

I didn't feel I deserved the compliment, considering my current act of manipulation and I felt a pang of remorse. But I had to go on. "Well, since I'm not looking to go to law school, my concern is that I'll stop learning new things. I need to be challenged to feel good about myself and my contribution to the firm. So, I'd appreciate your suggestions as to how I can prevent my job from getting stale and I've also come up with a few of my own."

"I'm sure I can think of some ways to keep things fresh, but let's hear what you've got."

I looked at my legal pad on which I had made a list of goals. "I'd like, if possible, to increase my direct contact with clients. Obviously, it will depend on the subject matter but I really don't think all contact needs to be through an attorney and since my billing rate is lower, the clients would probably appreciate it. And, it would show that the firm has confidence in my written and verbal communication abilities."

Gerard didn't saying anything and so I continued. "And I'd be interested in mentoring some of the entry level paralegals. As an experienced paralegal and one who has worked at BP&W for several years, I think it would be helpful to them and interesting for me as well." I looked up at Gerard.

Playing with the cap of his pen, he nodded. "Anything else?"

"Just one more," I said. I gripped the legal pad more firmly to keep my hands from trembling and licked my dry lips. Gerard was slouching in his chair and so I focused on his gangly legs, which were stretched out under his desk. "I really enjoy working on closings. Being involved in so many aspects of a deal, it's great to actually help close it. If possible, I'd like to attend more closings." *Almost finished, Stephanie. Don't quit now.* "I know most of our bigger deals close in the New York office and I wondered if you might consider sending me there again to help out. Traveling always keeps things fresh." I let the legal pad drop into my lap and, feeling a rush of relief to be finished, said, "That's it!"

Gerard was beaming at me so brightly, I knew I had done good and wondered if my childhood aspiration to be an actress wasn't something I should have taken more seriously. "Well, Stephanie, I'm very pleased that you've taken such initiative. I'll keep everything you said in mind. I'm pretty certain all can be arranged."

I waited for him to go into details but he just looked at me with a shit-eating grin on his face. I took his silence as a sign that the meeting was over, stood up and said, "Okay. Thanks for listening to me, Gerard. I appreciate it."

"And I appreciate you and all you do. See you later."

As I walked out of his office and back to mine, I felt totally stupid for thinking he might actually send me to New York on the spot. I wondered what exactly I had accomplished as a result of our meeting. I'd probably wind up mentoring a bunch of teeny-boppers whose only prior employment experience was babysitting. And I'd start receiving phone calls from asshole clients who thought their shit smelled like cherry blossoms. But, with my luck, I'd never attend a closing in New York ever again.

When I got back to my office, I closed the door and tried not to mope. My plan had totally tanked but there was nothing I could do about it except proceed with Plan B. That meant I had to come up with a Plan B. I wished I could get the answer by inserting "how can I see Hille again sooner rather than later?" into www.ask.com. For shits and giggles, I tried it. The first ten results were references to the phrase "sooner, not later." I tried Google and got the same results. Giggling, I debated whether to try Bing or Yahoo next when I heard a knock on my door. I quickly maximized the window for Moodys.com, the ever-popular business information site, said, "Come in" and tried to look professional.

It was Gerard and I prayed that three fresh-faced young paralegals were not standing behind him waiting to be mentored. I sat up straighter in my chair in an attempt to slickly see who he was with and said, "Hi, Gerard."

"Hi again. I wanted to talk to you about something." He was alone.

"Sure. Do you want to sit down?" I looked around, hoping he wouldn't notice the obscene amounts of paperwork cluttering my office.

Gerard sat in my guest chair and smiled at me. "I see you're keeping busy."

"Gotta keep those billables up!" I joked. I guessed he noticed the obscene amounts of paperwork cluttering my office.

"Well, hopefully, you're not overwhelmed."

Paralegals were, by definition, supposed to be overwhelmed, but since it was an unspoken rule not to admit it, I swallowed down the truth and responded, "Not at all. What can I do for you?"

"Well, coincidentally, I think we'll be able to implement one of your new goals sooner rather than later."

I tried not to laugh at his mention of 'sooner rather than later' and said, "Great!" as enthusiastically as I could muster, nearly certain whatever it was did not involve a trip to New York.

"How would you like to go to New York for a closing on Wednesday?"

"Wha, what?" I practically leaped out of my chair. "You serious?" My pitch was a little higher than I had intended and so I sat back in my chair, cleared my throat and added, "I mean, absolutely. For what case?"

"The Franklin General deal. One of the paralegals on the case is on maternity leave and another is on her honeymoon. They were going to hire temps, but after we spoke this morning, I called and mentioned your willingness to travel. So, assuming your cases can lose you for a couple of days, you're good to go."

I calmly responded, "Great. I need to work out the logistics, but it shouldn't be a problem." *Is two days enough notice for Hillie? What if he already has plans?*

"The associate on the deal in New York is Adam Ginsberg. Call him for details."

"Will do. Anything else?" *What should I wear at dinner?*

"Nope. You can use the firm's travel agent to get a round trip ticket on the shuttle and a hotel room for a couple of nights."

"Great. I'll do that right away."

Gerard stood up. "Well, that's that. Thanks, Stephanie."

I was smiling so hard my face hurt. "Thank you! I'm so grateful for your support."

As soon as Gerard left, I stood up, closed the door and did a victory dance around my office. Then I called Adam from the New York office and got the details regarding the closing. After making my hotel and flight reservations, I went to call Hille. I scrolled through my phone's address book for his number and realized I had never entered him into my phone. I considered getting his number from Paul but if he decided to spontaneously fly to New York to join us at dinner, I'd be pissed. I decided to call Eric instead, since he had a wife at home and was far less likely to pick up and travel to New York with two days notice.

He picked up after one ring. "Yo."

"Hey, Eric. It's Stephanie."

"I know that. If I didn't have caller i.d., I wouldn't answer the phone, 'yo'."

"Gotcha. So, what's going on?" I couldn't believe I was actually nervous to ask Eric for Hille's number but aimed to sound as casual as possible—just hoping to meet a friend for dinner—no big deal.

"Not much. What's wrong?" he asked.

"Nothing, why?"

"You sound weird. Nervous or something. What's up?"

I spit out the piece of fingernail I had bitten off. "Not nervous. Just swamped at work. Found out I'm being sent to New York for a closing. Leaving late tomorrow. I wanted to call Hille and see if he's available to go to dinner with me on Wednesday. Do you have his number?"

"Sure I do. Hold on."

After Eric gave me Hille's number, he laughed and said, "You think you have enough to talk about with Hille to take you through an entire dinner alone?"

"Of course! Why would you say that?" I wasn't entirely convinced either but alcohol always helped.

"He's as buttoned-up as his business shirts, that's all. But then again, you never shut up so I guess it could work. But keep the drinks flowing."

"Are you calling Hille boring, Eric?" I was surprised Eric would say anything bad about a fraternity brother.

"No. He's definitely not boring. He's my brother and I love the guy. But I doubt he was watching *The Love Boat* in his formative years, like you."

Eric had a point. We didn't have much in common. But there was always baseball and I knew Hille was also a Yankees fan.

"But there's always baseball!" Eric said.

"You scare me sometimes, Eric."

"Why's that?"

"Never mind. I should go."

"Okay, have fun and don't do anything I wouldn't do."

Considering Eric was quite the wild child before meeting Jess, I grinned.

"Which leaves your options wide open," he said.

Still grinning, I said, "Thanks, Eric. Talk to you soon." "See ya."

Once I crossed "Call Eric" off my "To do" list, I went to the Yelp website to choose a place to eat dinner. I wanted the restaurant to be close to my hotel so Hille wouldn't simply put me in a cab after dinner. I could spend more time with him if he walked me back to the hotel and I stood a much better chance of getting him inside my room. I didn't want to waste a free dinner on Applebee's, but since the firm would review my expense account, I couldn't exactly justify going to Per Se either. After much deliberation, I chose Del Friscos; men loved steak houses.

Pleased with my decision, I started dialing Hille's number and immediately felt my intestines in my throat and wondered how I was going to disguise my eagerness to hang out with him. I wished I could do a shot first but that would be really desperate, even for me. And, it could get me fired.

After the phone rang three times, his voicemail picked up. I listened to his outgoing message. "You've reached Craig. Leave me a message and I'll call you back." It was exactly the same as Paul's except that Paul included "maybe" before "I'll call you back."

"Hi Craig, it's Stephanie. It's Monday afternoon and I'm calling to let you know I'm actually going to be in New York this week for a closing. If you're around, I thought we could get together for dinner on Wednesday— my treat, well, my firm's treat. If you already have plans, no biggie, but it would be great to see you." I concluded the message by leaving my phone number at work and my cell. I was pretty certain I sounded very casual and nonchalant about the whole thing.

After I hung up, I didn't know what to do with myself. I wanted to make an appointment for a mani/pedi and wax but would have felt much better if I knew for certain I'd see Hille. I scheduled the appointments anyway and forced myself to get some work done. I was resigned to having a very low billing day but had to account for at least eight hours of my time and there was no billing number for contemplating outfits, and getting up to date on current events so I could easily converse on Hille's level. It also occurred to me that it might be a good idea to familiarize myself with the Franklin General deal.

After two hours, I hadn't heard back from Hille and I picked up the phone to cancel my appointments. But then I placed the phone back on the receiver. I was going to New York, the most amazing city in the world, or at least in the United States. The trip was worth the pain of an eyebrow wax whether or not I got to see Hille, even though the bikini wax was more likely to come in handy if I did. He was probably too busy at work and hadn't gotten my message yet. Back in school, Hille always thanked the driver before exiting the crosstown bus, even when he was drunk from free beer at the Towne Tavern's happy hour. He was raised too well to simply blow off my call.

Finally, as my day wound down and I was getting ready to log off my computer, my phone rang and it was a 201 number. I silently prayed, "Please be Hille. Please be Hille."

"This is Stephanie." *Please be Hille.*

"Hi, Steph, it's Hille."

"Hey there! Did you get my message?" No, a guy who has never called me before randomly decided to call me out of the blue on the same day I left him a voicemail that I was going to be in his town. Sometimes I was such a dork. But at least I was very much in touch with my dorkiness. "So, does that work for you?" Hille asked.

I realized I was so busy berating my dorkiness I hadn't heard a word he'd said. "Um, I'm sorry, Craig. My colleague was talking to me at the same time you were speaking. I missed what you said." *Smooth Steph!*

Hille chuckled. "Nice. I get ignored at work all the time. Didn't expect it from you."

"Sorry," I muttered. "So, what'd you say? Will you be around on Wednesday night?" I held my breath.

"Yeah. I don't have plans so that would be great. What time were you thinking?"

Trying not to let my voice give away my excitement, I evenly responded, "I'm honestly not sure what time I'll be through but I made, I mean I can make a reservation for eight. I'll certainly be finished by then and we can always get a pre-dinner drink or three if we're early. Have you been to Del Friscos?"

"No, but it's right near my office and I've heard all good things."

Moving my hands in a horizontal circular motion, I did the Cabbage Patch dance in my chair. "Cool. I'll make a reservation for two and will call you on Wednesday afternoon when I know what time I'll be there."

"Perfect. Looking forward to seeing you, Steph. Twice in one week. That hasn't happened since college."

"I know! Okay, talk to you soon."

After I hung up, I played his words in my head over and over again, *looking forward to seeing you, Steph.*

FIVE

MY MOUTH WATERED as I sat in my aisle seat and watched everyone around me munch on snacks they were smart enough to either bring from home or buy at the airport. I forgot that passengers on shuttle flights didn't get any food, not even those tiny bags of pretzels. So I sipped my tomato juice and looked forward to the room service I would order when I got to the hotel. I had planned to go to bed early so I'd be refreshed for the closing and my night with Hille but I'd never be able to sleep through the sounds of my stomach growling. And it wasn't as if I thought I'd be able to fall sleep easily anyway. I'd be too busy imagining Hille's face as he moved in to plant his juicy lips on mine.

I wondered what the others would say if we started dating. Would they be psyched or think it was weird? I didn't think we were any weirder a couple than Paul and Hope, although I had to admit they were pretty cute together despite the almost ten-year age difference.

I was picturing my family's Chanukah dinner with Hille as my date when the flight attendant announced we had started our descent. I had only gotten to the portion of the daydream when Sam and I tried to stifle our giggles while lighting the menorah and reading the prayer. I couldn't decide whether Hille would be bothered by our mockery of the Festival of Lights or if as a goy (my mom's word), he'd find it as amusing as we did. I knew my mom would be thrilled I finally brought a date to one of the Jewish holidays. She was always on my back, but each time I had contemplated asking someone, we'd broken up by the time the dinner came along.

Since it was too late to nap, I removed my MP3 player from my carry-on bag and shoved the bag underneath the seat in front of me.

I returned my seatback to the upright and locked position and closed my eyes and listened to the songs I had downloaded the night before to inspire me to go for it with Hille for the last twenty minutes of the flight. I had already listened to Natasha Bedingfield's *Unwritten* and Van Halen's *Right Now* when we landed. Michelle Branch's *Breath* had just started when I walked through the gate into LaGuardia and headed to baggage claim. Carry-on was not an option since my toiletries alone took up an entire bag.

*   *   *

When the fat guy waved me over, I faked a smile, walked to where he was sitting at the head of the large conference table and proceeded to notarize a set of documents for at least the fortieth time that day. I had assumed an 8:00 reservation would give me plenty of time to finish the closing, go back to the hotel and take my time getting ready but it was already past 4:30 and Gina, the other paralegal on the deal, had just left to bring more coffee. I started tapping my foot impatiently until I felt the fat man's eyes on me and silently reminded myself to chill out. I had asked to come to New York to attend the closing and so I had to suck it up. It would all be worth it when Hille and I admitted our feelings and laughed about how much time we'd wasted crushing on each other silently. And besides, the less time I had to get to ready, the less time I had to stress out. It was all good.

I applied my notary stamp and seal to the last document in the large pile, turned to the fat man, who I knew from witnessing his signature was named Neil, and said, "These are all done."

Neil reached out his hand. "Thanks so much for your help today."

Hoping he didn't notice my head jerk back at his expression of gratitude, I smiled, shook his hand and said, "It was my pleasure." I blushed, feeling guilty for calling him fat, even though it wasn't out loud.

"Stephanie's actually from our DC office." I looked up to see Adam, the associate on the deal, standing at the table with us. "We were lucky she was available to step in at the last minute when two of our local legal assistants were unavailable." Adam flashed me a wide grin. "Thanks, Stephanie! You were really helpful."

Trying not to notice how cute he was, I said, "No problem. I'm glad I could be here."

"We're pretty much through so you can leave if you want. I need to talk to you about something, though. Do you have a minute?" Adam asked.

"Sure." A minute sounded awesome to me, certainly better than an hour since I was anxious to get back to the hotel room and shower.

Adam, who was only about two inches taller than me but looked exactly like Casey Affleck, down to the green eyes, brown hair and even the beauty mark under his lip, walked me to the corner. He scratched his head and my eyes automatically darted to his left ring finger. It was bare. Not that it mattered, of course, since I only had eyes for Hille.

"Is something wrong with my hand?"

Feeling the pink rise in my cheeks, I quickly looked away and pretended to scan the room while ordering myself to think fast. When I turned back towards him, I frowned and said, "I think I lost my lucky ring. I didn't realize it was missing until I looked at your hand."

Adam looked at me thoughtfully. Then he pointed to the conference table. "Maybe it's under the table. You were sitting there before with Neil."

I remained silent as I looked in the direction of the conference table and pretended to consider Adam's suggestion. Then I widened my eyes and, feigning surprise, said, "Actually, I just remembered! I left it at home. I was afraid to bring it to the big bad city." I exhaled deeply and smiled. "Crisis averted!"

I couldn't believe how quickly I recovered. Much faster than the time I met this cute guy at a bar and asked his sister to set us up. Since it was actually her husband, it didn't go over too well.

"So, can you make it?"

Staring at Adam blankly, I asked, "Make what?"

Grinning, Adam said, "Carmines. Everyone on the deal is going out to dinner tomorrow night to celebrate. Can you make it?"

"Sounds great. I was planning on coming in tomorrow to do some post closing work so I'm not going back to D.C. until Friday anyway." If all went well, I'd be hanging out with Hille again tomorrow but I wasn't going to jinx myself by saying I had other plans.

"Awesome. Well, enjoy the rest of your night. Anything fun planned?"

"Yes! Dinner with my friend, Craig." I looked at my watch. "I should get back to the hotel and change soon. I don't like to wear panty hose any longer than necessary!" Wondering if that was too much information, I bit my lip and anxiously scanned the room searching for a subject change.

Adam laughed. "I can't stand wearing panty hose either." Winking at me, he added, "But it's okay for special occasions."

"Your secret is safe with me," I joked. Scrutinizing Adam as nonchalantly as possible, from his shiny black shoes through which I could almost see my reflection, his neatly pressed navy suit and pink tie, his clean-shaven face and his ring finger sans wedding ring, I questioned his sexual preferences.

Smiling warmly at me, he said, "Okay. Have fun."

Figuring it was perfectly acceptable to flirt with a guy before going on a date with someone else if the first guy was gay, I offered an enthusiastic, "That's the plan" and threw in a wink for good measure.

As I waited for the elevator, I took my phone out of my bag and called Hille. I told him I'd meet him at Del Frisco's at 7:30 which meant I had at least two hours to get ready.

*　*　*

During my long, hot shower, such senseless thoughts as "the next time I shower, my night with Hille will be over," "the next time I shave my legs, I'll know whether Hille shares my attraction" and "the next time I flush this toilet, I might have finally hooked up with Hille in real life instead of in my imagination" ran through my mind.

I wanted to look sexy but not skirt up to my crotch with-fishnet stockings and fuck-me-pumps sexy. After emptying my closet and most of my dresser drawers at home, I decided to wear a simple black A-line dress. It fell to a little above my knees and was cinched at the waist with a skinny red patent leather belt. I wore it with red patent pumps for an additional pop of color. I also packed two pairs of jeans and about five possible tops in the event I changed my mind at the last minute, but stuck to the original plan because the dress enhanced my best attributes and detracted from what I considered my worst. In other words, it showed off my small waist while hiding my ample tushy. And I had never tripped and fallen when wearing those particular shoes.

With shaky hands, I applied my makeup, using at least thirty Q-Tips in the process. I practiced looking at Hille seductively from under my eyelashes and licking my lips without looking like I was auditioning for a Pearl Drops toothpaste commercial. And I smiled at myself to see how widely I could grin without showing too much gum.

Make-up finished, I removed the towel from my head, applied my favorite anti-frizz serum and patiently blow dried my thick head of hair until the spot on the back of my head that tended to stay wet even hours after showering was bone dry.

I turned my suitcase upside down and couldn't find my flat iron. I stood up and circled the hotel room frantically. Realizing I must have unpacked it before I showered, I ran into the bathroom, relief washing over me, until I saw the only electronic appliance in the room besides the hotel-provided blow dryer was my cell phone. My heart palpitating, I sat on the toilet bowl and took deep breaths in and out. I refused to have a heart attack before I even got to kiss Hille. And then I remembered. I thanked God for small favors and ran back to my suitcase where I removed the flatiron from one of the shoe pockets I had shoved it in when the suitcase wouldn't close with it on top.

I continued practicing facial expressions in the mirror until the flatiron heated up and I was at last able to continue my beautification process. But after all that, I wasn't convinced I couldn't look better. I always knew I needed a haircut when my hair didn't look good even after I used my expensive "reserved-for-dates" shampoo and conditioner. I was tempted to wear it up but most guys I surveyed preferred my hair down and, unless Hille was in the minority, he hopefully wouldn't even notice that my long layers were a bit too long. And since it wasn't raining out or humid, it was unlikely to look any worse as the night went on.

When I was ready to go, I stood up on the bed and checked out my body from all angles in the mirror. I couldn't get a perfect view of my butt without risking breaking my neck but I felt pretty confident that I looked kind of hot. I smiled at myself in the mirror and sprayed some Binaca even though I had already brushed my teeth twice. Before I let the door close, I took one last look at the hotel room and wondered if Hille would be with me when I walked back in.

SIX

UPON ENTERING THE RESTAURANT, I was bombarded by a group of men on their way out. They were dressed in corporate attire and carrying leather briefcases and I guessed they were either business executives or lawyers. All but one had salt and pepper hair and I had a feeling the other one probably used Just for Men. They were attractive enough but probably too old for me, although my mother constantly told me to keep my options open with respect to men in their early forties.

I accidentally brushed up against "Just for Men guy" as we crossed paths.

Beaming at me, he said, "You're going in the wrong direction! We're headed over to Connelly's around the corner."

I gave him a wide grin. "No can do. On a date!" *At least I hope so.*

Shaking his head, "Just for Men guy" said, "Too bad for me!"

I smiled. "Thanks for the offer, though." As I walked into the restaurant, I couldn't resist turning around to see if he was still looking at me. He was, and I took it as a sign that the extra care I took getting ready did not go unnoticed.

Still smiling and feeling pretty, I climbed the staircase up to the bar. At the top of the stairs, I scanned the crowded restaurant. Paul would call this place a "sausage fest," albeit an upscale one. Among the men of different ages but sporting the same basic uniform, I quickly spotted Hille sitting on one of the stools at the bar. He had a clear drink in front of him and was staring intently at his Blackberry. I wasn't entirely convinced he received that many emails and wondered if the constant checking of his Blackberry was not a nervous habit or a crutch for when he had nothing else to do. I took a deep breath as I walked toward him and tapped him on his back. "Jeez, Craig, do you *ever* put that thing down?"

He turned around and smiled at me. Placing the Blackberry on the bar, he said, "I will now." Then he stood up and kissed me on the cheek. "Wow. You look nice, Steph."

"Thanks, Craig, I try." Then I sat down on the stool he had saved for me and just smiled at him, searching for my personality. My heart was slamming against my chest and I hoped the bartender would find me fast for some liquid courage.

"I know you said dinner is on you, but can I at least buy you a drink first?" he asked.

"I'm expensing everything, remember? But, hey, if it makes you happy, sure, buy me a drink. What are you drinking"?

Hille raised his drink in the air. "Sprite."

I felt the blood drain from my face as I realized Hille would be sober all night. "Sprite? Wow, you're living on the wild side tonight, Craig!"

"Just kidding. I'm drinking gin and tonic. What do you want?"

The blood returning to my face, I said, "Not gin and tonic!"

Looking amused at my strong reaction, Hille asked, "What, you don't like gin?"

I cringed as I flashed back to the night I drank gin and tonics at a work function a few years back. My memory wasn't entirely clear, but I recalled gushing at each attorney, telling him he was my favorite, and rubbing the belly of a senior partner as if he was the Buddha. And I had to wake my neighbor to let me into my apartment later that night when I couldn't focus to fit the key into the lock. Grossest of all were the cornbread crumbs in my hair the next morning. I still had no idea how they got there. "Let's just say the combination of me and gin is lethal," I said.

"So, gin and tonic it is then?" Hille teased.

Hoping that meant he was looking forward to taking advantage of me later, I shifted my bar stool a bit closer to him and said, "Funny. No, I think I'll go with Stoli Rasberry and soda." I had already put much thought into my drink of choice for the night. Beer was out because I didn't want to get too full, red wine was out because I didn't want my teeth to turn blue, and I was afraid a fancy martini would go straight to my head. I wanted to be seductive, not sloppy. After the bartender poured my drink, Hille asked, "So how was the closing?"

I turned my body sideways so I was leaning in towards him. "Totally exciting. I felt very important and all. I mean, it takes a very talented paralegal to take coffee orders. Aside from serving a light and sweet coffee to a guy who had asked for it black, I managed to stay out of trouble."

Giving me a high five, Hille said, "Atta girl!"

I giggled but then admitted I actually liked being involved in closings. "It's nice to witness the documents I prepare all day being signed. They might mean nothing to me when the day is through, but millions of dollars are exchanged upon signature of a document I drafted. Kind of cool in a geeky sort of way."

"I understand. You're talking to the king of geeks."

"You're not a geek, Craig. Just a brain!" I patted Hille's knee but quickly removed my hand, fearing I was coming on too strong so early in the night. And besides, I needed a bit more booze before I attempted any PDAs. "What time is it?"

Hille glanced at his watch. "Just about 8:00. You think our table is ready?"

"I don't know. I'll check." As I walked with my back to him towards the hostess, I wondered if Hille was watching me and tried very hard to walk normally as if I was not at all self-conscious that he might be looking at my butt. The hostess was a pale woman, probably in her late twenties. She wore her hair slicked back in a bun and with just red lipstick to add color to her face, reminded me of one of the girls from Robert Palmer's *Addicted to Love* video. After she handed two menus to a waiter and directed the men in front of me to follow him to a table, she turned her attention to me and smiled politely. "Can I help you?"

"Yes. I have an eight o'clock reservation for two. Cohen." I turned around to make sure Hille was still where I had left him.

The hostess looked down at her book and back up at me. As if reading from a script, she dryly asked, "Have both members of your party arrived?"

"Yes." I pointed to where Hille was still sitting at the bar. "My date is at the bar."

The waitress nodded and motioned for another waiter. I waited for Hille to turn away from the bartender and look in my direction. When he did, I waved him over. As I admired his lean but athletic body approach me, the room got warmer and I knew it had nothing to do with the actual temperature in the restaurant.

After we were seated, I asked, "So, any vacations planned, Craig?"

"Unfortunately not, but I'm trying to round up the troops for a trip to New Orleans in early spring. You up for it?"

"I could be, although I'm not sure I'm wild enough to flash my boobs to collect beads!"

"C'mon. You're way prettier than most of the girls who have no problem showing their skin."

I flipped my hair, tried to smile demurely and said, "You think?"

"Of course! Don't be silly."

"Are you ready to order?"

I wiped the stupid grin off my face and turned my attention from Hille to the waiter, a gangly college-aged kid covered forehead to toenails in freckles, at least from what I could see peeking out of his tuxedo shirt and vest.

After listening to the specials, Hille motioned for me to go first and I said, "I'll have the bone-in rib eye, rare, please."

The waiter turned to Hille and said, "And you, sir?"

"I'll have the rib eye as well, but well done. Wanna share the potatoes *au gratin*, Steph?"

Even though I'd heard the creamed spinach was to die for, I said, "Absolutely."

After the waiter left, I turned to Hille and narrowed my eyes. "Well done? How can you order steak well done? Rare or medium rare is the only way to go."

Hille shrugged and said, "I don't like any blood."

"The blood is the best part!" I insisted.

"Cohen, how about you pay attention to your own dinner or I'll tell the bartender to secretly replace your vodka with gin so you pass out?" Hille joked.

"Touché," I said. "But it's so much better rare."

Hille reached over, grabbed my drink and motioned like he was going to spill it on me until I said, "You win! Let's agree to disagree." Extending my hand across the table, I said, "Deal?"

Hille shook my hand. "Deal. So, read any good books lately?"

"I'm reading *Blink* at the recommendation of my boss," I said. I figured it was a more impressive title than *The Skinny Bitch*.

Hille's face lit up. "I just read that, too. I thought the stories were nicely written, informative and entertaining at the same time, but in my opinion, they didn't add up to anything terribly profound. What did you think?"

Since my thoughts on the matter were equivalent to a big fat zero, I looked around, hoping the waiter would bring our food over soon. "Uh, actually, I'm almost finished and haven't quite formed an opinion yet. But, yes, very entertaining." I took a sip of my drink. "So, I can't believe the Yankees won their twenty-seventh world championship! And the first year in the new stadium too."

"I know. It was a great season," Hille enthusiastically agreed. "It was nice to see A-rod step up to the plate in the post season."

Chuckling, I said, "I suppose Kate Hudson deserves some of the credit! Kind of concerned about the pitching for next season. Can't rely on three starters all year." I figured Hille would be impressed with my knowledge of baseball and hoped I wouldn't run out of material.

"Agreed. So, how'd you become such a Yankees fan, anyway? Being from Maryland and all, I would have thought you'd be an Orioles fan."

"I do like Cal Ripkin Jr."

"Of course you do," Hille interrupted with a knowing smile.

"Haha. Seriously, though, my stepfather and brother are die-hard Yankee fans and, since they taught me the game as a kid, I was subtly persuaded to share their allegiance. You know, a Reggie Jackson baseball card for Chanukah instead of a Barbie doll, my loyalty in exchange for not getting my butt kicked—that sort of thing. And my real father was originally from Massachusetts and is a Red Sox fan. Since he was a deadbeat, I was even more motivated to root for the Yankees to piss him off."

Hille nodded. "So, how's your steak? Besides raw?"

"Delicious. How's your leather, I mean steak?"

Hille laughed and I felt like the female Jerry Seinfeld.

Although the steak was delicious—juicy, just the way I like it, I wasn't all that hungry. I didn't want Hille to think I was one of those girls who didn't eat on dates, even though he didn't know we were on a date, so I forced down a good portion of it for appearances. When the waiter removed my plate, Hille leaned towards me and pointed at the table. "You sure you had enough to eat, Steph? It looks like you got more food on the tablecloth than in your mouth," he said laughing.

Feeling my face get hot, I said, "Shut up, Craig!"

Although I had enough solid food, I needed more liquid courage and, after dinner, Hille and I stopped at one of the many Irish pubs we passed between the restaurant and The Millennium hotel. A live band was playing Irish songs, none of which Hille or I knew but before long, we were swaying to the music and singing "Yes, we drink. And drink and drink. And drink and drink. And drink and drink. And if I might see a pretty girl I'll sleep with her tonight." When singing the last line, I was pleased that Hille kept his eyes on me.

As an older man and a girl who looked young enough to be his daughter separated from a lip-lock and got up, we took their spot at the end of the bar. "Let's do a shot of tequila," I proposed.

"Don't think so, Steph. I don't do shots on a school night."

Under my breath but loud enough for Hille to hear me, I muttered, "Wimp."

Scowling at me, Hille said, "What did you call me?"

"You heard me," I said.

"I'm not a wimp," Hille insisted.

"I call 'em like I see 'em and what I see before me is a w-i-m-p— wimp!"

"You're trouble, Steph. Fine. I'll do a stinkin' shot of tequila." Hille motioned to the bartender. I was glad it was the old man and not the scantily dressed Elisha Cuthbert look-alike on the other side of the bar.

The bartender nodded to Hille. "Two shots of tequila, please," he said.

I added, "Can we also get salt and lime, please?"

Hille turned to me and said, "Now who's the wimp? Salt and lime?"

Removing the salt shaker from the bar, I smiled sweetly at Hille and said, "I'm a girl, Craig. Calling me a wimp doesn't have the same effect. Sorry."

Hille smirked at me as I licked the underside of my wrist and poured the salt. "Cheers, Craig. Lick it, slam it, suck it!"

After the shot, we agreed another drink was probably a bad idea and Hille escorted me to my hotel.

Before he had the opportunity to initiate the end of the night, I said, "Come in for a minute. Check out my cool hotel room. It's got a great city view." Then I paused before adding, "Unless you're in a real hurry to get going."

Hille stroked his chin, appearing to contemplate. After a brief hesitation, he shrugged. "I guess I can hang out for a bit."

I wondered if he knew what I hoped would happen. I was so nervous I incorrectly inserted the magnetic room key into the slot twice before Hille chuckled, took it from me and opened the door. I glanced at him shyly, feeling my face get red, and said, "Blame it on the tequila shot."

Hille laughed again. "Whatever you say."

Even though we had basically been alone together all night, the dynamic changed as soon as we were enclosed within the four walls of my tiny hotel room and my hands were shaking. I told Hille to help himself to the mini bar and went into the bathroom to channel my inner cheerleader. I looked at myself in the mirror and, with the water running so Hille wouldn't hear me, said, "Get a grip, Stephanie. You look damn good tonight and you know it. Craig Hille would have to be an absolute fool not to want to hook up with you. He wants you and you know it. Now go out there and get him!" With that, I left the bathroom and found Hille sitting on one of the guest chairs staring at his Blackberry.

I tried not to laugh at his predictability. "Lots of emails, Craig?"

As he put the Blackberry back in his briefcase, he said, "Always, but nothing important or remotely interesting."

I sat down on the foot of the king-sized bed, which faced where Hille was sitting and said, "I'm glad we did this, Craig."

"Me too, Steph. It was fun. Thanks again."

"No. Thank *you*. I'm so glad you were free tonight."

There was a brief moment of awkward silence until I took a deep inhale and said, "Craig?"

"Steph?"

"This is kind of embarrassing." *And really fucking scary.*

Hille shifted his body in the chair. "What's wrong?"

"Uh, well, the thing is, I'm totally attracted to you right now." I swallowed hard thinking even the teenagers on *Gossip Girl* were probably more seductive than me.

Hille looked at me, eyebrows raised. Then he let out a shaky laugh. "That's probably just the vodka and that shot of tequila talking."

I bit my lower lip and shook my head. "Mmm, I don't think so. I felt the same way before we had our first drink."

Hille's eyes were closed as he pinched the bridge of his nose. "I'm flattered, Steph. I am. But, uh, what about Paul?"

I jerked my head back in surprise. "What about Paul?"

Hille stood up and said, "He's one of my closest friends—your ex-boyfriend? Wouldn't it be weird?"

"Paul hasn't been my boyfriend in eleven years, Craig! He's had many girlfriends since me and I seriously don't think he'd care what we did. It's not like he asked *my* permission before he started dating Hope."

Now pacing the length of the bed, Hille said, "Steph, I don't feel comfortable with this. The fact that you dated my best friend for two years kind of freaks me out—despite that it was eleven years ago. It's nothing personal—just doesn't feel right. I'm sorry."

I swallowed my dinner back down. This was not how it was supposed to happen and I wished I'd never said anything. I wished I could say "just kidding — psych!"

Defeated but forcing myself not to cower, I looked Hille in the eyes and said, "That's okay, Craig." I gave him a closed mouth smile and shrugged my shoulders. "I'll live."

Hille looked at me kindly and repeated, "Sorry."

Willing myself to play it cool, I jabbed him lightly in the arm. "Stop apologizing! You're only making me feel worse. And anyway, you don't know what you're missing."

"I can only imagine," Hille said with a soft smile.

We stood there in the middle of my hotel room in silence until Hille finally said, "It's getting late. I should get out of here."

"Okay, it was good seeing you, Craig." It was actually a nightmare and I wish I'd wake up already.

"Same here, Steph. When do you leave?"

"Day after tomorrow." *Not soon enough.*

"You staying here again tomorrow?"

" Yup." *Please just go!*
"Okay, maybe I'll call you.
"Cool."
Hille grabbed his briefcase, kissed me on the cheek and said,
"Bye, kiddo."

SEVEN

I WAITED UNTIL THE DOOR CLOSED behind him and said, "Well, that was humiliating" out loud to myself.

I got undressed, put on my pajamas—my ratty and faded Phi Alpha t-shirt and a pair of shorts—and went to the bathroom to wash my face and brush my teeth. As I washed off my makeup and stared at my reflection, I remembered the night the brothers made me an honorary member of the fraternity after I allowed them to give me a swirly. Apparently, sleeping with a brother wasn't a good enough exchange for wearing his letters. So I stuck my head in the toilet bowl merely to earn the right. And I still held it against Paul.

After requesting a wakeup call for the next morning, I turned down the white comforter on the king-sized bed I considered too big for just my 118-pound frame, got inside and turned on the television set. *When Harry Met Sally* was on TBS but I wasn't in the mood for my favorite chick flick. I was also in no mood to watch Samantha Jones have sex with her real estate agent. I usually enjoyed Jay Leno but Alisa Milano was on and I couldn't help but wonder if Hille would have turned *her* down. Finally, I decided on *Bull Durham* until it occurred to me that Hille looked like a younger version of Kevin Costner.

I turned off the television set, assumed the fetal position and closed my eyes, but sleep would not come. I replayed the evening with Hille in my mind: the pre-dinner cocktail, our playful banter at dinner, flirting at the bar afterwards and the rejection otherwise known as the most embarrassing moment of my life. I knew Paul wouldn't give a crap if Hille and I hooked up and wondered if Hille was trying to protect my ego by using that excuse. Why had I thought he liked me? Maybe Hille always winked at girls and I had never noticed. Maybe he was just being friendly when he asked when I was coming to New York again. Maybe my crush back in college had been completely one-sided. Looking up to the freshly painted ceiling, still visible thanks to well-lit Time Square peeking through the window, I offered a sarcastic, "Thanks, God. Thanks for nothing." Then I buried my head under the oversized pillow and prayed the whole night was just a bad dream.

* * *

When I woke up the next morning with a tequila-induced headache, I instantly flashed back to Hille promising me his rejection was "nothing personal," turned over on my stomach and cried until I forced myself to get in the shower and go to work.

I had done embarrassing things before and, although I beat myself up over them, the mortification always subsided in time. Once, I walked into Union Pub in D.C. only to discover that my skirt was tucked into my jacket and the entire bar got a bulls'-eye view of my ass as I walked to the back to meet my friends. I didn't go back to that bar for almost a year. I had a feeling this bruise would take even longer to heal, especially since Hille was a staple in my crowd of friends and, unlike a bar I could simply replace with another, he was not someone I could easily avoid. My head felt like it had been stomped on repeatedly by Big Foot and I wondered how I was going to get through the day. On top of that, everyone on the Franklin General deal was going to dinner that night. It was going to be a long day.

I fought my way through the crowds of people on the street, including rush hour corporate-types like myself and halted tourists, mesmerized by billboards, office buildings and other attractions of which I, also a tourist in my own right, was too hung over to notice. The two block walk took close to ten minutes and when I finally made it to my firm's building, I stopped at the little store in the lobby to pick up a sample packet of aspirin and a bottle of water.

"Smile, little lady. It can't be that bad."

I looked up into the deep-set sapphire eyes of the elderly man behind the counter, smiled and said, "You're probably right, but it sure feels that way."

The man grabbed a copy of *Cosmopolitan*, handed it to me with my change and said, "On me. Enjoy. But promise to smile."

For the first time since returning to my hotel room after dinner the night before, I managed a genuine smile and said, "Thank you so much. You just made my day." And although I meant what I said, I honestly had no desire to learn 139 ways to drive my man crazy in bed and would have much preferred a copy of *Bon Appetit*.

Part of me was desperate to be comforted. I wanted to tell one of my friends what had happened so she could tell me it wasn't as bad as I thought—that Hille was a dumb fuck who wouldn't recognize a sexy girl if she was sitting on his face. I even imagined crying to my mother over hot chocolate and a bottle of Reddy Whip. She would shrug it off and say, "Next!" But I decided to keep my misery to myself. A friend dragged me to a cheesy seminar once about finding true happiness and the quirky moderator encouraged the attendees to "fake it until you make it." I decided to fake not giving a shit about being rejected by Hille in the hopes that eventually I really wouldn't give a shit.

I immersed myself in boxes of closing binders with Gina, only taking a short break at lunchtime. I felt like ordering the entire menu at TGI Fridays but decided on an egg roll from the Chinese restaurant across the street, relying on the logic that it would satisfy my craving for fried food, yet leave me hungry enough to take advantage of the free dinner later.

And I was definitely hungry when I arrived at Carmines and inhaled the aroma of garlic and tomatoes. I glanced over at the hordes of people sitting at the bar, probably waiting for a table to become available, and breathed a sigh of relief that our crew had a reservation. I was entranced by the giant menu mounted on the wall when I heard someone call my name. I looked up to find Adam walking toward me from the back of the restaurant with a grin, his dimples out in full force.

"Hey, Steph. We're in the back. Follow me."

As he led me through the packed restaurant, I became instantly revitalized by the energy of the place. Waiters in all white uniforms were bustling about, carrying enormous platters of food. And the conversations among the separate parties, although I couldn't make out any of the words, created a buzzing sound I found invigorating.

Steve, the partner on the deal, ordered a feast of appetizers and entrees and, thanks to flowing bottles of red wine and a little hair of the dog, my persistent headache from over-imbibing the night before made a complete exit. By the time the Carmine's salad and fried calamari were served, I was no longer thinking about Hille either. Instead, I basked in the attention of the twelve attorneys and paralegals that comprised the Franklin General team, especially Adam who was sitting next to me.

"So, Steph, is the D.C. office as cool as the New York office?" he asked.

As everyone at the table looked in my direction, I swallowed the piece of chicken marsala in my mouth and gave the only acceptable answer, "Of course not! It's pretty cool but New York is my favorite."

"You did a great job on the deal, Stephanie. You're welcome to bill more hours from the New York office anytime," Steve said.

Although I doubted my notarizing skills were better than anyone else's, I said, "Thanks so much. Glad to be of help."

Adam whispered, "If I didn't have to go back to the office tonight, I'd take you for a drink. Next time?"

I felt the blush rise in my cheeks and said, "Sure," relieved he was too busy to go out. Adam was seriously adorable (and apparently not gay), but I'd probably make a fool of myself, assuming he was actually interested in me. It wouldn't be the first time that week. Yes, better to leave it at harmless flirting than psych myself up for more and watch Cupid laugh his ass off while shooting his arrow in some other girl's direction.

When the first group of associates left to go back to the office, I got up as well. I waited for Steve to look in my direction and said, "I've gotta head out, too. Thanks so much for dinner."

"It was great to have you, Stephanie. I'll put in a good word with Gerard," Steve said.

"I'd appreciate it!" Then I turned to Adam and said, "Let me know if you have any questions regarding the closing binders I prepared."

"Will do. Thanks for your help, Stephanie. Have a safe flight back."

"Thanks! Don't work too hard tonight." I waved one last time to the folks remaining at the table, weaved my way through the closely spaced tables and exited the restaurant onto crowded 44th Street.

Back in my hotel room, I decided to take advantage of the mini-bar and, since I didn't have to get up too early the next morning, I cracked open a bottle of merlot and relaxed in front of the television set. I was contemplating changing into my pajamas when I was startled by a knock on my door. I grabbed my cell phone, ready to call 911 if necessary. "Who is it?"

The voice on the other side of the door replied, "Hille."

Taken by surprise, I dropped my phone on the floor, called out, "One second" and ran my hands through my hair. I quickly put my phone back on the dresser, took a deep breath and opened the door to find Hille standing there in his suit and tie with a sheepish grin on his face. "Can I come in"?

Wondering what the hell he wanted, I stepped to the side to give him room to enter. "Of course."

"I was in the neighborhood."

"Cool. I was just helping myself to the mini-bar. Want something?" *Fake it till you make it.*

Hille walked to the mini-bar and kneeled down. "Let's see what you got." When he stood up again, he was holding a Toblerone and a bottle of Miller Lite. "Is this okay?"

"It's not on my dime, Craig. Although the partner might wonder how I could possibly eat a Toblerone after the large quantity of food we absorbed at Carmines."

"Carmines, huh? Good stuff," Hille said with an easy grin.

"Yeah, it was good. What did you do tonight?" *And why are you here?*

"I stayed late to do an upgrade on the phone systems and went for a beer with a colleague."

Hille and I just looked at each other for a bit until I said, "Craig" at precisely the same time he said, "Stephanie."

"You first" we both said, again at the same time.

"No, you first," I insisted.

"I feel kind of crappy about how we ended things last night, Steph."

So much for "fake it till you make it." "Geez, Craig. Could you let it go? I think it would be less painful for both of us if you just let it go." Hille shook his head. "That's the problem. I can't let it go. I've been thinking about it all day."

I sighed and waited for him to continue.

"I spoke to Paul," he said.

I sat down on the edge of the bed. "Lovely. I was kind of hoping we could keep this to ourselves, but I should've known better. Let's get this over with. What did he say?"

His tone serious, Hille replied, "He said it was a good thing I didn't go for it because it would've been the end of our friendship."

"Shut up! Seriously?"

Hille's lips curled up. "No. He just called me a dumb ass. Correction— first he thanked me for being so loyal and *then* he called me a dumbass."

Laughing, I said, "I knew he wouldn't care. My breakup with Paul could go into the *Guinness Book of World's Records* of amicable breakups."

Hille chuckled. "That's sort of what Paul said."

Still curious as to why Craig showed up at my doorstep, I said, "Craig, you didn't have to come here to tell me that."

"I know, but I wanted to. I didn't want to leave things weird between us."

"If things are weird between us, it's my fault, not yours. I shouldn't have told you I was attracted to you. None of this would've happened." And I could go back to my deluded reality that we're star-crossed lovers waiting for fate to bring us together at last.

"No, I'm glad you did - tell me you're attracted to me, that is."

Looking down at the carpet, I said, "I'm glad one of us is happy. But it would have been nice if the feeling was mutual."

"My attraction to you is not an issue, Stephanie."

I looked up hesitantly and asked, "It's not?" I worried that I heard him wrong and willed my legs to stop shaking,

"No, it's not. I'm totally attracted to you."

I still wasn't convinced and scanned the room for a hidden camera, probably planted by Paul so he could personally witness me make an ass out of myself this time. Tilting my head up towards him, I asked, "You are?"

Hille nodded, smiled and said, "Yeah."

"Really?"

"Yes, really!" Hille said, laughing.

I couldn't think of anything witty or meaningful to say so I just grinned and said, "Good."

Hille put his bottle of beer on the dresser and approached the bed where I was sitting, feet dangling over the edge. "So, how was dinner?" I felt my heart pounding and wished I could rip it out of my chest temporarily. "It was good."

Hille sat on the bed next to me and held a strand of my long hair in his fingers before placing it behind my ear. Then he kissed my neck and asked, "What'd ya eat?"

Feeling a bit breathless, I answered, "chicken," and closed my eyes as Hille continued to kiss my neck and nibble on my ear.

Between kisses, he asked, "What else?"

My heart was still racing from being so close to him and feeling his breath on my face and his lips on my neck that my usual steel-trap memory suffered a power outage and I could not for the life of me remember what I had eaten less than an hour before. Apparently, lustful feelings also caused me to stutter as I answered, "I don't re-re-member."

I was still reeling over my speech impediment when Hille stopped kissing my neck, looked at me for a moment and kissed me on the lips. I had psyched myself up for being with him the night before, but my bravado disappeared the instant he declined my advances, and fear and insecurity took its place. In the first moments of kissing him, my inner voice expressed an hour's worth of concerns: *Does he think I am a good kisser? Will he think my boobs are too small or my ass too big? Is my bikini wax still fresh?* And I wished I had taken the time to read that article in *Cosmopolitan.* I usually liked to hook up with music on to drown out my deafening thoughts.

But then I remembered I was actually making out with Hille, the guy I had fantasized about kissing over ten years ago and I started enjoying it. I opened my eyes to see if Hille was enjoying it as much as I was. His eyes were closed and so I closed mine again, too. Despite the beer, his breath was cool and sweet, like a Peppermint Pattie and his lips were buttery and soft. He definitely used Chapstick and I made a mental note to ask him what flavor so I could buy it later.

Hille wasted no time before reaching under my sweater and expertly unclasping my bra. When I felt his warm hands caressing my skin, I figured two could play at that game, so I stopped kissing him, and when he opened his eyes I smiled and began unbuttoning his shirt from the top down while my fingers roamed the patch of soft dark hair that covered the top of his tanned chest. He looked even better with his shirt off in real life than he did in my daydreams and I whispered, "I've been dying to do this since yesterday, Craig." It had actually been longer, but he didn't need to know that.

I ran my hands up and down his arms and gripped his defined biceps. I could have held onto them all night but before I knew it, Hille had pushed me onto the bed, unbuttoned my pants and pulled them off my legs. Things were moving faster than I had intended but I hadn't hooked up with a guy I actually wanted to sleep with in so long, there was no way I was going to tell him to slow down. And the wetness between my legs told me there was no reason to wait. I was about to ask if he had something when he got up and removed a condom from his wallet, and I didn't even have a chance to check out the size of his package before he was inside me. But he fit just fine and as we began to move together, I kept thinking "I'm having sex with Hille. I'm having sex with Hille!" until I finally stopped thinking and lost myself in the rhythm. I bit his shoulder to stop myself from calling out his name when I came but I might have done it anyway. I figured as long as I didn't scream, "Fuck me!" at the top of my lungs, I could live with it.

Afterwards we both lay on our sides facing each other.

I waited for our breathing to return to normal and, hoping to keep him occupied until we were ready to do it again, said, "So, Craig, tell me, what's your favorite color?"

Hille cocked his head to the side and repeated, "My favorite color?"

"Yep."

"Uh, I'll go with blue. What's yours?"

"Mine's blue, too. Not a light blue, but a dark, almost purplish blue. What about food? What's your favorite food?" I asked.

"Hmm, anything fried, I guess. Or anything with cheese. Fattening and artery clogging is the way to go."

"Interesting," I said. "I don't know where you put it. Okay, what's your favorite movie?"

Hille didn't say anything and I figured he was thinking about it. "Okay, I'll go first. I have a few. *Field of Dreams* is one. *When Harry Met Sally* is another. *Godfather Part II* definitely. And, don't laugh, *Saturday Night Fever*. Okay, your turn."

Hille didn't say anything and so I whispered, "Craig?" When he still didn't answer, I peered closer at his face and saw his eyes were closed and his mouth was slightly open. When I heard the faint snore escape his lungs, I knew he had fallen asleep. Proud to have worn him out, I chuckled, kissed him softly on the lips and closed my eyes.

EIGHT

WHEN I WOKE UP THE NEXT MORNING, Hille was sitting on the edge of the bed looking at his Blackberry. He was fully dressed in his work clothes.

Wishing I had kept a bottle of eye drops on the nightstand, I rubbed the corners of my eyes and said, "Hey. What are you doing up so early?"

Hille turned around to face me. "Getting ready for work," he said, yawning. "I used the shower. Hope you don't mind."

"Of course I don't mind. But what's the hurry?" Patting the side of the bed where Hille had slept, I said, "Don't you have time to hang out a little before you go?" I was hoping for a round of morning sex.

"I wish I did, Steph, but I can't afford to be late for work, not with all of the recent layoffs."

"Why didn't you wake me?" *We could've had morning sex.*

"I knew you didn't have to get up early today. You were sleeping so soundly, I didn't want to wake you up unnecessarily."

"I would've gotten up," I insisted, but fearing I sounded desperate, added, "But I do love my beauty sleep!"

Hille grinned. "I figured as much. Anyway, I had a great time."

"I had a great time too, Craig."

Hille stood up and walked over to me. "I really have to go. What time is your flight?"

"Not until 2:30ish."

"Good, you have time to go back to sleep for a bit. "

"Yup," I said.

"Anyway, if you get bored waiting for the plane, give me a call, okay?"

"Sure. Have a great day, Craig."

Hille sat on the edge of the bed. "Thanks, kid. You too." Then he gave me a quick kiss on the lips, stood up and said, "Bye, Steph."

I was afraid he smelled my morning breath so I nodded and gave him a closed mouth smile. When I felt he was a safe enough distance away to open my mouth again, I said, "Bye Craig" and watched him walked toward the door. Before leaving the room, he turned around one more time and gave me a quick wave goodbye.

After he left, I jumped out of bed and checked myself out in the bathroom mirror. I breathed a sigh of relief that my bed-head was not too bad and my mascara from the night before was not running down my face. Sitting back on the bed, I wondered what Hille was thinking. Was he glad he had changed his mind about hooking up with me or did he have regrets? Was the sex as good for him as it was for me or did he think I sucked in bed? Did he think I was relationship-worthy or just another name to add to his little black book? Why was he in such a hurry to leave? Did he really need to get to work so early?

Since morning sex with Hille was off the table, I forced myself to stop thinking about him and, after counting backwards from 100, I fell asleep. When I woke up a few hours later, I immediately worried that it was my morning breath that had turned Hille off. I blew on my hand and couldn't smell anything but it was normal to have bad breath first thing in the morning! I was incredibly charming, not to mention passionate in bed and if something as lame as morning breath could turn Hille off, I didn't want him anyway. I threw my clothes and toiletries in my suitcase and, after I completed the express check-out, I quickly glanced at my cell phone to see if Hille had called.

During my brief plane ride from LaGuardia to Reagan, I decided to chalk the night up to a good time between friends of the opposite sex. I refused to play the desperate girl hoping to turn a one night stand into a relationship. And besides, if Hille didn't like me, it was his loss. Feeling better and infinitely more powerful, I closed my eyes and dozed for the remainder of the trip.

After we arrived in D.C., I made my way to baggage claim and, as I waited with the others for the buzzer to go off and the bags to make their way around the carousel, I turned on my phone to see if Hille had called.

NINE

I WAITED PATIENTLY FOR MY DRINKS at the shiny red circular bar and chuckled silently, watching the guy next to me purposely flex his muscles as he raised his arm to get the bartender's attention. Catching me off guard, he turned to me and said, "Did anyone ever tell you that you look like the girl from *Gremlins?*"

Although I had heard this one before, I played dumb and asked, "Which girl would that be?"

He momentarily looked away from me and flashed his $5 bill in the bartender's face. I had a feeling the bartender was intentionally ignoring him since $5 wouldn't even buy a Diet Coke during happy hour specials at Lounge 201. He repeated, "Guy! Guy!" multiple times before turning his sunless-tan-gone-bad face back in my direction. "You know. The actress from *Fast Times at Ridgemont High.* The hot one."

Knowing the answer, I said, "You mean Phoebe Cates?"

"Yeah! That's her."

As I wondered why the only guys who seemed to hit on me were the ones I didn't find the slightest bit attractive, I gave him a sideways smile and said, "I actually have heard that a few times but, other than the dark hair, I don't see a resemblance. But I'll take it as a compliment. Thanks!"

Cutting in, Suzanne said to the guy, "Does that mean we'll catch you jerking off in the bathroom later?" Grabbing our drinks from the bar, she turned to me and said, "I got us a table."

I called out, "Nice talking to you," before making a quick escape with Suzanne to our table in the brightly lit lounge, which was decorated with posh booths and bright red couches.

Before we got halfway through our first round of mojitos, Suzanne asked if my membership on Match.com was still active. She met her fiancé Luke online and whenever I complained about a horrible first date, she'd recite her favorite cliché: "It only takes one!"

"Yes, Suze, my profile is still up." My membership had actually expired but it wasn't technically a lie since I could still receive emails. I just couldn't open them.

"But are you actively searching or sitting around waiting for guys to email you?" she asked.

"What do you think?"

Suzanne gave me a disapproving look while I sank my butt lower into the leather seat cushion. "I'd prefer to meet someone the old fashioned way, that's all," I said. Like in college, I thought, as my mind wandered to Hille.

"Hmm, not sure if I should be insulted since I didn't meet Luke the old fashioned way."

"Suze, I totally didn't mean that as an insult to you, but I can't stand online dating anymore and you've already snagged the one decent guy! For now, I think I'll take my chances and see what the universe throws my way."

"Like that goon at the bar?" Suzanne joked.

"Please. Seriously, can we please drop the subject? It's a buzz kill and these mojitos are too good to waste."

"I just don't want some bitch stealing your husband because she was looking for him while you were waiting for the universe to drop him at your doorstep!"

"You sound like my mom! I promise not to let some bitch steal my husband, okay! Now can we get another round of drinks? I have some information to share." I decided that maybe Suzanne would be less concerned about my single status if she knew I'd had sex recently.

"Information, huh? I'm sufficiently intrigued." Standing up, she said, "Okay, I'll buy another round and you can spill when I get back."

The deafening sounds of Beyonce's *Single Ladies* reverberated in the air as I watched Suzanne maneuver her way through the packed lounge area until her blonde curls disappeared in the crowd of Capitol Hill staffers and lobbyists. Despite spending so much time together, our love lives were not nearly as in sync as our menstrual cycles. Suzanne ended one long-term relationship, joined Match and only went out with two other guys before meeting Luke. My only long-term relationship was Paul and most of it took place under the influence of alcohol.

When Suzanne returned with our drinks, she sat down and said, "First of all, I hate this song—sets women back decades. Second of all, and more importantly, what information do you have to share with me?"

Laughing, I said, "First of all, I'm surprised you don't love this song considering that Luke 'put a ring on it'! Second of all, you don't waste any time, do you?"

"You started it, girlfriend. What's up?"

"Okay." I paused dramatically. "Since we were on the subject of my love life—"

Interrupting, Suzanne said, "A subject I promised I'd drop!"

"Yes, but if I initiate the conversation, it's okay."

"Okay, I am now fully aware of the rules. Keep going."

Raising my voice facetiously, I said, "Please, no more interruptions! What I'm trying to tell you is that I actually had a little fling in New York."

Looking at me with surprise, Suzanne said, "Seriously? Wow. Who with? One of the attorneys?"

"No. No one from the firm. Someone I went to college with. Have I ever mentioned Hille to you?"

Suzanne shook her head in answer, but then her eyes widened. "Hille! Yes! The serious one who's the Tony Randall to Paul's Jack Klugman, right?"

"Nice memory, Suze! Yes, that Hille."

"You fucked him?"

"You're so crude, but yes, we had sex." Suzanne wasn't one for beating around the bush.

"This is definitely turning into a more interesting drink night than I was expecting. I might have to tell Luke not to wait up. Give me the scoop. How'd it happen?"

"Well, Hille put his penis in my..."

Crossing her eyes, Suzanne said, "Du-uh! I know *how* it happened. You know what I meant, loser!"

"I actually thought that was pretty funny but, yes, I know what you meant."

Suzanne looked at me expectantly. "So?"

I started to tell her what happened the first night.

"He's gay," Suzanne interrupted.

"What the fuck are you talking about? He's not gay!"

Suzanne stood up. "A guy who turns down sex with a girl who is not a dog is gay. Period," she said, matter-of-factly.

"Can you let me finish? And, by the way, I'm so flattered you don't think I'm a dog." We stared each other down for a few seconds before I broke the silence. "Um, why are you standing?"

Suzanne sat back down. "Finish."

"As I was saying, he initially turned me down since Paul and I used to date."

"A hundred years ago!" Suzanne cut in again.

"Which is exactly what I said, but he was adamant."

After interrupting me several more times, Suzanne finally allowed me to conclude my story.

"We started kissing and, before I knew it, we were drenched in post coital sweat."

Suzanne raised her eyebrows. "Before you knew it?"

"Figure of speech, Suze! No, it was good. Really, really good." I felt my face flush and a tingle in my pants as I flashed back to Hille's body hovering over mine, my hands gripping his firm butt cheeks.

"Damn, Stephanie, you're full-on beaming right now!"

"I know," I said, smiling. "Weird, huh?"

"No, not weird. I like seeing you excited about a guy!" Leaning over the table in interest, Suzanne asked, "So, what was so good about it?"

"Suze, it wasn't just the sex. Kissing him was like butter. Literally, his mouth was smooth like melted butter and my lips practically slid off his. So many guys have rough lips. I don't know why soft lips aren't as important to guys as they are to girls!" I closed my eyes. If I concentrated hard enough, I could still feel Hille's lips on mine.

"Stephanie!"

I opened my eyes. "What?"

Laughing, Suzanne said, "I lost you there for a minute. Tell me more!"

Feeling the heat rise in my face, I said, "Oops. Where was I? Oh, yeah, his mouth tasted like butterscotch. A butterscotch flavored Altoid!"

Looking at me skeptically, Suzanne repeated, "Butterscotch?"

"Yes, I tasted butterscotch."

"Maybe he ate a bag of Werther's Originals before he got to your hotel," Suzanne said smiling. "So, do you like the guy or was it just great sex?"

"I think I like him, Suze. He makes me nervous in a good way and I feel the need to impress him like I haven't felt around a guy in ages."

"Impress him how?" Suzanne asked.

"With my smarts."

Before I could continue, Suzanne snorted and I waved my hand in protest, almost knocking over my drink. "Seriously, he's a brain and, although I love chick-flicks and repeats of *The Brady Bunch*, I want him to know I'm not one dimensional."

"Stephanie, he's known you since college. I'm sure your deeper side has surfaced at least once or twice in that time," Suzanne said before breaking out in laughter.

"Don't laugh at me!" I begged. "C'mon. I actually have feelings for a guy that go beyond tepid for the first time since you've known me and you laugh. Nice."

Finally serious, Suzanne said, "I'm sorry, Steph. I admit, I am having too much fun with this. I'll stop."

"Thanks."

"So, when are you going to see Butterscotch again?"

"I don't know. I haven't heard from Butterscotch since he left my hotel room five days ago." And I had double checked to make my sure my phone was charged and on at all times. And since Hille had responded to the "joke of the day" email Paul had sent to all of us, I knew he wasn't trapped under a dresser in his apartment.

Tapping her perfectly manicured pointer finger on the table, Suzanne said, "You know what I always say?"

Hoping for sage advice, I asked, "What's that?"

"Don't put all your eggs in one bastard."

TEN

THE FOLLOWING NIGHT, Hille still hadn't called and I needed an excuse to put distance between me and my phone so I went to the gym. Running was a much better stress reliever than sitting in front of the tube with a pint of Cherry Garcia and I wanted to be in good shape in case Hille called and wanted to see me naked again. I stepped on the treadmill, entered my stats and began my two minute warm-up of walking briskly. Although I was usually pretty focused at the gym, I decided to actually look around and see if there was any eye candy. I needed to prove to myself that Hille was not the only guy I found appealing. To my left, a girl who weighed next to nothing was running vigorously. She was probably better off strength training or eating something more than raw carrots. To my right, a plump guy, probably close to my age, was jogging at a slow pace. He was perspiring so profusely that some of his sweat landed on my treadmill and I scanned the room for another open machine. There weren't any so I focused on not vocalizing how disgusting I thought he was. Next to the row of treadmills, the resident meatheads showed off their massive biceps by lifting heavy weights, but none of them did it for me. I was never attracted to the beefy muscular type. I preferred guys who were in shape, like Hille, but didn't look like they spent all of their free time at the gym.

Just thinking about Hille made me horny and as the beginning notes of U2's *Where The Streets Have No Name* played on my MP3, I increased the speed of the treadmill to 8.0. I quietly sang along to the music, hoping to drown out thoughts of him but it didn't work. The faster I ran, the more vividly I could imagine him cheering me on, screaming "That's my girl!" as I crossed the finish line of the National Marathon.

After my run, I walked to the floor mats to stretch and do some sit-ups. As I passed the row of Nautilus equipment, I stopped short in my tracks and banged into one of the male fitness instructors.

The instructor, a tall guy wearing a black t-shirt with the word 'Trainer' printed across the left breast, put his hand on my shoulder and asked, "Are you okay?"

Flustered and distracted by another guy who, from the back, looked exactly like Hille and was wearing a Phi Alpha Omega t-shirt, I turned to the instructor. "Oh, God. I'm so sorry. I thought I recognized someone. Sorry about that."

"No worries. There's some heavy equipment here, though, so you should be more careful."

"Definitely. Really sorry." The instructor walked away and I immediately turned back to the Hille look-alike who was now facing me and looked nothing like him. I shook my head in embarrassment and left the gym without doing my sit-ups. On my way home, I stopped at Safeway to pick up dinner - Ramen Noodle Soup. I was in the mood to indulge in serious MSG.

Later that night, I picked up the phone to call my mom just as it rang. "Hello?"

The male voice on the other end of the phone said, "Hello."

I immediately recognized his voice and felt a pulsing in my throat like my heart had relocated to my mouth. To waste time while I swallowed my heart back down to my chest, I asked, "Who is this?"

"It's Hille."

"Hey there." I said before taking a deep breath in and out to calm my nerves.

"That was weird. I didn't even hear the phone ring."

"I don't know. I had my hand on the phone, ready to make another call and picked it up mid-ring. Maybe that's why."

"Do you want me to call you back?"

"No, that's okay. It wasn't urgent." I knew my mother would gladly come second to an eligible bachelor. "What's up?" Hoping his call would be worth the long wait, I sat down on my favorite reclining chair, kicked my feet up and muted *Bones* on my television set.

"Nothing much. Just wanted to say hi."

"Hi back at you. What's going on?"

"Nothing. It's pouring here so I'm looking out the window and watching the trees sway in the wind."

"You have trees in New York?" I joked.

"One or two. But I live in New Jersey. We have lots of trees in Hoboken. We even have flowers."

"Is that why they call it the Garden State?"

"No. I think the Garden State was a reference to New Jersey truck farms that provided floral and agricultural produce to cities in the area back in the 1930s."

I smiled to myself. If anyone would know the origin of a state's nickname, it was Craig Hille. "You're a wealth of information, Craig."

"So, I had fun last week."

Picturing him naked, I said, "So did I."

"I actually wanted to call you sooner but we're building out the 44th floor of my building and I've been in charge of the computer installation. It's been crazy."

"No worries. I've been so busy lately, too." Yes, I had been very busy anxiously waiting his call.

"I didn't want too much time to go by—I don't want things to be awkward the next time we see each other, you know?"

"Why would things be awkward?" I asked.

"It's just, we've been friends a long time..."

As I heard the word "friends" escape Hille's mouth, my lips started to quiver and I readjusted the recliner to the upright position.

"And I don't want what happened to get in the way of our friendship," Hille continued.

As I recalled the many times I offered a guy my friendship as a gentle letdown, I knew what was coming and felt moistness behind my eyes I couldn't hold back.

"We're friends, right, Steph?"

Wiping my inner eyes with the knuckle of my pointer finger, I thought to myself "fake it till you make it, swallowed down my tears and said to Hille in my brightest voice, "Of course, we're friends! Don't be silly!"

ELEVEN

THAT WAS A FIRST. A guy had never pulled the friend card on me. Sure, I had crushes on guys who never asked me out and there were plenty of times I was too afraid to even strike up a conversation with one, but I had never actually hooked up with a guy who afterwards said he didn't like me "that" way. And why did he wait until after we'd had sex to tell me? Was it because the sex was bad? I thought it was hot! Was it because he wasn't attracted to me? He called me pretty at dinner and then said his attraction to me "wasn't an issue." Was he lying? I didn't get it. Was this my comeuppance for all the times I had told a guy I didn't feel romantic potential but would love to be friends?

After silently wallowing in self-pity failed to make me feel better, I grabbed a can of Diet Coke from my refrigerator, sat at my two-person kitchen table and called Hope to vent.

"Maybe it's the distance," she said. "I mean D.C. and New Jersey aren't exactly in walking distance."

"Maybe you're right. But why did he bother coming back to my hotel room in the first place? If he was so concerned with our friendship, why didn't he just leave it at 'I don't feel comfortable sleeping with my best friend's ex-girlfriend from three billion years ago?' Did I do something wrong to turn him off?" I took a gulp of my soda, wishing it was beer. There was silence on the other end of the phone, which made me paranoid. "What?" I demanded.

"I don't know what to tell you, Steph. I don't get men either. Apparently, they're from Mars or something. Paul leaves me guessing all the time."

"How are things with you guys?" I felt a pang of envy as I said "you guys" since no one was likely to describe Hille and me that way.

"It depends on the day," Hope said glumly.

"Dating Paul is like a box of chocolates, Hope—You never know what you're gonna get!"

"That's an understatement. Last time he came here, he pulled out all the stops—took me out to Davios for steaks and got us a room at the Hotel Sofitel. He was actually romantic. But the last time I went there, he left me in his apartment alone all day while he golfed with his work buddies. Not so romantic."

"That's because Paul is clueless," I said. "One year in college, he made his pledges take me out for Valentine's Day. He thought I'd be psyched. Granted, I have nothing against being the only girl in the company of men, but on Valentine's Day? I don't mean to laugh at your expense, but it's just Paul being 'Paul' and it's not a reflection of his feelings for you. I can assure you of that."

"So, I guess I should just be happy that he didn't send *me* out to golf with his work buddies while *he* watched football at home alone? Is that your point?"

"No, my point is that guys suck."

"No argument there," Hope said.

From out my window, I observed a couple walking down my street holding hands. Since they couldn't see me, I flipped them the bird and cursed their happiness. "So, onto another subject! What else is new with you? How's Claires?"

"Same 'ole: chock full of accessories! Can't wait to be an Occupational Therapist and get out of the retail biz for good."

"Only one more year until you graduate!"

"Yup."

"So, did Paul say anything about me and Hille?"

"Not to me."

My stomach felt queasy as I imagined Paul and Hille laughing about me and comparing notes on my sexual aptitude. Not that they'd ever do that to me. Some random chick they both picked up, maybe, but not me. *Or would they?* "Promise you're not lying?"

"I promise! Are you okay about this Steph?"

"Aside from feeling stupid, yeah, I'm okay," I said.

"Why do you feel stupid?"

"Uh—I don't make a habit of throwing myself at guys."

Hope laughed but didn't comment.

"Anyway, what's done is done. The sex was great, but I don't think we'll be triple dating with you, Paul, Jess and Eric anytime soon."

"Is that what you want?"

"Kind of. He's so damn sexy, not to mention how convenient it would be since we're already friends." Paranoid again, I got up from the table and started pacing my kitchen floor. "Hope, don't say a word to Paul. I mean it! If you even talk in your sleep about it when sharing his bed, I'll kill you."

"I won't breathe a word. I promise."

"I mean, it's not like he promised to love me till the end of time or anything. But I'm disappointed. And totally embarrassed."

"Don't be! You were two consenting adults. There's nothing to be embarrassed about." Hope giggled and said, "You didn't ask him to go steady, did you?"

"Haha. No. But I did pin him!"

"You crack me up. So, you'll still be there on New Year's Eve, right?"

"I'll need to grow some serious balls to deal with the endless teasing which will undoubtedly come at my expense for doing the nasty with Hille. Good thing I have a month to prepare, but yes, I'll be there with balls on."

Hope chuckled. "I just need to sleep with Hille, or you with Eric and we can start our own reality show— *Incestuous friends!*"

"That's gross, Hope. Anyway, about Paul. I wouldn't worry about it. He's totally into you. And he should be! You're a hot, twenty-five-year-old chick with a kick ass body, your partying skills could rival Lindsay Lohan's, minus the DUIs and lesbian tendencies, and you have a heart of gold—no, platinum! He'd be hard-pressed to find better than you and he knows it. If anything, you'll find a hotter, younger, richer guy and dump *his* ass!"

"Doubt it, but thanks for the vote of confidence."

Kind of hoping she'd return the favor, I said, "Anytime."

"And by the way, you're way too cool for Hille anyway."

Smiling, I said, "Thanks, Hope. I sort of hoped for someone to kiss under the mistletoe this year, though."

Her tone gentle, Hope said, "I know. But look on the bright side."

"What bright side?"

"You're a Jew. And Jews don't have mistletoe!"

"Oh. That bright side," I said, laughing.

Hope was right. Being a member of the tribe, I could probably avoid the mistletoe.

But I couldn't avoid my Jewish mother.

TWELVE

AS WE WERE FINISHING CHANUKAH DINNER, our coffee cups drained and mere remnants of my mom's homemade chocolate rugelach left on our plates, my mom asked, "So, have you been out on any dates lately?"

Since I was the only single person at the table of "dating" age, I knew the question was directed at me. "Yeah, Mom. I was out on 12/13, 12/18 and 12/23. Are those dates okay with you?"

My mom rolled her eyes. "Hardy har har."

"You walked into that one, Mom," Sam said.

Ignoring him, my mom said, "Why don't you try one of those speed dating events?"

"How do you know I haven't?"

My mom smiled brightly, her sky blue eyes twinkling with hope. "Have you?"

"Nope."

"Will you?"

"Probably not," I said.

I looked away before I could witness my mother's smile fade and her eyes go dull. I figured she was silently lamenting her only daughter's failure to graduate college and beyond without earning her "MRS." Sam had done his job getting married nine years ago at the socially acceptable age of twenty-seven. "As much as I love talking about my love life, it's really not fair of me to hog the spotlight." I turned towards my stepfather and said, "So, Al, how 'bout those Redskins?"

Before he could answer, my mom continued to grill me. "So what's your plan for New Year's Eve, Stephanie?"

I wondered what made my life so much more interesting than the NFL standings but responded, "Going to Jess and Eric's house. They're having a little shin-dig."

"Will there be any single guys there?"

"Sure, but I already slept with all of them," I said.

Without missing a beat, my mom asked, "Are they Jewish?"

I saw Sam glance my way with his hand covering his mouth as if to keep the hysterics from escaping. When we were little, my mom tended to do things which would strike Sam and me as hilarious and the second our matching hazel eyes locked, we would lose it and my mom would be completely oblivious as to why. Like the time she bragged about being a great dancer and got down to Bill Wither's *Lovely Day* in the middle of the kitchen. Sam and I laughed so hard, I almost choked on my tuna casserole.

I was certain if Sam and I made eye contact at that moment, we would start laughing like we did as kids and so I picked up my dishes and brought them to the sink. I also wanted to change the subject since I actually had slept with two of the single men who would be in attendance at the party. Although I wasn't sure if Paul could technically be considered single since he was dating Hope.

As soon as I sat back down at the table, I was approached by my six-year-old niece Lillie, who stood next to me and put her delicate hand on my shoulder. Her doe eyes wide and inquisitive, she asked, "Can I be the flower girl at your wedding, Aunt Stephanie?"

"Of course you can, sweetie. If you don't get married before me, that is." I could almost picture myself at her wedding: the spinster aunt, standing next to her roommate from college and her future sister-in-law, all of us wearing matching puffy bridesmaid dresses.

My mom stood behind me and put her arms around my neck. She kissed the top of my head. "See? I'm not the only one who wants you to get married."

Scratching his gray beard, Al said, "Susan, can you cut the girl some slack? She's young and beautiful. She makes good money and takes care of herself. When she meets the right guy, she'll settle down. For now, let her have fun."

"Thank you, Al." I knew there was a reason I was glad my mom married him eighteen years ago, besides the fact that he used to buy me Hello Kitty stickers when they were dating. And besides, it wasn't as if I wasn't trying. I had hoped Hille was the right guy and I would have been more than happy to settle down with him but our damn friendship put a wrench in those plans. When Lillie asked us to go around the table and state what we were thankful for at Thanksgiving dinner, only a few weeks earlier, instead of my good health and supportive family, I should have expressed my gratitude that Hille was my BFF!

As I continued to pout about my bad luck with men and my mom's inability to give the subject a rest, my sister-in-law chimed in her agreement with Al. "I'll second that!" she said.

"Thank you, Amy!" I turned to my mom and gave her my best "so there!" look.

Relenting, my mom said, "All right. I'll lay off." Pretending to wipe the sweat from my brow, I said, "It's about time!"

"I just want to have more grandchildren."

As Amy tried to stifle her giggles, Sam let out a snort and said, "I did my job. It's your turn, kiddo."

Sam's use of the word "kiddo" immediately made me think of Hille and I wondered what his family talked about at the dinner table and if they were as nuts as my clan. Then I remembered Hille and I weren't dating and I probably shouldn't care what his family talked about at the dinner table. It wasn't like they'd ever invite me over.

THIRTEEN

ON NEW YEAR'S EVE DAY, Jess and Hope picked me up at the train station. In all of the holiday madness, I never did find the time to get my balls on for the teasing I assumed was awaiting me so, sans balls, I threw my bags in the small trunk of Jess's silver Saturn Sky, got in the back seat and leaned over to give both girls a kiss.

I had nervous knots in my stomach but Hope said no one had even mentioned my tryst with Hille. In disbelief, I asked, "Really? No one has given Hille a hard time about it?"

Jess looked at me through the rear view mirror and said with mock jealousy, "Well, Eric wouldn't dare introduce a conversation that might result in his precious Stephanie being teased."

I laughed and asked, "Since when? It's not like he doesn't make fun of me all the time."

"Yeah, but he doesn't like when others do it. It's the older brother syndrome. He can beat you up, but will fight to the death if someone else does." As Jess pulled into the driveway of the redwood split-level house she shared with Eric, she said, "You know, everyone treads lightly around Hille for some reason. He never gets the brunt of the abuse. The worst they ever say is he's an egghead!"

"The guys might be waiting for you to get here before they start in," Hope suggested as we all got out of the car.

Opening the trunk to remove my bags, Jess said, "Or maybe they've just matured."

After contemplating Jess's statement for a moment, we collectively exclaimed, "Nah!"

As we walked into the small foyer, which led to stairs up to the kitchen, living room and three bedrooms, or down to the family room, Jess shouted, "We're home!" She went upstairs to check out the food situation and Hope and I went downstairs to greet the others who were spread out on the two matching caramel leather couches surrounding the entertainment center. Eric was a music junkie and racks of CDs lined the walls of the room.

Corky approached me first. "Hey, hot stuff," he said hugging me fiercely. "We gonna make out later?"

"Do I have to decide right now?" I asked.

Walking back toward his spot on the couch and his open can of Miller Lite, Corky replied, "Nope. Take all the time you need in the next five minutes." At twenty-six, Corky was goofy with a capital G. The first time we met, he repeatedly chanted, "Lose the zero. Get with the hero!" while pointing to me and my date for the evening, my ex-neighbor and not-quite boyfriend Stephen. I hid from him all night until Eric told me Corky said the same thing to every girl who walked by with a guy and was not, as I feared, stalking me.

Interrupting my thoughts, Paul pointed to the large laundry bag I had dragged with me down the stairs and asked, "What's with the gynormous blue bag, Steph?"

"It's gifts for you!" I had purchased gifts from Sephora for all of the girls and customized plaques from the Yankee's website for the guys. I was afraid any gift I bought for Hille might send a message that I was either totally crushing on him or trying too hard to look like I *wasn't* crushing on him so, forsaking all creativity, I bought everyone the same gift, depending on his/her sex.

Shaking his finger at me, Paul said, "It's blue. Not very Christmas, ya know."

"I'm Jewish, remember? I wanted to share some of the Chanukah spirit. I even brought a dreidel. We can play a drinking game with it!"

"Hey missy, when you hang out with the followers of Christ, you leave your tribe's customs at home. You got that?"

"I got it, Paul. How 'bout I leave your gift at home next time, too! By the way, do I get a hug or what?"

Out of the corner of my eye, I had seen Hille observe the preceding interaction with amusement. As I embraced Paul, he finally approached me. *You've seen me naked.* "Hey you, Happy New Year." *We had sex.*

Not looking nearly as uncomfortable as I was feeling, Hille responded cheerily, "Back at you. How was the train?"

He didn't move in for a hug and so neither did I. "It was long. I'm just glad to be here and so ready for a beer."

"Anyone need a drink?" Paul asked.

Directing his attention to Paul, Hille said, "I do, but I'll make it myself. Last time I trusted you to make my drinks, I wound up passed out in some stranger's bathroom."

I left Paul and Hille to recount the events of that apparently fun-filled night and went to find Eric. He was outside on the back deck smoking, grilling some burgers and singing to himself what sounded like John Cougar's *Jack & Diane*, his thick mane of blonde curls peeking out from his red winter hat.

"Holy shit—it's freezing out here, Eric! Why are you grilling on New Year's Eve?" I asked as I hugged myself to keep warm.

"Because I can, Stephanie, because I can." Eric put out his cigarette in an empty beer can and kissed me hello. "When did you get here?"

"A few minutes ago. I saw everyone except Andy and Rachel. Where are they?"

"I really can't stand her, Steph. They're fighting because Andy wants to hang around tomorrow to watch football and Rachel wants to go to the outlets."

"Oh, God. I could never understand girls who insist on dragging their boyfriends shopping. The Rose Bowl is only once a year!" Even though I personally hated football, I totally sided with Andy on that one. "And I think the outlets would be closed anyway!"

"Don't ask me. She's a dog, too. He can probably only get it up in the heat of makeup sex." Raising and lowering his eyebrows at me, Eric said, "Speaking of sex, what's up with you and Hille?"

"Nice segue, Eric. We had sex. End of story. I think you need to flip that burger."

"What's wrong?"

"Nothing's wrong."

"You're lying. What's with you and Hille?"

"It's nothing," I maintained, letting out a loud exhale. "It's stupid, Eric."

Eric removed his focus from the grill, looked at me and said, "Probably." Continuing to gaze at me intently, he said, "But tell me anyway."

Too embarrassed to make eye contact, I looked down and mumbled, "I sort of like him."

"I knew it. Shit, Stephanie. Hille's a good guy and everything, but he might be quite the challenge—he's socially inept sometimes."

Surprisingly feeling better after my confession, I joked, "He seemed quite adept to me."

"TMI, Steph."

"Anyway, I'm sure I'll get over it." Determined to change the subject this time, I said, "Ya think I should go for Corky instead"?

"Sounds like a plan. And while you're at it, get yourself a drink already! It's New Year's Eve, for Christ's sake!"

On my way back to the family room, I grabbed a bottle of heffeweizen from the fridge and poured it in a pilsner glass with a slice of lemon. As I headed towards the stairs, I ran into Andy and Rachel coming out of one of the guest rooms. Pretending to have no idea they had been fighting, I called out cheerfully, "Hey, guys! Happy New Year!"

Rachel, smiling brightly, greeted me with a hug and kiss and said, "Hey, Stephanie. You look great! Are those jeans Miss Sixties? I wish I could fit into those!"

"Thanks, Rachel. You look great, too! Good to see you, Andy!" I leaned in to kiss him on the cheek.

"Good to see you, too," Andy said.

Before he could say anything else, Rachel placed her head on his shoulder, looked up at him from under her eyelashes and said, "Hon, can you pour me a glass of wine, please? Stephanie and I will see you downstairs."

Flashing me a defeated smile, Andy said, "Sure thing. You need anything, Steph?"

I held up my full glass of beer. "No thanks. I'm good." Then I followed Rachel down the stairs. So far the party was pretty weak. Paul and Hope were sitting in the corner of one couch staring intently at a laptop and Hille was on the other couch watching the television. Michael Jackson was playing in the background.

"Nice music, guys," I said.

Paul looked up at me from the computer. "What? You don't like *Beat It*? That's not what I heard. Or what I remember," he said with a wink and then added, "What about you, Hille?" Hope jabbed him in the arm. I ignored him and Hille, expressionless, shook his head and continued to stare at the television. I wasn't drunk enough to act normal around Hille so I went back upstairs.

Eric had the video camera out and was taping Jess and Corky dancing to *Bust a Move* in the living room. "Oh, my Lord. Did I jump into a time warp or something? *Thriller* downstairs, cheesy nineties rap upstairs?"

Corky approached me with his awkward dance moves and chanted, *"She's dressed in yellow, she says 'Hello, come sit next to me, you fine fellow"* and eventually took my hand and dragged me onto the "dance floor" to join him. I pushed away my initial self-consciousness as well as thoughts of Hille and danced along with Corky and Jess until I braved a solo. Swinging my hips in time to the music, I crooned, *"She thinks you're kinda cute so she winks back And now you're feelin' really fine cus the girl is stacked,"* turned around and saw Hille staring at me with a close-mouthed grin. I immediately stopped dancing, feeling my face turn bright red.

"Please don't stop on my account," he teased. "I'm enjoying the show."

Mortified, I said, "Show's over" and walked passed him into the kitchen. As I grabbed another beer, I felt his presence behind me. I turned around to face him and leaned against the refrigerator. *Fake it till you make it. We're friends, nothing else.*

"The party is really lame downstairs," he said. "Paul is showing Hope his Myspace page and Rachel is showing Andy her favorite jewelry in Jess's Tiffany's catalog. I came upstairs thinking it had to be an improvement." Then he started laughing and said, "So glad I did."

"Whatever I can do to provide some entertainment, Craig. You're up next," I joked.

"Not gonna happen, Steph—not without a lot more of this, at least," he said, holding up his drink.

Motioning for him to follow me downstairs where everyone else had finally gathered in the family room, I said, "Let's see what we can do about that."

For the next couple of hours, we sat around drinking and basically ripping each other apart. (Our motto: If we don't make fun of you, we obviously don't know you.) At 11:59 and 49 seconds, with a glass of champagne in one hand and a shot of tequila in the other, we chanted in unison: "Ten, nine, eight, seven, six, five, four, three, two, one—Happy New Year!"

I averted my eyes from the kissing couples and looked over at Hille and Corky. Raising my glass of champagne, I said, "Happy New Year, guys!" Corky wrapped me into a bear hug and planted a wet one on my lips. After he released me, Hille and I locked eyes and awkwardly moved in for a hug.

My face in his chest, I said, "Happy New Year, Craig!"

"Happy New Year, kid," he said before quickly detaching himself from our embrace.

By then, the couples had separated and after each person hugged and said Happy New Year to everyone else, Eric brought out the karaoke machine.

Paul performed the opening act—*Tangled Up In Blue*. Paul, Eric, Corky and Jess were always the most eager. Hope, Andy and I usually waited until the tequila had worked its magic and Hille's participation was usually limited to insulting Paul's performance.

After almost everyone had a turn, Eric looked at me and said, "You're up next. What are you singing?"

Suddenly I felt completely nauseated and I looked over at Hille, who was laughing at Corky's rendition of *"Gold Digger."* I wiped my sweaty palms on my jeans and said, "I'm not ready yet."

From across the room, Paul called out, "You're not wimping out are you, Cohen?" and suddenly all eyes were on me.

I had to do this. Hille had seen me in the throes of passion. Karaoke was trivial in comparison. "Not wimping out. Just deciding on a song." *Think of something, Stephanie.* "Okay, *Down Under* by Men at Work." It was easy, had no high notes and needn't be accompanied by dancing.

I felt as if I were wearing 100-pound ankle weights but somehow made it off the couch to the center of the room where Eric handed me the microphone. I couldn't remember the first words *"Traveling in a fried-out combie"* leaving my mouth but by the time I got to *"She just smiled and gave me a Vegemite sandwich"* (and maybe it was because Paul kept lifting his shirt and flashing me his pot belly), I was fine. In fact, when the song was over, I swear Hille looked upon me with admiration. Unless, of course, I was simply beer goggling on myself.

Although no one officially announced it was "bed time," as the sun began to peek through the shades, we all got ready for bed. Paul and Hope and Rachel and Andy called dibs on the two guest bedrooms, so Jess brought out pillows and blankets for Hille, Corky and me, who were stuck sleeping in the family room. Hille offered to sleep on the floor so Corky and I each got a couch.

I was beat and couldn't wait to go to sleep. Corky already appeared to be out cold when I got out of the bathroom after getting ready for bed and Hille was snoring—loudly. I didn't think the snoring would keep me awake but I was wrong. At first I was calm and just assumed that Hille would stop snoring eventually. I mean, who snored non-stop?

Apparently, Hille did and I counted how many hours I had until the others would wake up if I fell asleep at that precise moment. "Shut up," I screamed inwardly. I turned from my side to my stomach and then back to my side. Then I covered my head with my pillow and kicked my feet in annoyance. "Oh, God. Shut up! Please," I cried, this time out loud.

Hille stirred in his sleep, abruptly sat up and asked, "What's wrong?"

"You're snoring," I answered in frustration.

"Sorry, Steph."

"You sound like a cat trapped in a vacuum cleaner."

"And what exactly does that sound like?"

"Fucking annoying!"

Hille laughed. "You didn't complain about my snoring in New York."

Too tired to censor myself, I said, "Well, you had just given me an orgasm. You sort of had a get out of jail free card."

"I can give you an orgasm now if you want."

Whoa. "Come again?"

Totally deadpan, Hille responded, "That's the idea."

My heart began to beat at the pace of an Olympic runner. "Uh, will the real Craig Hille please stand up?"

"Why do you say that?" Hille asked lightly.

"So not like you."

"Why? Because I don't do karaoke, I have no sense of adventure?"

"No, just not what I expected you to say. I mean, first you needed Paul's permission and now—just not what I expected. That's all."

Hille shrugged. "I don't know. We've done it before—it's not like we'd be making history. And the sex was..." Hille stopped speaking before completing the sentence.

"The sex was what, Craig?"

"Really good."

Grinning despite myself and glad the room was too dark for Hille to see me, I said, "It was, wasn't it?"

Like a middle school bully trying to get his smaller friend to smoke a joint, Hille said, "So, what do you say? I promise you'll sleep better afterwards." *All the kids are doing it.*

"That's as good a reason as any, but what do we do about Corky?" Even as the words escaped my mouth, I couldn't believe I was saying them.

"Leave him here. Let's go in the bathroom."

Oh, God. What am I doing? "Do you have something?"

"I've got it covered, Steph," he said and with that, I followed him to the half bath.

As soon as he kissed me, I felt a flash of heat from the top of my head all the way down my body and any reluctance I had to be with him again disappeared just as quickly. Miraculously, I was no longer tired either. I was not a member of the mile high club and certainly wasn't experienced having sex in bathrooms. It was dark and quite uncomfortable at first as we tried to make the most of the cramped space but it felt so good. Even in those moments, I was aware that I had never before allowed a physical need to take over the voice in my head telling me I was probably headed down the wrong path. Before Hille, I had never even had sex outside of some sort of relationship, but I just wanted to cling to him like Saran Wrap and stay like that in perpetuity. I kept repeating, "Don't stop. Don't stop." The voice in my head tried to stop me from saying it out loud, but I couldn't help myself.

After we finished, I held onto him tight and when I felt him pull away, I said, "Not yet," my voice so breathy that I almost didn't recognize it.

Hille said, "Okay."

We stayed like that, not speaking and just breathing heavily until finally, I whispered, "I've never had a fuck buddy before, Craig."

Hille whispered back, "We're not fuck buddies, Steph."

Although I wasn't quite sure I wanted to know, I asked, "What are we, Craig?"

After a brief hesitation, as if pondering the answer, Hille pulled away and looked at me. Then he looked down and rubbed his thumb gently along his clean-shaven chin. Looking at me again, he smiled and said, "I got it. Friends with benefits!"

I didn't note a trace of disrespect in his voice or malintent in his eyes and, although I wanted to tell him that friends with benefits wasn't good enough for me, I was not ready to hear that my only choices were "friends with benefits" or just "friends." I also felt like a hypocrite telling him I wasn't "that kind of girl" while naked in a bathroom after having sex with him, so instead, I said, "I never had one of those either." Then we left the bathroom, went back to our respective make-shift beds and I wondered what the hell I was doing until I fell asleep.

FOURTEEN

THE NEXT MORNING I WOKE UP to the sound of clanking pots and muddled voices coming from upstairs. I looked around, saw I was alone in the room and figured I was the last one up. I went to the bathroom to brush my teeth and comb my hair and tried not to think about what I had done in that room only a few hours prior. Then I joined the others upstairs. Everyone was either standing in the kitchen or sitting in the living room drinking coffee, which I needed bad.

"Hey, sleepyhead," Eric called from the top of the stairs as I made my way up. "I thought you might have died."

"And you were so concerned you just left me there, huh?" I spotted Hille in the kitchen behind him, grinning at me when we made eye contact. I smiled at him a bit self-consciously and he asked if I needed a cup of coffee. "Yes! Desperately," I answered.

Holding the coffee pot in his hands, he asked, "How do you take it?"

"Lots of half and half and two Equals. Thanks, Craig." I sat down at the kitchen table with Hope and Paul and when Hille handed me my coffee, I said, "Thanks." He winked in response and went into the living room.

"How'd you sleep, Cohen?" Paul asked.

"Fine, why?"

"Just making conversation. Hung over?"

"A little," I lied. Sleeping with Hille had sobered me up pretty quickly and I wasn't even drunk by the time I went to sleep.

Later, we were all in the living room watching the Rose Bowl. Everyone was psyched that the Nittany Lions were beating the Trojans, except Paul.

"Any team named after a condom is the team for me," he said.

Looking up from Eric and Jess's wedding album (which I had already viewed at least twenty times), I said, "Is that so? Then why did you always try to guilt me into having sex without using one back in college?"

"Paul!" Hope shouted. "Were you trying to knock up a college freshman?"

"Nah. I had heard it felt better without one and, at the time, I hadn't tried it before. Chillax, Hope. I never knocked Stephanie up."

They continued to mock-argue while I tried to figure out what Hille was thinking. He was standing by the staircase typing on his Blackberry. I wondered who would email him on New Year's Day. I followed him with my eyes until he sat back down on the couch and took another sip of coffee. He caught me, smiled and stood up again. This time, he went to the bathroom and, with the door half opened, washed his hands. *Did it even register that we'd had sex in there?*

Cutting into my meditation of the night's events, I heard someone say, "Earth to Stephanie."

I looked up and saw Eric standing over me with a train schedule. Waving it at me, he asked, "What time do you need to be back?"

Shrugging, I said, "I don't know. Not too late. I hate getting home late when I have work the next day."

"There's a 4:30 that gets you into Union at 6:25. Does that work?"

"Yeah, that sounds perfect. Do you mind if I shower first? I feel dirty." I felt my face flush as I said that, although I knew no one except Hille would think anything of it. Still, I couldn't bring myself to look at him.

Getting up from the couch where she was sitting, Jess said, "Come with me. I'll get you some towels."

"I know where the towels are, Jess. Sit down. I'm okay."

Falling back down on the couch, Jess said, "Good! I'm too tired to walk upstairs!"

During my shower, I decided I didn't regret having sex with Hille again. Sure, Hille had made it clear he wasn't looking for a relationship with me, but he liked me and I liked him. We were attracted to each other and shared explosive sexual chemistry. Had Hille been some stranger I picked up at a bar, I'd feel regret. But Hille was my friend—a friend with benefits. There was nothing to regret.

I toweled off, combed my long, wet hair into a ponytail and threw on the t-shirt and sweatpants I had brought for the train ride home. I didn't bother with makeup, figuring it was unlikely I'd meet anyone interesting on the train. My mother would probably have berated that decision but I lacked the motivation to care. When I got downstairs, everyone was still sitting where I'd left them.

Jess, still staring straight ahead at the television as if in a trance said, "Hille said he'd drive you to the train station. I'd do it but I'm beat and he's gotta get going anyway. You don't mind, do you?"

I shook my head. "Don't mind." Then I forced myself to look at Hille, who I could see out of the corner of my eye was looking at me, and asked, "You sure you don't mind?"

"It's no trouble," Hille said. "But, we should get going soon. You just about ready?"

"Yep." Gesturing to the clothes from the night before in my hands, I said, "Just gotta throw this stuff in my bag."

We hugged and kissed everyone goodbye and then I walked with Hille to his car, a dark blue Nissan Altima parked across the street. After he put our bags in the trunk, he opened up the passenger side of the car to let me in. Then he walked around to the driver's side, got in and started the car.

Playing with his GPS, Hille said, "Now let's see if we can figure out how to get to the train station."

"Thanks again for driving me, Craig."

"It's not a problem. Plus I could tell Jess didn't really want to do it." Hille turned his head to face me, his lips curled into a smile. "No offense."

"None taken. I wouldn't want to take me to the train station either if I was comfy on my couch, recovering from a hangover."

"You hung over?" Hille asked.

"Thankfully, no. Just tired. You?"

"Trying not to think about it. I've got a two hour drive ahead of me. Then I'll sleep."

As he said this, Hille reached down to scratch his right leg and I had an overwhelming desire to scratch it for him. He was wearing long shorts and I couldn't help but notice how muscular his calves were. He looked like he played soccer, but actually wasn't much of an athlete at all. And his legs were always tanned as if he lived in a warm climate instead of New Jersey.

"So, Paul and I were talking about renting a house at the beach somewhere over Memorial Day weekend."

I tore my eyes away from Hille's legs and looked up at him. "Wow, I didn't know things had gotten so serious between you guys."

Hille's ears turned red as he rolled his eyes and said, "Seriously, if we rented a big house, would you want in?"

"I thought you were planning a trip to New Orleans?"

"I thought about it, but I like this idea better. If we got something on the east coast, maybe Charleston or Myrtle Beach, no one would have to fly and it would probably be cheaper."

"Well, count me in. I have four more weeks of vacation beginning today, plus a week carried over from last year. And I love the beach."

"It wouldn't be anything fancy. Just eating, drinking and lying on the beach."

"Are you suggesting I'm high-maintenance, Craig?"

"Not at all, although I did overhear a conversation between you and the girls this morning about some bare naked makeup. Probably not much need for makeup at the beach."

"Bare Minerals, Craig, not naked. Get your mind out of the gutter. And stop eavesdropping on conversations which don't involve you while you're at it!"

Hille smiled. "Guilty as charged. Maybe I was hoping to hear something a little bit more interesting."

"Like what?" I paused for a moment. "Details about our hot sex last night?"

As I tried to make light of our friends-with-benefits relationship, Hille looked like I pulled down his pants in front of the whole class. His face instantly turned the color of the traffic light we were approaching. But he quickly recovered. "Is that how you'd describe it—hot?"

And just like that, the tables were turned and I was the one blushing. Also recovering quickly, I said flirtatiously, "Maybe yes, maybe no. But, out of respect for our friendship, that's what I'd tell everyone."

Hille nodded. "Most appreciated. Would hate to get a reputation as being bad in bed, a premature ejaculator or any other cruel thing you girls say about us guys behind our backs."

"Like you have a teeny weenie?" I suggested.

"Nope, wouldn't want that either," Hille said with a laugh.

Definitely no worries there. "No worries."

Pulling into the train station, Hille said, "We're here." He drove up to the entrance and parked his car temporarily to let me out. As he opened the trunk to remove my bag, I watched a young couple exchange a tearful goodbye. Hille handed me my duffle bag. "Here you go. Are you okay waiting here by yourself?"

I wanted to say, "No. Wait with me. Tell me things about you that, after all these years, I still don't know." That's what I *wanted* to say. But what I said was, "I'll be fine." Then I glanced around and added, "Looks like a pretty tame crowd."

"Okay. Well, have a good trip."

"Thanks. Thanks again for the ride—to the train station." As I felt my face turn rosy, I wondered why I had to be such a loser. Hille smiled but didn't respond. Hurriedly, I reached up, grabbed his arm to steady myself and gave him a quick kiss on the cheek. "Okay, bye." Then I hightailed it into the train station without looking back.

The train to Union was already on the track and after I found a car with seats facing in the forward direction, since riding backwards always gave me a headache, I put my duffle bag in the overhead compartment and re-lived my last few moments with Hille. *"To the train station?"* Why did I have to say that? It reminded me of when Baby told Johnny she "carried a watermelon" in *Dirty Dancing.* I laughed out loud and quickly glanced around hoping no one heard me. I had a feeling the train might be crowded since it was New Year's Day. I was relieved that so far no one had sat next to me but, as if reading my thoughts and saying "not so fast," a woman looking to be in her mid-to-late forties stood over me.

"Is someone sitting here?" she asked.

I shook my head, smiled and said, "No. Be my guest." I made an initial judgment based on her appearance that my luck could have been worse. She was thin and therefore unlikely to encroach on my space and, after putting her bag next to mine above our seats, the only item she carried was a James Patterson novel. I held my breath for a few seconds in fear she would reach up and grab her cell phone, but after getting herself comfortable, she smiled at me, leaned back and closed her eyes, her arms wrapped around the book. Sleep. Now that was a novel idea. I hadn't gotten much the night before, although after my encounter with Hille, I was at least able to sleep through his snoring. Four hours of sleep just didn't do it for me, though, and with nowhere to go for another two, exhaustion took over. Within seconds of closing my eyes and allowing my body to relax, I was out. A tap on my shoulder jolted me awake and I realized what felt like hours was only a few minutes and the conductor was asking for my ticket. I apologized for keeping him waiting, clumsily reached into my bag for my ticket and handed it to him. Then I closed my eyes and instantly fell back asleep until I was again awakened, this time by the beep of my cell phone indicating I had a text message. It was from Suzanne.

"How was the party?"

"It was fun. Always is. How was your first New Year's Eve with Luke?"

"Extremely X-rated. Don't want to put details in writing lest they fall into the wrong hands and wind up on the Internet. How were things with Hille?"

Frowning, I debated my next response; I didn't want to keep it a secret from Suzanne that we'd slept together again, but I didn't know how she'd react, especially since my own feelings on the subject changed every five minutes. I decided there was no time like the present, typed my response and hit send. "X-rated, too."

Within seconds, my phone rang. Suzanne.

"Hey, I can't talk," I said. "I'm on the train."

"Drinks tomorrow."

"I'll see how work goes and let you know."

"It wasn't a question. Drinks tomorrow."

I sighed loudly and the woman next to me gave me a sympathetic look as if she could hear the other end of the conversation. I bit my fingernail and contemplated the value in arguing with Suzanne. There wasn't any. "Fine. Drinks tomorrow. Call me in the morning."

"I knew you'd come around. I love you, sweetie."

"Love you, too." It was almost impossible not to love Suzanne, and after we hung up, I chuckled softly.

The conductor announced that we were arriving in Baltimore and the woman next to me got up, grabbed her bag from the overhead bin and gave me a slight smile. "Happy New Year," I said.

"Same to you. Enjoy your drinks tomorrow."

"I'll try." After she left, I leaned back, stretched my legs out under the seat in front of me and slept for the remainder of the trip.

FIFTEEN

SUZANNE HELD the practically overflowing Pomegranate Martini to her lips and carefully took a sip before putting it back on the bar and turning to me. "Friends with benefits, huh? How convenient for him."

"Suzanne, stop. You make him sound like a total prick."

"No, I think he does that just fine on his own."

I glanced behind me as if someone who knew Hille might actually be at the Round Robin Bar at the Willard Hotel and whispered, "Look, it's not like Hille promised one thing and delivered another. I knew what I was getting into and walked in with my eyes wide open." I laughed and said, "And legs wide open."

Looking doubtful, Suzanne asked, "So, you're okay with this 'arrangement'?"

I wasn't really sure how to answer that question and took a sip of my drink as if the answer would come to me via flavored vodka. But as I felt the perfect balance of sour and sweet slide down my throat, I still had nothing. "Honestly, I have no idea how I feel. I'm totally attracted to him, Suze. I swear I want to rip off his clothes every time I look at him."

Suzanne smiled. "Well, it appears he's pretty fond of seeing you naked as well. Maybe things aren't as bad as I thought."

"He was all concerned about me being alone at the train station. It was sweet," I said.

Suzanne raised one eyebrow, a trick I never mastered, and said, "Nope. Things aren't as bad as I thought. They're worse. Much worse." Then she emptied the rest of her drink into her mouth in one swig.

"What?" I asked. Suzanne was always urging me to embrace my single status and whore around while I had the chance. I had hoped for a different reaction to this latest development.

Suzanne twirled one of her blonde curls around her finger and smiled at the bartender. "Can we get another round, please?" Then she turned back towards me, placed her hand over mine and looked me in the eyes. "Stephanie. I think this is a bad idea."

"Why do you say that?"

"When a guy says he's not looking for a relationship, he's usually not looking for a relationship. And 'Friends with Benefits' is not a relationship. I'm afraid you're going to fall in love with this guy."

"That's a bit premature, isn't it? And, by the way, it might not even happen again. It's not as if I plan on knocking knees with Hille every weekend. If things head in that direction the next time we get together, I'll deal with it then." I sincerely hoped things would lead in that direction sooner rather than later, but when it came to dating, Suzanne and my mom worshipped from the same bible and I knew exactly how to answer her prayers. "And in the meantime, I plan to date other guys."

Suzanne's face lit up. "Promise?"

"I promise." If I happened to meet another guy I liked, of course I'd date him. "So, how are the wedding plans going?"

Suzanne's face lit up even brighter as she told me about her latest dress fitting. "I lost a few more pounds and they have to take in the dress a few inches in the waist."

"Since when are you dieting?" Suzanne was my only female friend virtually void of body-image issues. As a student counselor at the Duke Ellington School of the Arts, she was a shining example to the weight-obsessed aspiring singers, dancers and actors.

"I love my womanly curves and I'm not technically on a diet. I'm just so busy with the wedding plans I don't have time to plan the wedding *and* eat. I've been eating Luna Bars for lunch at least two or three times a week. Honestly, I wouldn't mind losing five more pounds. As long as they don't come off my boobs."

As Suzanne said this, she cupped her 36Cs in each of her hands, oblivious to the twenty-something guy standing behind us who I guessed was a tourist by his drink order, a Rob Roy and a mint julep. I, however, was keenly aware that he was smiling from ear to ear, his eyes focused on the front of Suzanne's v-neck cashmere sweater. I stared at him until he noticed me, shrugged and said, "They're nice. I wouldn't change a thing."

Finally acknowledging the attention being paid to her cleavage by a third party, Suzanne smiled at the guy and said, "Thanks, buddy." Pointing at me, she said, "My friend's boobs aren't bad either—small, yet perky. Don't you think?"

To my knowledge, no one had ever said "nice rack" when referring to my 34Bs and the only reaction I could muster was to kick Suzanne in the leg.

"Ouch! The kick was not necessary, Cohen!"

Shaking his head, probably in awe of Suzanne's balls, the guy said, "I'm sure they're very nice, although I think my girlfriend would probably kick me too if she knew I was having this conversation. And I doubt she'd choose my leg as her target." After throwing a couple of singles on the bar, he said, "Enjoy your evening, ladies," grabbed his drinks and walked back to his table.

Still embarrassed by her blatant attempt to pimp me out, I said, "You're a piece of work, Suzanne."

"Damn. I didn't think he had a girlfriend. A little young, but dorky cute - probably good boyfriend material."

"No offense, but I really wouldn't be interested in a guy who noticed your tits before he noticed me anyway."

Grabbing her boobs again, Suzanne said, "Good luck with that!"

SIXTEEN

LATER THAT WEEK, I was in the middle of preparing an email to outside counsel, attaching copies of signed pages of an agreement they had requested, when I received a notification on the bottom right of my screen that I'd received an email from Hille. I saved my email to outside counsel into my drafts and quickly opened Hille's. It was addressed to everyone who was at the party on New Year's Eve.

> *Hey guys,*
> *Had a great time this weekend. I've attached the link to my album so we can re-live the night. We should do it again soon. Paul's birthday is next.*
> *Hille*

Happy for a break from doing real work, I immediately clicked on the link and watched the slideshow of Hille's album. Since I'd arrived at the party late, I hadn't seen Corky strip down to his boxers and hula hoop in Jess and Eric's living room and I laughed out loud looking at the pictures. There were a few of Hope draped across Paul's lap on the couch. As always, Hope's smooth red hair and bright green eyes practically jumped out of the pictures. The photos of Hille didn't do him justice and I decided not to even show them to Suzanne. No one ever believed you when you told them someone was way cuter in person but Hille really was. I didn't remember posing for many pictures and started to wonder if I was even in any when I saw it.

It was a picture of Hille, Hope and Paul standing by one of the couches. Hope was in the middle and Hille and Paul were both kissing her on the cheek. It was a great picture except when I took a second look, I saw myself in the background, to the left of Hille, looking at him in a dream-like trance. I could almost remember what I was thinking at that precise moment and it probably wouldn't take any paranormal ability to read my mind. I was undressing him with my eyes, recalling our night in New York. At the time I had no idea that history would repeat itself in a few hours.

I covered my face with my hand, wishing I could hide or at least destroy the picture. I closed my eyes, leaned back in my chair and prayed no one would look too closely at it. I hoped that like me, the others would pay more attention to how they looked in the pictures and would quickly breeze through the ones they weren't in. I mean, I didn't examine the pictures of Corky and the only reason my eyes so easily focused on the picture of Hille, Hope and Paul was because I was in the background. How likely was it any of the others would even notice I was staring at Hille? I opened my eyes, took a sip from my water bottle and exited the album. I'd finish looking at the pictures later.

I closed Hille's email and saw I had received a new one from Paul, also addressed to everyone.

> *Cohen, I think you've got some drool in the corner of your mouth.*
> *You might want to do something about that.*

I shook my head in disgust, wondering why Paul had to be such an asshole. If he hadn't said anything, the others might not have even noticed. Hille might not have noticed. Now they would all peer closely at each picture until they found the picture of me "drooling." So much for playing it cool like I was totally fine with the way things were going with Hille. The picture stated the obvious. I had it bad. I seriously hated Paul.

My head hurt and I grabbed the bottle of aspirin from my pocketbook just as my cell phone rang. I didn't recognize the number but the area code was 201 - New Jersey.

"Hello?" I said.

"Hey Steph, it's Hille."

My heart began to flutter at the sound of his voice even though I was pretty certain it was him before I answered. If he mentioned the picture, I'd die. "Hi," I said.

"Sorry to bother you at work."

"No bother. I actually wasn't doing much work anyway." *I was actually debating jumping out of my eighteenth floor window and you probably just saved my life.*

"I was hoping you could do me a favor," he said.

As long as it doesn't involve our mutual 'friend' Paul. "Sure. What's up?"

"I'm trying to gather information about the management of IT groups at other firms."

"Why?"

Hille laughed. "Don't sound so disgusted! It's not for fun, Steph. I'm trying to compare how other large firms are dealing with the economy and whether they're laying anyone off, outsourcing, cutting salaries. That sort of thing. Can you help me out?"

"I'll see what I can do." I couldn't believe Hille was so nonchalant.

"Thanks, kid."

"So, uh, have you seen the pictures from New Year's Eve?" I muttered "loser" under my breath when it occurred to me that, of course, Hille had seen the pictures. It was his album.

"Yeah, they came out pretty good. I especially liked the ones with Corky. Although the pictures didn't do justice to his performance with the hula-hoop. Eric should've used his video camera. The rest of the pictures were pretty boring. Not my best album."

Flashing back to the lust-struck look on my face in one picture in particular, I said, "Definitely not!" I bit my lip as I realized that probably came out wrong. Quickly correcting myself, I said, "I mean, uh, it was an okay album."

"Paul looked fat. I'll be sure to bring that to his attention," Hille said.

Figuring Hille's phone call was his way of telling me not to sweat the picture, I giggled. "Please do. Would serve him right." I didn't think I needed to specify why. "Thanks, Craig." I wished I could kiss him through the phone.

"So, you'll get me that information about your firm's IT group?"

"Huh? Oh, that. Of course I will. No problem." If Hille was sweet enough to come up with such a lame excuse to call me, I could at least pretend to go along with it.

"I gotta get back to work, but thanks again for helping me out."

"Back at you. I feel so much better now, you have no idea"

I waited for a response but Hille was already gone and I was left staring at the phone.

After we hung up, I went to make copies of a corporate binder for a client. As I unstapled the documents and ran them through the copier, I hoped the paper wouldn't jam. And I thought about how nice it was of Hille to make up a lie so he could call and make me feel better about Paul's obnoxious email. I smiled as I recalled our dinner in New York and how the cleft in his chin became more defined when I made him laugh.

Copies finished, I went to grab an empty black binder and a three-hole puncher. The small supply closet reminded me of the half bath in Eric and Jess's house where Hille and I had sex and I remembered how he poured my coffee the next morning.

One of the other paralegals at work did the "with benefits" thing. She talked about drunk text messages and late night booty calls, but as far as I knew, there was never any coffee involved. And she never mentioned anything about the guy going out of his way to protect her from an insufferable ex-boyfriend.

SEVENTEEN

AFTER WORK THAT NIGHT, I walked through the front door of my apartment, threw my keys on the kitchen table and removed my cell phone from inside my pocketbook. Pacing the length of my living room, I hit number three on my speed dial.

"What did you mean when you said Hille could be a challenge?" I asked.

"Huh?"

Exasperated, I raised my voice and repeated, "When you said Craig could be a challenge, what did you mean?"

"Relax, Stephanie Lynn Cohen. Don't get touchy with me."

"Sorry, Eric."

"What is this about?"

"On New Year's Eve, we were outside and you were smoking and grilling burgers. By the way, you might not want to smoke and cook at the same time. I think I tasted ashes in my burger. Anyway, I told you I sort of liked Hille and you said he could be a challenge."

"Perhaps I gave you one of the hashburgers—could explain your sex with Hille in the bathroom later than night."

"Haha, Eric. Seriously, what did you mean?"

"I just threw the word 'challenge' out there. I don't really know what I was thinking at the time."

"You must have been thinking something, Eric." Tired from pacing, I sat down in my reclining chair and with my free hand, began twirling pieces of hair around my index finger. "Is there something I should know about him? Beyond his quiet reserve, is Hille a bastard to women? Or a player? Does he have some sexually transmitted disease?"

Laughing, Eric responded, "No! Not at all. It's not that. But I've never seen him ga-ga over a chick. In fact, I've never seen him make much effort at all for a girl. In fifteen or so years of friendship, wouldn't you think I'd see that?"

Practically ripping the hair from my scalp, I said, "Maybe that's because he hasn't met a girl worthy of being ga-ga over. Doesn't mean he's not capable, does it?"

"Are you saying you want to be that girl, Stephanie?"

Of course I did, but hoping I sounded convincing, I said, "No, I just wondered what you meant by 'challenge,' that's all."

"Look, Steph, if Hille does it for you, by all means, have fun. Just be safe."

Laughing at Eric's mature advice, I said, "Yes, Dad!"

"And be careful."

"Careful? Is that different from 'safe'?"

Eric simply repeated, "Just be careful."

"Aw! You love me, don't you - you big sap!"

"Yes. I - love - you - all - over," Eric responded robotically.

"I love you, too."

After we hung up, I thought about what Eric said. It was true Hille didn't have any serious girlfriends in college but, then again, neither did most of my friends. For most people I knew, college was a time for having fun. I wasn't all that privy to details regarding his love life after college, although I knew he dated girls here and there. Although I didn't really see a problem with the fact that at the ripe old age of thirty-four, Hille had not yet been "gaga" over someone, between his categorization of us as friends with benefits, the absence of any real behavior on his part to suggest he felt otherwise and Eric's warning, I decided it was time to move on and focus my energies elsewhere. I decided to renew my Match.com subscription.

EIGHTEEN

IT WAS A WEDNESDAY NIGHT, my weekly "Girl's Night" with Suzanne, but we weren't in the mood to go out and decided to order in and watch *Criminal Minds* at my apartment instead. It hadn't started yet so I muted the television and showed her my amended dating profile.

After reading it, Suzanne cocked her head to the side and gave me a puzzled look. "You seriously plan on posting this?"

"What? It's not good?"

"I wouldn't go that far. But..."

"But what?"

Suzanne rolled her eyes. "Do me a favor. Read it out loud."

"Okay. Move over." We were sitting on my couch and after Suzanne shifted to the right to give me better access to my laptop, I leaned over my glass coffee table and started reading.

Physical attraction is, obviously, very important to me as it should be to you. I don't expect every guy to think I'm hot but I would hope my boyfriend would. Similarly, you don't have to be a GQ model but if we meet and I have no desire to kiss you much less see you naked at some point, it won't work. I would say my physical type is tall, dark and handsome. And brains are a turn-on. If your brain is small, the size of other parts of your body is moot. I think a guy who knows his way around a computer is hot. I prefer someone quiet and reserved over loud and obnoxious as long as you know how to have fun. I love baseball and although I'd prefer to date a Yankee fan, as long as you're not a

Red Sox fan, we might make it through a baseball season without killing each other. My friends are extremely important to me and any guy I date will need the intelligence and sense of humor to fully comprehend how awesome they are and how fortunate he is to be granted access to the fold. His friends, pending approval, are welcomed too.

I turned away from the computer and looked at Suzanne who, in the thirty seconds it took for me to read my profile, had managed to tie her curly blonde hair up in a bun without even using a ponytail holder. It always amazed me how good she was with her hair. I didn't acquire the coordination to put my hair in a simple ponytail until I went away to college and could no longer ask my mom. "I don't see the problem."

"You don't think it's a tad bit specific?"

"I'm not sure I follow you."

Suzanne got up from the couch and stood in front of me with her hands on her hips. Then she held up one finger and said, "Tall, dark and handsome, huh?"

I nodded. "Yeah, so?"

Holding up two fingers. "Knows his way around a computer, huh?"

I shrugged my shoulders. "I'm technically-challenged. It might be convenient to date a computer geek!"

Three fingers up, she said, "Quiet and reserved?"

I pursed my lips and remained silent.

Very loudly, Suzanne said, "Stephanie. Unless Hille or his doppelganger subscribes to Match.com, I don't think you need to join Match to find this person."

I crossed my arms defensively. "Not true!"

"Name one thing on this profile that doesn't describe Hille to a T."

I couldn't think of anything off the top of my head and felt the color rise in my cheeks. Determined, I read the profile again. "Got it!" I wrote that I *preferred* a Yankees fan but anything except a Sox fan would be fine! That doesn't limit it to Hille!"

Suzanne shook her head at me, turned around and walked towards my kitchen.

I knew she was right and followed her. Sitting at my kitchen table, I said, "I didn't do it on purpose. I just have Hille on my mind, I guess."

"If you're going to move on from this infatuation with Hille, you need to really move on," Suzanne insisted. "He's not the only guy in the world!"

I put my elbows on the table and covered my eyes with the palms of my hands for a few moments as I contemplated Suzanne's statement. A few seconds later, I looked up and said, "You're right. When you're right, you're right. And you're right. Time to move on. If Hille wanted me to be his girlfriend, he would do something about it. But he hasn't and so I must assume he's not interested."

Suzanne nodded in approval and I followed her back to the living room. "And, if he is interested, he needs to up his game," she said. "Shit or get off the pot, ya know?"

"Absolutely," I said. "Except it couldn't be just a coincidence that Hille called me mere moments after Paul's email. Why would he play hero like that and make me feel better if he didn't like me? And besides, he was the one who suggested hooking up again. I had no intention of making two moves in a row and had resigned myself to being 'friends' until he offered to give me another orgasm!"

I waited for Suzanne to offer up an explanation that might make sense out of all of this, but she had turned the volume up on the TV and was no longer listening to me. That's when I realized even the psycho-killing "un-sub" of the week on *Criminal Minds* was probably thinking more clearly and I promised to change my profile again and renew my subscription as soon as possible.

And then my phone rang.

NINETEEN

ALTHOUGH ONCE AGAIN, I did not recognize the 201 number, I once again knew instantly it was Hille. I was going to save his number to my contacts but had this fear that doing so would be presumptuous and result in his never calling me again. I had just turned on *Grey's Anatomy* but decided that Hille was McDreamy enough for me and muted the television. Nervous as usual, I picked up the phone with one hand and with the other began instinctively twirling my hair. After initial pleasantries, Hille got to the point of his call.

"Did you happen to get that information for me?" he asked.

"What information?"

"About your IT department. Remember?"

I repeated, "About my IT department?" and then I remembered. "Oh shit. I forgot, Craig."

"Oh. That's okay. Do you think you can get it, though?"

"You mean you really need it?" I could've sworn he had only asked as an excuse to call me.

"Well, it's not absolutely necessary. I was able to compile information from other firms."

I knew it. "Oh, good."

"So, Paul's birthday is coming up," he said.

I was glad he was finally changing the subject. "Uh huh. I thought about buying him sensitivity, but Target was all out of it."

Amusing Hille was becoming one of my favorite pastimes and when he laughed, I tried to contain my own grin and continue the conversation as if I hadn't noticed. "What's up for his birthday?"

"No one's seen my new place and so I was thinking about inviting the gang over to Hoboken to celebrate his birthday there. There's no shortage of bars. I just wanted to make sure you'd be up for it."

I was beginning to wonder if it was mere coincidence that the gang was getting together more frequently since Hille and I first had sex. "I'd be up for it," I said.

"Awesome!"

I measured Hille's response on my imaginary enthusiasm-meter. He thought it was "awesome" that I was up for a road trip to Hoboken. Not quite "ga-ga," but not too shabby at all.

The renewal of my Match.com subscription would have to wait.

TWENTY

A VENDOR HAD TAKEN a few of the paralegals out for a three
hour lunch, during which I drank three-plus cocktails. During lunch,
I silently vowed to speak coherently to Hille while in Hoboken and
not simply to say, "Yes. I'll have sex with you again." I was going to
ask him questions and not just whether he had a condom. I was
going to try to solve the mystery of Hille. There was more to him
than his penetrating dark eyes and almost genius IQ and I wanted to
know everything.

Due to my long lunch, I missed my mother's daily phone call,
and in my tipsy condition, was eager to talk to her. My mom was not
entirely unaccustomed to seeing or hearing me under the influence
of alcohol. Although she would sometimes "tsk, tsk" me for getting
drunk or for my occasional drag of Al's cigarette after too many glasses
of wine, she once confessed to enjoying my drunk proclamations that
she was the best mother in the whole wide world.

"Sorry I couldn't call you back sooner. I took a long lunch and
just got back," I said.

"Just now? Go anywhere good?" my mom asked.

"Yup! A vendor took me and a few other paralegals to Perry's."

"Very nice. What did you eat?"

"Lots of sushi and lots-o-wine."

My mom chuckled. "Aha! I knew you sounded more excited to
speak to me than normal. I was hoping it was because you missed me."

"Yeah, I'm a bit buzzed. But, I do miss you!"

"I miss you too, sweetheart. When will I see you again?"

"Maybe I can come over for dinner on Sunday." *And maybe you
can make your famous baked ziti parmesan.*

"I have a mahjong tournament on Sunday, but what about next weekend?"

"Can't. Going to New Jersey," I said.

"What's all the way in New Jersey?"

"Hille lives there. In Hoboken. It's supposed to be like a mini-New York City. Lots of bars and stuff. We're going to celebrate Paul's birthday."

"Is Paul still dating Hope?"

"Yes."

"So, I assume she's going too? And Jess and Eric?"

"I'm pretty sure."

"And who else?"

"Hille."

"So, it will be all couples except for you and Hille?" my mom asked.

It hadn't even occurred to me that Hille might invite some of his local friends, too. I hoped not since that might include girls. "I think it's just the core group, Mom. But we're all such good friends, it hardly matters. Hold on. I want to close my door." After I put the receiver on the desk, I got up to shut my office door. Then I walked back to my desk, took a sip from my water bottle and put the phone on speaker. "Okay. I'm back. What were we saying?"

"What are you going to do in Hoboken?"

"Probably go to the bars. We always play things by ear though."

"Don't you have any single friends, Steph?"

My mom tended to ask the same questions whenever I brought up my friends in conversation. I'd often thought about recording my responses to save my voice but I hadn't gotten around to it yet. "Of course I do, but I am closest with these guys." *But how could you know that since I've only told you two million times?*

"Well, can't they introduce you to anyone? Don't they know any single men?"

I knew I would be opening myself up to a whole new topic of conversation with my next words, but said them anyway. "Hille's single."

"Hille's the smart one, right? You could do worse. But, you're not interested in him, are you?"

When I didn't say anything, she asked, "Are you?"

I quickly debated telling my mom the truth. I usually didn't. "I don't know."

"But there's a possibility you might like him? Isn't he Paul's best friend?"

I giggled into the phone.

"What's so funny?"

"Nothing, Mom. It's just that Paul and I broke up in 1998. Many life-changing events have occurred since then. You became a grandmother, for one!"

Ever focused on my love life, my mom released a barrage of questions. "So you like Hille? Does he know? Has anything happened there?"

"Yes and no." How could I possibly explain to my mom that Hille and I were friends with benefits?

"What does that mean?"

"It's complicated, Mom. We're attracted to each other, but I don't know what's gonna happen there. Currently, we're just having fun."

"So, you're fuck buddies?"

I shouted, "Mom!" as my water bottle spilled across my desk. Searching my cabinets for extra napkins I had saved from eating lunch in my office, I asked, "How do you even know what that means?"

"Stephanie," she said, speaking slowly and clearly annunciating my name. "I'm not ancient and I've been around the block once or twice. Probably more than you."

At that statement, I grabbed the package of pink anti-nausea tablets I kept in my cabinet along with the stash of napkins and popped one in my mouth.

"And besides," my mom continued. "I think it was on an episode of *Sex and The City*. So, are you and Hille fuck buddies or not?"

"Not! We're friends with..." Deciding not to go there, I interrupted myself. "We're friends! But we've, uh, we've hooked up a few times. That's all."

"Isn't that the definition of a fuck buddy, Stephanie? Friends who hook up?"

I muttered, "I suppose."

"So, can I assume you'll be hooking up with him this weekend?"

I couldn't believe we were having this conversation even though I had started it. "I guess it's a possibility."

"Is Hille the reason you're so opposed to speed dating?"

"Oy veh! What's your obsession with speed dating, Mom? I'm fairly certain no guy I'd ever want to date would do speed dating. But, anyway, Hille is not the reason. I just want to try to meet someone in a less forced way." It occurred to me I had almost the same conversation with Suzanne.

"I understand. But do you think Hille will decide to upgrade your status from fuck buddy to boyfriend and girlfriend if you travel across states to have sex with him?"

Finally appreciating the humor of my sixty-two year old mother's repeated use of the phrase "fuck buddy," I laughed into the phone. "For the last time, he's not my fuck buddy, Mom."

In between chewing something, my mom said, "Okay."

"And, besides, it *could* lead to more."

"I guess." I heard a cracking sound and knew it was gum. One nasty habit I had managed not to inherit.

Hoping for more positive reinforcement, I pressed on. "Stranger things have happened, right?"

"As long as you're happy."

It was not quite the support I was seeking and as my buzz began to fade, I wondered who exactly I was trying to convince.

TWENTY-ONE

IN KEEPING WITH MY VOW to learn more about Hille while I was in Hoboken, I prepared a list of questions I wanted to ask and in the nights preceding the weekend, I read it over and over again, adding and deleting questions. Some of the questions were silly: What is your favorite television show? If you could only listen to one CD for the rest of your life, what would it be? What is the first concert you ever went to? Who would play you in the movie of your life? Some of the questions delved deeper into his psyche: What is your biggest fear? Have you ever been in love? If you had to be either blind or deaf, which would you choose and why? I also made sure I had my own answers to these questions in case he asked: *Criminal Minds,* "The Joshua Tree," George Michael, Zooey Deschenal, dying alone, I don't think so, deaf because I could learn to read lips and use sign language. I knew I couldn't whip out the list and ask these questions to Hille all at once without looking like a psycho, so I hoped to ease them into the natural flow of conversation. If I had to ask the others the same questions to make it look less obvious, so be it.

I took the train to Philadelphia on Saturday morning and drove the rest of the way to New Jersey with Eric, Jess and Hope. Paul was meeting us there. I hadn't spoken to him since the "drool incident" but since it was his birthday, I decided not to hold a grudge. He was turning thirty-five, the oldest of the group. I figured that was punishment enough.

While stuck in traffic on the New Jersey Turnpike, Jess called Hille to give him a progress report.

"We just passed East Brunswick so at least we're in Jersey," she said to him. "Shouldn't be too much longer, should it? I'm starving. What are we doing for dinner?"

I turned to Hope and whispered, "How could she be hungry? It's been less than an hour since we stopped at McDonalds. I still feel like I'm gonna hurl."

Before Hope could respond, Jess called out from the front seat, "I heard that."

"I didn't say anything bad, Jess! I just can't imagine eating again. I want to digest so I can actually drink later. So, what did Hille say?" *For instance, did he ask about me?*

"Not much, as usual. Paul is there and started drinking already."

"Great," Hope said sarcastically. "He'll be nice and wasted before we even get there."

"Too bad. I always find him less annoying when we get drunk at the same time," I said.

Flashing me a mischievous grin through the rear-view mirror, Eric said, "You'll just have to catch up quick then. I brought a bottle of whisky—a couple shots should do the trick."

Although my plan was to watch my shot intake so I wouldn't get too drunk to ask Hille any of my questions, I dryly responded, "Can't wait."

We didn't get much farther before Jess requested a bathroom break.

"We're less than forty-five minutes away, Jess. Can't you wait?" Eric asked.

"Unless you want your plush leather seats stained yellow, I don't think that's a good idea," Jess said.

"Jesus Christ. I'm buying you a catheter for your next birthday." Looking over his shoulder quickly, Eric pointed at me and Hope and asked if either of us had to go too.

"I can pee on demand," I called out as Hope said, "Sort of."

Eric shook his head and muttered, "Too many women in my life. I better have a son someday."

Jess scooted to the center of the front seat and sat closer to Eric. She kissed him on the cheek and said, "I can't wait to have a mini-you." She sat there until we reached the Thomas Edison rest stop and I noticed she would occasionally rub his right thigh or reach up to run her hands through the curls in his hair. I remembered my urge to scratch Hille's leg when he was driving and wondered if I would ever be in a relationship where I could satisfy such an urge without a moment's hesitation. I absently smiled upon them until Eric caught me through the rear-view mirror and gave me the loser sign. I shot him the finger in response and turned my head to look out the window.

An hour or so later, we finally made it to Hille's apartment in one of the three identical rust-colored high-rise apartments near the Hudson River. Although it housed its own parking lot, Hille only got one spot and his own car was parked in it. We spent about twenty-five minutes searching for a parking spot on the street with no luck and finally called Hille and Paul to come down and take up some of our stuff, including several six-packs of beer, bottles of alcohol and munchies. As we waited for them, Eric got out of the car to smoke and I, high on nervous energy, joined him to stretch my legs. Hope and Jess stayed inside.

When Hille exited the building, casually dressed in faded jeans and a navy sweater that complimented his olive complexion, he looked at the bags of supplies and started cracking up.

I flashed back to the moment he looked me deep in the eyes and proclaimed us friends with benefits and my stomach dropped. "What's so funny?" I asked.

"You'll see for yourself when you go upstairs, but let's just say, if we experience a remake of the Great White Hurricane and..."

Hille paused, probably in response to the lack of recognition on my face. "You know. "The famous Blizzard of 1888?"

Still clueless, I nodded, "Gotcha."

Hille shrugged. "Well, anyway, if a blizzard results in Hoboken being buried under fifty foot snow drifts, we'll still have enough food and drink to survive in my apartment for at least a month. I stocked my fridge and Paul brought two bottles each of vodka and tequila." Nodding to Hope, who had stuck her head out of the window, he said, "And he brought cranberry juice for you, but told me he plans to use very little of it in your drinks, so watch out."

"Consider me duly warned." Gesturing to the rows of cars parked bumper to bumper along the street, Hope said, "So, Hille, what's up with the parking? We drove all over and found nothing."

Nodding, Hille said, "Yeah, parking is brutal in Hoboken. Why don't you guys bring up some of this stuff and I'll go with Eric to park? I'll tell the doorman you're with me—16L. Paul will let you in."

"What? He couldn't come down and greet us?" I asked.

Smiling at me, Hille said, "He hasn't moved from the couch since he got here. I swear he'd ask me to use the bathroom for him if he could."

I wondered if Hille would think I was strange if I took the opportunity to ask about his favorite CD of all times. I decided the timing was off and let it go.

After Jess, Hope and I entered Hille's one bedroom apartment, I ignored Paul who had simply called out "It's open," and ran to the window, which overlooked the river and a stunning view of the New York City skyline. Turning around to face the others, I said, "Wow, Hille's view is breathtaking!" Then I walked over to where Paul was standing with his hands in the pockets of his brown cargo pants. I jabbed my pointer finger into his doughy beer belly and said, "Happy Birthday, you."

Paul lifted me up into an embrace, squeezed me hard and said, "Thanks, Cohen, my favorite ex-girlfriend ever! You know why I love you?"

I looked at him skeptically and said, "No, why?"

"Because you can take a joke, that's why."

"Oh. That's why. I thought it was because I have dirt on you that I'm kind enough to keep to myself."

"That too," he said, before walking over to Hope and dipping her Hollywood-kiss style.

You could tell a lot about a person by the books he read so, as Hope canoodled with Paul on the couch and Jess peed again, I perused Hille's bookshelf. As far as I could tell, the only books we had in common were *A Separate Peace* and *Yankee Century-100 Years of New York Yankees*. Hille owned *The Origin of The Species* and I made a mental note to work Charles Darwin into a conversation later. He also owned *New Ideas for Dead Economists* and I was pretty positive he could probably give me some great investment advice. I turned to the back cover of *The Universe in a Nutshell*, couldn't even understand the synopsis and quickly put it back on the shelf. I was so amused by the highly intellectual nature of his book collection it took me a few moments to realize he had returned. His stainless steel refrigerator door was opened and he was kneeling down, rearranging items on the bottom shelf. I wanted to bend down and kiss the back of his neck but took a more conservative approach instead.

"Great apartment, Craig," I said.

Standing up to face me, Hille grinned. "Thanks. It better be, considering it's sucking over $2500 a month out of my soul."

"Wow, I thought my rent was bad." Cheaper rent might be a good incentive for Hille to move to D.C. And maybe I could get him a job in my firm's IT Department.

Interrupting my wishful thinking, Hille asked, "So, you want something to drink? I figured we'd drink a bit here before we head out to the bars."

"Sounds good. You mind if I check out your fridge?"

Hille shook his head. Moving away to allow me access, he said, "Help yourself."

As I bent down to check out my options, I noticed a six-pack of Blue Moon. "I love this stuff! You mind if I take one?"

"That's why it's there. I sliced up some limes for the Corona and I think there are some lemon slices in there, too. They go with wheat beer, right?"

Blue Moon was typically served with orange slices but lemon would be fine. "Yup! What's your favorite beer, Craig?" The question wasn't on my list but I figured it fit nicely into the conversation.

"Tossup. Sometimes I crave a dark beer. Other times, a Bud Light does the trick," he said.

I brought the glass to my nose, inhaled the citrus aroma and took my first sip as Hille watched me. "Mine's definitely wheat beer. Do you like it?"

"Never tried it, actually."

I was about to ask Hille if he wanted to try mine when Eric and Jess came out of what I assumed to be Hille's bedroom. I hadn't even noticed they were gone.

"Time to make a toast to the birthday boy," Hille said. "Does everyone have a drink?"

"You have any champagne?" Eric asked.

"Champagne? Since when do you drink champagne outside of New Year's Eve?" I asked.

"In the mood to celebrate, that's all. I'll settle for a beer, though."

Hille handed Eric his beer, turned to Jess and asked, "What about you, Jess? What's your poison?"

"You have any orange juice?" she asked.

"Yeah, you want me to make you a screw driver?" Hille asked.

"No, just orange juice. Thanks."

"Why aren't you drinking, Jess. You okay?" Hope asked.

"She's fine." Eric said. Then he turned to Jess, smiled brightly and put his arm around her. She buried her face in the crook of his neck while the rest of us looked at them in silence. I was confused and wondered if I was the only one.

"What the hell is going on?" Paul asked. "Fuck the OJ! Let's do shots."

Eric rubbed Jess's back and whispered something to her. She removed herself from his embrace and turned to face us, her eyes watery. She looked at Eric and said, "You tell them."

"You sure?" Eric asked.

Jess nodded. "Positive. I can't keep anything from these guys."

Eric locked eyes with each of us one at a time until he got to Paul. "Paul, I know you love to be the center of attention but I have to steal your thunder tonight. I promise to make it up to you next year." He paused dramatically. "Jess just gave me some big news and, well, she said it was okay to tell you guys so...."

"We're pregnant!" Jess shouted.

There was a delay between Jess's words and any reaction from the rest of us, almost like we were speaking through a trans-continental telephone line. I wasn't even sure I had heard her correctly since I didn't even know they were trying. But then again, I'd never seen Eric's face quite that bright before, and Jess's excessive hunger and constant trips to the bathroom certainly made more sense now.

My feet were still frozen to Hille's wood floor, but the sounds of everyone else screaming "Oh my God!" and "Congratulations!" awoke me from my stupor and to the realization that my best friends were seriously having a baby. And that we were actually old enough to be parents, something I hated to admit. Since I couldn't seem to maintain a relationship, having a family was something unlikely to happen for

God only knew how long. I made my way over to the dad to be, pushed Paul to the side and pulled Eric into a tight hug. I whispered, "Congratulations" in his ear and, after we separated, said, "Wow. Eric Fitzgerald—Dad. That's some crazy shit!" It was hard to imagine the same guy who organized naked slip 'n slide at a college party changing his own child's diapers.

"I know. I'm still in shock myself. Jess has been trying to tell me since last night but said she couldn't find the right moment." Eric then looked over at Jess, who was talking to Hope, and said, "She's got some strange timing but I'm not complaining. That woman can do no wrong right now."

"You'll make a great dad, Eric. You always took care of me when I puked in the fraternity house." Mock glaring at Paul, I said, "My loving boyfriend at the time just directed me to the bathroom and lifted the toilet seat. You, however, actually held my hair back once. Yes, you will make a great daddy!" *Naked slip 'n slide participation not withstanding.*

Laughing, Eric responded, "My kid isn't drinking until he's thirty. And, if she's a girl, make it forty."

"Good luck with that, Dad," I said before turning to Jess who had finally separated from an extremely long embrace with Hope.

I remembered the night I had met Jess, my junior year of college. Eric, a senior, was bartending at the Longpost on a Monday night and the bar was empty save for me, Paul and the spunky red-head freshman Eric had met earlier that weekend. Eric fed us free drinks all night, which led to Jess's drunk confession that she thought Paul and I were an odd match. Prophetically we broke up the following month, deciding we'd be better off as friends.

Pouncing myself on Jess, gently of course to avoid hurting the unborn baby, I exclaimed, "My turn!" After we hugged, I said, "I'm so happy for you guys. Truly."

"Thanks, Steph. You ready to be an aunt again?" Jess asked.

Wiping a tear from my eye, I said, "Really? You want me to be an aunt?"

"Absolutely!"

I turned to Hope. "And Hope doesn't mind sharing the title?"

Wrapping her arms around me, Hope said, "Hope doesn't mind! We can have fun buying baby clothes together. If it's a girl, we can teach her about men. And if it's a boy, we can teach him how to treat women!"

Eric joined us and said, "Uh, the child is not even born yet. Can you refrain from discussing him or her in the context of sex at least until we know what sex it is?"

"Speaking of which, how far along are you?" I asked. "You're certainly not showing."

"Only seven weeks. I know you aren't supposed to tell people during the first trimester but I couldn't imagine keeping something like this from you guys, especially when I'm in an apartment full of alcohol and drinking juice!" Jess then rubbed her belly, something I had a feeling she'd do often during the next seven or so months—at least if she was anything like my sister-in-law and every other pregnant woman I had ever known.

"If you guys don't mind, I think Jess and I are going to try to check into a hotel and do our own celebrating," Eric said.

"You're seriously gonna blow off my thirty-fifth birthday? Some friends you are!" Paul said.

We all looked at Paul in disbelief until we noticed he was grinning.

"You're such an ass," Hille said. Then he took an unopened bag of Doritos from the kitchen counter and threw it at Paul. Eric followed Hille's lead with an unopened bag of potato chips and Hope joined in with an unopened box of Bavarian-style pretzels. Feeling left out, I grabbed the closest bag I could find—Fritos—and tossed it in Paul's direction.

Except the bag I grabbed was opened and the chips went flying all over his oak parquet floor.

Everyone started laughing and Paul, of course, said, "Could you *be* more of a spaz, Steph?"

Bending down to pick up the chips, I responded, "No." and looked up at Hille red-faced. "Sorry, Craig."

Clearly trying not to laugh, Hille said, "No worries" and bent down to help me.

I decided it was not a good time to ask him his biggest fear.

TWENTY-TWO

HILLE GOT JESS AND ERIC a reservation at the Sheraton Suites in Weehawken and after my initial disappointment that Jess and Eric weren't hanging out, I decided going out with just Hille, Paul and Hope could be a good thing. Although Paul and Hope had been dating for about six months, the long distance extended the newlywed stage and they tended to sneak away a lot. Alone time with Hille could mean more time to ask him questions.

Aside from Hille, none of us had ever been out in Hoboken, so we trusted his judgment when he suggested Scotland Yard, a European-style pub around the corner from his building. On the way, we passed rows of brownstones and at least one real estate company and two bars on every block. As we walked, Hille and I slightly ahead of Paul and Hope, I got a positive vibe and had a feeling it would be a good night.

"It's that one over there," Hille said, gesturing towards a bar with a bright red telephone booth at the entrance. "Sometimes they have live blues bands here, but I'm not sure about Saturday nights."

Taking a sideways glance at Hille, who was staring straight ahead towards the bar, I said, "I'm sure it will be fun. I'm all about the company anyway."

"And they have a great beer selection, too," Hille said.

When we got inside, we headed directly for the bar and Hille bought the first round. As suspected, it wasn't long before we lost Paul and Hope. Once Hille and I found an empty corner to park ourselves, I held up my beer. "Cheers, Craig."

Hille repeated, "Cheers," clinked his glass against mine and smiled at me.

"So, Hoboken seems pretty cool. You happy here?"

"Happy enough, I guess, and certainly happier than I was before. My commute went from over an hour to less than thirty minutes and there's much more to do here at night than there was in Newton, where I used to live."

"Is this where you want to settle down? I mean, in New Jersey?"

"Probably not, but I make more money working in New York than I would in most other places, so for now, it's good. If money wasn't an issue, though? That would be a different story."

"Where would you live if money wasn't an issue?" Another question not on the list but certainly worth asking.

Hille put his beer down on the built-in shelf on the wall and looked at me thoughtfully. "I don't know, maybe Richmond, Virginia. Or out West, like Washington State or San Diego."

"Remember Lori Wasserstein from my dorm sophomore year? She lived in San Diego—loved it. It's supposedly beautiful there and never gets too humid in the summer, unlike D.C." Yes, I could definitely see myself relocating there someday. I'd rarely have to worry about bad hair days.

"Isn't Lori the one who married a baron or something?" Hille asked.

"A baron? I don't think so. Lori? A baroness?" Laughing, I said, "Lori's claim to fame was mooning strangers at every opportunity."

Hille assumed a serious expression. "Maybe the baron was so impressed with her ass, he fell in love at first ass-sighting?"

"If Lori's white ass can hook a baron, there might actually be hope for me."

Hille nodded. "I'm sure if you dropped trough right now, you could hook a baron, too."

"Yes, cuz Scotland Yard is just bursting to the seams with barons."

"You never know. It *is* a Scottish bar."

We laughed together until Hille noticed my beer was empty and offered to get me another one. I followed him with my eyes and let out a sigh of contentment. Things were looking good.

A few minutes later, our eyes locked as he walked towards me with our drinks and I smiled at him and widened my eyes, hoping I looked flirtatious and not like a bugged-eyed tree frog. "Thanks, Craig. One of these days, you'll have to let me buy you a beer, okay?"

"Okay. I promise that if..."

Suddenly Hope appeared at my side and said, "You've got to get me out of here, Steph."

I looked up at Hille, who looked at me and then at Hope.

"What's wrong, Hope?" he asked.

Hope stood with her hands on her hips and said, "What's wrong is that your best friend is an asshole. That's what's wrong."

"Umm hmm. Okay, then. Let me find Paul," Hille said. And before I could say anything, he had walked away and was lost in the crowd.

I wondered why Paul had to ruin my night but forced myself to snap out of it and tend to my friend.

"What happened, Hope?"

Hoped pulled her long red hair into a ponytail and clipped it into a bun. "Nothing 'happened,' Steph. We were just talking about stupid shit—nonsense really—and he started telling me what he had planned for the next several months." Hope stopped speaking and stared at me.

"And?"

"*And*, do you know that Paul has his weekends planned for the next six weeks and doesn't seem to think there is anything wrong with the fact that none of those weekends involve seeing me?"

"Oh."

"Oh is right. So, Steph, do you still think Paul is so into me?"

I knew if I told Hope that I did believe Paul was still crazy about her, she wouldn't believe me or she would ask me to explain why he would plan six weekends without a woman he was crazy about. I had no answer for her. "Let's go someplace else and get hammered," I said.

Hope smiled, the color back in her face. "Where?"

I put down my half-empty beer and motioned for Hope to follow me to the exit. "Did you see how many bars we passed between Hille's apartment and here? I'm sure we'll find a place. Let's just go."

I had tossed aside my paranoia about saving Hille's number to my phone and as we walked across the street and into the nearest bar, I sent him a text, "Took Hope to Hobson's Choice. See you later :)."

By some stroke of luck, we found two spots at the bar and sat down. I bought us SoCo and lime shots and two beers and before we did the shot, we recited our favorite chant: "*Here's to the men who we love. Here's to the men who love us. And to the men we love who don't love us, fuck the men and here's to us!"*

After we did the shot, Hope got silent, her eyes focused on the filthy floor of the bar. I patted her shoulder gently. "So, what exactly are these plans Paul has for the next six weeks?" I selfishly wondered whether Hille was involved in any of these plans and if Hope's lack of involvement would translate into six weeks without any excuse to see him.

"I don't want to talk about him, Steph." She pointed at the crowd, specifically at a group of boys playing pool a few feet away. "Lots of cuties here. Check 'em out."

I took note of the cuties in the bar. "Too bad they all look like jail bait," I said.

"I'm sick of dating old men. Maybe it's time I found a more age-appropriate boyfriend."

"He's only thirty-five, not exactly a senior citizen. Plus, his maturity level is that of an eighth grader. Doesn't that kind of balance things out for you?" I joked.

"I love him, Stephanie." She was not joking.

Pretending I knew even the slightest bit about love, I offered my best advice. "Love is a battlefield, Hope. Suit up."

"I'll do that," she said somberly. Then she got up and said, "Going to the bathroom. Be back in a sec."

I took the opportunity to check my cell phone. I didn't want to care whether Hille had returned my text but I did. He had, but it wasn't much better than no text at all. All he said was, "Okay. See you later." I put my phone back in my bag and imagined how the night would've gone if Hope and Paul had not fought. We would've talked for hours, moving seamlessly from topic to topic. As the time went by, we would stand closer to each other and look at each other's lips while we spoke. When he excused himself to go to the bathroom, he would put his hand on my shoulder or on the small of my back before he walked away. Or, better yet, we would go to the bathroom at the same time and, rather than find Hope and Paul when he was finished, he would wait for me and be standing outside the girl's bathroom when I walked out, ready to pick up where we had left off. If only Hope and Paul hadn't fought.

When Hope returned, she was smiling. "Paul called."

"Yeah? What did he say?"

"He said it was all a big misunderstanding and he wanted to talk about it face-to-face."

"Where are they?" I hoped they were still at Scotland Yard so Hille and I could get back to our talk.

"Heading back to the apartment."

"I guess that means you want to get going, too?"

"Are you mad?"

"Of course not. Let's get out of here."

When Hille let us into the apartment, Paul stood up from the couch and Hope walked over to him slowly. I could tell she was nervous. She loved him. I kind of had a feeling, but to hear her say it was strange. I wondered if she had ever said it to him. Paul and I had never said, "I love you" in the two years we were together. We said it all of the time now, but, of course in a different way. Hope was now sitting next to Paul on the couch and he was holding her hand. I decided it was time to stop watching them and looked for Hille. He was in the kitchen throwing empty beer bottles in the trash.

"Need some help?" I asked.

"Nope. I'm good. Want another beer?"

"Sure. Strange night, huh?"

Hille poured a bottle of Blue Moon into a glass and placed it in front of me on his granite countertop. Then he grinned and said, "Aren't they all?"

Hope and Paul were now kissing. As I tried not to look in the direction of the living room, I said, "I feel kind of like a voyeur."

"A bit awkward, huh? Why don't we bring a bunch of beers into my room? We can watch TV."

"Okay." I had a feeling I would be spending the night in Hille's room—not that I was complaining—so I grabbed my bag on the way. I didn't want to be in need of my toothbrush later and too afraid to leave the room at the risk of catching Hope and Paul going at it on Hille's pull-out couch.

Hille's room was scantily furnished with a queen-sized bed, a mahogany dresser and chest set and a small television. There were no chairs, so when he sat on the bed, I followed suit. As I watched him flip through the channels, I wondered what he was thinking and tried not to fidget.

"Seinfeld okay with you?" he asked.

"Absolutely. I love Seinfeld." I looked at the television and immediately noticed one of my favorite episodes was on. "I love this episode!" I said.

Hille looked from me to the television set and back to me. "You sort of remind me of Elaine, ya know?"

I wasn't sure how to take that. I thought Julia Louis Dreyfus was pretty but didn't think I looked anything like her.

As if reading my mind, Hille said, "Not her looks."

I hoped Hille wasn't referring to my dancing abilities. I wasn't likely to try out for *So You Think You Can Dance*, but I had a modicum of rhythm. "In what way then?"

Hille motioned towards the television where Elaine was trapped on the subway and cursing into oblivion. "I can see you doing that."

I laughed. He had me pegged and I was pleased he was so observant. "You, on the other hand, are so calm. You probably never lose it," I said.

"You'd be surprised, Steph. I've had road rage many times. It's not pretty. Trust me."

"Glad to hear it. You seem so put together sometimes, you make the rest of us look bad."

Hille shrugged but didn't say anything and I returned my attention to the television. While pretending to watch, I thought about how to work some of my questions into the conversation. I turned back towards Hille and said, "So, Craig, have you ever been in love?" I didn't know what caused me to choose practically the deepest question on my list and wished I'd asked about his first rock concert instead.

Hille looked pained as he turned to face me. Feeling stupid, I bit my lip and hoped he didn't think I'd asked because I thought he was in love with me.

"No," Hille said. "Never been in love." Then he leaned in, planted a soft peck on my lips and pulled away to look at me. He still looked pained.

I wanted to know why he chose that moment to kiss me and why he looked pained but I didn't have the guts to ask.

"What?" I whispered.

"Nothing." Then he chuckled. "Can I kiss you again, Elaine?"

As I nodded my permission and opened my mouth against his, I told myself that Hille initiating meant he really wanted me and so what if he wasn't into drawn out conversations?

A few seconds later, while flat on my back with my eyes shut, I felt his hands on my waist gripping the bottom of my shirt and I sat up slightly so he could pull it over my head. I opened my eyes to his bare chest but avoided eye contact because I was still trying to justify sleeping with him again despite any effort by him to "up his game." I promised Suzanne I would move on. I promised myself I would move on.

Mere moments later, as I rocked back and forth above him, I fought the urge to let him slip out of me so I could curl into a ball on the opposite side of the bed. I looked down at him, his eyes were closed tight and his teeth were clenched. I knew an orgasm wasn't in the cards for me this time and whispered, "Can we switch positions?"

When Hille opened his eyes beneath me, I said, "I'm tired" and laughed to avoid crying.

Hille flipped me over so he was on top and a few thrusts later, we were both flat on our backs—Hille satisfied, me not-so-much, but it wasn't his fault.

"You okay?" Hille asked.

I looked up at the ceiling. "Yeah, I'm fine. Been a long day, that's all."

Hille said, "Get some sleep then. Tomorrow will be here before you know it." Then he turned his back to me and said, "Night Steph."

To his back, I said, "Goodnight, Craig."

TWENTY-THREE

THE NEXT MORNING, I woke up before Hille. The apartment was so quiet, I figured Hope and Paul were still sleeping too. I glanced over at Hille who was snoring with one arm over his head and a pillow between his knees and quickly jumped out of the bed, grabbed my bag and went to his bathroom to shower. I didn't want to be alone with him and have to make forced conversation. It was too hard and I always seemed to make most of the effort anyway. Well, duh, Steph. Of course I put more effort into it. I was the one with the crush. He was just along for the ride.

As I was getting dressed in the bathroom after my shower, I heard voices from the living room. I did a half-assed blow-dry of my hair, stuck it in a clip above my head and put on a little make-up before joining the others.

Still in his sweatpants, Paul yawned loudly from the couch. "Don't you look pretty, Steph. How nice of you to make so much effort for us."

Hille was standing by the window talking on his cell. I tried not to care who he was talking to. "You never know who I might meet on the train. Gotta be prepared," I said.

"Yes, and that includes wearing nice panties" Jess said. "No period granny panties."

Hille, no longer on the phone, walked over, shook his head in disgust and said, "Nice, Jess."

"You're so uptight, Hille. You hate the period, farts, doody talk, don't you?" Jess asked.

"All the above are kind of personal bodily functions and I think they should stay that way," Hille said.

"Tell that to Paul," I said. "He seems to think his farts are for the world to experience with him."

"Aren't they?" Paul asked. "I'm off to shower, peeps, but before I do, I want to leave you with something to remember me by."

I knew what was coming and shielded my eyes with my hand as Paul dropped his pants and showed us his business. Admittedly, I peeked through my fingers a little but I'm pretty sure Jess and Hope did too.

Eric wanted to head back early but first we went to the Malibu Diner. It was packed and I stood outside with Eric and Paul while we waited for our table. They wanted to smoke. I just didn't want to be near Hille.

"You have fun last night, Steph?" Eric asked.

"Um hmm. Not exactly what I had expected. I barely spoke to Paul at all, though, so I can't really complain," I joked. Looking at Paul, I said, "Seriously, this was supposed to be your birthday celebration and we didn't even celebrate."

Shrugging, Paul said, "I know. I didn't exactly plan on fighting with Hope and the whole pregnancy thing—well that was unexpected, too."

With some force, Eric pushed Paul but laughed and said, "Pregnancy 'thing?' If Jess hears you call it that, she'll go ape shit on you."

"Joking. Besides, Steph, you had more time to throw yourself at Hille," Paul said.

Disgusted, but more at myself than at Paul, I couldn't think of anything to say. I looked up at Eric, forced a smile and said, "Eggs or pancakes? Protein vs. carbs. That's my dilemma."

Laughing, Eric said, "You have that dilemma every time, Cohen!" Then he softened his voice and added, "Follow your gut. It's not life or death. You know what I mean?"

"I think so, Eric. Thanks." From inside the diner, Hille knocked on the window and motioned for us to come inside. Eric squeezed my shoulder gently, smiled and said, "Let's get some breakfast."

* * *

On the way home, I spent most of the time looking out the window but instead of noticing the waving kids in passing cars, I saw myself on top of Hille and felt like I'd swallowed a lump of coal.

"Steph?"

I turned away from the window to look at Hope and said, "Yeah, what?"

"You just grimaced. You okay?"

I faked a shiver and said, "I'm fine. Kind of cold, that's all." Then I forced a smile. "Thanks."

It was past nine by the time I got home and after putting on my pajamas, I brushed my teeth, washed my face and got right into bed. I stared at the ceiling, contemplating whether to get up and pour a fresh glass of water to keep on my nightstand. I glanced over at the half-filled glass already there and decided it wouldn't kill me to drink two-day old water and closed my eyes.

Four hours later, my eyes bolted open and I immediately pictured myself looking at Hille admiringly, my eyes fully dilated and so clearly into him, my tongue might as well have been hanging out of my mouth. And then I remembered the questions. The stupid questions. By the grace of God, I hadn't had the opportunity to ask most of them.

As I buried my head under my pillow in shame, I wondered why I had to be so fucking stupid, so fucking transparent and so fucking easy.

TWENTY-FOUR

A FEW DAYS LATER, I had ordered sushi, poured myself a glass of Riesling and was in the middle of watching *General Hospital* on Soapnet when Suzanne called. I stopped screaming at the television set at some nurse who was making her crush on Prince Nicholas Cassadine too obvious and told Suzanne I couldn't make our drink night for the following evening. Suzanne wouldn't have it.

"Steph, I don't know what happened last weekend, but you're clearly upset about it."

I jammed a chopstick into the center of a piece of my Naruto roll and removed a chunk of salmon. "Nothing happened, Suzanne. I'm fine. Just in a funk."

"The best way to get out of funk is to go out and get your mind off of it. Self-loathing is only helpful for forty-eight hours. It's all diminished rewards after that," she insisted.

I took a sip of wine. "I really don't want to go out." *And if I drink alone and make an ass out of myself, no one will know about it except me.*

"Okay, how about you come over for dinner? Luke has a poker game tomorrow night. It'll be fun. I'll make you anything you want."

Drawing to memory the velvety taste of her homemade sauce, I said, "Penne Alia Vodka?"

"If that's what you want," Suzanne said.

Being thin had not served to make me any luckier in love thus far, and figuring it didn't matter if I gained ten pounds gorging myself on pasta and cream sauce, I relented. "Okay. Count me in."

* * *

The following night, Suzanne prepared the main course while I sat at her breakfast bar sipping a glass of Cabernet and nibbling on mozzarella and tomato salad. To her credit, Suzanne actually waited until I started my second glass of wine to grill me about my sullen mood. She tried to tell me I was being too hard on myself. As the pasta cooked, she poured herself a glass of wine and sat down next to me.

"Do I think it was smart to sleep with the guy again? No. But, Stephanie, you had sex with the guy a few times, and you said it was great sex. It's not that big a deal. Why are you so upset?"

"I'm not upset it happened the first time, but I feel so stupid that even after it was obvious it was just sex, I didn't stop. And it was only great sex the first two times. The third time sucked because I couldn't stop thinking it was wrong. God, you make the best tomato and mozzarella salad ever." I started giggling. "I don't know how you cut the cheese so perfectly."

"Yes, Luke always says that no one cuts the cheese quite like I do, but I say he takes the cake in that regard."

"Gross. Does he take books into the bathroom, too?"

"All guys do. I don't know if the crapping process actually takes longer or if it's because they love to sit on the bowl for a while even after they finish." Suzanne's face turned serious again. "Do you know how many girls have done the same thing? C'mon, Stephanie. Show me one girl who's never let lust cloud her judgment, aside from the nuns at Sacred Heart. And some of them are probably sporting Ben Wa balls under their habits! Anyway, you should be glad you figured it out before you got too vested."

After I swallowed my last bite of layered tomato and cheese, I said, "I guess. But I still feel shitty that he doesn't consider me relationship-worthy."

"Crap on a cracker, Stephanie! What makes you think Hille's disinterest in a relationship has anything to do with you not being 'relationship worthy?' Even Eric said Hille was not the relationship type, right?"

"No. Eric said Hille was not one to go ga-ga over a girl"

"Exactly," Suzanne said.

"Yes, exactly." My bottom lip protruding in a pout, I said, "I obviously don't have 'ga-ga' appeal."

"To Hille, maybe! But there are plenty of guys who would disagree with him and you know it!"

I placed my elbow on the table and dropped my chin into the palm of my hand. "If I'm so great, why am I terminally single? Why is everyone coupled up but me? And why doesn't Hille like me enough to be my boyfriend?"

Suzanne poured the remaining wine into my glass and got up to throw the now empty plate of appetizers into the dishwasher. When she returned to the table, she sat down and said, "What's this about, Steph? Are you upset about Hille not wanting to be with you because you like him or because your ego is bruised?"

"Why can't you believe that I actually like the guy?"

"I don't know—from what you say, he seems like a withdrawn prick who knows how to fuck. You deserve better." Suzanne stood up again, walked to the cabinets above her sink and pulled out a green box. When she returned to the table, she handed me a box of Girl Scout cookies.

Ignoring the box, I said, "There's more to him than meets the eye. I saw some of it but each time we started to make progress, something got in the way. I just wanted more time."

"Well, you can always take more time. I'm sure he'd be fine maintaining your friends with benefits status while you continue to try to figure him out." Pulling out the tray of Thin Mints, she said, "Take one."

I popped a cookie in my mouth, but the cool minty flavor served to bring back memories of Hille's fresh breath when he kissed me. "No," I said, shaking my head. "I thought we were fated to be together after all these years, but I guess not. I can't do it anymore. It's not worth it."

"You said it. Not me. Perhaps you're right—maybe there is more to him than meets the eye. But you don't know that for sure, so you're really not losing anything except great sex, which by the way, you'll find with someone else eventually. And if it's fate, it's not in your control anyway. Time will tell," she said.

"Fair enough. Okay, I must pee!"

As I ran to the bathroom, I heard Suzanne shout, "While you're in there, take a look at yourself in the mirror. You're a smokin' hottie, girl!"

I smiled at my image in the bathroom mirror, noting my blue teeth thanks to the red wine. I shook out my head of thick, long, dark hair and peered into the reflection of my big hazel eyes. Smokin hottie? I never really thought of myself that way. Cute? Okay. Pretty? I guess. Hot? I didn't think so, but God bless Suzanne for saying so. I was unlikely to be discovered by a model/talent agent, but despite my limited relationship experience, I had attracted the attention of quite a few men in my thirty-two years and Hille wasn't exactly being charitable by screwing me either. Some might say he got pretty lucky, too. So no more negativity, I decided. Suzanne was right; self-loathing was not the way to go.

I just hoped my new found perspective on the situation would not fade with my buzz, leaving me back at square one tomorrow, along with a red wine migraine.

TWENTY-FIVE

THINK POSITIVE. So my past experience with the online dating scene was less than successful. As Suzanne said, "It only takes one!" He seemed kind of cool on the phone and his pictures were decent. And if there was no spark, at least I'd get a free drink out of it. *Unless he was cheap.* I let out a sigh, ran my hands quickly through my hair and walked into Rhino Bar & Pumphouse in Georgetown. I hoped he'd be there before me. I hated the awkwardness of waiting and, unlike Hille, had no Blackberry to look at in the meantime. *I will not think about Hille. Will not think about Hille.*

I pretended to be self-assured and not at all anxious as I scanned the bar packed with frat boys in Red Sox baseball caps and girls wearing navel-bearing sleeveless shirts and designer jeans. In what was clearly a sports bar, I felt over-dressed in my straight-from-work black pencil skirt, white blouse and black pumps.

We planned to meet in the upstairs bar and when I saw him sitting on one of the couches, I recognized him immediately except that he didn't do justice to his pictures. He was heavier, looked like a poster child for the before pictures in a ProActiv commercial and was just plain dorky looking. I knew instantly he would not be my rebound guy from Hille. We made eye contact and I smiled, hoping it looked sincere as I approached him.

He smiled back and stood up. "Stephanie?"

"That's me. Kenny, I assume?"

He offered me his hand and said, "Good to meet you."

Shaking hands with a perspective soul mate was the opposite of sexy. As I shook his hand, I noticed the wiry, pubic-like black hairs that ran up and down his arm. I sat down next to him, leaving ample personal space between us and said, "Same here."

Pointing to his left eye, he asked, "Does my eye look red?"

I peered at his eye, which did look very red. "Kind of."

Kenny rolled his contact lens in the palm of his hand. "I'm legally blind in my right eye which makes it more vital that my left functions at full capacity."

"Oh." In the realization that it was going to be a long night, I scanned the room. But then I remembered that even though a romantic relationship was out of the question, the date might still be fun. *Must think positive.*

"Do you want something to drink?" he asked.

"What are you drinking?"

Kenny coughed while I awaited his answer. Then he coughed again. "You okay? Need some water?"

Kenny took a sip of his drink, looked at me as if to say something and resumed coughing. With one hand covering his mouth, he got up and gestured with the other hand that he'd be back in a minute and walked over to the bar. In his absence, I scanned the room again, hoping no one thought he was my boyfriend. And then I felt guilty for caring what anyone else thought and decided to be nice again. When he returned, he had stopped coughing and handed me a bottle of Sam Adams Light. I smiled. "Glad you're okay. I hate coughing fits." I took the beer from his hand and took a long sip. Raising the beer in my hand, I said, "Thanks for the beer."

"Yeah, I swallowed my gum with the beer." Angling his body toward mine, he said, "So, if I avoid eye contact, it's only because I have difficulty focusing with sight in just the one eye."

Leaning backwards, I said, "No problem."

Kenny ordered mozzarella sticks and fried calamari to share and I told him about the Pub Crawl I did on St. Patrick's Day with some friends from work. "I love green beer!"

"The food coloring has no taste," Kenny said dryly.

"I know. But the fact that it's green makes it more festive. Don't you think?"

Kenny gave me a blank stare. "The food coloring is poison."

Unable to think of a verbal response, I shrugged.

Interrupting our awkward silence, a waitress stopped in front of us and asked if we needed anything."

Pointing at the plates already on our table, Kenny yelled, "We already ordered!"

I passed an eye over the room again and hoped I wouldn't wind up with whiplash. There were plenty of cute guys in the bar, smiling and having a grand old time with their friends watching college basketball on the enormous television screens. I wished I was out with one of them. Or with Suzanne. Or at home watching *Survivor*. Where was the pleasant guy from the phone? Why did I waste forty-five minutes getting to know him when the in-person version was a completely different model?

About an hour later, Kenny and I stood outside of the bar. "Thanks for treating," I said.

"My pleasure," he said. "Can I kiss you?"

I took two steps away from him. "I had a nice time, Kenny. But I don't feel a romantic vibe. I hope we can be friends, though." As I flashed back to hearing almost the same words from Hille, I discovered that giving this speech was almost as bad as receiving it. I wanted to go home.

Kenny gave me a wry look and a half smile. "No problem."

I started to hail down a taxi when Kenny said, "Can we do this again sometime?"

At that moment, I hated dating more than doing my laundry. I turned away from the street, looked at Kenny and said, "Okay," hoping a cab would read my mind and stop at my feet at that precise moment.

"But you didn't want me to kiss you."

I raised my hand in the air and as the taxi approached, said, "If we go out again, it would have to be as friends." I crawled into the cab. "I hope that's okay."

Looking disappointed, Kenny said, "Sure," and as the cab drove in one direction, I turned around and saw him walk in the opposite one.

Never again, I vowed, which is what I told Suzanne when I called her from the cab on my way home.

"That bad, huh?" she said.

"Yes, that bad," I confirmed.

"At least you got free drinks and food—a girl's gotta eat!"

"A bottle of Sam Light and a mozzarella stick, Suze. I was afraid to eat off of the same plate in case he started coughing again. I'm thinking of ordering Chinese when I get home. Seriously, the only thing we had in common was a disinterest in golf. And he took me to a Red Sox bar even though there are pictures of me on my profile wearing a Yankee baseball cap! And I mentioned I was a Yankees fan on the phone, too. Thankfully we still have a few weeks before baseball season starts because if there was a game on against the Yankees, I'd probably have gotten my ass kicked."

Laughing, Suzanne said, "They say opposites attract, you know."

"Sure, but there was no attraction of any kind."

"That's bad. How'd you end things?"

"He asked if I wanted to go out again and I responded with an unenthusiastic "Okay." Hopefully, he'll get the hint and not call. We had nothing to talk about. I have no clue why he'd want to go out again anyway."

"Cuz you're a smokin' hottie. What did I tell you? Anyway, better luck next time, girlfriend."

"Like I said, there won't be a next time."

"It only takes..."

As the cab stopped in front of my apartment and I paid the driver, I said to Suzanne, "One. I know. It only takes one."

TWENTY-SIX

IT WAS LATE but pre-closing meetings sometimes lasted all night. I tried to keep my eyes open while Gerard and the counsel for the other side reviewed the long list of documents which would be signed at the closing. I yawned and stretched my arms over my head. As I dropped them back to the sides of my body, I locked eyes with Gerard. He nodded, indicating I could take a break. I quietly left the conference room and went to my office. I debated whether to call my mom or take a nap, but I knew a nap would be of no benefit unless it was at least seven hours in duration. I startled my mom by phoning so late but after I assured her that I hadn't been mugged, raped or hit by a car, she was happy to hear from me.

"I'm sorry I haven't called you much lately. Things have been crazy at work. I'm still here," I said.

"It's almost eleven! Are you going home soon?"

Her voice sounded groggy and I worried that I'd awoken her or, worse, interrupted her having sex with Al. "Not likely. The overtime is great, though."

"What else is new?"

"Nothing."

"Anything interesting to share?"

"No."

"Are you okay, sweetheart?"

Although my token answer to that question was "I'm fine," when I attempted to say the words, I started sobbing. No words came out, just gasps of air.

"Stephanie, what's wrong?"

I no longer heard the television in the background and I knew my mother was sitting upright on the bed. She was scared and I hated that I frightened her, especially since I had no idea what had come over me. I wiped my eyes with my hands, ignoring the mascara on my fingers, which was probably running down my face as well. "Nothing's wrong," I gasped.

"You're crying! Is this about work?"

I shook my head as if my mom could see me. "No."

"Is this about Hille?"

"I feel like a slut! I went against every relationship how-to book in publication. What's wrong with me?"

"Honey, you're not a slut."

"I'm pathetic," I insisted. "He said we were friends with benefits and I didn't listen."

"So you had a little fun," my mom said. "You're entitled! And maybe he'll come to his senses."

"He won't."

"Then you'll find someone else and forget all about him."

I blew my nose and moaned, "I'm not so sure."

"Well I am and I'm your mother," my mom said sternly.

My mom's certainty was not convincing, but it was nice to hear. "I hope you're right."

"I am right. You're a beautiful, intelligent, wonderful young woman. Now go home and don't worry about meeting someone."

"From the lips of the woman who bribed me into joining eHarmony last year."

"I'm not going to bug you about it anymore."

"Really?"

"Not until tomorrow, at least. Too bad Eric married Jess. I like him for you."

My mother was nothing if not consistent. I shook my head. "Mom, Eric is my friend. That's all."

"I know, but he's such a nice guy and he loves you."

"And I love him too, but not in that way."

"I know. Okay, you get back to work. I love you."

"I love you too. Thanks Mom."

After we hung up, I went to the bathroom to wash my face. The tears made my eyes look greener and I wondered why they had to look prettiest when the rest of my face was swollen from crying. I also wondered what exactly Hille had done to deserve my tears. I couldn't think of anything, but the idea that I had spontaneously erupted into hysterics over nothing didn't exactly make me feel better. The next time I cried over a guy, I hoped I'd have a better reason. I wasn't proud of my behavior with Hille, but I had a weak moment. Okay, I had several of them. But I felt better. I truly did. Maybe it was my mom's pep talk or maybe it was simply the realization that I wouldn't be nearly as hard on a friend going through this as I had been on myself. The truth was, nothing I had done would be considered punishable by imprisonment or death under the laws of any country and certainly shouldn't receive a lifetime sentence of self-hatred. It was time to deem it a lesson learned and move on.

Glancing at my watch, I realized forty minutes had passed since I left the conference room and I hurried back to work.

TWENTY-SEVEN

IT RAINED THAT SUNDAY and I was home with John Cougar Mellencamp's Greatest Hits, my cleaning music, blasting. The phone rang while I was on the floor by my closet, bopping along to *Rocking in the USA*. I was trying to decide which shoes I really would never wear again and which I was likely to regret tossing in a month when I was wearing the perfect outfit but missing the perfect shoes.

It was Hille calling, and when my stomach didn't leap at seeing his name on my phone, I knew I was making progress.

"Hi, Craig."

"Hey, kid," he said cheerfully. "How's it going?"

He probably hadn't even noticed that the last time we spoke one on one or even acknowledged the other directly was in the minutes after screwing. "It's going okay," I said. "No complaints. You?"

"I have complaints, but I won't bore you with details."

"I'm cleaning my apartment. The urge strikes me so infrequently, I feel like I should take advantage."

"Or hire a cleaning lady. That's what I do."

"Nah. I'd feel too lazy hiring someone to clean a measly five hundred square feet."

"You work hard, Steph, you deserve it. Eric said you've been working tons of hours."

"Part of my job." *And a nice distraction from feeling like a loser for throwing myself at you.*

"Well, speaking of lazy, how do you feel about a lazy week at the beach? Paul and I found a place in the Outer Banks. We were thinking of extending Memorial Day weekend."

A week at the beach with Hille? I wasn't sure how I felt about it. "It sounds fun. I'm not sure I can get the days off, though." I was getting quite skilled at lying.

"Check with your boss. You said you got four weeks and you wouldn't even need a full one since I'm sure you already get Memorial Day. It'll be a blast. Eric, Jess and Hope are already in. Corky is checking with his department and I've asked a few other brothers."

"Wow. Must be a big house!"

"It's three floors and seven bedrooms of varying sizes."

"Who would I room with?" I immediately regretted asking and hoped Hille wouldn't think I was trying to flirt.

"Not sure, but we'd work out details later. You have to come. It wouldn't be the same without you."

Why? Because you probably wouldn't get any? "Glad you think so. Okay, I'll check with Gerard and let you know."

"Great."

The CD finished playing and I thought about what I should put on next. Maybe Steely Dan or The Fray. "I should get back to cleaning before I lose my motivation."

"Okay. Good talking to you. Happy cleaning."

"Thanks. Have a good one."

TWENTY-EIGHT

I FORGOT MY SISTER-IN-LAW'S BIRTHDAY. Well, I didn't technically forget, but had I remembered earlier, I wouldn't be in a bookstore buying her a last minute gift mere hours before her birthday dinner. I couldn't decide between a gift card from a bookstore or Sephora, but chose the book store since I didn't want to give Amy the wrong impression that I thought she needed to wear more makeup.

On my way to the check-out line, a book caught my eye. I looked at my watch, and since I had some time, picked it up. I was fascinated by Maureen McCormack's story. I had heard rumors that McCormack and Barry Williams slept together from third party sources but wasn't sure if they were based in fact and didn't think I could ever watch *The Brady Bunch* again without being haunted by visuals of Marcia and Greg having sex.

"What's your favorite episode?"

Startled, I looked up from the book into the twinkling blue eyes of a baby-faced guy, probably around my age, with dark hair cut close to his head and a spattering of freckles on his fair skin. He was so darn cute, I wanted to give him a bear hug on the spot. It suddenly occurred to me that he was probably acutely aware I was checking him out so, regaining my composure, I responded, "George Glass."

"George Glass? No way!"

I chuckled at his strong reaction. "Why? What's yours?"

"Definitely the three-parter in Hawaii."

"No way! With the stupid taboo idol and the oh-so realistic tarantula? I don't think so."

"But Vincent Price was in it. C'mon!" He winked at me. "And don't tell me you weren't hot for Greg in his bathing suit?"

"No, but I bet you liked Marcia in her bikini."

"Actually, I thought Carol looked pretty hot in her grass skirt," he said, grinning.

Shaking my head, I said, "I wasn't thrilled with those episodes. I might have even enjoyed the Grand Canyon ones more."

"Bobbeee!! Cindeee!!" He raised his voice as he said this and a few people turned around to look at us.

Barely containing my laughter, I put my finger to my lips. "Shhh. You're causing a scene."

Shrugging, he took a quick glance around. "Sorry. I guess I got a little excited."

"The Brady Bunch gets you that excited, huh?"

He smiled again, flashing a great set of teeth. "Just excited to meet a fellow fan, even if her taste in episodes is not quite up to par. I'm Ryan, by the way."

I couldn't help returning the smile. "Nice to meet you, Ryan. I'm Stephanie." Turning his gaze from me to the book in my hand, he said, "So, you think you'll buy the book?"

"I think I will. It figures, I come here to buy a gift for my sister-in-law and end up buying something for myself." Suddenly, I remembered that I had to get to Bethesda by 6:00, it was 5:15 and I still had to pay and get to the Metro. "Shit, I need to get in line."

"Ya gotta be somewhere?"

"Yeah. Bethesda for dinner with the family."

"Well, how do you feel about *Three's Company*?"

"Huh?"

"Well, I was wondering if you wanted to get together sometime to discuss preferences—Chrissy, Cindy or Terry?"

Although it was a no-brainer, I responded, "I'd love to."

After he put my number in his cell, we said goodbye and I made my way to the cash register to pay for the book and Amy's gift card. I added ten dollars to Amy's gift as a special thank you for her being the catalyst to my meeting Ryan.

As I left the store, I took one backwards glance inside. Ryan appeared to be deeply engaged in conversation with an elderly couple in the sports section. I smiled to myself and walked out. I'd probably be late for dinner but it wasn't every day an adorable guy asked for my phone number.

TWENTY-NINE

AFTER WE LAUGHED at the Benihana chefs traditional "shrimp in the pocket" trick, Sam turned to me and asked, "Are you pregnant, Steph?"

As Amy exclaimed "Sam!" in protest of his question, I shouted, "No! Where the hell did *that* come from?" I glanced over at the strangers sharing our table, thankful they appeared to be too engrossed in their own meals to overhear.

"I'm just asking because you're kind of glowing," Sam said, smiling at me.

"I am?" I hoped I was already glowing when I met Ryan.

"Yeah. Is it that Hille guy?"

"I'm not pregnant, Sam! For the love of God!"

I knew our neighbors heard me this time when the mustache-clad Tom Selleck look-alike sitting clockwise to us began distracting his kids, pretending to drink his entire bowl of spicy mustard sauce.

"That's not what I meant. Mom told me you were hanging out with Hille." Mimicking my mother's voice, he said "The genius in the group." Then he deadpanned, "Is it serious, sis?" but the sarcasm was not lost on me.

"Not quite. I guess Mom hasn't given you the latest update! Shocking. Anyway, we're just friends." Glancing over at my mother, who was still working on her Miso soup, I whispered, "I actually met a guy this afternoon at the book store. I know nothing about him other than his name and his favorite *Brady Bunch* episode though, so let's keep it on the down-low, okay?" I motioned towards my mom. "I don't want to get her all excited."

Looking up from her soup, my mom asked, "You don't want to get mom all excited over what? Did Hille come around? Should I order a subscription to *Bride* magazine?"

"Not unless you and Al are planning to renew your vows." I glanced at Al for his reaction but he was slurping up the rest of his soup and wasn't paying the slightest bit of attention.

"I'm sure you'll tell me after a little more sake," my mom said.

"There's nothing to tell, Mom. Hille did not come around, but a guy asked for my phone number at the book store today. Before you ask, I don't think he's Jewish and I have no idea what he does for a living. Let's wait for him to call before we discuss wedding plans, okay?" I was actually totally psyched, but didn't want to jinx myself by talking about it too much.

"How old is he? Where does he live?" my mom asked.

The chef gave us all an equal amount of noodles and scooped the rest onto my plate. Since I loved the noodles most of all, I looked up at him and smiled. He winked in response and I wondered if maybe he had a Jewish mother too.

THIRTY

I WAS EMPTYING OUT my dishwasher the following night when my phone rang. I didn't recognize the number, hoped it was Ryan and said, "Hello?"

"Is Stephanie there?"

I recognized his voice but feigning ignorance, said, "This is she. Who's this?"

"George"

Grinning, I said, "George who?"

"George Glass."

"Wow, and all these years I thought you were imaginary."

"Nope. I'm flesh and blood. Actually, it's Ryan. George isn't available at the moment."

I closed the dishwasher still containing clean utensils, and walked to my living room. Sitting lengthwise on the couch, I said, "That's too bad. Did something suddenly come up?"

Ryan laughed. "Something like that. So, how are you? How was dinner in Bethesda?"

"It was good. We went to Benihana for my sister-in-law's birthday."

"I love that place. Did the chef do the shrimp in the pocket trick?"

"Of course. It was the highlight of my meal!"

"Nice."

"And how was your night?"

"Uneventful. Walked my dog and watched some college basketball."

"What kind of dog do you have?"

"A pug. Do you have a dog?"

"Nope. I always wanted one, but my mom didn't think my brother and I would take care of it so she lied and said she was allergic.

Then she would torture us by bringing us to pet stores so we could look at all of the puppies she wouldn't let us have."

"Oh, man. That's cruel. What about your dad? Couldn't talk him into it?"

"Parents are divorced. My stepfather didn't come into the picture until later but my mom wears the pants in the relationship anyway, although Al's awesome."

"Glad you get along with your stepdad," Ryan said. "I've heard some horror stories."

"He's been good to me. More of a dad than my real one, who certainly won't win any Father of the Year awards in this lifetime." I hoped it wasn't too soon to share personal information and held my breath for Ryan's reaction.

"Some people get two shitty parents, at least you only got one." Ryan chuckled. "Although that mom of yours sounds like a tough cookie!"

Giggling, I said, "She's a spitfire, all right. I like to think some of it got passed along to me. But I'd let my kids have a dog!"

"So, I could ask you all the usual questions like what you do for a living, where you're from originally and your biggest fears and greatest desires but then we'd have nothing to talk about on our date."

"Hmmm, I don't recall planning a date." I felt my heart beating rapidly in anticipation for what he would say next.

"Aha. That's why I'm calling, actually. Wanna go on a date with me?"

If I was glowing at Benihana, I was probably fluorescent by now and was glad Ryan couldn't see me through the phone. Smiling like the proverbial Cheshire cat, I said, "Sure."

Because Ryan wanted to save his best material for face-to-face contact, we quickly nailed down the plans for that coming Friday and hung up. After I saved his number into my contacts, I got up from the couch and walked back to the kitchen to finish emptying my dishwasher. I was still grinning as I sang, *"Everybody's Smiling, Sunshine Da-ay!"* into a spoon.

THIRTY-ONE

"SO, HOW'S THE MOM-TO BE?" I asked Jess the following night. I had increased my bi-monthly phone call to once a week to check on her.

"Vomitous."

"Morning sickness?"

"Morning, noon and night sickness is more accurate," Jess said.

"Oh, no. Wow, that sucks. It's normal though, right?" I didn't remember Amy getting sick at all when she was pregnant with Lillie.

"It falls in the range of normal. No worries, Aunt Stephanie."

"Cool. Still sucks, though."

"You don't know the half of it. Hold on a sec."

"Okay." While I waited, I scrolled the TV guide channel. I had about 500 channels, yet there was absolutely nothing on.

Returning to the phone, Jess said, "Sorry about that. Eric wants to talk to you."

"Okay."

"Hey. What's up?" Eric asked.

"Nothing. Just checking in on your wife. What's new?"

"Not much. What's up with the beach house? You're in, right? Hille asked me to check with you."

"I completely forgot." Not quite accurate.

"What's the hold up, Cohen? You wanna go, right?"

"I guess."

"Steph, it's probably the last time we can party together before I'm a dad and things change forever."

"I hadn't thought of it that way."

"So, can I tell Hille you're in?"

I knew once Jess had the baby, things would change. While I was having one-date wonders and pining over unavailable (or just disinterested) bachelors like Hille, my friends were falling in love, getting married and making babies like real grownups. I couldn't miss this. I had hoped to avoid temptation to hook up with Hille but at what expense? And maybe I'd be totally over him by then anyway. Maybe Ryan's boyish charms were precisely what I needed to wash Hille's quiet yet sexy reserve out of my hair once and for all. "Yes, count me in."

THIRTY-TWO

SUZANNE CAME OVER to help me get ready for my first date with Ryan but mostly she finished off an opened bottle of wine and leafed through my collection of *In Style* magazines. She looked up occasionally to give me the thumbs up or down sign regarding the different combinations of jeans and tops I tried on.

Lying stomach down on my bed with her head near the edge, she asked, "What were you thinking, waiting till the last minute to decide what to wear?"

"When was I supposed to decide, Suze? Last month? It's not like it's the prom. It's just a date. Been on at least a hundred of them."

"Yeah, but you're actually psyched for this one!"

She was right and without a will of their own, my lips curled into a grin. I held up a short-sleeved purple tunic with a somewhat plunging neckline. "I should show a little skin, right?"

"Absolutely. It puts the idea of sex in his head without you saying a word. Not too much, though. Save that until you're ready to drive it home. I assume not tonight?"

"Definitely not. My slutty days are over. Anyway, he's definitely kissable but whether he's fuckable has yet to be determined."

"I still don't think your 'slutty days' ever began, but if it makes you feel closer to Samantha than Charlotte, go with it. So, what does he look like?"

"He's shorter than Hille and more stocky." I buttoned up a pair of dark blue jeans and turned my back towards Suzanne. "How does my butt look in these?"

"You've got a great ass, Cohen, but those jeans are too dark for that top. Try a pair that's more washed. Got more wine?"

"Yeah—in the fridge."

"Coolio." Climbing off the bed, Suzanne lost her balance and plummeted knees first onto my wood floor. "Fuck a duck. Your bed is too high."

"Or maybe you're just drunk." I pulled up a new pair of jeans and asked, "These better?"

Returning from my kitchen with the bottle of wine in her hands, she nodded. "Perfect. So he's short and stocky?"

"Not really—just compared to Hille. He looks like a little boy in a man's body. Nothing like Hille."

With one hand on her hip, Suzanne said, "I asked what he looked like. Not for a side by side comparison of him and Hille." Thrusting the bottle towards me, she asked, "Wine?"

"No. I don't want to be drunk before I get there."

"Smart. By the way, if there's even a chance you're gonna bring this dude over, you might want to do something about that."

I followed Suzanne's gaze to the piles of jeans, sweaters and shirts, which had been pulled from my closet and strewn haphazardly in accidental piles in the vicinity of my closet.

I had no intention of inviting Ryan home with me but just like I had gotten a bikini wax in case I changed my mind, I picked up the clothes in one shot, threw them in the closet and quickly closed the door before they could fall off the shelves. Although I liked to think my experience with Hille had taught me not to spread my legs prematurely, if this was the date from heaven and I decided to release slutty Stephanie, I didn't want clothes on my floor or an ungroomed vagina to be my cock block.

After I brushed my teeth for the third time, applied lipstick and showed a three-sheets-to-the-wind Suzanne out the door, I pushed the clothes, which were peeking out from my dresser, back into the drawers where they belonged, grabbed my bag and headed out to meet Ryan. According to my calculations, I would be seven minutes late. Perfect.

THIRTY-THREE

ALTHOUGH WALKING WAS AN ACTIVITY I tended to take for granted, as I approached Rosa Mexicana and saw Ryan waiting in the entrance, I was consciously aware of each step and hoped I would make a good second impression. He was leaning against the wall, dressed in a black sweater, slightly washed black jeans and a welcoming grin.

Taken aback by how truly nervous I was, I smiled shyly. "Hey, Ryan."

Ryan leaned in and kissed my cheek. "Hey there, Brady fan. I put our name down but we should have time for a drink first. You game?"

I couldn't wait to have that first drink in my hand and watch it disappear along with my first date jitters. "Absolutely." I looked through the glass door behind him into the restaurant. It was packed with crowds of people surrounding the hostess area and seeping into the bar.

"After you." Ryan opened the door to the restaurant and motioned for me to go first. As I walked past him, he momentarily placed his hand on my lower back, where my shirt fell above the low rise of my jeans. The warmth of his hand felt good on my bare skin. From behind me, I heard him say, "I was going to wait for you at the bar but it's kind of a madhouse in there."

Still walking, I turned slightly backwards and said, "Good thing I'm an expert at navigating my way through crowded bars then!"

"Are you now?"

"Yup. Years of practice in college and only one casualty."

Ryan looked at me appreciatively. "Casualty, huh?"

I shrugged matter-of-factly. "Yeah, I killed someone once, but she was a bitch anyway. And it was last call."

Laughing, Ryan said, "Remind me not to get on your bad side. Especially in a bar at the end of the night.

After we made our way to an area at the bar just wide enough for him to squeeze his way in to order us a round, Ryan turned to me. "You a margarita drinker?"

Nodding, I said, "Definitely. Not frozen, though. I like them on the rocks, no salt."

"Me too. What do you think?"

I cocked my head to the side and quickly pondered my drink of choice as Ryan awaited my answer. I was well aware that margaritas could be lethal. On the other hand, if we both drank the same thing, it might lend itself to splitting a pitcher with dinner and I liked the idea of sharing. I'd just make sure to drink one glass for every two he drank. "Let's do it."

While he worked on getting the bartender's attention, I pretended to look at the festive Mexican masks mounted on the wall. It was the first time in years I felt excitement around a guy whose name wasn't Craig Hille and I wanted so badly to have a good time.

Interrupting my thoughts, Ryan said, "Here you go" and handed me my margarita, which was poured beyond capacity into the glass.

"Thanks so much. A warning though, I'm a bit clumsy. Promise not to hate me if I accidentally spill some of this."

"I promise not to hate you. But I'll laugh."

"I'll accept those conditions." Raising my glass in the air, I said, "Cheers, Ryan."

Clinking his glass against mine, he said, "*Salud.*"

"Wow. You're bilingual, huh?"

"*Si.*"

*   *   *

By the time I was a quarter finished with my drink, I was entirely at ease in Ryan's company and decided tequila should be a required beverage on all first dates.

"Do you like being a guidance counselor?" I asked.

"Definitely. Middle-school kids are an interesting bunch. The land of the 'queen bees' and 'wannabes.' And boys getting boners while giving oral presentations in class always adds to the drama."

Laughing, I said, "Good times!"

"Honestly, my part-time gig as a soccer coach is more up my alley, but you can't make much of a living that way."

"I suppose not."

"And what about you? Are all lawyers scummy or is that just a stereotype?"

"Nope. Some are pretty scummy! But I work with some really nice folks. I've been at the firm since I was twenty-five."

"And how long is that exactly?"

I quickly answered, "Seven years," before it occurred to me that we'd never divulged our ages. "How old are you?" I quickly prayed that he was older than me or at least the same age.

"I'll be thirty in July. Practically your age."

Wishing he was older, but relieved he didn't seem put out by the age difference, I joked, "I'm surprised you actually remember the old seventies sitcoms. Were you even born?"

"Repeats. And, if I'm not mistaken, The Brady Bunch was a bit before your time, too."

"True. So, have you ever dated someone older than you?"

"I dated my sister's college roommate for six months. She's thirty-four—older than you. No worries."

"So, you've got experience with mature women, huh?"

Ryan raised an eyebrow. "Yeah, but something tells me the gap in our maturity level isn't that wide."

"I might be insulted by that if I actually wasn't kind of a late bloomer."

Ryan smiled. "I was merely pointing out that I'm wise beyond my years. What about you? Into younger men?"

Locking eyes with him, I said, "Depends on the man."

"I see." Ryan looked at me as if to say something else, but the pager lit up and whatever he intended to say was replaced by, "That's us! Ready to eat?"

Glancing down at my almost empty margarita glass, I figured solid food was probably a wise idea and the aroma of Chile peppers permeating the restaurant was almost as inviting as tableside guacamole service. "Starving."

I noticed how many people occupied the space between where we were standing and the hostess and was not entirely comfortable with my ability to navigate a clear path. "You lead the way this time," I said. As I followed Ryan, it occurred to me that I had never seen him from behind and so I took the opportunity to check out his rear end. I figured he'd already checked out mine on our way into the restaurant so it was only fair. I was pleased to note that unlike most guys, he actually had a butt. Not too big, not too small. I giggled quietly, comfortable he wouldn't be able to hear me over the loud conversations taking place around us.

The hostess led us through the restaurant, a vibrant pool of pink, red, blue, aqua and orange, to our cramped but cozy table and, after we got comfortable in our brightly colored webbed chairs, we quickly agreed to order guacamole and a pitcher of margaritas to start.

The margaritas went down very well and with each glass, the conversation got sillier.

Ryan swallowed a chip, put down his glass and gave me a serious look. "So, Zach or Slater?"

Of course, I knew exactly who he was referring to and was psyched that Ryan and I clearly had one thing in common—television trivia. "What about them?" I asked.

"Who would you rather have sex with?"

Without hesitation, I said, "Zach." I thought about it for another second, nodded and repeated, "Definitely Zach, which is odd since I don't usually go for blondes. What about you? Kelly or Jessie?" I guessed he would say Kelly.

"Neither. Turtle was my favorite. She was a cutie." Ryan popped another chip in his mouth, swallowed and turned serious again. "Okay, Potsie or Ralph the Mouth?"

Laughing, I said, "I had a secret crush on Potsie when I was younger but now I think I'd like Mouth—he was funny." I lightly tapped my hand over Ryan's across the table. "By the way, I'd actually prefer neither."

Ryan shook his head. "Not an option in this game. You have to choose. Your turn to ask me."

I figured it would be my turn at some point and so I had already given it some thought during our *Happy Days* discussion. I quickly asked, "Laverne or Shirley?"

Even quicker, Ryan responded, "Laverne. Shirley is prettier but doesn't strike me as much fun. Okay, which staff member on *The Love Boat*?"

"That's a tough one. Dr. Bricker was a ladies' man but only because he was a doctor. Isaac was gross, but he had access to all of the booze on the ship, which could help. I used to dig Gopher but not so much anymore." Grimacing, I said, "This sucks. Please don't make me choose!"

Ryan was unrelenting and didn't even crack a smile when he insisted I choose.

"Fine!" I pictured each of my choices leaning in to kiss me and shivered inwardly until I remembered something. "I got it! Ace the photographer! He was actually handsome, although I think he might be gay. Anyway, I've got one for you." I paused dramatically as Ryan waited. "Mrs. Garrett or Cloris Leachman from *The Facts of Life*?"

"I think I need a shot of tequila before I even consider that one."

"You have to choose!" I mocked.

"I choose tequila. Let's do a shot."

Extending my arm across the table, I said, "Twist my arm."

By the time the food came, I was more interested in whether Ryan was going to order another pitcher of margaritas than I was in eating my crabmeat enchiladas. I was also finding it very difficult not to "accidentally" brush my legs against his under the table. Each time I smiled at something Ryan said, I worried I had salsa in my teeth. And I really had to pee but was reluctant to interrupt the flow of the conversation. I put it off as long as possible but eventually excused myself to go to the bathroom. I got up from my seat and when attempting to squeeze past the table next to us, knocked over the basket of chips.

I said, "Oh shit" and bent down to pick the basket off of the floor. When I looked up, the two girls at the next table smiled at me sympathetically. I turned to Ryan, mortified, but he chuckled and said, "You warned me that you were clumsy. At least the basket was almost empty."

I was definitely buzzed, and as I walked to the bathroom, I concentrated on not tripping or banging into any waiters. As always, there was a line for the bathroom and when it was finally my turn, I let out a sigh of relief while I peed for longer than the squatting position was comfortable. Before returning to the table, I ran a brush through my hair and, although I considered reapplying my lip gloss, I decided against it. It would just end up on my glass anyway.

I must have made a wrong turn after leaving the bathroom because I couldn't find Ryan. After I circled the restaurant in a panic, I finally spotted him. As I sat down, I said, "Anything interesting happen while I was gone?"

"Actually, yeah," he said. "The entire restaurant did the Macarena. It was awesome."

I placed my hands on my hips and pouted. "Damn. Why do these things always happen when I'm not around?"

Ryan winked. "It's a conspiracy."

When the check came, Ryan immediately picked it up. Being cheap was a deal breaker for me and so I hoped he would pay but didn't want to make assumptions. Hoping I didn't sound as awkward as I felt, I asked, "Do you need any money?"

Ryan looked up at me from the bill. "No way."

Happy that I didn't have to stop liking him, I smiled. "Thank you."

"My pleasure. Ready to go?"

As we left the restaurant, I wondered what would happen next. I didn't want the night to end, but I was already experiencing mild stomach spasms from the two pitchers of margaritas we shared and figured they wouldn't be so mild if I continued to drink. *So much for drinking one glass for his every two.*

When we got outside, Ryan walked to the edge of the sidewalk and I followed him. As we stood face to face, he smiled and said, "I'm impressed."

Surprised, I said, "With what?" Recalling that confidence was supposedly a turn-on, I quickly added, "I mean thanks, but why are you impressed?"

"You can handle your tequila."

"Not really. I'm kind of buzzed," I admitted.

His eyes sparkling, Ryan repeated, "Kind of buzzed, huh?"

I laughed. "Drunk girls never admit to being drunk. Just buzzed or maybe 'feeling it.' I'm feeling it."

"And I'm still impressed. And it only took you two laps around the restaurant to find me after your bathroom break. You've got a stellar sense of direction."

I blushed at the realization that nothing got past this guy and he seemed to like me anyway. My lips tingling to feel his, I said, "I'm glad you're impressed. I am too."

Moving closer to me, Ryan asked, "With what?"

I took a small step closer to him and replied, "With you."

"What about me?"

Not removing my eyes from his, I took his hand in mine. "Just you. Period."

It felt like minutes that we stood there looking at each other but I think it was only a few seconds before Ryan sealed the remaining space between us and planted a soft kiss on my lips. Wanting more, I released his hand from mine, wrapped my arms around his neck and pulled him in for another kiss, this time more passionate. The beginnings of stubble on his chin felt rough against my face, but I didn't care. He smelled like spiced vanilla and his hands in my hair felt sexy. I wanted to swallow him whole.

When we finally separated, I squeezed him fiercely and said, "I've wanted to hug you since the moment we met!"

Ryan smiled and softly caressed my earlobe with his thumb and index finger before leaning down and planting a kiss on top of my diamond stud earring. "I think I'll refrain from confessing what I've wanted to do since we met, at least for now," he said. "I'd suggest another drink but since you're already 'feeling it,' it might get you drunk. Wouldn't want that."

I was ready to go home and sleep off the tequila but I hoped he'd mention going out again first. "I had fun, Ryan. Thanks again."

"Me too. Do it again? We never did discuss *Three's Company*."

"We'll add it to the agenda for next time then," I said, happily.

After one more kiss, Ryan hailed me a cab. I smiled all the way home and even with the room slightly spinning, fell asleep thinking I just had one of the best first dates ever.

THIRTY-FOUR

ON OUR SECOND DATE, a few days later, we went to an Orioles/ Rays game. Ryan was an Orioles fan and, since they weren't playing the Yankees, I rooted for them too. Ryan barely reacted when I accidentally spilled some of my beer on the head of the guy sitting in front of us. The guy was really pissed off, though. I apologized profusely and even offered to buy him a drink, but ten minutes later, he was still running his hands through his hair as if it was soaked with beer.

"It's just a little beer," Ryan whispered to me. "The guy's a pussy. Don't sweat it."

Nothing seemed to bother him. Not my endless stories about my college glory days. Not my insistence that Eric knew more about music than anyone. He didn't even flinch when I referred to the Philadelphia Flyers as a basketball team. It was only after the date that Sam informed me that the Flyers were a hockey team but Ryan was kind enough to let it pass without comment. On our third date, I told him my mom wished I'd fall for a Jewish guy to see how he would react.

"That's okay," he said with a laugh. "My sister converted to Judaism two years ago. That makes me sort of Jewish by association."

But he wasn't a kiss ass. He made fun of me plenty. Especially the collection of sappy music on my Ipod like Five For Fighting's *100 Years* and Bonnie Rait's *I Can't Make You Love Me*. And when I enthusiastically sang along with the jukebox to Def Leppard's *Pour Some Sugar On Me*, he hid one arm behind his back while pretending to play the drums to mimic Rick Allen. He was plenty obnoxious, but on our fourth date, when we befriended tourists from Scotland who wrapped their arms around his shoulders while singing Journey's

Don't Stop Believing at the top of their lungs, I felt his charm deep in my loins and I had to have him.

Our beers were empty and when he asked if I wanted another one, I shifted my bar stool so I was leaning into him, put my hand on his thigh and said, "No. I don't want another beer. I just want you."

Ryan's lips curled up slightly but did not quite make it to a smile. He nodded, turned to the bartender and said, "Can we close out our bill?"

We didn't say a word during the few blocks walk from The Dubliner to my apartment. Holding hands, we walked as briskly as possible. We hurried into the elevator and just as the door was about to shut, a hairy arm shoved its way inside and the door opened again to allow entrance to a man and his dog, two young girls and an older woman. Ryan and I stood on opposite sides from each other and as the elevator stopped on every floor before mine, we'd sneak glances at each other trying not to laugh. When at last we made it to my floor, I grabbed Ryan's hand and pulled him towards my apartment at the end of the hall. I started to unlock my door but when he began kissing my neck from behind, I dropped my pocketbook, turned around, put my arms around his neck and kissed him. We sucked face like horny teenagers for a few minutes until Ryan moved aside some hair near my right ear and whispered, "Think we should go inside?"

I held his face in my hands, kissed the top of his nose and then his chin before saying, "If that's what you want."

"That's what I want."

"My wish is your command."

With a devilish grin, he said, "You mean 'your wish is my command'?"

"Whatever. Get your ass inside."

We didn't bother turning on any of the lights in my apartment, but I insisted on background music. "I don't like fooling around in silence," I said. "Is that weird?"

"Nah. But I don't think I can perform to Barry Manilow or Babs." Ryan sat on my couch and straightened the pile of direct mail catalogs I kept on my coffee table. I couldn't bring myself to throw them out on the off chance I might decide to order the stainless steel bakeware set from Crate & Barrel or the new bra from Victoria's Secret.

As I walked towards my CD player and pondered our choices, I said, "Really? I thought we'd dance to the Copacabana first to get in the mood. Not for you?"

My back was still toward Ryan, but when I felt him tap me in the back with his finger, I spun around to face him.

"Stephanie," he said. "I'd listen to a CD of you singing at your Bat Mitzvah if it meant I could see you naked."

"That's the nicest thing anyone has ever said to me. Seriously. You've never heard me sing."

"Uh, yes I have." Assuming a high-pitched, completely off-key tone, Ryan began to sing *"Take the bottle. Shake it up. Break the bubble. Break it u-up!"* until I pushed him. "Do you want to see me naked or what?"

His fingers already working the buttons on my blouse, he said, "Hells yeah."

And with that, Ryan and I had sex for the first time, but not before I put on the *Saturday Night Fever* soundtrack. We simultaneously made out and undressed to *Staying Alive* and I nearly lost it when Ryan started dancing in his boxers. During *How Deep is Your Love,* Ryan admired my nipples for an extended period of time. We kissed some more during *Night Fever* and I started cracking up.

He was leaning over me, one hand on the bed and the other softly caressing the side of my face. "You know I'm not laughing at you, right?" I asked. "But I've never hooked up to the Bee Gees before. Kind of amusing."

"You can laugh at me all you want. So long as it's not right after I take off my boxers. That would be bad, Steph."

I could tell by his expression that he wasn't really concerned. "Moment of truth time?" I asked.

"I'm ready when you are."

"Flip over so I can do my thorough examination."

"My wish is your command."

He was now on his back and I placed my thumbs on the elastic of his boxers and very slowly pulled them down. With each gentle tug, I looked up at him and smiled wickedly. Finally, I planted a kiss on his belly where there was a trail of dark hair leading downward. I ripped the boxers the rest of the way, exposing a perfectly acceptable sized package. "Whew." I wiped my brow in jest. "You had me worried there for a moment, but this will do just fine."

Since I was down there already and his penis was staring right at me, practically saying "please," I decided to extend my kisses beyond his belly. I always wondered if I was very good at it but I had read enough articles on the art of the blow job to be fairly confident. And no one had ever complained. Ryan certainly seemed pleased.

His face flush, he said, "Your turn" and started to inch down the length of the bed. Suddenly, I felt nervous. I tapped him on the head and when he looked up at me said, "Can I take a rain check?"

Looking slightly offended, he sat up. "Uh, sure. You okay?"

I sat up too and pushed the blankets off of the floor so there was nothing between our naked bodies. Pushing him on his back, I said, "I'm more than okay. I just want to be with you. I mean, really be with you. But I'll definitely turn in that rain check another time." And I meant it. I just found oral sex more intimate than intercourse and wasn't ready.

The smile back on his face, Ryan said, "Works for me!" Then he flipped me over so I was on my back and kissed me. I kissed him back until kissing turned into kissing and groping, and we kissed and groped until kissing and groping turned into kissing, groping and fucking. And when the fucking came to an end, we both lay on our backs, spent and looking up at the ceiling. But then Ryan poked me in the belly.

I turned my head to the side to face him. He was propped on his side smiling at me. I poked him back. Knowing full well why he was so giddy, I asked, "What are you smiling about?"

Ryan shrugged. "Orioles won tonight."

I glared at him. He glared back and we attempted a staring contest. Within seconds, I started laughing. Ryan had more practice keeping a straight face, thanks to his weekly poker night with the guys but moments later, started laughing too.

Afterwards, we stayed up for hours watching infommercials. I was this close to buying a fruit dehydrator but Ryan had one and wasn't impressed.

I sat up and looked at Ryan who was lying on his back propped up against both of my pillows. "So, who did you sleep with before *buying your* fruit dehydrator?" I asked.

"Wouldn't you like to know?"

I thought about it for a second before responding. "Actually not. So long as she's no competition for me now."

"No worries, Steph."

"Good. Now I can sleep peacefully. 'Night, Ryan."

Ryan inched closer and curled his body around mine. "Good night, Stephanie."

I closed my eyes but knew I wouldn't fall asleep right away. I was totally fine staying up, playing the night back in my head over and over again. I was at the point in my flashback where Ryan and I left the bar when he whispered from behind, "Steph?"

Without moving, I said, "Yeah?"

"I heard somebody say."

I wiggled out of his embrace and turned around to see Ryan lying perfectly still with his eyes closed. "You heard somebody say what?"

Without opening his eyes, Ryan answered, "*Burn Baby Burn, Disco Inferno! Burn Baby Burn, Burn that mama down!*"

THIRTY-FIVE

LATER THAT WEEK, I met Suzanne at Starbucks for an afternoon snack. She already knew I had slept with Ryan since I sent her a text from my bathroom as soon as Ryan had fallen asleep, but over full fat white chocolate mochas with whip, I spilled the dirty details. Our chairs were side by side and facing the window so we could watch the suits walk by on their lunch hours

I took the first sip of my drink, extra careful not to get whipped cream on my nose. "Did your high school have superlatives, like Best Looking or Most Likely to Succeed?" I asked.

Suzanne nodded. "Yes. I won Most Talkative."

"Not surprised," I said rolling my eyes.

"Neither was anyone in my class. Anyway, why?"

"Well, if I could give out superlatives for my sexual partners, Ryan would win 'Most Fun Lay' hands down."

Suzanne scooted her chair closer to mine, and turning sideways to face me, asked with interest, "What was so fun about it?"

"Everything!" There was a lot to tell and I didn't know where to start. I figured I'd start with foreplay and move forward from there. "Well, we were listening to the *Saturday Night Fever* soundtrack and I had told him that hooking up in silence made me uncomfortable, so whenever too much time went by without us saying anything and the only sounds were us breathing and kissing, he would start singing along to the music to lighten the mood."

Suzanne smiled and took a sip of her coffee. "Keep going."

I flashed back to the night in question and started laughing. "Okay, you know that joke about guys reciting baseball team lineups in their heads to stop from coming too soon?"

Suzanne nodded.

"Well, he was ready to come and I wasn't quite there yet and when I told him, he proceeded to call out the roster from the soccer team he coaches. Out loud. It was priceless."

"Insert important question here: Did you come?"

"Yes, I did, thank you very much," I said, blushing.

Suzanne responded flatly, "Sounds hot, Steph."

Feeling protective of my new beau, I said, "I had hot, intense sex with Hille in the bathroom and you know what? I don't recall laughing once!"

"Speaking of Hille, what does he think about your new boyfriend?"

"He doesn't know about him."

Looking at me like I went outside in the rain without an umbrella and was surprised to get wet, Suzanne said, "Trust me. He knows. If Eric knows, he knows."

"Eric doesn't know either."

Suzanne put down her cardboard coffee cup and crinkled her nose at me. "Really? Does anyone know?"

"Just you. And my mom. She calls me every day at work and always wants to know what I'm doing later and it's too hard to lie. I've given her a slightly skewed version of reality, though. She thinks we've only gone on two dates and that I'm on the fence as to whether I like him." I was afraid if I confided my true feelings for Ryan to my mom, she would start looking at diamond cuts. Not to mention that almost every time I had told my mom I was excited about a guy in the past, the relationship was over within a week, case in point, Craig Hille, and I didn't want to get her hopes up.

Looking agitated, Suzanne said, "We'll get to your mom later. I'm still trying to understand why you haven't told any of your other friends."

"I don't know. It hasn't come up."

"Bullshit. You talk to those guys all the time and I'm certain they ask 'What's new?' each time. I'd think that would be an appropriate time to say 'Actually. I started dating a guy.' Stephanie, you like him enough to sleep with him! How are you possibly keeping him a secret and why?"

"I actually haven't spoken to any of them! Why are you getting so worked up over this?" I was kind of insulted that Suzanne seemed more intrigued by the fact I hadn't told the gang about Ryan than she was about my sleeping with him.

Faint wrinkles appeared on Suzanne's forehead as she scrunched her face to look at me but she didn't say anything.

"What?"

"Please don't tell me you're keeping the news from Hille in case he suddenly decides he wants an actual relationship with you."

"That's ridiculous." My last thoughts before going to sleep had been of Ryan since practically our first date. And Hille was clearly not interested in having an actual relationship with me anyway. Reaffirming my prior statement, I said, "Completely ridiculous."

Without blinking, Suzanne locked her eyes with mine, almost daring me to look away. "Yes, it is. But just a couple of months ago, you thought Hille was your fate. I hate to hurt your feelings but Hille probably won't care all that much that you're dating someone, except maybe disappointment that he won't have a built in fuck buddy for the Outer Banks."

"Thanks, Captain Obvious. I'm under no false illusions that Hille is secretly in love with me or anything." I picked both of our empty cups up off the counter and stood to throw them out. "Haven't heard from Craig in over a month and don't really care," I said before walking away. I hoped she'd change the subject when I got back but could feel her eyes boring into my back and wasn't holding my breath.

"Then tell them about Ryan," she said the minute I sat back down. "He sounds awesome, by the way. When do I meet him?"

"It seems too soon to introduce him to friends, don't you think? It's only been a few weeks." And just like telling my mom about a guy made him magically disappear, so did introducing him to my friends. "But soon, I promise. You'll love him!"

Finally smiling, Suzanne said, "I like him already. He makes you happy and that makes me happy. But you should tell those guys soon. If you kept me in the dark for that long, I'd be pissed."

"I'll tell them soon," I promised.

Suzanne looked at her watch and grimaced. "Shit, I've gotta get back to work." Grabbing her jacket from the back of her seat, she asked, "So, when are you seeing Ryan again?"

"Friday night."

"Suggestion?"

"Always open to those."

"The *Grease* soundtrack. I heard *Summer Lovin'* drives the men wild."

Chuckling, I said, "Great idea."

"Okay, talk to you later, sweetie." And with a kiss on the cheek, she was gone.

THIRTY-SIX

IT WAS AN UNSEASONABLY WARM DAY for April, and Ryan and I were in Stanton Park tossing around a softball. We started with a football but Ryan said I threw like a girl so we borrowed a softball from a group of kids.

I collapsed on the grass. "I'm tired! Let's take a break."

Ryan sat down next to me and tousled my hair. "Tired! I guess that's what I get for dating an older woman."

I rested my head on his shoulder hoping he'd keep playing with my hair. "Actually, I'll be four years older than you next week. My birthday is May 5th."

Ryan tossed the softball in the air and caught it. "A Cinco de Mayo baby, huh? Awesome. We'll have two reasons to celebrate that day!"

I removed my head from his shoulder and turned to look at him. "What kind of celebrating did you have in mind?"

"I'll surprise you."

"Okay, but nothing big. I just want to do something fun."

"I can arrange for that," he assured me.

"I know you can," I said, before tackling him to the ground. Planting kisses up and down his neck, I repeated, "I know you can."

* * *

All I wanted to do when I got home that night was put on my pajamas, curl up on my couch and watch my Sunday television line-up of *The Amazing Race*, *Cold Case* and *Entourage*, but when I removed my cell phone from the bottom of my bag, I noticed I had a voicemail.

And then learned I had four of them. Since I'm rarely that popular, my first thought was that something happened to my mom or Al. My heart beat rapidly as I dialed into voicemail and I looked upwards and prayed they were okay.

The first message was from Hope. What's the plan for my birthday? Am I coming to Philly? The second message was from Eric. Was I coming to Philly for my birthday? The third message was from Hille. He didn't know what the plan was for my birthday. Should he keep the weekend open? And the last message was from Paul. I'm a loser, soon to be old hag, but he loves me anyway and is sorry he won't be able to hang out for my birthday this year— will make it up to me in the Outer Banks.

I immediately called Eric.

"Hey, stranger," he said.

"Hey you. Sorry I missed your call. I was in the park and didn't hear the phone ring."

"No biggie. What was in the park?"

"Grass, trees, me!" *And my adorable sort-of boyfriend.*

"Nice. What's up for your birthday? Do you mind if we're more low key than usual? I don't want to bring my pregnant wife to a crowded bar."

"I understand completely. I was actually thinking we could skip my birthday this year. We can celebrate it late at the beach or something."

"Are you sure? Is this because of Jess, cuz we still want to do something with you."

And if they knew I was blowing them off to hang out with a new guy—would they still want to celebrate with me? "I know. Not about Jess. Just swamped at work and not sure I have the energy for a crazy weekend." As I waited for a response, I rubbed the spot on my head that was sore from twirling my hair so hard.

"Whatever you want, Cohen. I could really use a drinking buddy, though. One who can actually hold her alcohol, which leaves out my sister-in-law."

"I'm sorry. I promise to drink you under the table in the OBX, okay?"

"I guess I don't have a choice. So what else, everything okay with you? Haven't heard much from you lately."

"I've been good, Eric. Busy with work." *Oh, what the fuck.* "And dating."

"Dating, huh? Any prospects? Don't get too serious until we approve!"

I could easily see Ryan concocting stupid drinking games with Paul and hogging the mic at karaoke. "You guys will approve of him."

"Do you mean that in the general sense or is there an actual 'him'?"

"I've actually gotten past the third date with someone, yes."

"Wow, I might have to call Ripley's. Who is he?"

"His name is Ryan. No more questions. Too early!" Along with telling my mom about a guy and introducing him to my friends, talking about him too much was another no-no.

"Jeez, Steph. Withhold much?"

"Not from him," I said, laughing.

"Not too early for some things, I guess, huh?"

"No comment. Oh, by the way, Hille called me about my birthday, too. Do you mind letting him know I'm skipping the birthday celebration this year? I'm so busy— not sure when I'd get to calling him back." I felt my body tense and quietly prayed Eric wouldn't comment on my recent history with Hille.

"Sure, Steph. I'll pass the info along."

Instantly feeling my body relax, I said, "Thanks."

"So, I guess we won't see you until the end of the month?"

"Probably not. You're going to pick me up on the way to North Carolina, right? I'm on the way." I wasn't entirely sure that was true, although D.C. was south of Philadelphia and north of the Carolinas so how far out of the way could it be?

"We'll work it out later. Someone will pick you up, though."

"I can't wait." As the words came out of mouth, I realized how much I meant them.

"Me neither."

"Okay, kiss Jess for me."

"I'll even slip her the tongue," Eric said.

Giggling, I said, "Just don't knock her up! Oops—too late!"

THIRTY-SEVEN

I NEVER REALLY CARED about not having a boyfriend on my birthday. Sure, when I blew out the candles on my cake, my wish was always, "I wish I'd fall in love this year," but it actually didn't bother me that for the past several years, I'd taken the train to Philadelphia to drink my face off with my friends who, at the end of the night, or more typically, the beginning of the morning, tucked me into my borrowed bed-for-one. I actually considered myself incredibly lucky. And I still did. Only, having a boyfriend on my birthday was *so* much better!

Ryan got us tickets to the Orioles/Yankees game and the Yankees won. Ryan said he'd arranged for a fix and I didn't have the heart to tell him it was because the Yankees were a better team. After the game, we went back to his place and snuggled on his couch for a brief nap. When Ryan woke up, he bolted off the couch and almost took me with him.

"Whoa!" I said, regaining my balance. "What's the hurry?"

Standing over me, he said, "Sorry, I didn't realize what time it was. I made reservations for dinner. We've gotta take showers and don't have much time."

I stood up and put a hand on each of Ryan's shoulders. "I know how we can make up time."

Ryan held my hair into a mock ponytail. "Not blow dry all this hair of yours?"

"I was going to suggest we shower together, but if you'd prefer I go to dinner with a wet head, that would work too."

Ryan paused as if debating the pros and cons of both options and then said, "No. I think it's really important that your hair look extra nice on your birthday. So, let's go with your plan."

I thought we'd take turns going under the shower head, but when it was Ryan's turn, I was cold so I pushed my way under the hot water. "I never realized how hard it was to take a shower with someone. They make it look so easy in the movies," I said.

Looking surprised, Ryan asked, "You've never showered with someone before?"

I bent my head back to rinse the shampoo out of my hair and, with my eyes closed, said, "Not since Paul and we were always drunk."

"Paul?"

"My college boyfriend, I thought I told you about him." I opened my eyes and moved aside to let Ryan back under the water.

Ryan kissed my wet shoulder. "The only Paul you've mentioned is your friend from Virginia, the King of Quarters."

"One and the same."

"You're still great friends with your college boyfriend?"

I moved out of the water, grabbed the conditioner I had brought from home and poured some on my hands. Running it evenly through my hair, I said, "Yes. Do you have a problem with that?"

"No. No need to get defensive. I just didn't know you went out with the guy."

"It was a long time ago. Like another lifetime."

"So, no lingering feelings?"

"No way! In fact, I can't believe I ever thought of him that way. I love him as a friend but, eww, no way." I thought it was adorable that Ryan was slightly jealous, but the thought of Paul as a threat to our relationship was laughable. And sort of gross. "Anyway, kind of awkward being naked with you talking about another guy."

"Yeah. If it was another girl, though, it would be hot."

"How come guys love hearing about two girls but I don't get the slightest turned on thinking about two guys?"

"Cuz girls are hot and guys are, well, not hot."

"You're hot," I said.

Smiling, he said, "I'm so glad you think so."

I stood on my tippy toes and, nibbling Ryan's soap-scented ear, whispered, "I was thinking. Do we have time for me to maybe take you up on that rain check?"

"What rain check?" he whispered back.

"I'll give you hint. How do lesbians have sex?"

"Strap on?"

Laughing, I said, "Another way."

"Oh that! Not really, but it's your birthday, so I'll make the time."

"It might take a lot of time. We might have to be late for our reservation. It's not a surprise party, is it?"

Ryan turned off the faucet and took my hand to help me out of the shower and we walked towards his bedroom, dripping water all over his floor. Pushing me onto his bed, he said, "No. Just fondue. It can wait."

I closed my eyes and tried to push aside all thoughts except how good Ryan was making me feel but before I succumbed, I smiled in the certainty that an orgasm was a much better birthday present than even free shots of the finest quality tequila.

THIRTY-EIGHT

WHO WOULD HAVE THOUGHT it would be so difficult to find a beach towel? After looking in TJ Maxx, Filenes Basement and Bed Bath and Beyond with no luck, I enlisted my mother to help me track one down. We had only been in Target for ten minutes before my basket was filled with over $50 worth of merchandise, but no beach towel.

From the center of a pile of neatly folded bath towels in various colors, my mom pulled out a burgundy one and handed it to me. "Here," she said.

"I don't need bath towels, Mom. They're supplied at the house. I just need a fricken beach towel! Where the hell do they sell them?"

"This is crazy. Why are you killing yourself looking for one? Why don't you borrow one of ours?"

I kissed her on the cheek. "You're a genius, Mom! I hadn't even thought of that."

My mom released a chuckle of amusement. "I'm glad I'm good for something. So, when do you leave?"

"The Saturday of Memorial Day weekend. I'll be back the following Sunday."

"How does Ryan feel about your trip?"

A couple of weeks earlier, my mom had called me on my way home from happy hour with Suzanne and I had confessed my feelings for Ryan. Afterwards, I decided it was a good thing our daily phone calls were usually in the middle of the afternoon, when I was less likely to be under the influence and tell her all of my deepest feelings.

"I planned it before I met him."

"You didn't want to ask him?"

"I'm not ready to bring him around those guys. They're brutal. Plus, I kind of like having him all to myself"

"Okay. It's totally up to you. I was just asking."

My mom and I continued to walk up and down the aisles, stopping every few minutes to pick something up and put it back down again. When we got to the DVD section, I immediately spotted *Saturday Night Fever* and felt a pang of conscience. "Mom?"

"Yes sweetie?"

"Do you think it's a bad idea not to ask Ryan to the beach with us? We've only been dating six weeks, but now I feel sort of bad. I don't want him to think it's because I don't like him enough."

My mom put down the box set of *Curb Your Enthusiasm's* second season and looked at me. *"Do* you like him enough?"

"Definitely. I'm just not ready to immerse him in that crowd. I want to make sure he really likes me before I subject him to Paul who might scare him away. He'd probably make comments about me and Hille." And since I hadn't even told Ryan that Hille was my ex-friend-with-benefits, it would be more than a little awkward.

"It might be nice to see Hille's reaction to you being with another guy."

"He'd probably be happy for me, not jealous."

"I wouldn't bet on it. I think you give him too much credit. He couldn't do better than you and he'll regret it someday. Maybe sooner than you think. Maybe it's a good thing Ryan won't be there. A little visit from the green-eyed monster might be all he needs."

"Why do you care what Craig thinks? I thought you didn't approve of our 'fuck buddy' status. Anyway, Craig's a good guy and all, but he's not the jealous type." I was almost positive I was right on this issue, but even though Ryan was awesome, I would not have minded being wrong. But it was gratifying to hear that my mom thought I was a catch despite wishing I was not still single at my "advanced" age. "And besides, I'm not interested in making Hille jealous. We weren't all that compatible, except..." I didn't know if I should complete my sentence.

Doing it for me, my mom said, "In bed?"

I nodded my answer. "It was really good, yeah." Always more embarrassed than my mom when discussing sex, I felt my face get warm.

Raising her voice, my mom said, "What about Ryan? Is he good? Because you can't start a relationship with a guy who sucks in bed!"

Mortified, I whispered, "Yes, Ryan knows what he's doing! I have no complaints there. And we have loads of fun outside of the bedroom too, unlike with Hille. With Hille, it was just sex and he knew it. It was me who didn't."

My mom and I resumed our walk to the cash register and after we stopped at the end of the shortest line, she said, "Okay. I just know how much you liked Hille. You would make really smart children. And it would be nice to have someone in the family who could teach me how to use the computer."

"Mom, please."

My mom laughed. "Anyway, I hope you've stopped beating yourself up over sleeping with him. You're not a slut. You enjoyed yourself. No harm done. But if Ryan makes you happy, I hope it all works out. I can't wait to plan the wedding."

Ignoring her last words, I said, "He does make me happy. I just hope I don't blow it."

"If it's meant to be, you won't blow it." My mom paused. "Unless you break up with him over something stupid like the way he wears his socks."

I broke up with a boy in middle school because he insisted on rolling down his socks like donuts. "I was thirteen, Mom. Let it go." Since I rarely had the opportunity, or a reason to have serious discussions with my mom about relationships, woman to woman, I decided to milk it. "Anyway, how will I know it's meant to be? I thought Hille and I were kismet." I rolled my eyes. "How wrong I was!"

Giving me her "mommy knows best" look, my mom said, "Well, if it's right, you should feel safe with him."

"Safe how?"

My mom looked straight ahead as if the right words were somewhere in the distance and then nodded. "Have you ever been infatuated with someone to the point that you practically walk on eggshells fearing he'll stop liking you at any time?"

I thought back to almost every guy I had ever liked. "Uh, yeah!"

"Well, when it's right, you shouldn't feel that way. You should feel safe and secure in his feelings for you." Pointing her finger at me, she said, "Unlike my relationship with your father."

I was pretty confident Ryan wasn't on the verge of losing interest in me. "Cool."

"And when it's the right man, you should also feel confident he'll take care of you."

I should've known this was coming and waved my hand in protest. "I'm not looking for a sugar daddy, Mom."

My mom shooed my hand away. "That's not what I meant." Chuckling, she said, "Well, that's not entirely what I meant. I don't want you marrying a man who can't support you and your children economically. Does Ryan do as well as Hille?"

"Mom!"

"I was just asking. But what I meant by 'taking care of you' was that a man who loves you will do whatever is necessary to protect you from dangerous people and dangerous situations. Even with his bad knee, Allan insists on taking out the garbage if it's after sunset so I don't have to walk outside in the dark."

Maybe that's why Ryan always insisted on coming with me when I got drunk and wanted to leave a bar to grub a cigarette from a stranger. "Okay. What else?"

Looking thoughtful again, my mom said, "He should accept and adore you the way you are while at the same time encouraging you to be even better."

Ryan still liked me no matter how often I knocked over my drinks. And he was trying to persuade me to train for a half marathon. This was looking good. I beamed at my mom. "You amaze me, Mom. You're so wise."

Laughing, my mom said, "Not really. Just experienced. I've had two husbands, remember? Anyway, if Ryan's not the right one, someone else is. Maybe even Hille. You never know. He's at that age where he might want to settle down soon."

I was fairly certain Hille wasn't "the one"' I just hoped I could make it through a week at the beach with him without doing something I'd regret.

THIRTY-NINE

IT WAS A WEDNESDAY NIGHT and after take-out Chinese food and rough headboard-banging-against-the-wall sex at my place, Ryan had fallen asleep, his body partially draped over mine. I was watching the last few minutes of *Top Chef* when he woke up, sat up in the bed and asked, "Whatchya watching?"

"*Top Chef.* I love this show."

"Kind of ironic since your top dish is grilled cheese."

"Shhh. They're at judges table. It's almost over."

"Okay. Let me know when it's okay to speak."

We sat in silence until the panel of judges made its decision. "You can speak now," I said to Ryan. He didn't say anything and when I looked over at him, he was staring straight ahead at the television. I poked him in the arm. "Did you hear me? I said you could speak."

Still staring at the television, he looked at me out of the corner of his eyes. "I heard you. I don't have anything to say now."

"Can I speak then?"

"I don't know. I think *Bernie Mac* is on TBS. Can you wait until it's over?"

"Ha ha."

After I pouted in silence, Ryan put down the remote control, turned to me and grinned. "Okay, sexy. I should get out of here."

"Why? Don't go."

"I honestly had no intention of falling asleep here. You wore me out!"

Still pouting, I asked, "Is sleeping here so horrible?"

Ryan brushed my bangs from my face and kissed me on the forehead. "You're cute when you're needy."

My heart stopped at his use of the word needy. One of my favorite dating books, *Why Men Love Bitches,* warned women against being needy. "I'm not being needy. It's just, I'm leaving for the beach soon and won't see you for a week. I don't want you to miss me too much." I gave myself an imaginary pat on the back for my speedy recovery.

"Oh, yes. Your upcoming week of chicanery with your crazy friends." Ryan pointed to the pile of bathing suits and trial size toiletries placed next to my empty suitcase in the middle of the floor. "I see you've been diligently packing."

"I work best under pressure." Tickling his arm, I said, "And besides, I've been a little busy."

"Maybe someday I'll meet these infamous friends of yours."

"I hope so. I think you'll like them." I paused a second, visualizing Paul in his usual state of obnoxiousness. "After they grow on you."

"Yup. While I'm busy counseling the leaders of tomorrow regarding which colleges to attend, you'll be drinking Coronas on the beach. Life's not fair."

"You live such a tortured life, Ryan. So, you wanna stay over or not?"

"I don't know. Ask me nicely."

I hesitated, looked in the direction of my coat closet and pictured my copy of *Why Men Love Bitches* packed away at the top, along with *He's Just Not That Into You* and *The Rules.* I turned back to Ryan who was gazing at me expectantly.

He adopted a feigned wounded look. "Did you change your mind or something?"

"No. I was weighing the pros and cons of honoring your request."

"Nice. What did you decide?"

Batting my eyelashes, I said in my sweetest voice, "Please stay over, Ryan—pretty please with a cherry on top?"

Ryan lowered his hands between my legs and I closed my eyes as I felt the gentle pressure of his fingers inside me. "Okay. But only because you asked me nicely," he said. "And because I'm gonna miss you next week."

"I'll definitely miss you too."

FORTY

I WAS STILL PACKING when Eric called from downstairs at 10:30 and said they were outside.

"Don't you guys want to come upstairs and see my place?" I asked.

"No," Eric said. "I want to get there and start drinking!"

I threw another pair of jeans and a dress in my suitcase, just in case we decided to actually go someplace nice. "Doesn't Jess have to go to the bathroom or anything?"

"You're not finished packing, are you?"

"Yes I am! I thought Ms. Preggars might need to empty her bladder though. Why go to a gross rest stop when she can pee here?"

I heard Jess call out, "Let's go up and see her place. And I have to pee anyway!"

"Okay, we're coming up," Eric said. "But you better be ready to go. Or is this your lame attempt to get me to carry your suitcase? "

In frustration, I shoved all of my clothes deeper into my suitcase. Hoping to make more room, I kicked off my flip flops and put them inside, took out my bulkier running sneakers and put them on my feet. "No, I can carry it myself but I might need you to sit your fat ass on it so I can get it closed."

As soon as we got in the car, Hope and Jess wanted to hear all about Ryan. After I described what he looked like, told them what he did for a living and bragged that he had 500 friends on Facebook, Hope asked, "How old is he?"

"Twenty-nine," I said.

And all of sudden Eric, who started laughing, was interested. "Stephanie the Cougar."

"I'm not a cougar! And his thirtieth birthday is in July." Weren't cougars women over forty who dated guys in their twenties? "We're only three years apart." I leaned over the passenger seat and tapped Jess on the back. "I'm not a cougar, right, Jess"?

Jess nodded. "Not a cougar, chickie."

Still laughing, Eric said, "Jess, do me a favor, grab me the box of CDs from under your seat. I want to change the music."

Handing him the box, Jess asked, "What do you want to put on?"

"You'll see," he said.

"Well, I think he sounds great, Steph. Good for you," Hope said.

"Thanks, Hope." I shot Eric a nasty look. "I'm glad some of my friends are happy for me."

"I'm happy for you too, Steph," Eric said. "In fact, I dedicate this next song to you and Ryan. Drum roll please."

I asked, "What song?" but the answer came quickly when I heard the first few notes "*dee dee dee dee dee dee dee dee dee dee dee dee dee*" followed by Eric's annoying, although admittedly perfect pitched, singing voice, "*And here's to you, Mrs. Robinson, Jesus loves you more than you will know.*"

And the rest of the drive was more of the same as Eric referred to me and Ryan as Demi and Ashton respectively, and played Mrs. Robinson every hour on the hour. I was relieved when we finally arrived at the beach house until it occurred to me that if Eric was this relentless with the jokes, Paul would be impossible. It was going to be a long week.

FORTY-ONE

IT WAS A THREE-STORY white Victorian-style house with the kitchen, living room and master bedroom on the top floor, a few more bedrooms on the second floor and a laundry room, pool table, two more bedrooms and a garage on the ground floor. After several trips up and down the stairs lugging our suitcases, bags of groceries for the week and enough cases of beer and bottles of alcohol to open our own liquor store, Eric, Jess, Hope, Hille, Paul, Corky, Denise (the younger sister of Bill, Eric's big brother in the fraternity) and I finally got to relax with drinks on the ocean-overlooking back porch. Our plastic deck chairs were spaced in a close circle just wide enough to fit a square weathered wood table in the center to hold our empty beer bottles and an ashtray.

"How do you like your virgin Bay Breeze, honey?" Eric asked Jess.

Her cheeks already puffy from the middle stages of pregnancy, Jess said, "Most delicious. But can I tell you how much I'd love to spike it with some vodka?"

I loved drinking during the day and with an entire week off from work ahead of me, I was without a care in the world and my first beer went down nice and easy. Standing up, I said, "Getting another beer. Anyone want something?"

"Not me," Paul said. "But Corky here wouldn't mind a handjob."

"I think I saw a few in the fridge. I'll check for you," I said.

Standing too, Corky said, "That's all right. I'll check myself. But you walk first so I can stare at your ass."

"It would be my pleasure. I've been using the stair climber at the gym. Can you tell?"

Only because he was Corky, I let him squeeze my ass. "Sweet," he said.

We grabbed our beers and a container of salted mixed nuts and headed back to the patio. Through the screen door, I could see Paul laughing.

"Did I miss something?" I asked.

"Who's Ryan?" Paul asked.

"Who's—Wait, is that my phone?"

"Yeah. Who's Ryan?"

"Why?"

"Cuz you just missed his call." As Paul said this, he raised his hand, along with my phone, in the air and out of my reach.

"Give me my phone!" I jumped up and grabbed the phone from his hand. "Jackass."

"Who is he?"

I should have known the topic would come up quickly. "He's the guy I'm dating. Satisfied?"

"I got one word for you, Steph," Eric said.

Praying he was about to change the subject, I asked, "What?"

"Plastics."

"You lost me," Denise said.

"*The Graduate* reference. Steph's new boy toy is a youngun," Eric said.

"How old is he?" Hille asked. He directed the question to me and not Eric and with his eyes on mine, I felt myself blush and figured old habits died hard.

"He's eighteen. Totally legal."

Hille continued to look at me as if inviting further details. His expression reflected amused interest, but not signs of jealousy.

"He's turning thirty in July! Older than three people sitting right on this balcony. Give it a rest. So when are Andy and Rachel getting here?"

"Monday afternoon," Paul said. "I need to find a way to return his porn collection without Rachel seeing."

Jess took a deep inhale of Eric's rum and coke. "He lent you his entire porn collection?" she asked. "I thought he needed it to fall asleep at night."

Hope leaned over, rubbed Paul's leg and said, "He didn't lend him the entire collection—just a bunch of DVDs. Right, Hon?"

"Yup," Paul said.

"You knew about this?" I asked Hope.

"Kinda."

Hille stood up and said, "Thanks for the insight into your sex life, Hope. My turn to refill my drink. Anyone?" When he turned to look at me, I shook my head. "No thanks. But I'm going in for a bit too."

In an almost accusatory tone, Paul asked, "Calling your boyfriend?"

"Yes, in fact, I am. You got a problem with that?" Without waiting for the answer I turned back towards Hille but he had already gone inside. I followed his lead, sat on one of the couches in the living room and called Ryan back.

"Hey you," I said when he answered.

"Hey. I wanted to make sure you got there alive."

"Just barely. Sorry I missed your call. Paul stole my phone."

"Interesting. Doesn't he have his own?"

"He does. But it's more fun to torture me. In full disclosure, they're mocking me endlessly over the fact that you're younger than me." I looked up in time to catch Hille on his way back outside. He smiled and closed the screen door behind him, leaving me alone to talk to Ryan.

Ryan chuckled. "From what you told me about those guys, I'm not surprised. Don't let it get to you and, whatever you do, don't get back together with Paul."

"You're not sincerely concerned about that, are you? Not gonna happen."

"Not really concerned. Okay so I'm guessing you guys are already drinking heavily?"

I glanced at the almost empty beer in my hand. "Starting to, yes."

"You go imbibe. Drunk dial me later."

"Will do!"

"Cool."

I could clearly visualize him holding his phone while playing hacky sack in his living room. "Miss you," I said.

"Me too. Talk soon."

"Bye."

After we hung up, I joined the gang outside. Hope and Paul were showing the others the gift bag they had made for Andy. Among other "treats," it came with an inflatable cow, vagina flashlight, balloon boobies and masturbation cream.

Yes, my friends were some sick folks.

FORTY-TWO

LATER THAT NIGHT, after several beers and a family-style dinner of spaghetti and garlic bread, courtesy of Jess and Hope, a few of us decided to take a walk to the ocean. The pathway to the beach was a few houses down.

Navigating the rickety wooden bridge running from the house to the beach reminded me of my two summers at Camp Pocono Hills when I was a kid. Aiming my flashlight at the path in front of me, I said, "I feel like I'm in sleepaway camp and sneaking my way to boys' campus in the middle of the night."

"Andy's vagina flashlight would come in handy right about now," Paul joked.

"Paul, can I grub another cig?" Hope asked. She was wasted and I was positive she'd be puking later.

Grabbing Hope by her tiny waist, Paul asked, "In exchange for what?"

Cupping his butt, Hope answered, "Anything you want."

With that statement, they started groping each other and I took it as my cue to walk away. Although it was dark and I could barely see two inches in front of me, I could hear the sounds of the waves crashing on the beach. I sat down in the sand with my beer, closed my eyes and breathed in the scent of the salt water.

"What are you doing here all by yourself?"

I looked up and saw Hille standing over me. "Just taking a rest," I said.

"Want some company?"

"Sure. Pop a squat." After Hille sat down, I clinked my bottle against his. "Cheers."

"Cheers. To a week at the beach with no work."

I took a swig of my beer. It was getting warm. "I'll drink to that."

We sat there quietly looking towards the water until Hille broke the silence. "So, tell me about this guy Ryan"

I looked at him in surprise. "What do you want to know?"

"How'd you meet him?"

"We bonded over *The Brady Bunch* at a book store."

Hille chuckled. "*The Brady Bunch*? Really?"

"Strangely enough, yes." I thought back to Ryan's public display of enthusiasm over the Grand Canyon episode and smiled.

"You like him, huh?"

"Yeah. I do. He's a good guy. Lots of fun too."

Rubbing his hands together as if trying to warm-up, Hille looked at me and asked, "I guess he'd fit in with this crowd?"

"Definitely. He's not quite as obnoxious as Paul, but he could hang."

Hille nodded. "That's cool, Steph. I'm glad for you. You deserve it."

Just as I thought—happy for me. "Thanks, Craig. That means a lot. I feel the same way about you." In all honesty, I wouldn't be happy if Hille started dating someone for real after relegating us to "friends with benefits" status, but what else was I supposed to say?

"Thanks, Steph." Hille stared out at the waves, letting the sand sift through his fingers. "Okay, my beer is ass warm. Time for a new one."

"I was thinking the same thing."

Hille stood up and when he extended his hand to me, I grabbed it and stood up too. Then I released my hand from his and said, "Let's go."

*   *   *

It was a surprisingly early night and I was in the room I was sharing with Denise. I didn't relish sleeping in a twin bed for a week, but we had our own bathroom so things could have been worse. The gender-neutral room was generically decorated from the white painted walls, to the clean looking but unobtrusive white furniture set to the drab gray carpeting. I was in bed but kept the light on for Denise who was still washing her face and brushing her teeth. When she got in her bed, I reached over to the lamp on the night table and turned the light off. "Goodnight, Denise."

"Night, Steph."

I closed my eyes and wondered what Ryan was doing at that moment.

"Steph?"

"Yeah?"

"You had a fling with Hille didn't you?"

I opened my eyes and turned on my side facing Denise's bed. "Not sure I'd call it a fling, but we hooked up a bunch of times, yeah." I had prematurely thought it was old news since no one else had mentioned it so far. Not even Paul. "Does anyone *not* know?"

Denise laughed. "I'm guessing it made the alumni newsletter. Just kidding, but you know how word spreads around the brothers."

"It's kind of ridiculous how they never grow up." I couldn't help but smile since immaturity was one of the characteristics that bonded us together.

"Seriously I can't believe Bill's a dad. So, is it weird being in the house with him?"

"With who? Hille?" *Why are you so interested?* I sat up in bed. "Why? Do you like him?" With her long dark curly hair and flawless figure, Denise was attractive enough, but braces in your late twenties were probably not at the top of Hille's wish list in women. I cursed myself for being petty.

Denise sat up. "No! I mean, I think he's good looking, but I can't go for anyone from Bill's pledge class. It would be like incest or something."

I wasn't sure I bought it. It seemed very "the lady doth protest too much" of her.

Denise continued, "I saw you guys come in from the beach together and was wondering."

"We're just friends. He's totally cool that I'm dating someone." Not wanting Denise to think I'd feared otherwise, I added, "Not that I thought he'd be any different."

Lying down again, Denise said with her eyes closed, "That's great. It should always be that uncomplicated. If it was my life, there would probably be crazy drama." Turning on her stomach, she muttered, "You're lucky."

I fell back in bed and turned to my side, this time facing away from Denise. "Yes, I guess I am lucky— lucky and soon to be tanned. I can't wait to be on the beach tomorrow! Night Denise."

"Goodnight, Steph."

As I drifted off to sleep, I thought about what my mother had said in Target. As suspected, she was wrong. Hille wasn't at all jealous about my dating Ryan and it was just as well.

FORTY-THREE

THE NEXT MORNING, I woke up in an empty room. I stretched out in the bed and lay there for a minute staring at the ceiling. I was so happy it was only Sunday and I still had an entire week of vacation. But I felt guilty that Ryan had to work. His soccer team also had its championship games that week. He was pretty competitive and, as I recalled his face after I beat him four times in a row in Spit, a bit of a sore loser. He was probably nervous.

I didn't want the others to go to the beach without me so I reluctantly got out of bed. I peeked out the window and jumped up and down when I saw how sunny it was. Then I brushed my teeth and went upstairs to the kitchen. Eric was spreading peanut butter on toast and the others were outside on the balcony.

"Morning, Eric," I called out.

"Supp, Steph. Coffee's ready."

"Just what I need. Throw a piece of bread in the toaster for me, will ya?"

Eric looked at me as if making my breakfast was the last thing he wanted to do but a moment later, grabbed a slice of wheat bread from the loaf and placed it in the toaster oven.

"Thanks Eric." I kissed him on the cheek, poured a cup of coffee and went outside.

"Morning, folks." I sat down in the first empty chair I saw, took a sip of my coffee and grimaced. "Ugh. I can't stand regular milk in my coffee."

Sitting in the chair next to mine, Hille said, "I bought you half and half."

"You did?"

Hille nodded. "Uh-huh." Looking up from the computer on his lap, he said, "It's in the back of the fridge somewhere."

"Thanks, Craig. You've saved me from a week of shitty coffee."

Paul stood up and pulled up his sweatpants which were at least a size too big. "And you saved the rest of us from a week of hearing Stephanie complain about how awful her coffee tasted. Thank you. Thank you. Thank you!"

Eric came outside and handed me a plate. "Here's your toast, Steph. I put peanut butter and grape jelly on it. If you didn't want that, tough shit."

I took a bite, relished the perfect combination of salty and sweet and wished I could personally express my gratitude to the inventor of the PB&J sandwich. "This is great. Thanks Eric. You'll make a fine papa!"

"Yes he will. As long as he doesn't smoke up in front of the child," Jess said.

I swallowed another piece of toast and repeated, "Smoke up?"

"Paul brought pot which Eric is more than a little excited to smoke later," Jess said.

"I gotta get it out of my system. After the baby's born, no more illegal drugs. You've got my word!"

"Yeah, just Vicodin, Percocet and Valium. All legal," Hille joked.

"And maybe some Viagra," Paul added.

"My honey don't need any little blue pills!" Jess insisted.

"Not yet, anyway," Paul said.

Bored with the conversation, I looked at my pasty white arms poking out from the Jorge Posada Yankees t-shirt I'd worn to sleep. "When are we heading down to the beach?"

* * *

The songs on my Ipod drowned out the sounds of the guys' constant laughter as they traded insults back and forth and I let the warmth of the sun woo me into a semi-dream state. The heat made me horny and I tried not to wiggle in my beach chair as I imagined

Ryan thrusting into me with slow, long strokes as his body covered mine. I opened my eyes in time to watch Hille walking back from the water, his skin already tanned and I turned over onto my stomach. When I felt cold drops of water on my back, I flipped over and he was standing over me. I squinted my eyes to see him through the bright sun and removed my headphones. "What's up?"

"Why aren't you in the water? You were so anxious to get down to the beach."

"Yes, to get some color on my milky white body!"

"Steph's afraid of the waves," Eric called out from his chair.

"For real?" Hille asked. "Why?"

"Bad experience," I said.

Hille pulled his beach chair next to mine and sat down. "Tell me about it."

"It's stupid." I sat sideways on my beach chair with my feet in the sand facing Hille. "When I was younger, I was fearless. I used to swim pretty far back in the ocean and ride the waves. I loved it."

"So what happened?" Hille asked.

"One time my family was in Virginia Beach. I must have been about twelve and I was in the water with Sam. The waves were pretty high but I was cocky and wasn't even looking at them. I was facing the other direction waving at my mom and Al on the beach. Sam called out 'holy shit' and I turned around and saw a huge wave coming toward me. There was no way I'd be able to jump over it and I freaked out. Sam kept chanting, 'swim through it, swim through it' but I was too scared."

"So, what'd you do?"

"I stood there paralyzed until the wave hit me and knocked me down. I swear, I flipped upside down at least twice. I finally got my bearings just in time for another wave to crash into me. I think it happened three times until I was pushed toward the shore. I had sand and seaweed everywhere and it took an hour for my breathing to go back to normal. Since then, I've never gone in the ocean except to get my feet wet."

As I told the story, I felt like I was reliving the experience and actually got goose bumps, but Hille just looked at me blankly. "So, that's it?"

I stared at him dumbfounded. One of the scariest experiences of my life and this was his reaction? "What? Obviously, I lived to tell the tale. What else were you expecting?"

Still looking at me incredulously, he said, "You don't plan to ever go in the ocean again because of something that happened when you were twelve?"

"That's correct."

Hille stood up, put his beer bottle in the koozie and reached out his hand. "Let's go."

"Go where?" I knew exactly where he wanted to go and my blood ran cold. There was no way.

"To the ocean." He waved his hand at me. "C'mon. I promise I won't let you drown."

My heart throbbing, I said, "Are you serious?"

Hille laughed. "Deadly. C'mon."

As everyone else encouraged me to go with Hille, there was a chorus of "c'mons" until I finally decided dying might be a better fate than listening to everyone else tell me to face my fear head-on. I grabbed Hille's hand, dug my fingernails into it and threatened, "If I die, you're so coming with me."

"I'll take my chances, but I promise you won't die."

We walked down the beach in silence and I heard Corky shout, "Go Steph!" and then Paul scream, "Jews don't believe in cremation, right?" I stopped and put my hand on Hille's arm. "I'm scared shitless, Craig. Don't make fun of me."

"I'm not making fun of you. You'll be fine."

We continued walking and when we reached the water, I jumped in shock. "Jeez, it's freezing!"

"That's cuz it's not even June. It will feel good once you're used to it."

"Like sex?" I bit my lip, afraid introducing sex into the conversation would make things awkward.

Hille chuckled. "I didn't need to get used to sex. Always felt good."

"Cuz you're a guy!" I was pleasantly surprised by his apparent comfort with the topic of fornication.

Hille winked at me. "Can't help that—was born that way. Ready to go farther?"

I was just happy his wink no longer made my nipples stand at attention. "Not really, but it doesn't look like I have a choice."

"Nope, but I'll hold your hand if it makes you feel better."

I grabbed his hand and reasoned that it was okay since I was terrified.

Matter-of-factly, Hille said, "The waves are pretty calm. But we can stay here for now if you want."

I noted this was the most serious conversation I'd ever had with him. "Why are you being so nice?"

Hille looked at me in surprise. "Why? Am I not usually nice?"

Embarrassed at the question, I shook my head. "Not what I meant. But why do you care if I overcome this fear?" We were standing knee deep in the water. Far enough to ride the smaller waves but close enough that my life didn't feel threatened. It felt nice and I floated on my back, still holding Hille's hand.

Hille leaned back and floated too. "I just think that some fears are reasonable and others aren't. Life's too short to live in fear."

I motioned towards the water. "And could be shorter if we seek out danger!" I was relieved not to see any enormous waves coming toward us.

"Yeah, but riding waves close to the shore is not the same as jumping into shark infested waters in the middle of the ocean. I'm terrified of heights and so I bungee jumped last year."

"Did you piss in your pants first"?

"No. For a while there, I thought I might shit in them though!"

I giggled, surprised that Hille would even joke about a bodily function. "Did you have fun though?"

"Not one bit. But I felt great afterwards. Was a natural high.

"Cool," I said.

"Steph."

"What?"

"We're in pretty deep."

I released Hille's hand and stopped floating. Treading water, I asked, "What do you mean?"

He pointed out toward the water and let a wave move him along, "You're riding the waves and not dying."

I watched another wave approach me and jumped over. "You're right!"

Hille smiled. "Feels good, right?"

"Feels awesome!" I agreed. "Craig?"

"Yeah?"

"Can we go back now?"

"Already?"

"Yeah. I'd like to quit while I'm ahead."

Hille grinned at me. "Whatever you want. You did good, kid."

"Thanks. Thanks for being so nice."

"Not a big deal."

When we reached the shore, he asked, "So, you think you'll go in again later?"

"Don't push your luck!"

When we got back to the others, I high-fived everyone and grabbed a beer from the cooler. I felt like Super Woman. Hille was right. It was a natural high. I had to call Ryan.

As soon as he answered, I asked, "Guess what?"

"You're already drunk at noon on a Sunday?"

"Nope! I just rode the waves for the first time since I was twelve!" I looked at Hille and whispered, "Thank you." He shrugged his shoulders and mouthed, "Your welcome."

"Awesome. Why not since you were twelve?"

"Chicken shit. But I did it anyway!"

"Good for you! Must feel good. Wish I could celebrate with you."

"Me too, but you're here in spirit." I took a sip of beer in his honor and whispered, "And I had a little beach fantasy before."

"Was I in it?"

"Duh! You were the leading and only man. And you were really good. It was hot."

"Maybe we can act it out when you get back."

Looking toward the water, practically the same color as Ryan's eyes, I said, "I look forward to it. So, how's everything with you?"

"Oh, it's great. It's raining and I have soccer practice in twenty minutes and my goalie fell off his bike and hurt his knee. I doubt we'll win the playoffs this season."

"That sucks, Ryan. I'm sorry."

"Me too. But it's only soccer. I guess."

"I miss you."

"I miss you too. Go chug a beer for me or something."

"If you insist."

When we hung up, I chugged the rest of my beer and fell back in my chair with a smile.

"For Christ's sake, Stephanie. It's not like you climbed Mt. Everest. Wipe the goofy grin off your face."

I sat up and kicked sand towards Paul's chair. "You're *such* a buzz kill. I can't believe I actually dated you!"

FORTY-FOUR

AFTER CLEANING UP THE STEAK DINNER prepared by Denise, we sat around the large dining room table drinking and pondering the evening's festivities. Paul suggested a game of Trivial Pursuit and to determine teams, we pulled numbers out of a hat. Both Hille and I picked two.

"Not fair," Paul complained. "You got Hille. You're so gonna win."

"But it would be fair if you got Hille? Luck of the draw, Mister! And besides, I've accrued my share of useless information over the years too."

Laughing, Paul said, "Sure, in the category of television trivia from the seventies, eighties and nineties."

I turned to Hille. "I'm not that good at Trivial Pursuit, Craig, but I'll try."

Hille shrugged. "It's just a game. It doesn't matter who wins."

Paul placed a pitcher of beer in the center of the table and put a shot glass next to each of us. "To keep things interesting, anytime one of us answers a question incorrectly, he has to do a shot of beer."

"Why not a shot of tequila?" I joked.

"Just trying not to kill anyone, Cohen. But if you'd like tequila instead, it could be arranged."

"No thanks. What about Jess? She can't do a shot of anything."

We all turned to Jess who, looking apologetic, said, "I don't have to play."

It hadn't even occurred to me how bored Jess might be watching the rest of us drink. "Of course you can still play! How about you do a shot of juice instead?" I suggested.

"Oh, that would be swell, Stephanie. What a hoot."

Feeling helpless, I looked at Hille, shrugged and whispered, "It was just a suggestion."

He chuckled. "As you can tell, it went over real well."

Eric stood up. "I've got an idea. Since I'm the one responsible for the unborn genius, how about whenever Jess answers a question wrong, I do a shot?"

"How generous of you," Jess said. "You're already high, you might as well get extra drunk too. Maybe I'll even be lucky enough to clean the toilet when your aim is off later."

Eric sat back down again and turned his chair towards Jess who was staring towards the ground. "Do we have a problem?"

Jess shook her head but refused to look at any of us. "I'm fine. I just never realized how annoying you all are when you're drunk. I kind of wish you'd all pass out like Corky."

No one said anything and I figured that, like me, they didn't know how to respond. We sat there and quietly scanned the room making eye contact with each other while Jess continued to look down. Finally, Paul slammed down his shot glass, breaking the silence. He stood up, walked toward the kitchen and said, "You're absolutely right, Jess. We're all totally annoying when we're drunk." Returning to the table with the bottle of tequila, he poured himself a shot, and said, "Here's to being annoying." Then he poured Denise a shot. "Here's to being annoying," she said, before slamming it down. He then poured Hope a shot. Hope hesitated, looked at Jess and said, "I'm sorry sis!" before repeating the phrase and taking the shot.

Before Paul made his way to the other end of the table where I was sitting next to Hille, Jess stood up and took the bottle of tequila from his hands. She looked at me, Denise and Hope and said, "Someday you'll understand how hard this is. I only hope I'm drunk when that happens." Then she turned to Eric. "And as for you, my sweet husband, I'm sure I'll come up with appropriate revenge for you insisting on taking your pregnant wife away for a week of non-stop drinking." She poured Eric a shot, pushed it towards him and said, "Here's to being annoying!" Then she started laughing. Everyone else remained silent.

I elbowed Hille who turned to me and whispered, "What?"

I whispered back, "Does this mean Jess isn't mad anymore?"

"Not sure. What do you think?"

"I dunno." I turned to Jess. "Jess?"

Still laughing, Jess said, "Yeah?"

"Can the rest of us laugh now, too?"

Jess nodded. "Yes, Stephanie. My evil hormonal twin has left the building. Laugh away."

"Cool. Someone do something funny so I can laugh." I looked around the room and stopped at Paul, who stood up and began walking towards me with the tequila bottle.

"Obviously Trivial Pursuit is not in the cards for this evening. Since we all know who would have won, I suggest that we give them the prize anyway." Then he poured Hille and me each a shot. "Good game, guys."

Hille picked up his shot glass and winked at me. "Nice game, Steph."

I smiled, said, "Nice game, Craig" and winced when the tequila hit the back of my throat. I forgot how nasty tequila tasted without salt and lime.

FORTY-FIVE

AFTER TWO NIGHTS IN A ROW swallowing down feasts of home-cooked meals with beer, I felt enormous and decided I had to go running before getting back in a bikini. I was hung over but knew that if I worked out, I'd at least feel better in a bathing suit, even if I looked exactly the same. I had crazy heartburn and a stubborn pounding on the left side of my head, but took two aspirin and forced myself out of bed as Denise slept.

When I dry heaved each time I picked up the speed or hit a hillier patch of ground, my forty-five minute brisk run turned into a twenty-five minute slow jog before I gave up and headed back. I wheezed my way up the stairs through the front door of the house and heard voices I immediately identified as coming from Andy and Rachel.

"Someone's up," I heard Rachel say.

"Yup, it's me," I said. When I reached the top of the stairs and saw them standing in the living room, Andy casually dressed in a New Orleans Jazz Fest 2007 t-shirt and long shorts and Rachel dressed for the Kentucky Derby in a polka dot sundress and a white wide brim hat, I said, "I'd hug you guys, but I'm too sweaty. Welcome to the house!"

"Hey, Steph," they said in unison.

"Is everyone else sleeping?" Andy asked.

Eric stuck his head out the door of the master bedroom. "No, we're up. Give us a second, we'll be out." Then he closed the door behind him.

"Okay, I feel gross and need a shower big time. Make yourself comfortable." I so wanted to tell Rachel that mint juleps were being prepared on the balcony but refrained. "Eric, can you make coffee?"

Through the door, I heard him say, "Yes, I'll make coffee. I'm beginning to think you don't know how, Steph."

"Of course I know how!"

I had no idea how to make coffee unless it was instant. My firm served free coffee all day and when I wanted a special treat, I went to Dunkin Donuts. I was addicted to the coconut flavor. It wouldn't bother me if Eric knew, but I didn't think Rachel and Andy needed to be privy to how challenged I was around regular household appliances.

I felt much better after my shower and immensely skinnier in my bikini thanks to the long overdue run and the much needed tan from the day before. I couldn't wait to get back on the beach. I'd skip the pre-happy hour beers this time, though.

Mostly everyone was now awake and watching *Regis and Kelly* in the living room. As I approached the others with a cup of coffee in hand, I saw Hille and Denise talking on the balcony. I sat next to Corky on the couch facing the window and tried not to look outside.

Corky moved closer to me and rested his head on my shoulder. "Hey, hot legs. How was your run?"

"Awful. I was on the verge of throwing up the entire time."

Corky sat up and slid away from me. "You're not gonna puke now, are you?"

"No. But you're lucky you passed out early last night. Paul killed us with the tequila shots."

"I don't recall pouring them down your throat, Cohen!" Paul said.

"True. My bad." I peeked out the window and made eye contact with Hille, who smiled and motioned for me to come outside. Standing up, I said, "Going outside."

Denise was showing Hille pictures of Bill's baby and neither of them looked up when I sat down. I felt like I was intruding and wondered why Hille had asked me to join them. Maybe he was just waving hello. I was about to go back inside when he finally acknowledged me.

"Hey, Steph. I heard you went running this morning. Impressive. As I sit here getting fatter and fatter."

As he said this, he stretched his arms above his head and I got a glimpse of his toned belly and the trail of hair leading downwards. I quickly turned away and brushed aside the memory of fucking him. "Don't be too impressed. I only ran for twenty-five minutes and had to stop a million times to catch my breath. And I think I had a few cigarettes last night. Smoking doesn't mix well with cardio-vascular activity."

Hille started laughing. "You did smoke last night. Kept taking Eric's cigarettes. You thought you were being sneaky, but he saw you. It was cute."

"Shit! I'd better buy Eric a new pack! Kind of scary that I don't remember."

Denise stood up. "I don't remember much about last night either. Don't even remember going to bed. I'm going to put my album away." Then she looked at Hille, smiled and said, "Unless you're still looking."

Hille returned Denise's smile and shook his head. "Nope. Cool pictures, though."

Denise smiled at Hille again and walked back into the house. I didn't know why a measly photo album inspired so much smiling among the two of them. Had they hooked up the night before while I was busy stealing cigarettes? Surely Denise would have remembered that.

"So, what's on the agenda for today?"

I looked at Hille's face. There was no post-coital glow or any other evidence to suggest he'd gotten laid the night before. "The beach, I guess," I said.

"I meant after the beach—I think us guys might go fishing. I heard Rachel mention the outlets and I'm guessing Andy will be roped into going with her. So that leaves you girls with the house to yourself."

"I'm sure we'll find something to occupy our time."

"I'm sure you will too. Talk to Ryan lately?"

"Yeah. Apparently we exchanged a long round of text messages last night. But I don't remember sending them. My grammar was perfect though, if you can believe it."

Hille chuckled. "Wow. How'd you manage that?"

"I haven't a clue. Also don't know what possessed us to debate the best television theme songs but we did. I have the evidence to prove it."

"What's your favorite?" He asked.

"*Greatest American Hero*," I said.

"His?"

"*Dukes of Hazard*." I considered asking about Hille's favorite until I recalled the embarrassing list of questions I had once prepared.

"Funny stuff." Hille stood up and motioned towards the beach below us. "I'm about ready to hit the sand. You?"

I followed him back in the house, where the others were still mesmerized by the television. Rachel Ray was making one of her Thirty Minute Meals—Buffalo Club sandwiches.

* * *

Later that afternoon, Hope and I were sitting on Eric and Jess's bed watching Jess blow dry her hair and going through her makeup collection. The guys had left to go fishing a few minutes earlier. I was relieved Denise had gone to the Coach outlet with Andy and Rachel instead of joining the guys.

I removed a hot pink lip gloss from the case and unscrewed the cap. "I use this one too. Kind of cool the way the same shade looks different on everyone."

"I use it too," Hope said. "And so does Denise."

"How weird is it that all four of us use the same lip gloss? I thought it was my secret," I said.

Finished with her hair, Jess sat on the bed with us with her feet dangling over the edge. "So did we."

"So what should we do while everyone else is out?" Hope asked.

"Hmmm. How about we run around the house naked?" I suggested.

Hope giggled. "I think Paul did that last night."

"Want to get out of here? I wouldn't mind driving somewhere," Jess said.

"I'd suggest a bar if I wasn't afraid your evil impregnated demonic twin would kick my ass." As I said this, I held up my pointer fingers in the sign of the cross hoping my dead Jewish grandparents couldn't see me.

"Mwahaha!!" Jess said laughing. "Actually, both me and my evil twin wouldn't mind sitting at a bar. I'll order a fancy drink with an umbrella—hold the alcohol."

"Sounds good to me. Except for the 'hold the alcohol' part," Hope said.

MEREDITH SCHORR

"Cool. Let me throw on some of that lip gloss and grab my wallet." On my way out, I snuck a look at the master bath. "Have you guys used that awesome Jacuzzi tub yet?"

"Not yet. But Eric keeps mentioning it. I think tonight's the night."

"Is it hard to have sex in a bathtub?" I asked.

"I'll let you know tomorrow morning. Hurry up and grab your wallet before the guys come back and want to join us. I'm craving some girl talk."

About a half hour later, the three of us were sitting at Sundogs Sports Bar sipping our drinks—mine a Rum Runner, Hope's a Long Island Iced Tea and Jess's a virgin frozen Strawberry Daiquiri. We sat at the bar, Jess in the middle so that she had easiest access to the potato skins and nachos.

"Did either of you notice how weird Craig's acting?" I asked. I moved my stool back a few inches from the bar so I could see Hope better.

"Weird how?" she asked.

"He's being so outgoing and friendly and I've barely seen him with his Blackberry."

Jess eyed the last potato skin and looked from me to Hope. "Can I have it?"

"Go for it. I just want another drink," I said. "So, did either of you guys notice?"

After Jess slurped down the rest of her drink, she asked, "Notice what?"

"Craig's behavior!"

Both girls shook their heads.

I knew it was not a figment of my imagination. "You didn't notice how much more talkative he's been to me suddenly?"

Hope shrugged. "I guess. That was awfully sweet of him to take you in the ocean."

"Definitely. I was surprised."

"Maybe he likes you, Steph," Hope said.

"No way." I took a long sip of my drink. "You really think?"

"Why not?" Jess asked. "You've hooked up a bunch of times."

"And you know what they say about not knowing what you've got till it's gone," Hope said.

"Whatever. I practically threw myself at Hille before and he made no effort. Maybe he's just happy to be off from work for the week."

I waited for a response from the girls but none came and we quietly watched the bartender prepare our second round of drinks. "Do you think he likes Denise?" I asked.

"I doubt it," Jess said.

Gesturing towards me, Hope said, "He obviously has no issue with casual sex, though, so you never know what the rest of the week will bring."

Her comment elicited a hearty laugh from Jess. I didn't think it was very funny but I forced out a chuckle anyway.

FORTY-SIX

A FEW DAYS LATER, I stretched out on the couch and called Ryan. The first words out of his mouth were, "When are you coming home? I mean hi!"

Charmed by his enthusiasm, I said, "I'll be home soon enough and hi right back at you!"

"What's going on? I'm bored. Let me live vicariously through you."

"Hmm, okay, we dared Corky to run around the block naked last night and he did. Eric got completely stoned last night and offered to make us guacamole but wound up eating it all himself. Andy's still trying to hide his porn addiction from Rachel but Paul and Eric keep leaving his DVDs around the house. I finally turned over on my stomach today at the beach and my butt cheeks are sun burnt. Hope and..."

"Wait," Ryan interrupted. "Not so fast, woman. Your butt cheeks are sun burnt?"

Giggling, I said, "I figured that would interest you. Yes, my bikini bottoms are kind of small and my butt is, well, kind of big and it got burned."

"Your butt isn't big. It's perfect," Ryan said. "Man, I wish I was there to apply sunscreen."

Tickled pink by his reassurance that my butt was perfect, I said, "Me too. But if it still hurts when I get home, you can apply aloe to the affected area."

"I just got hard."

"And I think I'm gonna take this conversation into the bedroom while Denise is out and I have it to myself. Hold on a second."

As I walked away, I glanced over at Hille on the couch by the window. He was furiously typing away at his computer, seemingly lost in his own world. Figuring he must have overheard my conversation with Ryan, I recalled Hope's comment at SunDogs that he might like me and for a brief moment, wondered if he could be jealous.

*   *   *

We decided to go out for dinner that night. I was relieved since almost everyone besides me had already been assigned kitchen duty and I was afraid I would be forced to suit up and cook for the house. We went to an Asian Fusion restaurant that Andy, Rachel and Denise had passed on the way to the Coach outlet. We hung out at the bar while we waited for a table large enough to accommodate us.

Paul was the first to get the bartender's attention. "What's everyone drinking?"

"Vodka and cranberry. I don't want to mix drinks later," Hope said.

Corky shouted out, "Whatever's light on tap for me!"

I was contemplating my choices. I wasn't sure if I wanted to drink beer or wine. Still undecided, I looked up to find Paul glaring at me.

"Cohen! We don't have all day," he said.

I was about to order a glass of Riesling when Hille tapped me on the shoulder. "They have heffeweizen on draft, Steph."

I called out to Paul, "Heffeweizen," and then turned to Hille, "Thanks, Craig. I couldn't see the beer selections from here." In truth, I saw that there was heffeweizen on tap. I was in the mood for wine, but decided to go with the beer since Hille went out of his way to point it out to me.

When our table was finally available, I sat down next to Eric on one side and Hope on the other. I was starving and anxiously reviewed the menu until I was struck by a memory of being in Hoboken drinking wheat beer at Hille's apartment. None of the others drank it and Hille told me he had never even tried it, yet he had it in his refrigerator. And then there was the half and half. No one else had a problem with whole or even skim milk, yet Hille brought half and half to the house. I had told him on New Year's Day I took my coffee extra light with half and half! Had he purposely stocked the refrigerator with my preferences in mind?

I looked over at Hille on the other side of the table in surprise and knocked my beer over. I caught the glass in time to avoid a break, but a good portion of the beer spilled onto Eric's lap and he jumped out of his chair. "Shit, Steph! What the hell is wrong with you?"

Cheeks burning, I tried to blot the spill with my napkin and said, "I'm sorry, Eric. I don't know what happened."

Eric motioned for the waitress, who wiped down the table. "Don't worry about it," he said to me before looking at the others. "Anyone want to switch seats with me? For those looking to spice things up, sitting next to Steph is always an adventure."

FORTY-SEVEN

I CLEANED MY PLATE of spicy ginger beef and rice noodles, but if someone asked me what it tasted like or even if it was good, she'd be rewarded with a blank stare. I feigned exhaustion and went to bed early but I was actually wide awake long after Denise came stumbling in hours later.

As the old fashioned clock on the night table recorded each passing second with a loud tick-tock, the idea that Hille might be totally into me after all became less and less crazy. And it wasn't only because of the heffeweizen and half and half. Everyone else was completely unfazed by my fear of waves, yet Hille insisted I try to overcome my phobia. Even my mom, in her ultimate wisdom, said the right guy would help me overcome my issues.

On the other hand, my mom also said, with the right guy I wouldn't fear his losing interest at any given moment and Hille certainly kept me guessing. But then again, my mom was probably referring to an *existing* relationship. I couldn't possibly know whether I would be insecure in a relationship with Hille until we actually started dating.

But that raised another question—why weren't Hille and I dating? I thought I had made my feelings for him pretty clear so, if he liked me, why didn't he ask me out for real when he had the chance? Although Hope had suggested that maybe Hille didn't realize how much he liked me until it was too late. Even my mom guessed my relationship with Ryan would light a fire under Hille's ass.

I stared at Denise as she slept, probably dreaming about Hille.

Unless he thought I wouldn't be interested in a real relationship with him. I never told him I was opposed to being friends with benefits so maybe he thought that was all I wanted. And that would also explain why he looked so pained when I asked if he'd ever been in love.

I flipped over onto my stomach, my chin resting on the pillow.

And maybe he didn't think he was my type. I dated Paul for two years and Hille was the Anti-Paul. Maybe he assumed because he was quiet and not a ham like Paul, I wouldn't like him. In fact, he got awfully defensive on New Year's Eve when I said spontaneous sex in the bathroom was out of character for him. Maybe that's why he left the bar early all those years ago, practically tossing me in Paul's lap. He might have thought I'd never choose him over Paul so he didn't bother to compete. What if he was settling for Denise because he thought I'd never go for him?

I turned over onto my back and closed my eyes, hoping to clear my head of all thoughts of Hille.

And when he asked if Ryan would fit in with the gang, maybe he was wondering if Ryan was more like Paul than him. He might have been sizing up his competition. Maybe his quiet reserve was a cover for a serious inferiority complex.

With that last thought, I finally fell asleep and when I woke up the next morning, the house was empty. It was almost 11:00 am.

My immediate reaction to being left behind was pissed. What if everyone went out for breakfast without me? Or what if they decided to take a day trip somewhere cool and hadn't bothered to wake me? I stormed into the kitchen, cursing under my breath and then I saw the post-it note on the refrigerator with my name in big red letters. They went to the beach and hoped I wouldn't be upset they let me sleep late. They thought I needed a good night's sleep. I vowed to have more faith in my friends moving forward and to stop assuming the worst.

Aside from a two minute phone conversation confirming I'd made it to the Outer Banks in one piece, I hadn't spoken to my mom since I'd arrived. I poured a cup of coffee and took advantage of having the balcony to myself to talk to her without risk of Paul shouting expletives in the background. After closing the sliding door behind me, I sat in a plastic chair, stretched my feet across another chair and waited for her standard greeting from work.

Her voice sounded tired as she answered, "Noren and Company."

"Hi Mom, it's me."

"Hi! How's it going over there? Having fun?"

"Lots of fun," I said.

"Doing anything besides drinking?"

"I'm not drinking now! That's something, right?" I noticed I'd missed a spot shaving and made a mental note to run a razor over my knee before meeting the others.

"So, how's everything going? How are things with Hille?"

Upon further examination of my legs, I decided the top of my ankles could use a shave too. "Things are fine with Hille. In fact, he's been great."

Notably perkier, my mom asked, "Great how?"

"Dunno. He's just been really nice to me."

"What does he think about Ryan?"

"He hasn't met Ryan. Ryan's not here, remember?"

"I meant, how does he feel about you dating someone else?"

"He said he's happy for me. But..." I bit down on my lip as I remembered tossing and turning the night before in confusion over Hille's motives.

"But what? Is he jealous?"

Suddenly I heard a sound coming from inside the house. I stood up and peered into the glass. It was Corky refilling the cooler. I raised five fingers to signal I'd meet them soon and called out, "On phone with my mom."

"Hi, Mom," Corky said before heading back outside.

I sat back down and into the phone said, "Where were we?"

"I asked if Hille was jealous of Ryan."

"At first I didn't think so, but I don't know, Mom. He's been so nice. Super friendly. He's never been so talkative around me. Even the others noticed." I wasn't sure that was true, although Hope and Jess did mention how nice it was of him to take me into the water. "And he's done some really sweet things." I took a sip of my coffee, thankful we had half and half in the house.

"I told you, Stephanie. The green-eyed monster reared its ugly head."

Still uncertain, I said, "Maybe."

"What are you planning to do about it?"

"Nothing. I have a boyfriend!"

"Have you spoken to Ryan?"

"Of course. A bunch of times."

"I remember going to St. Baits with your father before you were born. With three other couples. Almost like you guys. Oh, to be young again. Have some fun on my behalf. Oh, before I forget, Allan won an Ipod in a sweepstake and can't seem to get it charged. Maybe Hille can figure it out."

I rolled my eyes but before I could protest, I heard a phone ring on my mom's end and she said, "Oh, crap. I have to take another call, Stephanie. Have fun. Be good. I love you."

"Love you too, Mom."

I ran upstairs to my bathroom, ran my razor under some cold water and did a half-ass shave, drawing blood of course. Then I threw a cover-up over my bathing suit, grabbed my beach chair and headed down to the beach.

I was mildly nearsighted but too vain to get glasses. I approached the fuzzy group of sunbathers and hoped they were my friends. I felt self-conscious as I watched them watch me, especially because it wasn't easy walking on hot sand wearing flip-flops and dragging a chair and beach bag. I knew I looked less than graceful. When I finally reached them, I dropped my bag and looked around for an empty space to put my chair. "Hey guys! Having fun yet?"

"Not as much fun as we'll have now that you're here, sexy mama. Sit next to me," Corky said.

"Thanks, Corky. Glad to be here. Grab me a cold one, will you? I need to catch up."

Corky opened and handed me a beer he'd grabbed from the cooler. I took a long sip and said, "Ahh! Now that's what I'm talking about."

The rest of that beer went down quite nicely as did the next one and the one after that. I sat in my chair and closed my eyes, feeling the soft breeze on my face. To anyone who was listening, I said, "I wish I could be buzzed all the time. Not drunk, just a little tipsy."

"I think you're drunk right now," Paul said.

I opened my eyes and shook my head. "Nope. Not drunk. Just feeling really peaceful."

Eric, who had gotten up to grab another beer, stood in front of me blocking the sun. "That's probably because you slept about twelve hours last night!"

"I didn't actually sleep all that time," I said.

Denise put down her book and looked at me curiously. "Yeah, you were doing a lot of tossing and turning."

I was glad Eric was also blocking my view of Hille, who was lying on his stomach on a beach towel, probably sleeping or listening to some geeky book on tape about economics. "I had a lot on my mind," I said.

"Like what?" Paul asked. "Worried about what you missed this week on *Gossip Girl*?"

"Shut up, Paul. You're such a dick sometimes."

"Shut up, Paul. Shut up." Paul mimicked. Then he looked at Corky. "Do you know what I'm thinking?"

"Negative. What are you thinking?" Corky asked.

"I'm thinking now that Cohen has overcome her fear of the water, she should go back in before she loses her nerve again."

Corky grinned at Paul and looked over at me. "I think that's a great idea. What do you think, Stephanie?"

"I think it's a horrible idea but appreciate your concern," I said.

Neither of them argued with me and I assumed the subject was closed. But then I heard the shuffling of feet and felt a shadow over me. I opened my eyes as Corky grabbed my arms and Paul grabbed my ankles and forcibly removed me from my chair.

"What the fuck?" I yelled. "Put me down, guys!" Not only was I afraid of being thrown in the water, I was scared I'd lose my bathing suit. I had saved my skimpiest bikini for when I was tan.

By then, we had already reached the water and as they swung me back and forth, they counted "One! Two! Three!"

"You ready, Stephanie?" Paul asked.

"No! Put me down. I'm drunk! What if I drown? Or throwup? Please!"

Paul started laughing. "I thought you were just buzzed?"

"I lied!"

"Of course you did," Paul said. "You're always buzzed until you're grubbing cigarettes or having sex in bathrooms. Then you blame it on being wasted."

They were still swinging me, although with less force and it felt almost like a hammock except I thought Corky might rip my arms from the sockets. "Please put me down, Paul. You loved me once. Remember the good times!"

"You must be desperate if you're pulling the ex-girlfriend card. Okay, let's put her down," Paul said.

They both released me at the same time and, as my butt landed on the ground and I got smacked by a wave crashing into the sand, Paul looked down at me, and said, "You're such a baby, Cohen" and walked away. Corky followed him, leaving me alone to regain my bearings.

From the edge of the water, I shook the sand off of my body. Corky and Paul were back by our spot on the beach and I could still hear Paul's obnoxious cackle at my expense. I walked past a young boy making sand castles and when I glanced over at his parents, the man asked, "You okay?"

Nodding, I said, "I'll live." Then I sat in the sand next to the boy and, pointing at his bucket, said, "Would you mind if I borrow this for two minutes?" I looked up at his parents. "I promise to give it right back." I glanced in the direction of Paul and Corky. "I just need to do something really quick."

The little boy reluctantly handed over his bucket and I could feel him follow me with his eyes as I walked back toward the ocean, filled the bucket with salty water and then added several scoops of sand. As I passed his parents on my return trip, I put two fingers to my lips, pointed at Paul and Corky whose chairs were facing the opposite direction and continued walking, the little boy shadowing me the entire time.

When I reached our spot, I stood silently behind Paul and Corky until Hope looked up at me from her issue of *Glamour* and joked, "How was the water?"

I splashed the entire bucket of mud across Paul and Corky's backs and said, "Very refreshing."

I returned the now-empty bucket to the little boy and mouthed, "Thank you" to his giggling parents, who gave me the thumbs up sign. Reclining in my beach chair, I closed my eyes with a smile and ignored the two morons who jumped out of their chairs and ran toward the water to wipe off the grime.

About an hour later, I was on my fifth or sixth Corona. I had lost count.

Jess stood up and pulled one of her bathing suit straps away from her skin, revealing the contrast of bright red against milky white. "Holy crap. If I stay out here any longer, the folks from Red Lobster might come after me to use as catch of the day. I'm heading in."

"I'll go with you," Hope said. "Too much sun for my Irish skin."

My arms and legs felt heavy. In fact, my entire body felt like it was trapped under one of those lead aprons used to protect against radiation exposure during x-rays at the dentist's office. I closed my eyes and fell asleep. When I opened them and lifted my head after what only felt like a few minutes, I was alone with Hille.

He smiled at me and asked, "Sweet dreams?"

"I'm not sure actually. I feel a bit woozy."

Hille grabbed a water bottle from the cooler and handed it to me. "Here. You're probably dehydrated."

After I drank about half of the water bottle in one gulp, I said, "Thanks. I can't believe I fell asleep. I usually can't sleep out in the sun. It's too hot."

"Probably the beer helped."

"Probably," I agreed. I watched Hille, who was sitting on his towel with his knees pulled towards his chest, staring straight ahead towards the ocean.

He must have sensed me looking at him, because he turned toward me and asked, "What are you thinking?"

I was too exhausted to lie. "I was thinking about the night I met Paul."

Hille nodded. "I remember that night. At The Longpost. If I recall, he impressed you with his rendition of Blind Melon's *No Rain*."

"Actually, it was *Cotton-Eye Joe*, but you were close!" I wondered if the night brought back painful memories since it was the night I chose Paul.

"You're right. I must be thinking about a different girl!"

"Yeah. Paul was some ladies' man," I said sarcastically.

"Girls always seem to fall for his charm," he said with a laugh.

I bit my cuticles and contemplated my next statement. "Confession?"

Hille turned to look at me. "You have a confession to make?"

"Yeah." I was slightly nauseous and wasn't sure if it was from too many beers on an empty stomach or the knowledge that what I was about to admit might change everything.

Hille looked at me quizzically. "Confess away."

"The night I met Paul, I had gone to the bar to meet you." There, I said it.

"What do you mean?"

"I sat behind you in class and thought you were hot. So, I went to the bar that night hoping to hook up with you."

Hille opened his eyes wide. "Really? Wow. I didn't know that."

"Yup. I had a massive crush on you but was too shy to talk to you in class." Suddenly bashful, I scanned the width of the ocean to avoid eye contact.

"That's too funny."

I didn't think it was funny at all. It wasn't funny that I came to that class in full makeup and in outfits tried on the night before and modeled in front of my roommate. I was guessing Hille didn't think it was humorous either but I had caught him off-guard. He was awkward like that.

I faced Hille head-on again. "I guess I'm trying to say Paul might have charmed me with his performance but you were the reason I was at the bar in the first place."

Hille looked at me, his mouth slightly open and his eyes still wide. Hoping to keep the conversation light and breezy, I joked, "Who knows what might have happened had you not left early that night!"

Hille scratched his head. "I guess things happen for a reason, though, right?"

"You should know that girls don't always like the hammy types like Paul. We also like the more quiet types, like you. You're mysterious." I smiled shyly.

Hille returned the smile. "Thanks for telling me. I had no idea you had a crush on me back then, Steph. I'm flattered. I take it Paul doesn't know about this, does he?"

"Nope. I didn't think he needed to know that the night we hooked up, I was insanely attracted to his best friend. Didn't think he'd appreciate it then. Don't think he'd appreciate it now."

"It'll be our secret then. Okay?"

"Sounds good to me, Craig. Shall we shake on it?" I extended my hand to Hille and he shook it firmly.

"Craig?"

"Yeah, Steph?"

"If I asked you to give my mom lessons on the computer, would you think I was nuts?"

Hille laughed. "Not at all. Too bad we don't live closer or I'd be happy to help out."

We gathered our stuff and walked back to the house in silence and I wondered why Hille didn't just admit he liked me back then, too. "Don't you think life would be so much easier if people said what they were thinking instead of hiding behind fear?" I asked.

"Where'd that come from, Steph?" Hille grabbed my chair and put it next to his in the garage before following me up the stairs to the house.

I stopped walking and turned to face him. "Life's too short, Craig. When you want something, you should go for it. That's all I'm saying."

"In theory, yes. Sometimes it's not that cut and dry, though. Some things aren't as simple as riding the waves or bungee jumping, you know?"

I thought about Ryan. Maybe *The Bachelor* wasn't as ridiculous as I had always thought and it *was* possible to develop feelings for two people at the same time. "You're right. Love's a complicated emotion, isn't it?"

Hille nodded. "Yes. And, if we had all of the answers ahead of time, our lives would probably take a completely different direction."

"Totally. That's exactly what I was thinking. You're so smart, Craig." My mom was right. We'd make really intelligent children. I looked Hille deep in the eyes, not sure of what to say next. It was an intense moment, interrupted when Hille broke out in a huge grin and said, "Enough waxing philosophical! We've got a lot of booze to finish before the week's over."

FORTY-EIGHT

AFTER DRINKING SEVERAL MORE BEERS and sneaking furtive glances at Hille who, as always, adopted a poker face as if everything was normal, I knew what I had to do. And I had to act soon since Denise, who had shifted her chair suspiciously close to his on the back porch, looked primed to make her move.

I grabbed my phone and walked toward the front porch for privacy, stopping in the kitchen for a shot of vodka on the way. I chased it with a cigarette I stole from a half full pack that was sitting on the kitchen counter. I sat on the top step and, hands shaking, called Ryan. He wasn't picking up. I couldn't leave this on his voicemail. I took a final drag on the cigarette as I listened to his outgoing voice message. Hearing his voice made me sad. I put out the cigarette and kicked the butt down the stairs.

"Hey Ryan, it's me. Um, Stephanie." I laughed. "You probably recognized my voice, though. Duh! Anyway, I need to talk to you. I really don't think I should leave this on a voicemail. That's kind of shitty. So call me." I paused. "The thing is, well, I really like you, Ryan. I mean, I really, really like you. You're awesome! And adorable and fun. And I really like you." I coughed. I didn't actually need to cough but the message wasn't going well and I wanted to stall. "But there's this guy. His name is Craig but everyone calls him Hille and we've..." Before I could finish, I was interrupted by a long beeping sound.

I shouted, "Fuck fuck fuck!" as I called him back. "Sorry about that. I was cut off. Anyway, I met Craig in college and we really liked each other but I didn't know he liked me and he didn't know I liked him especially since I was dating Paul but, well, now it's out in the open. This sucks because I'm totally into you." I recalled the last time I had kissed Ryan, in the doorway of my apartment, and I could almost smell the fresh and summery aroma of his aftershave. "God, I like you so much but I think I need to explore this thing with Craig. After all these years, we finally came clean about our feelings. That must mean something, right? Shit, I'm probably gonna get cut off again so I'll make this quick. I'm so sorry, Ryan." I wiped a tear from my eye. "Please don't hate me. Call me if you want to talk. Maybe we can be friends. I'm sorry. I'm sure you'll meet someone better than me." I tried to picture me and Hille on a double date with Ryan and another girl but the vision stung my insides. "Um, well not right away, right? But someday. Okay, bye. Sorry!"

I hung up and sat there for a minute watching my knees shake. I was queasy; probably nerves about telling Hille we could now be together and he wouldn't have to pretend it was just sex anymore. I wondered what he'd say. I wondered what Ryan would say or if he'd call me. I pictured Ryan in his big grey hoodie. It was so big, I got inside it with him once. He bet me we couldn't both fit into it but I knew we could. I laughed at the visual, stood and walked back in the house. I figured I would pull Hille to the side. Maybe we'd take a walk to the beach. We'd done our best bonding there. But first I'd freshen my face. Before heading into the bathroom, I glanced at my bed, warm and inviting. I'd just lie down for a minute and get my thoughts together. As I kicked off my shoes, got under the covers and pulled the crisp white top sheet up to my chin, I mumbled, "Just for a minute."

FORTY-NINE

I STILL FELT DRUNK the next morning and tasted smoke on my breath. Slightly dizzy, I walked into the bathroom to brush my teeth and wash off last night's makeup. Denise wasn't awake yet and so I took my phone into the living room, sat in the reclining chair and checked my messages. I thought maybe Ryan had called, but he hadn't. I heard the front door open and a second later watched Rachel and Andy walk up the stairs holding bags of groceries.

"We bought bagels and stuff," Andy said.

Although I almost puked in my mouth at the thought of eating, I forced out, "That was nice of you."

After Rachel put a few containers of orange juice in the refrigerator, she joined me in the living room and sat down on the couch. Bending down to adjust the strap of her stiletto sandals, she said, "Where'd you disappear to last night, Steph?"

The night's events were coming back to me in waves. "I must have passed out. Crazy night."

Rachel looked at me with concern. "You okay?"

Nodding, I said, "I think I might still be drunk. But not in a good way. I feel like the cat's ass."

"Did you take something?"

"No. It'll pass, I'm sure. Thanks." Standing up, I said, "I need to lie down."

As I walked down the stairs to my room, Paul and Hope were walking up.

Paul blocked my path. "Hey Cohen, what happened to you last night?"

Not in the mood, I pushed him to the side and kept walking. Feeling both sets of eyes on me, I said, "Not feeling well, guys. I'll be okay in a bit." I entered my room, closed the door behind me and jumped into bed at the same time Denise woke up. I covered my head with my blankets hoping she wouldn't try to talk to me. After she left the room, I grabbed my cell phone from the night table, placed it next to me on the bed and fell asleep.

When I woke up, I was no longer drunk or hung over and I hoped the others hadn't eaten all of the bagels. I took a quick glance at my phone and headed into the kitchen. I could see through the window that it was raining outside.

Eric called out from the living room. "Hey, Steph. You okay?"

"I'm fine. Just starving." After I spread cream cheese on my sesame bagel and poured a glass of orange juice, I walked into the living room and looked for a place to sit.

Jess moved closer to Eric on one of the couches. "There's room here, Steph."

I sat down and asked, "What are we watching?"

"What does it look like?" Paul asked.

I turned my attention to the television in time to see two blonde girls, probably no older than twenty-one, making out. They were wearing only bikini bottoms and fondling each other nipples. "*Girls Gone Wild*. Nice." Looking around the room, I asked, "Where's Craig?"

Hope gestured towards the balcony. "Outside. On the phone."

I followed Hope's glance and spotted Hille. His head was covered by the hood of a North Face raincoat but it didn't look like he was on the phone anymore. He saw me looking at him and waved. I waved back, got up from the couch and joined him outside, figuring we should talk.

"Lovely weather we're having, isn't it"? I said.

"Yeah, it sucks. But we had some great days here. Can't complain too much."

"You have such a positive outlook, Craig." And there were certainly worse qualities to be found in a soulmate.

Hille laughed. "I fake it well."

I couldn't think of anything to say and just stood there awkwardly.

"You all right?" he asked.

My voice shaking, I said, "Actually, will you take a walk with me?"
With a puzzled expression on his face, Hille asked, "In the rain?"
"Yeah, I kind of need to talk to you."
"Sure. Do you have a sweatshirt or something? Want me to bring an umbrella?"
"No umbrella. I want to grab a hoodie though. Be right back."
"Okay. I'll meet you on the front stairs."

I had no idea what I was going to say to him and hoped somehow the words I had spinning around in my head would turn into complete sentences as they left my mouth, circled the air and passed through his ear drums. I brushed my teeth again, grabbed a hoodie and made my way to the front porch where Hille was waiting for me, holding an umbrella. He raised it in the air, smiled and said, "Just in case it starts pouring."

As we headed down the driveway and made a right turn up the block where I had run a few days earlier, we didn't say anything. I thought it should be obvious why I wanted to talk to him alone since our conversation the day before had gotten so deep, but figured it was up to me to start. "So, Ryan and I broke up last night," I said.

Hille stopped in his tracks and turned to face me. "Really? What happened? Are you okay?"

"Yeah. I'm okay. It was my idea." I resumed walking and Hille followed me.

"I don't get it," he said. "I thought you really liked the guy. You seemed so happy."

"I was happy. Ryan's the best boyfriend I've ever had." I paused as I thought of a way to remove my foot from my mouth. "In the last ten years!"

Chuckling, Hille said, "Don't worry. I won't tell Paul. So, what happened?"

"I started thinking about us."

Hille repeated, "Us?"

I stopped walking, sat down and patted the curb for Hille to join me. "Yes, you and me."

"What about us, Steph?"

"I think we have something."

Hille didn't comment so I kept going. I was afraid I would stumble my words if I looked at him so I directed my gaze toward the house across the street. "Like I told you yesterday, I had a massive crush on you in college, before I started dating Paul. I put the crush to rest while I was with him and honestly didn't think much of it over the past several years, but when I saw you on Hope's birthday last fall, the feelings came flooding back. I'd never done anything like I did with you in New York— being so aggressive like that. But I had to. I had to find out if the feelings were mutual. And I was so happy when you admitted to being attracted to me, too. And then we had sex—great sex. But when I thought you just wanted to be friends with benefits, I forced myself to move on—and I met Ryan. I thought you and I were done, but you've been so nice to me since we've been here— buying me half and half, taking me into the ocean. I realized our story wasn't over yet. Why else would you do those things if you didn't really like me, too?" I turned to face Hille, both relieved to have said my peace and apprehensive as to how he'd respond.

But the only noise coming from Hille was the sound of his right foot tapping against the ground.

"Craig?"

Staring down at the pavement, he said, "Yeah?" He was still tapping his foot.

I planted my left foot on his right in a not-so-subtle effort to make him stop. "Say something. Please," I urged.

Finally, he looked at me and frowned. "Steph. I, uh, I don't know what to say to this."

A crooked smile on my face, I said, "You can start with 'I'm so happy you feel the same as me'!" I waited for Hille to stop frowning but his face was frozen still.

"Steph. You're an amazing girl. You're smart, fun, interesting and adorable." Hille kicked a pebble with his foot and watched it roll down the street.

I didn't have a good feeling. When I imagined having this conversation and pictured Hille's face, he never looked like he was constipated. I'd never actually imagined the conversation, but I was certain Hille would not have worn that expression. I put my hand on my chin to stop it from trembling. "But?"

"But, we're just not a match."

My mouth felt dry and I swallowed hard. As calmly as I could, I asked, "Why not? Is it Denise?"

Hille sighed loudly and averted my gaze. "No. Not Denise. I just don't think we're compatible."

My voice quivering, I asked, "Based on what? Am I not smart enough for you? I know I'm not the intellectual type but I'm definitely smart, Craig. I graduated college with honors and got promoted at work twice in two years. I'm not an idiot."

"It's not that, Steph. I know you're smart."

"Then what? You don't think I'm pretty enough?"

"No! C'mon, Steph. You know you're pretty."

"Then what is it, Craig? Why am I not good enough for you?" I knew I sounded desperate but only part of me cared and that part was no longer in control.

"You are good enough for me!"

"Clearly. Whatever. At least I know now. Good enough to fuck but not good enough to date." I lifted the hood of my sweatshirt over my head to cover my face.

Practically in a whisper, Hille repeated, "You're good enough, Steph."

"I heard you the first time. Let's go back. It looks like it's gonna start pouring any second." I stood up and began walking away until Hille tapped me on the back.

"Wait," he said.

I wiped the tears from my eyes and turned to face him. "What?"

"I'm gay, Stephanie."

Certain I'd heard him wrong, I did a double take. "What'd you say?"

Hille repeated, "I'm gay. We're not compatible because you're not a guy." Hille paused for a second and then said, "You can close your mouth now."

I closed my mouth and clenched my teeth to keep it that way.

"Say something," he said.

I wasn't sure if my legs would hold out and sat back down on the curb. "I had no idea." And I still didn't know if I believed him. I thought I read in *He's Just Not That Into You* that a guy would rather tell you he's gay than admit he doesn't like you.

Hille sat down next to me. "No one knows, Steph. I've been trying to figure out a way to tell you guys, but I didn't want you to think this was about you. It's not."

I wasn't convinced. "Then why did you sleep with me in the first place?"

"I never meant to lead you on. I'm so sorry, Steph."

"You didn't answer my question."

"I had never thought about it but when you hit on me that night in New York—"

Interrupting Hille, I rolled my eyes and muttered, "Don't remind me. Feeling kind of stupid right about now." From the look on Hille's face, he was feeling equally foolish. "Sorry. Keep going."

"I knew the Paul excuse was lame but I couldn't think of anything else," Hille continued. "But when I got home, I thought about how perfect it would be if you and I *did* get together. I already knew you, and liked you so much. I thought maybe I could really like you—in that way. I was deluding myself." Hille let out a nervous laugh. "No offense."

"None taken. Evidently, I'm an expert at deluding myself." My heart was still slamming against my chest as Hille's words reverberated in my ears. "But it didn't only happen once. And you initiated! New Year's Eve? Hoboken?"

"Yeah. I know. I knew after New York I just couldn't do it, Steph. But since we didn't see each other often, it seemed like a good way to keep everyone in the dark until I figured things out."

I couldn't believe what I was hearing. In disbelief, I asked, "So you used me to make everyone think you were straight?"

His face draining of color, Hille nodded. "I didn't think anyone would get hurt. I had no idea you liked me that much, Steph. I'm so sorry. I never meant to hurt you. I was desperate, I guess."

"So, why have you been so friendly to me this week? And don't tell me that you're always this friendly!"

Hille lowered his head and raised his shoulders, seeming to shrink his upper body in shame. "I don't know. Maybe I'm subconsciously more comfortable with you now that you have a boyfriend."

I nodded. "And you don't have to worry about me hitting on you. I see. So you didn't have a crush on me in Criminal Justice class?"

Hille pursed his lips and shook his head.

"And you weren't upset that I chose Paul?"

"Not really."

I buried my head in my hand in shame of my stupidity. Looking up, I gave him one more chance to make things right. "And you're not insanely jealous of Ryan?"

Hille finally smiled, wrinkles forming in the creases of his eyes. "Sorry, Steph."

We stopped talking momentarily to acknowledge a teenage boy who walked by with his Golden Retriever. Once the boy was out of earshot, I asked my final question. "I don't get it. You're so good in bed! How could you be so good at something you don't enjoy?"

Shrugging his shoulders, Hille said, "It's not that I don't enjoy it. Physically, it feels good. But Stephanie, I'm just not into girls. Let's put it this way, I'd rather date Brad than Angelina."

I chuckled despite myself. And then I thought about Eric's comment that Hille had never been ga-ga over a girl. It was starting to make sense. *In a really fucked up sort of way.* "So is that why you pretty much skipped over foreplay and got right to business? And never wanted to chit chat or cuddle afterwards?"

"Even straight guys can only do so much cuddling, Steph."

Not necessarily, I thought as I recalled nights spent spooning with Ryan. I twirled my hair into a knot and observed Hille. He looked miserable. Like someone stole his Blackberry, but worse.

I couldn't believe I felt sorry for a guy who pretty much used me as his "beard," but he was my friend and I felt way worse for him than I did for myself. "It's okay, Craig. I understand. It must be hard."

Nodding he said, "You have no idea. But I guess I'll have to deal with it now."

"Don't worry about me. I won't tell anyone."

Hille looked at me in surprise. "You won't?"

I shook my head. "Not my secret to tell."

"Thanks, Steph. I truly am sorry."

"I know you are."

"And Steph?"

"Yeah?"

"If I was straight, you'd be the first girl I'd want to go out with."

I playfully jabbed him in the shoulder. "I bet you say that to all the chicks."

We laughed and then walked back to the house in silence.

One fleeting thought in my head, I muttered, "I guess this means you actually did need information on my firm's IT department."

"Yeah. Why?"

"Never mind."

We found the others where we left them, watching television. Hille disappeared, probably to his room and I went to mine. I was dying to call Ryan until I remembered I had broken up with him. I returned to the living room, sat next to Paul on the couch and hoped he wouldn't ask where I had gone with Hille.

He gave me a suspicious look. "Where'd you and Hille disappear to? Sex on the beach? Did *Girls Gone Wild* get you that hot?"

"We took a walk. I needed his advice on computers. My laptop is on its last legs." As I said this, Hille walked in the room. He winked at me before sitting on the reclining chair. I gave him a closed mouth smile in return as it dawned on me that my lustful feelings for him had been replaced with more brother/sister-like emotions. I worried that it was homophobic of me to suddenly not be attracted to someone after discovering he was gay but realized that the last time I even fantasized about Hille was before my first date with Ryan so it had nothing to do with his recent admission. Relieved I wasn't a homophobe, I turned my attention to *One Life to Live*. I found it amusing how the guys were so into it and made a mental note to remind Paul the next time he made fun of my addiction to *The Hills*.

Nobody drank that night. I think we all needed a little de-tox from seven days of drinking practically non-stop. I was happy to lounge on the couch in my pajamas eating microwave popcorn. Hille cooked some frozen chicken nuggets and offered to share them with me. I figured he was trying to bribe me to keep my mouth shut. I meant what I said, though—I had no intention of outing him. But I ate some of the chicken nuggets anyway.

FIFTY

IT WAS ABOUT MIDNIGHT and we were watching *Late Night With David Letterman*. His first guest was Patricia Arquette and I guess no one was very interested because one by one, everyone excused himself to go to sleep.

When it was just Eric and me left, he said, "And then there were two."

"Yup. I'm not that tired."

"I'm beat. I'm gonna head in." He threw me the remote control. "Now you can watch whatever your little heart desires. Night, Steph." Then he leaned in and kissed me on the forehead. "You seem a bit off today. Let me know if you want to talk." Eric paused and added, "Tomorrow."

I shook my head. "I'm fine. But thanks for the offer. I stand by my statement. Your unborn baby has one heck of a daddy."

After he left, I pressed the guide button on the remote control and scrolled my list of choices. I could continue with *David Letterman* or switch to *Mama's Family*, *Law and Order SVU*, *Pimp My Ride*, *Road House* or *Saturday Night Fever*. I immediately turned on *Saturday Night Fever*. It was the part where Tony looked at himself in the mirror and chanted "Attica! Attica!" to his poster of Al Pacino. I laughed out loud but felt a dull ache in my gut. I missed Ryan. Watching TV with him was always interesting, especially reality shows. He'd get so aggravated when the characters did something stupid. I tried to explain that the shows would be boring if the characters weren't train wrecks, but it annoyed him to no end. He was adorable. My heart starting beating at a frantic rate as I realized what I'd done.

I couldn't fathom what had possessed me to do something so stupid but it was done and I had no one to blame but myself.

I'd broken up with the cutest guy in the world for a gay guy I didn't even want anymore.

Suddenly, I couldn't catch my breath. I started bawling and before I knew it, I was engaged in a full blown tantrum—the likes of which I hadn't experienced since my eighth grade home-economics teacher said I was disrespectful in class and my mom refused to take me on my semi-annual shopping spree as punishment. I threw all of the pillows off the couch, raised and lowered the volume on the TV and if there was a door in the living room, I would've definitely slammed it. I felt so helpless and wanted my mom. No, I wanted Ryan.

"Stephanie?"

I was face down on the couch with my head buried in one of the cushions but looked up to find Eric standing over me with his hands on his hips. "What the fuck, Steph?"

I sat up and hid my face with my hands. Shaking my head, I mumbled, "I'm so stupid."

Eric sat next to me and tousled my hair. "What happened? I just left you ten minutes ago—you said you were fine."

My face still covered, I said, "I thought I was. I broke up with Ryan last night and it was a huge mistake. Colossal."

"You get in a fight?"

I finally removed my hands from my face and looked at Eric. "Not exactly."

After I explained what happened, leaving out the reason Hille said we were not a good match, Eric stared at me in disbelief. "You're a piece of work, Steph," he said. "You complain all these years that you can't meet a guy you really like who likes you back, you finally meet one and you dump him for Hille? You guys have nothing in common except mutual friends. Horrible couple. You're nuts."

"I know. I've just liked him for so long. I guess I thought it meant something."

Looking at me questionably, Eric asked, "You've liked him for so long?"

I told Eric about my college crush. First he laughed and then he yelled at me for never telling him. Then he asked if I still liked Hille.

"No. I like Ryan," I said. "Seriously, if God could create the perfect guy for me, it would be Ryan. Well, from what I know about him so far. We're still in the honeymoon stage." I paused. "Correction. We *were* in the honeymoon stage." I started sobbing again.

"Stop it!" Eric yelled. "Just call Ryan and apologize."

The tears stopped. I hadn't thought of that. "Do you think he'd take me back?"

Scratching his head, Eric said, "I don't know. What you did was totally fucked up, Steph. But if you like him as much as you say..."

"I do!"

"And if he likes you as much as you like him, he might forgive you. It's worth a shot."

Excited, I went to grab my phone from the coffee table but Eric covered my hand with his. "Not now, Steph. You can't call him in the middle of the night. Wait till tomorrow."

"You sure?" I really wanted to call him now.

"I'm sure. Go to sleep and call him in the morning." He got up and started walking toward his room.

"Okay. Thanks, Eric. I love you."

"I love you too. Now stop crying and get some sleep."

I wasn't tired at all but figured the sooner I went to bed, the sooner I could wake up and call Ryan. I couldn't wait to apologize and get it over with. I wanted to see him. And hug him. And kiss him. And have sex with him. Yes, definitely that last one. I wondered why I thought sex was so great with Hille when it was amazing with Ryan. Hille wasn't even that good. I just thought he was because I was so damn into him! Ryan was so much better. Sex with Ryan reminded me of the Fleetwood Mac song *You Make Loving Fun*. I was going to start crying again. I couldn't bear another minute of him thinking I didn't like him anymore.

I looked at the clock. It was 1:47. Ryan liked to sleep late on Saturday mornings and so I didn't want to call him before 11:00. That meant I had at least nine hours and thirteen minutes before I could call him. I hoped he wasn't out late, especially if he was on a date. I had to apologize before he met someone else! Sure, the chances of him meeting someone else in the twenty-four hours since we'd broken up were slim, but what if his buddies took him out with the sole purpose of getting him laid? Oh God, what if he was fucking someone right now? Why hadn't he called me all day? Did he even care that I broke up with him? My stomach hurt. My heart hurt. Everything hurt and my breathing was labored. There was no point even trying to fall asleep. It wasn't gonna happen.

I dragged the comforter off my bed and brought it with me into the living room where I curled on the couch and turned on the television. I kept the volume low so I wouldn't wake Eric and Jess. I never understood people who liked to stay up all night watching television. There was never anything good on. I settled on an old episode of *Dallas* on Soapnet. I couldn't believe I used to love such a stupid show. And Charlene Tilton was freakishly short. I turned the TV off, flipped over on my side in the fetal position with my face towards the couch and imagined Ryan holding me. I could almost feel my smaller frame wrapped in his larger one, his hands covering mine and his breath in my ear gently lulling me to sleep.

With that image in mind, my heart slowly stopped racing, my breathing returned to normal and finally, I fell asleep.

FIFTY-ONE

I WOKE WITH A JOLT and immediately checked the time—8:11. There was no way I could wait another two hours and forty-nine minutes to call Ryan. I had to do it now. If anything, he'd appreciate my eagerness. No one seemed to be up yet, but it was about that time. Paul would probably come farting up the stairs any minute now. I took my phone outside to the front porch, like I had two days earlier. This time I skipped the vodka shot and cigarette, although the shot was tempting. With a mixture of excitement and sheer terror, I stared at Ryan's name on my phone contemplating whether to hit "send." The last time I was this nervous was the night I threw myself at Hille in New York. And I cried myself to sleep that night. This was different. I'd be fine. I'd have to suck it up for a few minutes while I apologized. But then he'd accept my apology, we'd laugh about it and I'd see him tomorrow night like originally planned. Just a few minutes of pain and then everything would be back to normal. I knew I could do it and, with that, I crossed my fingers, hit send and closed my eyes as I waited for the phone to ring and for Ryan to pick up.

I was vaguely aware I was holding my breath for the first two rings. Halfway through the third ring, I wondered if his voicemail would pick up. I couldn't hang up—he'd know I'd called. Fourth ring—maybe the initial apology over voicemail wasn't a bad thing. It could break the ice. Voicemail. I listened to him tell me he wasn't available but would call me back as soon as he could, heard the beep and took a deep breath.

"Hey Ryan, it's me, Stephanie. I know it's early and you're probably sleeping. I didn't want to wake you up or anything but I had to call you and couldn't wait any longer. I feel so incredibly stupid, Ryan. I made a huge mistake. I don't know what was going through my mind when I broke up with you but it's the last thing I want to do. When you get this, please call me, okay? I really want to talk to you and apologize. I'm still in North Carolina, leaving tomorrow but I have my cell." I glanced at the phone in my hand. "Obviously. Okay, talk to you soon. Okay...bye."

After I hung up, I stared at the phone and analyzed the message I'd left. At least I hadn't stuttered or said "um" a million times. It could've been worse, but it could've been better and I forgot to tell him that he made loving fun. I thought about calling him back but decided against it. He'd get the message when he woke up and would call me back. I just had to wait it out.

But what if his phone was broken and he never got the message? Or what if he lost his phone while he was out with his friends last night? Or what if the girl he was fucking deleted the message? I realized I was sweating and went back inside to take a shower, but then decided to wait a bit in case Ryan called. My legs were still shaking and I was afraid I'd pass out in the shower anyway.

Jess and Eric were sitting on my couch/bed.

Gesturing toward the pillow and comforter now on the floor, Eric asked, "Did you sleep here?"

"Uh, huh," I said.

"Why?"

"I couldn't fall asleep in my bed so I came out to watch television and fell asleep. What's the big deal?"

"I take it by your 'tude that you haven't spoken to Ryan yet?"

Not sure who I was trying to convince, I said, "I left him a message. He's probably sleeping, though. It's really early and he likes to sleep late on weekends—like me." I dramatically plopped myself on the other couch, stretched my feet on the coffee table and whined, "I wish he'd call me back already!"

Looking confused, Jess asked, "What's the urgency?"

I looked at Eric. "You tell her. I need some air." I stood back up and started walking toward the balcony before I realized I forgot something, did an about-face and grabbed my phone from the coffee table. As I headed outside, I pretended not to see Eric shaking his head at me.

The morning hours passed pretty quickly and when Ryan didn't call, I remained relatively calm. I even pretended to help Hille make French toast. As it approached 11, I became very anxious knowing Ryan was probably going to wake up soon and call me back. I kept my eye on my phone even as I put on my bathing suit for our last day on the beach.

I didn't want to be drunk when Ryan called so I decided not to drink any beers. And I didn't listen to my iPod because I wanted to hear the phone when it rang. And since I sat up every five seconds to make sure my phone was charged, I was pretty much guaranteed to leave the Outer Banks with an uneven tan.

I couldn't sit still. "Going to dip my feet in the water," I said. "Anyone want to come?"

Standing up, Hope said, "I'll go with you."

Denise was lying stomach down on her beach towel but flipped over and said, "Me too."

"I guess it's a girl thing. Count me in." Jess stood up and extended her hand to help me up. "Let's go chicky."

Grabbing her hand and pulling myself up, I said, "Cool." I bent down to pick up my phone but Eric took it before I had a chance.

"Leave your phone here, Steph. A watched phone doesn't ring," he insisted. "And with your luck, you'll end up dropping it in the ocean."

I was reluctant to part with my phone, but knew he was right. If I dropped the phone in the water, it would probably break and I'd never get Ryan's call. I couldn't bear that and so I threw the phone in my bag and leaned down to kiss Eric on the cheek. "Thanks."

Arms locked, Jess and I walked towards the water. "I don't know what I'd do without your husband, Jess. He's my voice of reason."

"My honey is pretty awesome, isn't he?"

"That he is. Ryan's pretty awesome too, but Eric is da-bomb!"

When we got to the edge of the water, we stopped walking. Hope and Denise had ventured out further and were riding the waves. I tried to erase the memory of riding the waves with Hille and thinking it meant he loved me.

Jess turned to me with a serious expression on her face. "Eric told me what happened with Ryan. Sorry, Steph."

I forced a smile. "It'll be fine. We'll straighten everything out once he calls me back." The smile fading, I added, "I just wish he'd call me back already. I'm losing it."

"Try not to think about it," Jess said.

"Easier said than done!"

"I know. Maybe you should drink a beer to relax." Patting her growing belly, she laughed and said, "Wish I could."

"You're right. He'll call when he calls. In the meantime, I don't want to waste my last day on the beach obsessing over it."

"That's my girl. Let's go. My feet are sufficiently cooled off now."

"Mine too."

When we returned to our chairs, I immediately went to check my phone.

Eric whispered, "It didn't ring."

Shrugging my shoulders, I said, "Oh well. No biggie." Then I grabbed a beer from the cooler and sat down. I looked over at Hille listening to his book on tape and tried not to hate him for ruining my life. It wasn't his fault and even if he wasn't gay, I still knew that breaking up with Ryan was the stupidest thing I'd ever done. Far more stupid than the time I did a lap around Fraternity Row as fast as I could, believing Paul and Eric were really timing me. When I got back to the front of the Phi Alpha house, huffing and puffing and sweating profusely, they were both smoking cigarettes and when I asked them how long it took me, they pretended not to know what I was talking about. Yes, I was the second most gullible girl at my college. I didn't know who was more gullible than me but there had to be someone.

I made a deal with myself that I wouldn't look at my phone until I finished my beer.

Beer finished, I checked my phone, threw it back in my bag and asked, "What time is it?" I could have checked the time on my phone but didn't want to look at it again so soon.

"Time to drink another beer," Paul called out.

"That too, but what time is it for real?"

Paul looked at his watch and said, "1:22."

"Thanks." I decided not to check my phone until at least 2:22. "Hand me a beer, please someone."

Two beers and three checks of my phone later, I was drunk from drinking on an empty stomach and Ryan still hadn't called. We headed back to the house to pack to go home the next morning. We had pretty much finished off the alcohol and eaten most of the food so we decided to bring in Chinese for dinner. I wasn't in the mood to eat. I also wasn't in the mood to pack. I was only in the mood to wallow in self-pity. I was losing faith that Ryan was going to call. None of the excuses I had given him had much merit anymore. Sure, he might have had soccer practice that morning but it should've been over by now. And even if it was his father's birthday, he could've taken a few minutes to call me back. And, yes, there was a .00000001% chance that he didn't get my message, but he probably had. My only hope was he was purposely making me suffer by waiting until later to call. After what I'd done, I could live with that.

I wasn't hungry but I sat with the others at the kitchen table. I grabbed the container of lo mein, poured some into my plate and started eating. When I was finished, I took some more. I wondered what Ryan was eating for dinner and if he was thinking about me. I wanted him to call me back more than anything in the whole world.

"Steph!"

I looked up from my plate to find everyone staring at me. "What?"

"Stop bogarting the lo mein," Paul said.

Confused, I said, "Huh?"

Speaking to me like I was a deaf child, Paul repeated, "Please Pass The Lo Mein."

"Oh." I picked up the container and was about to pass it down to Paul at the end of the table when I noticed it was empty. "There's nothing left."

"You ate the entire thing? I thought you weren't hungry," Paul said.

"I didn't eat it all!" I insisted.

Paul stood up. "Raise your hand if you ate any lo mein tonight?"

I raised my hand and looked around the room. No one else's hand was up. "Sorry guys. I eat when I'm nervous."

"What are you nervous about, Cohen?" Paul asked.

"Nothing."

"Then why are you eating like a fucking pig?"

"Because I feel like it. Go to hell, Paul. You've been a complete prick to me this entire week. I can't wait to get the fuck away from you tomorrow!" With that, I left the table and went outside to the balcony, slamming the sliding door behind me. I was afraid to look inside the house and knew they were talking about me. I lit one of the cigarettes Eric had left outside and took a deep drag. I promised myself when I got home, I wouldn't have another cigarette for at least a month. But I smoked when I was pissed. And I smoked when I felt out of control. And I was both pissed and out of control. Plus, smoking was less fattening than eating. Not that anyone was likely to see me naked in the near future. I heard the squeak of the sliding door, looked up and saw Paul standing in front of me.

He smiled softly. "The door could use a little WD40, huh?"

"I guess so."

"You hate me, Cohen?"

"Of course not. But you must admit you've been quite the dick to me this week."

Paul sat next to me. "That's my job! You're like my kid sister. I'm supposed to tease you. And by the way, I've been reasonably well-behaved, considering the little stunt you pulled yesterday on the beach."

"Stunt I pulled? You started it! And besides, I already have an older brother and he hasn't been that mean to me since I was about twelve. And I never slept with him."

"Thanks for confirming that piece of information. I'd always wondered about you two."

I hit Paul on the leg. "Shut up."

"What's wrong?"

"I'm in a fight with Ryan. I don't want to talk about it."

"Okay. You don't have to," Paul said.

"I think we're over."

"Why do you think that?"

"Because I'm a complete fuck-up, that's why." When Paul opened his mouth to speak, I put my hand against it and said, "I'm not in the mood for your sarcasm, Paul!"

Paul brushed my hand aside. "All I wanted to say is that couples fight. Look at me and Hope. One minute she wants to cut off my balls and the next she's..."

Laughing I said, "Massaging them?"

"And they say I'm the pervert."

"This is different. We've only been dating about two months. I don't have much goodwill in the bank."

Giving me a devilish grin, Paul said, "Do you massage them?"

Confused I asked, "Do I massage what?"

Paul responded with a knowing look and it hit me. Giggling, I said, "Yes, I do not neglect the balls!"

"There's your goodwill. My job is done." Paul stood up. "Let's go, Cohen. There's a pint of chicken chow mein with your name on it."

As I walked with Paul back in the house, I turned to him. "Ew, who ordered chicken chow mein?"

FIFTY-TWO

AFTER I FINISHED PACKING to go home, I double checked the washer and dryer to make sure none of my G-strings had accidentally gotten stuck to the side of the machines and, hoping for a distraction, returned to the living room to see what everyone else was up to.

Hille was clearing out the refrigerator. "Anyone want any leftover steak and mushrooms before I throw it out?" he asked. When no one answered, he asked, "What about salad?" and looked around. "Guess not," he said before chucking it all in the trash, plastic container and all.

Paul was collecting all the empty beer bottles and stacking them for recycling. He stood with his hands on his hips looking at the cardboard containers full of empties and muttered, "Bunch of drunks."

Wearing headphones and bopping around the kitchen singing, "*Under my umbrella. Ella, ella, eh eh eh,*" oblivious to everyone else, Denise was emptying the dishwasher and putting all of the clean dishes back in the cabinets above the stove.

And Corky was outside on the balcony, picking up the cigarette butts that had never made it into the ashtrays. I watched him take a final drag of his own cigarette, throw it on the ground and step on it, only to pick it up a second later and throw it in the garbage bag.

As I climbed up and down the stairs to bring the bags of garbage to the side of the road, it occurred to me that no one needed to be told to chip in cleaning the house—we all just took it upon ourselves to help out—and I tried to appreciate how well we all worked together as a team.

Later that night, when Eric blasted *Man in the Mirror* and we all sang along like it was the best song since *Stairway to Heaven*, I tried not to underestimate how blessed I was to have the most amazing friends in the world. And with Hope's arm around me as we swayed back and forth singing *"And no message could've been any clearer, if you want to make the world a better place, take a look at yourself and make the cha-ee-ange,"* I tried to truly believe that I, Stephanie Lynn Cohen, was one pretty lucky chick.

But all I truly believed was my life sucked and Ryan was never going to call me back.

When I closed my eyes to go to sleep that last night in the Outer Banks, I imagined asking my fairy godmother to grant me not three, but a measly single wish—that I had never broken up with Ryan. And I drafted in my mind a persuasive essay to Mr. Rourke explaining why I deserved a spot on Fantasy Island; a place where Ryan would certainly forgive me for my sin. And I thought about how great it would be if I could ask Bill and Ted to make one quick extra stop on their Excellent Adventure to forty-eight hours prior, before I had left that stupid fucking voicemail to Ryan.

In a last ditch effort, I sat up in bed and looked up to the ceiling. "Please God," I whispered, looking over at a sleeping Denise. "Please let there be a message waiting for me from Ryan when I wake up. If you let Ryan call me, I'll agree to gain five pounds I'll never lose. And I'll prematurely wrinkle. You can even give me a huge cystic pimple the day I get my period every month! Just please make Ryan call me back. Please." Then I closed my eyes and tried to sleep.

But after checking and double-checking my voicemail inbox the next morning, it was painfully clear that God was not interested in playing 'Let's Make a Deal' with me and I spent the entire ride home staring out the window and wishing I was someone else.

FIFTY-THREE

I DROPPED MY SUITCASE in the doorway of my apartment and immediately called for reinforcements. "I need you," I cried into the phone.

"What's wrong? How was your trip?"

"Not over the phone. Can I come over?"

"Of course. But I thought you had plans with Ryan your first night back."

Her words were like a dagger through the heart. "I'll be there in twenty minutes," I said before abruptly hanging up. I stared at the pile of mail I had received during the week. It could wait. I grabbed the keys I had just moments ago dropped on my coffee table and headed out. I paused briefly when I walked past my suitcase. I considered unpacking first but muttered, "Not now," walked out of my apartment and locked the door behind me.

A half hour later when we were sitting in Suzanne's living room, she said, "I told you he was gay!"

"No, you didn't!" I bit the head off of one of the sour patch kids I had scooped from Suzanne's candy bowl.

Suzanne pointed her finger at me. "Yes, when you told me he turned down your advances that first night in New York, I said he must be gay."

"I thought you were kidding and it's not really the point anyway. Ryan hates me. Do you have any more sour patch kids?"

Suzanne shook her head. "You finished them. I have sunflower seeds, though. Want some of those?"

Nodding, I said, "Yes. Thanks."

When she got up to grab the sunflower seeds from the kitchen, I followed her. Taking the bag from her hand, I asked, "Where should I put the shells?"

Handing me a customized photo mug from her trip to Key West with Luke, Suzanne said, "In here."

I glanced from the large bag of sunflower seeds to the small mug and figured I could always dump the shells in the garbage when the mug was full. I had a feeling I'd finish the entire bag. I turned the mug so the image of the smiling couple was facing away from me. "So, that's it in a nutshell. I blew it."

"I concur," Suzanne said matter-of-factly.

"Thanks for the support."

"Don't come to me if you want me to sugar coat things for you. What you did was completely self-destructive. I don't know what you were thinking."

We were back in the living room, sitting side by side on her coffee-colored leather couch. 60 Minutes was on the television, but it was muted. "I honestly thought Hille liked me. He was acting so nice, Suze. And he was so attentive to my needs. I just read him wrong, I guess."

With a furrowed brow, Suzanne asked, "But if you liked Ryan so much, why did you care how nice Hille was?"

My head hurt and I closed my eyes and pressed my fingers to my temples. "I don't know, Suzanne. It's like I lost all common sense. I swear, I don't think I had any idea what I was doing. I'd like to say I was drunk and I was, but it wasn't just that. It's almost like I had brainwashed myself to think Hille and I should be together and even though I didn't really want to break up with Ryan, I somehow truly believed I had to—like Hille and I were supposed to end up together. Even though I didn't even want him anymore." I opened my eyes and looked at Suzanne. "Does any of this make sense?"

Suzanne exhaled deeply. "If it was anyone else, I'd say absolutely not." Then she shook her and head and smiled. "But you're not like everyone else. So, yes, it sort of does make sense."

The tension in my chest loosening slightly, I exclaimed, "Thank God! I don't have the energy to try to explain it again."

Suzanne placed her hand over mine and looked me dead in the eyes. "To me, maybe. But what about to Ryan?"

Removing my hand from Suzanne's, I slid off the couch and onto her area rug, watching my fingers disappear into the black shaggy fabric. Pouting, I looked up at Suzanne. "Ryan doesn't want to hear it. He didn't call me back. Obviously he's done with me."

Standing up, Suzanne waved her finger in front of me. "That's it? You're gonna give up that easily?"

Looking up at Suzanne, I asked, "What am I supposed to do?"

Her eyes wide, Suzanne, in near-shout volume, exclaimed, "Call him again! Stephanie, you broke up with the guy to be with someone else. In a voicemail! That must have hurt. Did you seriously think it would be that easy to straighten this out? Shit, Stephanie—you called the guy once. Once. I think you owe him another attempt."

I wasn't so sure. Looking at her pleadingly, I said, "Really? I won't look pathetic?"

"No. You'll look like you actually care about the guy!" Suzanne sat down on the rug facing me. Calm again, she said, "Seriously, you screwed up big time and, honestly, if he had made it too easy, he'd be the one looking a bit pathetic. Did that ever occur to you?"

It hadn't. I hadn't even thought of what Ryan must be feeling. I was such a bad girlfriend. "You're so right. I can't stand that I made him feel second best. Fuck."

"So, you'll call him again?"

My head was still in a fog thinking about how utterly self-absorbed I'd been but I nodded, "Yeah."

"When?"

"Now." It wasn't as if the task would be easier tomorrow. "Will you sit with me? I'm scared."

Standing back up, Suzanne said, "Yes. I'll even hold your hand if you want." She offered me her hand and when I took it, led me back to her couch.

I reached into my bag for my phone, saying one last silent prayer that Ryan had beaten me to it, but he hadn't. So I wouldn't have time to get too nervous or chicken out, I found his number and called him immediately.

When the phone rang three times, I was positive he was screening but then he answered with, "What do you want, Stephanie?"

At least he hadn't deleted my number from his phone. Adopting a cheery voice and pretending I didn't note the annoyance in his, I said, "Hi! I, uh, just wanted to make sure you got my message."

"Which one would that be? Never mind, I got both."

"Ryan, I didn't mean it."

"Which one didn't you mean? The one when you broke up with me to be with another guy or the one when you changed your mind?"

Sniffling, I said, "The first one. I'm so sorry, Ryan."

There was silence on the other end and I was about to apologize again when he finally said, "I forgive you, Stephanie."

I whispered, "You do?"

"Yes. I accept your apology."

Grinning broadly, I stood up and gave the thumbs up sign to Suzanne's now smiling face. Thank God!

"But I have no desire to go out with you anymore," he said.

My heart sank, along with my body, back onto the couch. "Oh. You don't?"

"No. Listen, it's no big deal. It's not like we were serious anyway. We barely know each other. I appreciate the apology but it's just not worth it. Good luck to you."

I grabbed Suzanne's hand and squeezed it tight. "Ryan?"

"Yeah?"

I silently pleaded with him to say "Just kidding. Of course I still want you." But he didn't. "Umm, I..." *Think of something! Beg him to reconsider!* "Good luck to you too."

"Bye, Stephanie."

Before I could say my own goodbye, he hung up and, lips trembling, I looked at Suzanne's concerned face and shook my head. "It's done," I said. "He doesn't want to be with me anymore. He liked me so much and I fucked up. I wish I was dead."

"Stephanie! Don't ever say something like that. What did he say?"

"Basically he could care less. He said we weren't serious anyway. It's not a big deal. I feel so stupid." Once again, a relationship had ended before it really began. And I'd never even assigned Ryan a nickname like "soccer guy" or "the guidance counselor" or even "my young boyfriend." He was just Ryan. *Because, unlike the others, he mattered.*

I pushed away the bag of sunflower seeds. I wasn't hungry anymore. "I'm so sorry, Stephanie. I wish I had something comforting to say but this sucks."

Talking more to myself than to Suzanne, I said, "It's no big deal. It's just not worth it. That's what he said. He doesn't even care. I'd rather him hate me. He doesn't even care." I felt a rumbling in my lower stomach and bile in my throat and wanted to go home and crawl under my covers. I got up from the couch and grabbed my cardigan from Suzanne's kitchen. "Thanks for listening to me, Suze. And thanks for the food. I gotta go." I started walking toward her front door.

Following me, Suzanne tapped me on the back causing me to turn around. "Will you be okay? Luke should be home soon. We can drive you."

I shook my head. "No. I need to be alone for a while. Thanks though." Then I absently kissed her on the cheek and left.

As I walked to the Metro to get from Logan Circle back to Capitol Hill, I felt like I was at Ryan's and my funeral watching a montage of scenes from our brief but fun-filled relationship. When I first saw his goofy grin at the book store. The first time he leaned in to kiss me when I was drunk from too much tequila. His laugh when I got mustard all over my pants at the Orioles game. The look on his face right before he ejaculated. I couldn't get him out of my head. He was everywhere. I even thought I saw him in line as I walked past Subway and my heart stopped. I had seriously messed things up and the worst part was that it wasn't even because of an honest mistake. I couldn't justify my actions by saying at the time I thought I was doing the right thing because deep inside, I knew I was making a mistake. And I couldn't look at the bright side—that I'd learned something and would not make the same mistake again—because the likelihood of being in a similar situation ever again was slimmer than Kate Moss on Weight Watchers. No, absolutely nothing good came out of this mistake. And besides the fact that I felt like someone ripped out my heart, pulled my hair really hard and kicked me in the gut all at the same time, I had hurt Ryan. I visualized his face when he listened to my first voicemail and wanted to shrink to nothing. How could I have been so oblivious to his feelings? I didn't deserve Ryan, but I wanted him so badly. I wished he knew how truly horrible I felt and that I never wanted to hurt him. And I wished he knew how much I loved being with him—more than any other guy probably ever. Even more than wanting us to be back together, I wanted him to know I was sorry. Not just sorry for the ending of our relationship but for the decision leading up to it and for making him believe for one second I didn't think he was the epitome of adorable awesomeness.

And then I wondered if I was over-reacting considering we had only been dating two months. Maybe Ryan really didn't care and I was making more out of our relationship than there actually was. He'd never met my family or even any of my friends. We'd never said "I love you," we never even discussed exclusivity, although I assumed it was a given. Maybe he wasn't all that hurt by what I'd done. Maybe he really didn't care. And maybe I shouldn't either. But I did. A lot.

FIFTY-FOUR

I RESUMED MY REGULAR ROUTINE of going to the gym in the morning, working nine to ten hours during the day, coming home, microwaving dinner, watching television and going to sleep. Insert missing Ryan and beating the shit out of myself for ruining everything whenever my mind was not otherwise occupied, and that was my daily schedule. The schedule varied only once or twice a week when "coming home, microwaving dinner and watching television" was replaced with dinner and drinks with Suzanne or people from work. I didn't have much interest in socializing but was trying to fake some semblance of normalcy, mostly for my mother's sake.

It was a Monday afternoon and my mom and I were engaged in our daily afternoon phone call.

"Working late tonight?" she asked.

"Not sure yet. Too soon to tell if I need to."

"Any plans?"

"Nope. I'm tired. I can't wait to go home and watch *The Bachelor*."

"I guess you haven't heard from him?"

I didn't have to ask who she meant by "him" and I felt my insides tighten. "No mom! I don't expect to hear from him. There is no reason for him to call."

"I was just asking."

"Please don't ask that anymore. Don't you think I wish he'd call? He's not going to and you asking won't change that."

"Okay. I'm sorry. Where does he hang out? Maybe you can make a point to run into him."

"And then what? Mom, please stop," I pleaded.

"I just thought if you saw each other, you'd be able to talk face to face and maybe work things out. I'll stop, though. I hate seeing you this way, Stephanie. And I don't like the idea of you going straight home from work every day. It's not healthy."

"It's been less than two weeks, Mom. And I'm not going straight home from work every day. I'm going out with Suzanne tomorrow night."

"Good. Do you guys ever meet people when you go out? I know Suzanne's engaged but she encourages you, right?"

As if a gift from God, my other line rang before I got the chance to completely lose my patience. "Mom, I gotta go. I love you."

"I love you too," she said before hanging up.

I picked up the other line and said, "This is Stephanie."

"Hi, Stephanie. It's Adam from the New York office. We worked on the Franklin General deal together if you remember."

"Of course, I remember. How's it going?"

"It's going well. How about you?"

"I'm good," I lied. "What can I do for you?"

"I have some Security Agreements I was hoping to interoffice to you. Gerard said you could file them with the Trademark Office."

"No problem."

"Great. Thanks."

"Okay, I'll look out for the documents."

I assumed the conversation was over and was surprised when Adam asked, "So, any plans to visit the New York office soon?"

I recalled how horrible I felt when I had met Adam in New York. I had been rejected by Hille the night before and here we were talking again after I was rejected by Ryan. "Not that I know of," I said. "But if you want to put in a good word with Gerard, I'd be pleased. Wouldn't mind a change of scenery."

Adam laughed. "I don't have much clout with Gerard, but I'll see what I can do. It would be cool to see you again."

Suddenly I felt nervous as I wondered if he was flirting with me. "Thanks, Adam." I contemplated telling him I'd like to see him again, too, but couldn't do it.

"Okay, well, let me know if you have any questions about the documents."

"Will do."

"Take care and hopefully I'll see you soon."

"Yeah, that would be great." I tried to find the humor in my initial assumption that Adam was the gay one and not Hille.

After we hung up, I decided I'd tell Gerard I was dog sitting for a friend if he tried to send me to the New York office for another closing. A pug. Ryan had a pug.

FIFTY-FIVE

"**THAT GUY JUST CHECKED YOU OUT,**" Suzanne said. We were sharing a bottle of sweet German Riesling and a fruit and cheese plate at Sonoma Restaurant and Wine Bar.

I took a sip of my wine, licked the residual sugary taste from my lips and said, "Oh."

"Don't you want to see what he looks like?" Looking over my shoulder, she said, "He's cute, Steph."

Glancing around the lounge, I observed pockets of nondescript young male professionals. I turned back to Suzanne and blandly replied, "Sure. Which one?"

Suzanne rolled her eyes. "Don't sound so enthusiastic!"

Popping a dried apricot in my mouth and washing it down with a gulp of wine, I said, "I'm not enthusiastic, Suzanne. I'm not interested in dating right now. I just broke up with Ryan a couple of weeks ago. You act like I need a man to be happy."

Suzanne raised one eyebrow and asked, "Don't you?"

I topped off our glasses. "Sure. Relationships are all exciting when you're taking showers together and eating Chinese food in bed. But then you have too many beers, your imagination runs wild and poof,—you make one hasty decision and it's over." I pounded my fist on the table. "I got it! I'll start a Jewish convent for other fuck-ups like myself. We can swap designer handbags, share bottles of wine and watch *Sex and the City* on DVD all day." Confidently, I said, "It could work."

Laughing, Suzanne said, "Yes, except you'll all wish you were Carrie and could end up with your very own Big. Or you'll be so incredibly sex deprived that watching Samantha whore around will make you ridiculously jealous." Sounding more confident than me, she said, "It won't work."

Once again, Suzanne outplayed me. I placed my glass on the table and stood up. "Okay, you win. Which guy? I have to pee so I might as well give him a look-see." *Fake it till you make it.*

Suzanne grinned. "The fair skinned guy in the light blue button down and jeans. You'll pass him on the way to the bathroom. Smile at him."

"Okay, boss." I ran my fingers quickly through my hair and brushed the crumbs from the focaccia bread off my black jeans and headed past the exposed brick wall towards the bathroom. I immediately noticed the guy Suzanne had said was checking me out and he was looking at me. We made eye contact and he smiled.

I stopped short and sucked in my breath. Ryan had the same shirt. He actually owned four of them and wore one of them at least three times a week, including the last time I saw him. After I recovered, I looked away and walked as fast as I could to the ladies room where thankfully there was no line. Once in the stall, I sat on the toilet seat, not at all concerned with the long list of diseases I might catch. Then I put my head between my legs and started crying.

As we stood outside the restaurant to say our goodbyes before heading in opposite directions, Suzanne frowned. "So perhaps it's too soon for you to flirt with other guys."

"Thank you! Maybe when I stop thinking I see Ryan everywhere I go, I'll be over him. I swear I look for him in my lobby every time I come home from work, hoping he'll be waiting for me to declare his love." Sniffling, I said, "Wishful thinking, huh? And he'd probably just call anyway."

Suzanne hugged me and whispered in my ear, "I'm so sorry sweetie. But I do believe if it's meant to be, it'll be."

I held her embrace a few moments, thankful for the comfort and mumbled, "Unless it *was* meant to be and I screwed with the fates." Reluctantly separating, I said, "Anyway, I do believe in fate to a degree but free-will can get in the way and ruin everything. Damn free-will, never did me any good!"

Suzanne smoothed my hair like a mother to her child. "Have you spoken to Hille by the way? Does he know what happened?"

I looked down at my feet where someone had tossed a candy bar wrapper into the garbage and missed by a mere inch. "I'm guessing he knows we're not back together— everyone else does."

Hailing a cab, Suzanne said, "Gay or not, I don't like him. Ryan seems much warmer." Probably noting the expression on my face, she added, "Sorry," stepped into the cab and blew me a kiss goodbye.

I remembered the first time Ryan hugged me, outside of Rosa Mexicana. It wasn't one of those quick, pat you on the back and pull away hugs. He had really squeezed me tight. I blinked to hold back the tears and called out, "On that note, see you soon!"

I watched Suzanne's cab drive away and headed home. During my ten minute walk, I thought I saw Ryan at least three times.

FIFTY-SIX

I FLEXED MY MUSCLES, proudly noting hints of actual definition in my biceps. In the past week, I had developed more muscles lugging boxes from Gerard's office to the closing "war" room than I had over the last year doing three sets of bicep curls twice a week. The firm had taken over a new case and we had spent all weekend going through the files the client's previous counsel had sent over.

On the floor of Gerard's office, I stretched out my legs and tried to touch my fingertips to my toes. As I brought my hands back to my sides, I reached into the container of pork dumplings and popped one in my mouth. Extending the plastic container to Gerard's secretary, Stacey, I said, "Please take these away from me! I'm not even hungry, yet I can't seem to help myself."

Stacey, a dainty girl just short of five feet and probably less than 100 pounds, shook her honey-blonde bob and patted her stomach. "No more for me either. It's almost bathing suit season."

Getting up to throw the half-full container in the garbage, I said, "I think you can afford it."

"I think we both can, actually," Stacey said.

"Whatever. Let's farm it off on the others. Maybe it will make the news that it's gonna be another long night go down easier."

I began making my move to the closing room where three other junior paralegals were busy organizing documents when I saw Gerard walking towards me. Like us, he had spent all weekend in the office and I had a new respect for him as a real team player.

"Hey, Stephanie. I've been looking for you."

"Is everything okay?" I had been working so hard all week to make the transition of responsibility as smooth as possible. Long hours had other advantages as well. By the time I got home and in bed, I fell asleep before my mind had a chance to conjure up images of Ryan's blue eyes and miss the way he used to look at me when he thought I wasn't watching.

Gerard smiled. "Everything's fine. I have some good news for you."

"For me?" My first thought was Ryan was waiting for me in the lobby, but I quickly dismissed the possibility when I remembered that not everyone's world revolved around my love life. Gerard didn't even know I'd been dating someone.

I followed Gerard back to his office and after he asked Stacey to give us a minute, I sat in his guest chair. Even though he said it was "good" news, I had nervous knots in my stomach. And the exorbitant amounts of Chinese food I had devoured earlier probably didn't help.

Gerard took a sip of his canned iced tea and leaned back in his chair. "It's been a rough week, huh?"

I nodded. "Definitely. But taking over a big case like this is good for the firm."

"I've been thinking about your ideas," Gerard said.

I nodded, hoping he'd clarify since I had no idea to what ideas he was referring.

Gerard grinned at me. "You have no idea what I'm talking about, do you?"

Busted, I shook my head. "Not a clue."

"You came into my office about six months ago with a list of ideas on how to keep your job fresh and I've been thinking about how well things have worked out."

I most certainly remembered the list of ideas I had concocted. When I reflected on my business trip to New York City and the chain of events that followed, "successful" was not how I would describe the outcome. "I'm glad you think so."

"I'd like to reward you for your hard work, Stephanie."

Wait. What? "Really?" I sat up straighter in my chair.

"You're already a Senior Paralegal and I obviously can't promote you to lawyer."

"Obviously," I said, laughing.

Gerard took another sip of iced tea, leaned forward and placed his elbows on the desk. "Your leadership this week has not gone unnoticed.

You've demonstrated sharp delegation skills. The junior paralegals really listen to you."

I felt my face turn red. "I'm so glad."

"I'd like to see you continue in this direction. Being a point person for the other paralegals and directing cases. And if all goes well, although there are no guarantees, we can discuss a promotion to Paralegal Director at your next official review."

"Oh, my God. I'm so flattered that you'd consider me for a role like that." Paralegal Director had a nice ring to it. It sounded way more important than Senior Paralegal which just made me feel well, old, as in senior citizen. *Spinster senior citizen.*

Gerard smiled brighter. "And, of course, a promotion comes with a raise. In this market, the raise won't change your lifestyle but I think you'll be pleased."

I returned Gerard's sunny expression. "I'm sure I will be. Thanks so much, Gerard. I won't disappoint you."

Standing up, Gerard said, "I'm sure you won't, Stephanie. Keep up the good work."

I stood up too and shook Gerard's hand. "Thanks again." As I left his office smiling, I couldn't shake the realization that it was the first time I'd been genuinely happy since before I'd broken up with Ryan. And the first time in as long as I remembered that my happiness was not dependent on a guy but in my own hands.

FIFTY-SEVEN

ON MY WAY HOME THAT NIGHT, I called Suzanne to share the good news.

"I'm so happy for you, sweetie. You deserve it," Suzanne said.

"I guess," I said. "I really have worked hard but I wish it was because I was genuinely passionate about the work and not because I was trying to escape my own misery."

"Enough with the self-inflicted Jewish guilt, Steph. Your motivations aside, you worked hard and you deserve it. Enjoy it."

"I will. It's not a certainty, though. I have to prove myself over the next few months, but hopefully it will all work out. And it's not like I'm being promoted to partner or anything. It's just Paralegal Director."

"The self-deprecation is boring, Stephanie." I could almost feel Suzanne rolling her eyes through the phone.

"You're right. It's definitely a step in the right direction and I *do* deserve it."

"That's my girl!"

"I can't wait to tell my mom!"

"Okay. I'll let you go. Drinks this week on me to celebrate, okay?"

"Drinks this week for sure. And we have to plan someone's bachelorette party, too."

"True that. Do you think we're too old to drink from those penis straws? I saw them the other day at Spencers."

"We're never too old to drink from penis straws!"

"Cool. Bye sweetie. Talk soon."

I was about to hang up when I thought better of it. "And Suzanne? I'm sorry for monopolizing all of our conversations with my relationship drama. Let's make the next year all about you, okay?"

"No need to apologize. I'm constantly on your back about dating. That being said, you've got yourself a deal—all about me for the next year. And I'll hold you to it!"

"Please do! I love you, Suze."

"Love you too, Steph."

When I got home, I decided it was too late to call my mom and so, after washing my face and brushing my teeth, I watched an episode of *Man Vs. Food* on The Travel Channel. I fell asleep before finding out if Adam Richman finished the twelve-pound hamburger.

* * *

Right on schedule, my phone rang at exactly 3:30 the next afternoon. I answered the phone cheerily, "Hi Mom! How was your weekend?" Admittedly, I was more interested in telling her my good news.

"It was nice. Al and I saw a play at the Helen Hayes Theater on Saturday night. How was yours?"

"I worked all weekend."

"Again? You must be exhausted."

"Not really." I'd actually made it to the gym that morning for an early run.

"Sam and Amy invited us over next Sunday for a barbeque. You coming?"

"I don't know. Mom, I have some good news."

"You heard from Ryan?"

The excitement in her voice caused my spirits to temporarily plummet, but I shrugged it off. "No, Mom. But I'm up for a promotion at work!"

"That's great, Stephanie. What kind of promotion?"

I explained the position to my mother, careful to remind her that it was dependent on my continued hard work.

"Well, I hope the long hours don't get in the way of you getting out there and dating."

"I actually think it will be a good change for me. I'm trying not to focus so much on dating." In response to the silence on the other end of the phone, I said, "They always say it happens when you're not looking."

My mom laughed. "That's a load of bull, Stephanie. You can't sit at home and expect Mr. Right to knock on your door."

"Maybe I'm not looking for Mr. Right. Or maybe I found him and blew it."

"It wasn't meant to be, Stephanie. Maybe Hille will finally open his eyes."

"Hille's gay, remember?" I felt a lump in my throat. "Can't you be happy for me?"

"Happy that your heart is broken? Of course not."

"Happy that I'm getting a promotion, Mom!"

Calmly, my mom said, "Of course I'm happy for you."

"I worked really hard for this and you don't even care." I realized I was raising my voice, put the phone on speaker and closed my door.

"Of course I care. What are you talking about?"

"All you care about is my love life. And your constant reminders that I don't have one don't help. There is more to my life than dating." There was more silence. "I'm busy at work. Talk to you later." I hung up the phone and headed to the 4:00 staff meeting. I was fifteen minutes early so I sat alone in the conference room and closed my eyes.

When I got back to my office forty-five minutes later, there was a red light on my phone. I figured it was my mom yelling at me for hanging up on her and reluctantly listened to the message. It *was* my mother, but she didn't yell; she just asked me to call her back when I got a chance.

I felt my heart pounding as I dialed her number. I felt guilty for hanging up on her but couldn't bear to listen to her carry on about Ryan and Hille and "getting out there" anymore. "Hi, Mom."

"So you finally decided to call me back."

"I was in a meeting, Mom. I just got your message now."

"I wanted to apologize to you." Her voice sounded shaky.

My heart continued to beat rapidly. "For what?"

I heard her exhale into the phone. "I don't know. For being a Jewish mother, I guess."

"You forgot the word 'overbearing' between 'Jewish' and 'mother.'"

"You know I love you, right?"

"Of course, but..." My mom's love for me was never in doubt.

"But what, honey?"

I hesitated, searching for the right words. I knew they'd never come. Or at least not until later that night when I was alone in my apartment re-playing the conversation to myself. "Sometimes I think you'd be happier if I was more like Sam. You know, married with child."

"I *would* be happier, Stephanie. But only because I want you to find someone who loves and adores you the way you deserve to be loved and adored."

"I want that too, Mom. But wanting something doesn't make it so. It is what it is and your constant reminders just make me feel worse."

"I'm sorry, Stephanie."

"Ryan made me happy."

"I know dear."

"But the entire time we were dating, I felt like you compared him to Hille. 'Hille's so smart,' 'Hille makes good money.' Ryan's financially secure, too. And he's extremely intelligent—about stuff that really matters. Half the stuff Hille knows about is meaningless in the real world. Who cares that the first immigrant to Ellis Island was a fourteen-year-old Irish girl? And you wonder why I never want to tell you anything about my love life!"

"Oh, Stephanie. I'm terribly sorry." She sighed. "I'm afraid your mother isn't always the sharpest tack."

The sincerity in her voice urged me to continue. "I wish you were proud of me the way you are of Sam."

"Of course, I'm proud of you! I couldn't be prouder." This time, it was my mother who raised her voice and I glanced over at my office door, confirming that it was still closed.

"Even though I'm still single and apparently a failure at love?"

My mom laughed. "Yes. And you're not a failure at love. Your time will come." Before I had a chance to respond, she said, "But if it doesn't, I won't love you any less."

"But my time will come!" I was hopeless. I had expended all that energy insisting that my happiness did not revolve around my love life and yet the thought of being alone forever felt like a death sentence.

"Yes, it will. I'm certain of it."

"Are you really?" I knew the answer but I wanted to hear it again.

"I'm positive. But remember, the most important relationship is the one you have with yourself. I guess I failed to teach you that, huh?"

She most certainly had, but I was too old to blame my mistakes on my mother. I had broken up with Ryan of my own free will. "Not at all, Mom. I love you."

"I love you, too. And I'm proud to be your mother. Please believe me."

As I insisted I believed her, it felt good to know I was actually speaking the truth.

I treated myself to dinner that night. Sushi was expensive, but as I sat at the bar at my favorite restaurant with my three favorite rolls in front of me, I thought of the raise I had coming to me at the end of the year and felt no guilt. And I found a bright side to my experience with Ryan. I was capable of truly falling for someone who liked me just as I was and while it was too late to make things right with Ryan, someday I'd find someone else. And when I did, I'd be ready to take the next step. Until that happened, I wanted to embrace life and do the things that made me happy. I'd seen a sign-up sheet at the gym for a runner's group. Maybe I'd train for a half-marathon. Or maybe I would take a cooking class and learn to make something besides grilled cheese. And when Jess and Eric had the baby, I'd be the best pseudo aunt ever.

FIFTY-EIGHT

I WAS ON MY COUCH contemplating my next move. My apartment needed cleaning but I wasn't motivated.

I had three loads of dirty laundry but it was Saturday and I hated wasting my weekends doing laundry. And I knew the laundry room would be packed since everyone did laundry on Saturday and Sunday afternoons. I'd just stress out over whether there would be enough dryers.

I considered using the time to create a profile on Facebook. Suzanne was on my case about it, but I couldn't bring myself to reconnect with people from high school and would probably spend too much time stalking Ryan's friend list wondering if he was dating any of the pretty girls. I was feeling better about things but it was all about baby steps.

When my phone rang, I jumped off of the couch, psyched to have something to occupy my time. It was Paul. I hadn't spoken to him since we left the beach. "Hey, there," I said. I placed the phone in the crook of my neck so I could examine the ends of my hair at the same time. I needed a haircut.

"Wassup Cohen?"

"Not much. Bored. You?"

"Ditto. Just checking in. Thought you'd be interested to know that the *Brady Bunch True Hollywood Story* is on E. And I only know this because Hope told me."

My neck hurt so I stopped playing with my hair and held the phone to my ear. "Sure. I know you're a closet Brady fan. Admit it."

"Nah. Although Marcia was pretty hot in the movie. And those rumors of Cindy being a porn star are pretty intriguing. Her lisp has an entirely different effect on me now."

"You're disgusting."

"Yes I am. Here's Hope"

"Nice talking to you," I said to the air.

"Hey, Steph. How are you?"

"I'm good."

Sounding doubtful, Hope said, "Really?"

"I'm getting there."

"It'll get easier. I'm making Paul watch The Brady Bunch thing. *The Partridge Family* is next but somehow, I'm not as interested."

"I agree. Danny Bonaduce's drug problems are so last century. Are you at Paul's or is he with you?"

"He's here. We're going to Jess and Eric's for dinner tonight."

I felt a pang of jealousy. "I wish I lived closer."

"Me too. Okay, Paul is hitting me with the remote control. I gotta go."

I heard, "Bye, Cohen," in the background and said, "Bye, Paul," in response. "Thanks for the heads up about the Brady Bunch special, Hope. I've been trying to figure out what to do with my afternoon and can't think of anything better than spending it with the Bradys."

"Glad I could help. Love you."

"Love you too."

After we hung up, I turned on the E channel. The special was almost half over but I'd already seen it twice so I wasn't that upset about it. I grabbed a bottle of water and some pretzels and on my way back from the kitchen, noticed *Here's The Story—Surviving Marcia Brady* exactly where I left it the day I met Ryan, on my bookshelf between *The Devil Wear's Prada* and *Confessions of a Shopaholic*. I had forgotten all about it.

I put the water and pretzels on the coffee table and returned to my bookshelf. I removed Marcia's book and flipped to the back cover. There was a picture of the entire Brady family and it was definitely taken during one of the later seasons because all of the guys, except Bobby, had perms and Carol had a mullet. I couldn't help but giggle. Still standing, I turned to the front cover and sucked in my breath. There was a handwritten note and it was from Ryan. I quickly slammed the book closed. My knees a little wobbly, I walked over to my couch, took a deep breath, opened the book again and read Ryan's note.

Dear Marcia,

Thanks for introducing me to Stephanie. She's pretty swell and I'm so glad something didn't suddenly come up before our fourth date. It was a good one. I promise not to play ball in the house.

Ryan

I started cracking up. Then I read it again. And again.

Our fourth date. That was when we first slept together. He must have written it when I wasn't looking. He totally cracked me up. I felt my throat tighten and willed myself not to cry. I turned off the E channel and switched to the Yes network. The Yankees were playing the Orioles. My team against Ryan's. I wondered if he was watching the game, too and thinking the same thing. I hoped his team would win. I sighed and fell asleep with the book in my arms.

FIFTY-NINE

I WAS SICK OF BEING COOPED UP in my apartment, so the next day I grabbed my Marcia Brady book and walked to Cosi for lunch. While in line, I nibbled on a piece of their yummy bread I had taken from the large bowl of samples. I wanted more than one piece but since I was ordering a tomato, basil and mozzarella sandwich, I figured I could live without the extra bread. As the line moved and I was forced to walk farther away from the bread bowl, I changed my mind, reached behind me and took another sample.

The guy behind the counter, wearing a white apron and black cap with the words Cosi written in stylized white lettering, asked, "What can I get you?"

I swallowed the bread and answered, "The TBM please. And a medium coffee with room. Thanks." I looked around, wondering if I knew anyone. It amused me how put together some people looked on a Sunday afternoon. I was wearing khaki cargo pants from the Gap, a black tank top and Old Navy flip flops. The humidity was surprisingly low for early July and my hair was down. I took my sandwich and coffee from the barista and headed to a table at the back of the restaurant, my book in the enormous gray Cole Haan pocketbook I had treated myself to as a consolation prize for losing Ryan.

I was comfortable being alone but self-conscious at the same time. I loved people watching, but hated the idea of others watching me, especially when I ate. Eating a sandwich was especially challenging because I tended to get excess mustard or mayonnaise all over my face without my knowledge. There were no condiments on my sandwich that day and, after a few bites, my self-consciousness eased and I got lost in the book.

I finished the prologue and was about to start reading the first chapter when I realized my pocketbook was laying on the floor. My mother would kill me if she knew I'd carelessly left my new $345 bag sitting on the dirty floor of a public eatery, so I got up, picked the bag off of the floor and took the opportunity to throw my empty coffee cup in the garbage. When I returned to my seat, I placed the strap of my pocketbook on the back of the chair and was about to sit down when I heard a large crash right behind me. I jumped up in shock and turned around. My chair had toppled over from the weight of the bag and by the grace of God, it didn't happen when I was sitting down.

Since I was so accustomed to making an ass out of myself in public by wiping out or colliding with another person, I was relatively unfazed. But to minimize any embarrassment others in the restaurant might feel for me, I shrugged my shoulders, laughed and said, "Oops." Then I returned the chair to the upright position and casually looked around. A few people were looking at me but I hadn't caused that big of a scene. Relieved, I went to sit back down and out of the corner of my eye, saw another Ryan look-alike at a table toward the front of the restaurant, facing my direction. I was getting so sick of seeing him everywhere I went and so I muttered, "Get a grip, Stephanie. It's not Ryan. It's your imagination," and sat down.

As I tried to concentrate on the book, I couldn't help but wonder if fake Ryan was still looking at me. The words on the page eluded me and after reading the same ones over and over again with the reading comprehension skills of a preschooler, I folded the page I was on, closed the book and turned my gaze towards the front of the restaurant.

Fake Ryan was still looking right at me and if I was not mistaken, he had a half smile, half smirk on his face. I squinted my eyes to see him better. I continued to stare at him and him at me until it suddenly got very hot in the room and I realized that fake Ryan wasn't fake at all. I was looking directly at the real Ryan—my Ryan.

SIXTY

I WAS STANDING IN FRONT OF HIS TABLE with no recollection of walking there from mine. I felt a bit dizzy and rested my hand on the table for support. Also on the table was a black plastic plate with the remnants of whatever sandwich, probably turkey, Ryan had eaten and a water bottle. My face felt warm and I knew if my mom placed her lips against my forehead, she'd let me stay home from school. I swallowed hard. "Hi."

Ryan nodded his head. "Hi, Stephanie."

I didn't know where to start. "Small world, huh?" That's as good a place as any.

Ryan answered flatly, "Yup."

He was so damn cute it was painful to look at him, even more painful since his eyes didn't light up when he saw me like they used to. "How've you been?"

"I've been okay."

He was just looking at me, expressionless. It was so awkward and I sort of wanted to run away, but I also wanted to keep talking to him forever. "I'm glad you've been okay, Ryan. Not that you asked and, I guess I shouldn't expect you to, but I'm not okay."

Sounding bored, Ryan asked, "No? Why's that?"

I shrugged as if I didn't know the answer.

Ryan raised his eyebrows like he was waiting for me to either speak or walk away.

"Ryan, I'm sorry. I don't know why I'm bothering because you have every right to hate me but I want you to know. I need you to know."

"Know what?"

"The truth," I said.

"Which is?"

Feeling my legs spasm, I intensified my grip on the table and confided, "That breaking up with you was the dumbest thing I've ever done."

When Ryan continued to look at me with a blank expression, I kept going. I felt the words leave my mouth but couldn't hear them, like I did back in school whenever I had to give an oral presentation to the class. "You're probably wondering why I broke up with you if I didn't want to and seriously, I wish I had an answer that would make sense to you and if you had a few hours, I could try. But the bottom line is you're the only guy I want to be with. I miss you so much. And before you yell at me, if you care enough to bother, let me tell you that I've been kicking my own ass constantly." I stopped, took a deep breath and tried to gauge what Ryan was thinking but he was still sporting that damn poker face.

I was getting tired of standing, but didn't dare ask him if I could sit down. "I don't blame you for breaking up with me..."

Ryan interrupted me by raising his hand in the air. "Correction. You broke up with me. I just wouldn't let you retract the decision."

I felt my face turn a more purple shade of red. "I stand corrected."

"Keep going."

"Where was I? Um, oh yeah. I don't blame you for breaking up, I mean not taking me back. Why would you want to? But even if I never see you again, I want you to know how truly remorseful I am that I hurt you, although maybe you didn't really care that much. But, assuming you did care, I want you to know it kills me that I might have made you feel second best when basically I can't believe how lucky I was to have met you. You're perfect for me. And I fucked it up. I know that. Trust me, I know that. But if it makes you feel any better, I'm miserable, Ryan. I'm miserable and I'm a mess and I seriously think you've ruined me for other guys forever. No one will ever be as great as you. Two months we were together, Ryan. But it was the most fun two months I've ever spent with a guy in my life and I think I love you." I couldn't look at him when I said that last part but after I finished speaking, I stopped looking at the dirty floor and faced him. He was still looking at me with a fixed expression and I knew I couldn't hold back the tears for much longer. "Okay, that's all I wanted to say. Thanks for listening. I'll leave you now. Oh, and happy almost-birthday."

I started walking toward the exit but remembered my pocketbook was still at my table. I mumbled, "Fuck," did an about-face and sprinted towards the back of the restaurant. I had tunnel vision and didn't look to see if Ryan was watching me.

God had done me at least one favor that afternoon in that no one had stolen my designer bag while I was pouring out my soul to Ryan. It was still where I had left it, hanging off the edge of the chair. I grabbed it by the strap and did a quick 180, desperate to get as far away as possible from Ryan. I had barely put one foot in front of the other when I, once again, heard a large crash because, once again, I knocked over the fucking chair. I didn't think my day could possibly get worse but at that point nothing would've surprised me. I quickly picked up the chair and ran out of the restaurant, this time not bothering to see if anyone, including Ryan, had witnessed the scene.

SIXTY-ONE

WHEN I GOT OUTSIDE, I ran as fast as I could to the end of the block and stopped to catch my breath and contemplate what had just happened. I was surprisingly calm. My life still sucked but at least I had the opportunity to tell Ryan how I felt. I wouldn't have to wonder if things would have been different if I'd had the chance to explain myself. I'd still wonder what our life would have been like if I hadn't broken up with him—whether we'd stay together, get married and procreate—but I'd apologized and even told him I loved him, something I hadn't even realized until the moment the words came out of my mouth. I wished I'd realized it before it was too late but my life was a collection of Monday morning quarterback moments and hindsight really was 20/20. I shrugged my shoulders and muttered, "Life's a bitch and then you die."

I decided the tears would have to wait until I got home and I began the walk back to my apartment. I sat on a bench in Stanton Park and watched a couple tossing a frisbee. They looked almost like Ryan and me except Ryan was way cuter than the guy and the girl was probably smart enough to actually appreciate her boyfriend. I thought back to playing catch with Ryan and making out with him in the grass afterwards. I never once worried he would shoo away my kisses but it hadn't occurred to me until now. So much for holding back the tears. I got up from the park bench and walked the rest of the way home.

I was across the street from my building when my phone rang. There was no way I could hold a conversation and so I ignored it. Whoever it was would have to leave me a message. But as I approached my lobby, I heard the signal that I had a text message. Wishing whoever it was would leave me the hell alone, I removed the phone from my bag, prepared to throw it in the closest garbage. I had no desire to engage in text message ping-pong but curiosity got the best of me and I needed to know who exactly had the poor timing to text me in my moment of despair.

It was Ryan. My legs started shaking immediately and I felt lightheaded. Scared I might faint, I walked back outside, sat down on one of the concrete steps outside of my building and stared at my phone. What did he want? What if he wanted to yell at me? I thought about deleting the text without reading it, but I couldn't do it. He gave me the chance to explain myself and I figured he deserved the opportunity to let me have it if he so desired. But I couldn't bear to be yelled at right now. I was still too raw. I made the decision to wait until I was in a better state of mind. Then I clicked "open" on the message.

It said, "I have one more question for you."

One more question for me? What the hell did that mean? I remained fixated on the message until I felt someone standing over me, blocking the sun. But less than a second later, the shadow had passed and out of the corner of my eyes, I could see that someone was sitting next to me. When I looked up, Ryan was perched on the step within kissing distance, his blue eyes peering directly into my hazel ones.

I couldn't believe he was there. How was it possible to be both totally psyched to see someone and scared shitless at the same time? I was still shaking and aware that he knew it, but I couldn't stop. I opened my mouth, wondering if I still had the ability to speak and whispered, "You wanted to ask me something?"

Looking at me intently, he said, "It's a very serious question."

I wanted to kiss him so badly it hurt. "Ask away."

"Which blonde?"

I opened my mouth to answer before registering the question and then realized I had no idea what he was talking about. "What?"

Ryan's lips curled up slightly. "You never did tell me which blonde on *Three's Company* was your favorite."

I wondered if this was his idea of closure. "Chrissy." I tried not to look at his lips and asked, "What about you?"

"I prefer brunettes, actually."

"Janet? Really?"

Ryan shook his head and smiled.

As I pondered how he could possibly smile at a time like this, I asked, "Who then?"

"I like brunettes with *long* hair."

His proximity to me was overwhelming and, wracking my brain for another brunette on the show, I stood up. "Greedy Gretchen?"

He smiled again—this time a full-on grin that reached his eyes—stood up too and said, "No, Stephanie. No one on the show. Do you know of any other long-haired brunettes?"

The light bulb turned on. "*I'm* a brunette with long hair."

Inching closer to me, Ryan said, "Exactly."

I braved to say out loud the question dangling on the tip of my tongue, although I wasn't sure he'd hear it over the sound of my beating heart. "Does that mean you like me?"

Ryan paused and shook his head. I stared at him as he examined my face like he'd been blind until that very moment. Finally, he said, "It actually means I kind of love you."

I had cotton mouth but somehow managed to produce saliva, swallowed it and said, "You do?"

Ryan nodded his answer.

I remembered how psyched I was when he told me over the phone that he forgave me, but seconds later he said he didn't want to go out with me anymore. I refused to jump the gun again this time. Crossing my fingers behind my back, I asked, "And you want to be with me again?"

"Yes."

"Really?"

"Yes, Stephanie. Really."

"You're sure?"

Still smiling, he said, "I'm positive, Stephanie. You really pissed me off but, what can say, I'm a sucker for girls who knock over chairs, I guess."

I finally smiled back—wider than I did when Gerard told me about the promotion—the kind of smile that couldn't be contained. Then I shouted, "Yippee!"

Ryan shook his head and laughed at me.

Beaming shamelessly, I jumped into his arms and wrapped my legs around his waist, almost knocking us both over. Then I kissed him hard on the lips and whispered in his ear, "I love you, too."

My feet back on the ground, but still holding him tight and inhaling his scent, I sang, "*And if I can't have you, I don't want nobody, baby.*"

EPILOGUE

I TOOK A SIP OF MY CHAMPAGNE PUNCH and observed Ryan and Paul sitting on Jess and Eric's living room floor putting together the train set Eric's aunt and uncle had bought for Aidan. From the cackles of laughter, I could tell they were having a little too much fun playing and I hoped the train set would still be functioning by the time Aidan could actually use it.—he wasn't even born yet and the package said it was appropriate for ages three and up.

"Hey, Stephanie."

I turned my attention away from Ryan and Paul and looked at Hille, who was now at my side, along with a built guy with shaggy blonde hair and a bronzed complexion. I reached over and gave Hille a kiss. "Hey, Craig! Good to see you!"

Hille smiled widely. "Good to see you, too!" Gesturing to his friend, he said, "This is Thomas."

Deciding that Thomas looked like a human version of the cartoon character Fred Jones from Scooby Doo, I said, "Hi there. So nice to meet you."

"Same here. Craig's told me so much about you, I feel like I know you already." Thomas smiled shyly, making me question what exactly about me was discussed.

I grinned at Hille. "Not sure if that's a good thing or not!"

Hille smiled warmly. "It's all good, kid."

"Okay, I need a refill on my beer," Thomas said. "Either of you need anything?" He looked from me to Hille and when both of us shook our heads, he walked away, leaving us alone.

Hille took a sip of his beer. "So, how's it going, Steph?"

I looked over at Ryan, who caught my eye and winked. "Very well. Life's good, Craig. What about you?"

"Life's good on my end, too." Hille looked over at Ryan and Paul and turned back to me with a smile. "I'm so happy you and Ryan worked things out. I felt incredibly guilty for my part in your breakup."

"We've actually made it past the three and a half month itch. I guess we're in the big leagues now!" I giggled. "Anyway, it wasn't your fault at all, Craig. It was mine. And honestly, I think everything happened for a reason." I raised my shoulders in a shrug and turning my palms upward said, "Who knows? If I hadn't made a fool of myself with you, I might not have realized how much I cared for Ryan."

Hille patted me on the shoulder. "You didn't make a fool of yourself, Steph."

I looked at him doubtfully. "You're too kind."

He laughed. "Seriously. But, I agree, everything does happen for a reason. It's funny, just a few months ago I would have insisted there was no such thing as fate but I'm not so sure anymore. If it wasn't for you, who knows when I would've come out? I should probably thank you for making a fool of yourself over me."

Giggling, I said, "I'm glad I could be of assistance." I vaguely remembered the weeks spent crying over my enormous lapse in judgment but now it seemed like a lifetime ago—someone else's lifetime, in fact.

When Thomas returned with his bottle of beer in hand, I took the opportunity to excuse myself. I walked over to Ryan who was now chatting with Jess and Hope's dad.

"Okay, so we didn't have a great season. But the Orioles are going all the way in 2010," he said to a skeptical Mr. McElroy.

I put my arm around Ryan. "In your dreams, sweetie." I turned to Mr. McElroy. "My boyfriend is too loyal for his own good, John."

"Loyalty is a virtuous quality," John said.

After Mr. McElroy walked away, I looked at Ryan and actually felt my heart expand to make room for the feelings I had for him, which seemed to grow with each moment we spent together. "He's right, you know," I said.

Ryan put his hands on my waist. "Right about what?"

"Loyalty is a virtuous quality— in baseball fans and in boyfriends."
Ryan looked at me thoughtfully. "You can't give up on something just because it doesn't always perform the way you want it to. Sometimes even the best pitchers give up too many hits. Doesn't mean I'm gonna switch teams." He smiled. "And just because my sexy girlfriend sometimes breaks up with me for gay dudes doesn't mean I should give up on her either."

I hugged him and said, "I only did that once, Ryan."

"Uh, yeah. And once was enough," Ryan said squeezing me tight.

"Ya think? Cuz Thomas is awfully cute."

Ryan raised his eyebrows.

"Kidding! You're way cuter—no contest."

A few minutes later, Eric announced he wanted to make a toast. "I'll just be a few minutes, folks," he said. Directing his attention to Paul, he added, "And I promise to bring out the karaoke machine when I'm done."

After everyone gathered around, Eric continued. "I want to thank everyone for being here at our unisex baby shower. It wouldn't be a celebration without your drunk, I mean, smiling faces. I'd like to start out by expressing my love for my beautiful wife, Jess. Come here, honey." Eric paused until Jess made her way through the crowd to his side. He took her hand and resumed speaking. "The first time I saw you, when I was bartending and you ordered a slow gin fizz, I decided you were the most beautiful girl I'd ever seen and I vowed to make you my wife."

Wiping away tears, Jess laughed and said, "Really now?"

Eric chuckled. "Okay, so maybe I wasn't thinking that far ahead, but it wasn't long before I was convinced you were the one. And standing here today, carrying our child, you've never been more beautiful to me." After he bent down to kiss her, he turned his attention to the crowd. "Both Jess and I are well aware that the blessed arrival of our son Aidan wouldn't be nearly as blessed without our friends and family. I'm the luckiest man in the world to have Jess as my wife and the mother of my child but even luckier to have such amazing friends to share in our happiness. Anyone who says you can't have it all doesn't know shit! So, please raise your glasses. To having it all!"

We all repeated, "To having it all" and took a sip of our drinks.

After Eric finished his toast, I glanced around the room. Among the friends and relatives of Jess and Eric, I observed the smiling faces of the people who made up my world: Paul, my first boyfriend who was now like a brother to me—sibling rivalry and all; Hope, the little sister I never had who managed to make love out of a drunken hook-up with Paul; Corky, who initially frightened me but later proved to be about as scary as a newborn puppy; Jess, the only woman I could ever deem worthy of Eric; Eric, my best friend, voice of reason, hero and father figure rolled into one; even Hille—the guy I thought was the man of my dreams but wasn't. And finally Ryan, the real man of my dreams—my adorable boyfriend Ryan who I was convinced was created by God just for me. Ryan, who had immediately taken to my friends like I knew he would. Ryan, who was currently looking at me like he couldn't wait to go home and do The Hustle, our new code word for getting it on.

Eric was right. It *was* possible to have it all.

THE END

PREVIEW OF
BLOGGER GIRL
BY MEREDITH SCHORR

CHAPTER 1

I SLID MY MOUSE back and forth between 4 and 4.5 pink champagne flutes. I couldn't decide if the book, *Gladly Never After*, was 4.5 flutes worthy. The ending was a bit abrupt and the hero was kind of obvious from the beginning. At the same time, it was certainly an engaging story, so much so that I took every available opportunity to turn on my Kindle to see what happened next, even while squatting on the toilet between beers at happy hour.

"Long!"

I saved a draft of my review and stood up. "Yes, Rob?" I walked into his large fish-bowl shaped office knowing he wasn't going to come to me. "What's up?"

Rob handed me two sheets of paper. "Can you scan this to Bartlett?"

Removing the papers from his hand, I said, "No problem. Should I include a message?"

He scratched his thick head of brown hair. "Nah. He'll know what it is."

Rob's recent takeover of a high-profile litigation was definitely getting in the way of my blogging. I had four books scheduled for review in the next two weeks and had received several more on my Kindle from publishers and authors in the past couple of days. Then again, it was my day job as a legal secretary at a mid-sized New York City law firm that paid my $1800 rent, not my voluntary – albeit immensely more satisfying – side gig as a chick lit book reviewer/blogger.

"Also, send an email to the team about squad drinks around the corner at Banc Café at 5."

My heart skipped a beat. "Who should I include in the email?"

Rob was now facing his computer and without bothering to turn around, he said, "The whole team, Lucy, David, Nicholas, Blah, Blah, Blah, Blah."

Rob probably didn't actually say, "Blah, Blah, Blah, Blah" but that was all I heard after "Nicholas." Ordinarily, I preferred the company of friends over the partners, associates and paralegals that made up Rob's team, but I'd make an exception if Nicholas was going to be there. I took stock of my outfit, exhaling a sigh of relief that I was wearing a flattering low cut black top and form-fitting black skinny pants. I fingered my necklace, a platinum chain with an opal pendant that conveniently fell right in the line of my cleavage. "Sounds good. Uh, I forgot who else you mentioned after Nicholas." *Not that it matters.*

Rob waved me away. "Just the team. The usuals. Add a sentence at the end about inviting anyone I forgot."

"Gotcha."

When I got back to my desk, I emailed the team about happy hour, casually adding Nicholas' address somewhere in the middle. It was very short notice, but a) it was free drinks and b) Rob was the boss and by virtue of him being the boss, sufficient advance notice was not required. Once I confirmed that the email went through, I practically ran to the copy room to scan Rob's documents and quickly emailed them to Bartlett. I glanced at my Movado watch, a gift from my parents for my 28th birthday earlier that year. It was 4:42. After I grabbed my enormous leather pocketbook from the bottom drawer of my desk and told Rob I was stepping away, I headed to the bathroom and called Bridget.

She picked up after one ring. "Is everything okay?"

I ran a brush through my long light brown hair and shook my head from side to side to give it some bounce. "Why would you ask that? Because I called instead of texted?"

"Bingo!"

Bridget had been my best friend since the 7th grade. Text messaging often won out over actually talking on the phone, but it wasn't like telephone conversations were reserved for emergency trips to the hospital or anything. I removed the pink monogrammed makeup case I'd had since junior high school from the bottom of my pocketbook. "Having drinks with the team tonight after work."

"The team, huh? Does that include your work crush? What's his name again?"

"Nicholas!"

Bridget snorted. "I know! Nicholas *Strong*," she repeated. "Rhymes with Long. I remember."

"Ha ha. Be nice." Mentioning the rhyming of my last name with Nicholas' wasn't one of my proudest moments, but it was after two flirtinis, and two flirtinis for a 101 pound girl were like five flirtinis for an average sized woman.

"Well, have fun. Don't do anything I wouldn't do," Bridget said dryly. Gun shy after an uncharacteristic one-night-stand generously left her with a case of crabs, she hadn't done anything with anyone in over a year.

"I'm not entirely certain he sees me as anything more than that 'chick' who occasionally connects him to Rob's voicemail, but he's serious eye candy. Chances are, we'll exchange less than four words, I'll end up extremely frustrated and regret going in the first place."

"There you go, Ms. Positive! Good luck."

"Thanks. See ya." I hung up the phone and wiped the corners of my lips before applying a shiny but translucent gloss. I dusted a little powder over my nose trying unsuccessfully to hide the constellation of freckles that appeared at the tip. I zipped the case and returned it to my bag. I wished I knew how to apply dramatic makeup but every time I made an attempt, I looked like one of those freaky pageant kids.

When I returned to my desk, I noticed that Rob's light was off. It was only 5:05. *Someone needed a beer.*

I opened my saved post to finish my review.

> *In closing, I would highly recommend Gladly Never After to all lovers of chick lit, particularly those who prefer books with more action/dialogue and less description/ backstory.*
> *Rating: 4.5 Champagne Flutes*

I set my blog to post the review at 6 the next morning and logged off of my computer. At least I'd be fashionably late.

*   *   *

I spotted my crew immediately upon entering the dimly lit restaurant. They had taken over the left side of the semi-circular bar. I stood up as tall as my 4"11' frame allowed and approached the crowd. Although my eyes looked straight ahead towards Rob, always the center of attention at these events, I used my peripheral vision to confirm that Nicholas was in attendance. He was talking to Lucy, a junior associate in the group. Lucy was actually really nice, but her straight blonde hair was always pulled back into a tight bun and her daily attire consisted of stodgy business suits. She looked like a librarian and I couldn't imagine Nicholas being interested in her as more than a colleague. *On second thought, maybe Lucy is one of those stereotypical librarian types who's kinky in the sack.* I had often wondered if Nicholas had hooked up with any of the female associates in the office while pulling an all-nighter or after one of the many firm-hosted parties. As I glanced back at Lucy in jealous paranoia, I was surprised to catch Nicholas looking directly at me. Could he tell I was thinking about him? Bridget and I always said guys had radar.

"There she is. My right hand. What are you having?" Rob asked.

I tore my eyes away from Nicholas and focused my attention on Rob. "A glass of prosecco. Thanks." I considered asking for a cocktail menu but wanted a drink in my hand too badly to spend the time considering my choices.

Rob raised one of his thick dark eyebrows and took a sip of his lager. "Beer isn't good enough for you?"

"Not when the firm is paying." I giggled.

Rob handed me my glass and I casually looked around. I caught Nicholas' eye again and prepared this time, gave him a friendly wave.

"Hey you," he said, smiling wide as his brown eyes darted down to my chest and quickly back to my face.

His appraisal of my rack, while subtle, was unmistakable. Not that a guy checking out a girl's chest was an indication of actual interest. It was probably merely instinct for them, but I was still thrilled. I would be the first to admit that I drew attention to my chest since, being so short, I needed to give people a reason to look down far enough to see me. I raised my glass and smiled back. "Hey," I said before turning back towards Rob. I wanted more than anything to go over and cock block his conversation with Lucy but I didn't have the nerve. Checking out a girl's cleavage was not necessarily an invitation for conversation.

"Did you send that email to Bartlett?" Rob asked.

Without batting an eyelash, I responded, "Did you ask me to?"

Rob offered a bemused smile. "Touché. I thought you might be too busy working on your blog to attend to such menial tasks like getting your work done."

"When has my blog ever gotten in the way of attending to your business, Rob?" Rob loved to give me shit about my blog, but I knew he was joking. I had only worked with him at our current firm for four months, but had been his assistant at his previous one for close to two years. He had left our old firm more than six months earlier, leaving me behind with a promise to use his influence to get me hired as well. We worked well together. Although in his mid-fifties, Rob had the energy of a teenager and was extremely high-strung. I knew how to take him down a notch without threatening his authority.

"What blog?"

I felt a flush creep across my cheeks as I turned around to face the source of the question. I wasn't surprised, since I blushed whenever I talked to Nicholas, even when the phone rang at work and I saw his name on my caller ID.

"You didn't know about Kim's blog?" Rob asked, his blue eyes reflecting amusement.

Nicholas shook his head, not removing his eyes from mine.

All I could think about was running my fingers along the dark stubble on his jawline. Never completely clean shaven, he currently looked like he hadn't touched a razor in several days. I held his gaze willing my voice not to give away my crush, but the heat on my face suggested a crimson complexion that probably already had. "I have a blog where I write book reviews." I figured Nicholas didn't know about my blog since our opportunities to socialize outside of work had been few and far between in the four months we'd worked together. It was that unfamiliarity which I blamed for my chronic bashfulness in his presence. *Well, that and his overwhelming sex appeal.* Unable to maintain eye contact a second longer, I glanced back at Rob hoping he'd pick up the dialogue.

"It's incredibly popular. Publishers actually beg my secretary to read and review their client's novels on a daily basis." Rob beamed at me like a proud uncle as if he was somehow responsible for my blog's immense popularity.

I turned back to Nicholas and smiled shyly. "Every other day basis is probably more accurate but yes, it's a widely read blog. I have several thousand followers and get requests from authors, publicists and agents pretty often."

Nicholas looked at me with admiration. "Awesome. What types of books do you review?"

I hated this part of telling people from work about my blog. I never knew if the attorneys would raise their noses in the air and judge my taste in "literature." *Here goes nothing.* "Chick lit," I admitted.

Nicholas tilted his head to the side. "Like the gum?"

I giggled as if I'd never heard that one before. "Yes, it's called chick lit, like the gum. But it's also a book genre. Like *Bridget Jones's Diary, The Devil Wears Prada.* You know?"

Nicholas looked thoughtful as he rubbed his thumb along his chin. "My ex-girlfriend had a bunch of books with pink covers. Were those chick lit?"

Forcing myself to stay focused instead of wondering what his ex-girlfriend was like, how long ago they broke up and why, I smiled and said, "Probably." Although chick lit had certainly evolved beyond stereotypical pink covers, it wasn't the time to go into defense-mode.

Nicholas smiled wide. "Very cool, Kim!" Glancing at his empty glass, he said, "Time for a refill. Be right back" and walked towards the bar.

I tore my eyes away from the back of Nicholas' light blue business shirt and back to Rob. But Rob was now talking to Lucy about some guy she had deposed the previous day. *Boring work talk.* I downed the rest of my prosecco and walked over to the bar. After quickly getting the bartender's attention, I ordered another glass, on Rob's tab of course, and observed Nicholas finish sending a text. As he smiled into his phone, I felt my Hanky Panky thong practically melting off. At only about 5"7', his stature might have kept him off of some women's top five lists but since I was vertically challenged too, he was currently number one on mine. I couldn't even think of who would follow him in second and third place.

"Penny for your thoughts, Blogger Girl."

I snapped out of my list making and faced Nicholas, silently praying he was not a mind reader.

He looked at me expectantly.

I swung my free hand in dismissal and lifted my drink towards him. "Nothing important. Cheers!"

Nicholas clinked his glass against mine, said, "Cheers" and took a sip of his drink.

Following his lead, I took a sip of mine.

Nicholas inched closer to me. Speaking in almost a whisper, he said, "Having fun yet?"

Very aware that we'd never stood this close to each other and that these were practically the most words we'd ever exchanged one on one, I replied with faux nonchalance, "Can't really complain about free drinks. You?" The cuffs of his shirt sleeves had been pushed up to his elbows and I pondered whether the dark hair on his arms was coarse or soft. I wondered what it would feel like to run my fingers up and down his arm. I also wondered if he could hear my heart beating through my chest.

"Definitely can't complain about that," Nicholas agreed. "And a break from work is always welcome, especially these days." He smiled. "Doing anything good this weekend?"

I had practically forgotten it was Thursday night, which was odd for me since I lived for the weekends when my secretarial duties did not get in the way of my reading. "Not sure yet. Probably drinks with friends. And I need to catch up on some reading. For the blog. What about you?" *Please don't mention a girlfriend.*

"Oh, this and that." His eyes glowed, almost like he was holding back a secret.

I bit down on my lip and without thinking, blurted out, "Do This and That have last names?"

Nicholas gave me a once over before shaking his head laughing. "I'll probably spend most of it at work actually. So, tell me more about this blog."

I tipped my head to the side. "What do you want to know?"

"I don't know. Like, what made you start it?"

"The condensed version or the truth?"

Nicholas cocked an eyebrow. "How long of a story is the truth?"

"Why? Do you have a date to rush off to?" I swallowed hard. *Nice, Kim.*

Laughing, he said, "It's just that your answer was rather mysterious, you know?"

I shuffled my feet. "Well, I usually tell people I started the blog because I've always loved to read, blah, blah, blah."

"Blah blah blah. Gotcha."

After he said that, he winked at me and when my knees wobbled in response, I grabbed the bar with my free hand. "The truth is that one day I was bored at home surfing the internet and I found all of these blogs dedicated to romance books, like Harlequin stuff, and then I found some more devoted to science fiction, thrillers and so on. But I could barely find anything dedicated to chick lit and it pissed me off because I love it. I figured if I love it, there must be other girls who love it too and maybe if I started this blog, I'd find them and we'd bond." I paused. "Aren't you glad you asked?"

As his phone rang, Nicholas distractedly responded, "Yeah, that's cool," before bringing it to his ear. He whispered, "Sorry" before answering it.

I wondered if it was from "This" or "That."

Nicholas hung up his phone and frowned at me. "I knew it wouldn't last. I've gotta head back to the office."

"Oh that sucks." Of course, if he had to work late, there was less time for him to have sex with someone else later, except maybe Lucy the Librarian within the confines of one of their offices. Or maybe he didn't really have to go back to the office but all of my blog talk had bored him so intensely that he was happy for any polite excuse to be free of me. *Snap out of it, Kim.*

Nicholas shrugged. "The glamorous life of an associate. But it was nice talking to you, Kim! Don't be a stranger."

"You either. Don't work too hard."

"Tell that to him," he said, gesturing towards Rob. With one last smile and a light tap on my shoulder, Nicholas walked away. As I answered another co-worker's question about where I had bought my peep-toe bright red patent leather pumps, I saw him make his round of goodbyes and walk out of the bar.

Even though I was pleased that my banter with Nicholas had finally progressed beyond telling him that Rob was in a meeting or running late, I hoped I hadn't gone too far with the blog talk. It wouldn't be the first time. Served him right for asking, although he probably knew I wasn't prepared to converse with him about anything work-related. I looked inside my half empty glass. Rather than come out and chug almost two drinks, I should have used the time to read. I was too buzzed to concentrate on a book now and was positive I was incapable of writing a coherent review.

I grabbed my coat and walked over to Rob to say goodbye.

"You're leaving before my big announcement?" Rob asked, his shoulders dropping.

I pretended not to notice his disappointment. Rob had a "thing" for making announcements. I wasn't sure if the content of the speech mattered to him as much as the pleasure he seemed to derive from hearing his own voice against a backdrop of silence while he had everyone's rapt attention. "Are we all getting six figure bonuses? And by 'we all', I mean secretaries included?"

Rob smirked at me. "Yeah, right."

"Am I getting fired?"

"Not if you stay for my announcement."

I glared at him.

"No, you're not getting canned."

"Then what is the announcement about this time?" I bet he hadn't even written it yet.

Rob took a sip of his beer and looked down at the dirty floor. Looking back at me with a sheepish expression, he said, "I'm not quite sure yet."

Aha! I thought so. "Then I am going to excuse myself and you can repeat your brilliant announcement to me tomorrow." *Insert kiss ass comment here.* "And I'm sure it will be brilliant."

Rob gestured with his hand towards the entrance of the bar. "You're excused."

After I said my goodbyes to the rest of the squad, I walked out onto chilly 3rd Avenue. As I zipped up my jacket, it occurred to me that Nicholas had conveniently neglected to answer my question as to whether he had a date later. I walked back inside the first set of doors, removed my phone from my bag and texted Jonathan. I was as horny as a 15-year-old boy at a strip club.

MORE GREAT READS FROM BOOKTROPE

Caramel and Magnolias by **Tess Thompson** (Contemporary Romance) A former actress goes undercover to help a Seattle police detective expose an adoption fraud in this story of friendship, mended hearts, and new beginnings.

Tumbleweed by **Heather Huffman** (Contemporary Romance) When a cruel twist of fate threatens her new life in the Ozark Mountains of Missouri, Hailey must choose between rebuilding and fighting for love, or continuing to drift through life like a tumbleweed.

A State of Jane by **Meredith Schorr** (Contemporary Women's Fiction) Jane is ready to have it all: great friends, partner at her father's law firm and a happily-ever-after love. But her life plan veers off track when every guy she dates flakes out on her. As other aspects of Jane's life begin to spiral out of control, Jane will discover that having it all isn't all that easy.

Thank You For Flying Air Zoe by **Erik Atwell** (Contemporary Women's Fiction) Realizing she needs to awaken her life's tired refrains, Zoe vows to recapture the one chapter of her life that truly mattered—her days as drummer for an all-girl garage band. Will Zoe bring the band back together and give The Flip-Flops a second chance at stardom?

Next Year I'll be Perfect by **Laura Kilmartin** (Contemporary Fiction) Sarah's discovery of a list her younger self put together outlining what she wanted to achieve by the age of 30 turns her world upside down.

Discover more books and learn about our
new approach to publishing at **booktrope.com**.

Made in the USA
San Bernardino, CA
30 June 2015